PRAISE FOR VIVIAN AREND

"If you've never read a Vivian Arend book you are missing out on one of the best contemporary authors writing today."
~ *Book Reading Gals*

"The bitter cold of Alberta, Canada, is made toasty warm by the super-sexy Coleman brothers of Six Pack Ranch."
~ *Publishers Weekly*

"Brilliant, raw, imaginative, irresistible!!"
~ *Avon Romance*

"This story will keep you reading from the first page to the last one. There is never a dull moment..."
~ *Landy Jimenez*

"I definitely recommend to fans of contemporaries with hot cowboys and strong family ties.."
~ *SmexyBooks*

"This was my first Vivian Arend story, and I know I want more! "
~ *Red Hot Plus Blue Reads*

"In this steamy new episode in the "Six Pack Ranch" series, Trevor is a true cowboy hero and will make any reader's heart beat a little faster as he and Becky discover what being a couple is all about."
~ *Library Journal Starred Review*

ALSO BY VIVIAN AREND

The Stones of Heart Falls

A Rancher's Heart

A Rancher's Song

A Rancher's Bride

A Rancher's Love

A Rancher's Vow

The Colemans of Heart Falls

The Cowgirl's Forever Love

The Cowgirl's Secret Love

The Cowgirl's Chosen Love

Holidays in Heart Falls

A Firefighter's Christmas Gift

A Soldier's Christmas Wish

A Hero's Christmas Hope

A Cowboy's Christmas List

A Rancher's Christmas Kiss

A full list of Vivian's contemporary print titles is available on her website:

www.vivianarend.com

ROCKY MOUNTAIN FOREVER

SIX PACK RANCH: BOOK 12

VIVIAN AREND

This is a work of fiction. Names, characters, places, and incidents either are the product of the author's imagination or are used fictitiously, and any resemblance to any persons, living or dead, business establishments, events, or locales is entirely coincidental.

Rocky Mountain Forever
Copyright © 2021 by Arend Publishing Inc.
ISBN: 9781989507278
Edited by Manuela Velasco
Cover Design by Damonza
Proofed by Angie Ramey & Linda Levy

CAST OF CHARACTERS

Family units and children ages in December at the start of ROCKY MOUNTAIN FOREVER. [**Book where the couple's story occurs.**]

~**Six Pack Ranch Colemans**~

Parents: Mike & Marion. Married 40 years.

Blake & Jaxi [**Rocky Mountain Heat**]
- Married 8 years. Home is the SP homestead. Blake works Coleman land. Jaxi is a homemaker and overall mischief-maker for the family.
- Becca (Rebecca)(7½), Rae (Rachel) (7½), Lana (6), PJ (Peter) (4½), Justin (2)

Matt & Hope [**Rocky Mountain Desire**]
- Married 5 years. Home is in Rocky Mtn House. Matt works the Coleman land. Hope is a homemaker and runs the Stitching Post quilt shop.
- Colt (Colton) (3), Cam (Cameron) (1)

Daniel & Beth [**Rocky Mountain Haven**]
- Married 7 years. Home is in Rocky Mtn House. Daniel makes rustic furniture. Beth teaches high-school math online to homeschoolers.
- Lance (17), Nathan (15), Rob (14)

Travis, Cassidy, & Ashley [**Rocky Mountain Freedom**]
- Married 2 years (Ashley & Travis; Cassidy took Coleman name in private ceremony.) Home is the Peter's house, across the coulee from the SP homestead. Travis and Cassidy work the Coleman land. Ashley is a homemaker and sells art projects on commission.
- Daisy (2½), River (1½), Forest (3 months)

Jesse & Dare (Darilyn) [**Rocky Mountain Home**]
- Married 1½ years. Home next to Joel and Vicki on Sunset Ridge on Six Pack land. Jesse works the Coleman land. Dare is a homemaker and runs a popular homestead/farming blog.
- Joey (Joseph) (2)

Joel & Vicki [**Rocky Mountain Rebel**]
- Married 1½ years. Home next to Jesse and Dare on Sunset Ridge on Six Pack land. Joel works the Coleman land. Vicki is a homemaker and cooks during special events for a local catering company.
- Jess (Jessica) (1½)

~**Angel Colemans**~

Parents: Ben (died nearly 3 years ago) & Dana. Married 34 years.

Gabe & Allison [**Rocky Mountain Angel**]
- Married 6 years. Home is an expanded cabin Gabe built on Angel land. Gabe works the Coleman land. Allison is a

homemaker and helps with organic analysis and planning for the Colemans.
- Micah (4), Ariel (1)

Michael (d)

Rafe & Laurel [**Rocky Mountain Devil**]
- Married 2 years. Home is the homestead on Angel land, shared with Dana Coleman. Rafe works the Coleman land. Laurel works at the Rocky Mountain House Library.

~**Whiskey Creek Colemans**~

Parents: George & Sally (died 25 years ago) Married 8 years.

Karen & Finn [**The Cowgirl's Secret Love**]
- Married 3 months. Home is at Red Boot dude ranch in Heart Falls. Finn is an investor and co-owner of the dude ranch. Karen is the Red Boot ranch foreman.

Tamara & Caleb [**A Rancher's Heart**]
- Married 2 years. Home is the main homestead of Silver Stone ranch in Heart Falls. Caleb is the head of the Stone family and ranch. Tamara is a retired nurse and homemaker.
- Sasha (11), Emma (9), Tyler (9 months)

Lisa & Josiah [**The Cowgirl's Forever Love**]
- Together for six months. Home is a ranch outside Heart Falls. Josiah is the local veterinarian. Lisa helps her friends and family by doing odd jobs.

Julia* & Zach [**The Cowgirl's Chosen Love**]
- Married 3 months. Sort of. *Julia is discovered to be a missing Whiskey Creek sister in *The Cowgirl's Forever Love*. Home is a

cabin at Red Boot dude ranch in Heart Falls. Zach is co-owner of Red Boot Dude ranch. Julia is an EMT and medical officer for the Red Boot ranch.

~Moonshine Colemans~

Parents: Randy & Kate. Married 39 years.

Steve & Melody [**Rocky Mountain Romance**]
- Married 1 year. Home is a house Steve built on Moonshine land. Steve works for the Colemans. Melody is a homemaker and does part-time shifts at the Rocky Mountain Veterinarian clinic, usually for small animal work.
- Jay (Jason) (2½), Expecting in June

Trevor & Becky [**Rocky Mountain Shelter**]
- Married 4 years. Home is the "rental" that Uncle Mark Coleman gave to Becky to live in when he dropped her off five years ago. Trevor works for the Colemans. Becky works at the Stitching Post quilting shop with Hope.
Expecting in March

Anna & Mitch [**Rocky Ride**]
- Married 3 years. Home is in Rocky Mtn House near a large park. Mitch works at the Thompson & Sons garage with his brothers. Anna is a retired RCMP, now homemaker.
- Kay (Kasey) (2½), Expecting in June

Lee & Rachel [**Rocky Mountain Retreat**]
- Married 1½ years. Home is in Rocky Mtn House. Lee works the Coleman land. Rachel is a homemaker.
- Liam (1), Ava (2 months) (They did not expect to get pregnant while Rachel was nursing baby #1)

PART I

Tell me, tell me, smiling child,
What the past is like to thee?
'An Autumn evening soft and mild
With a wind that sighs mournfully.'

Past, Present, Future
Emily Brontë

SP Ranch Journal

~Michael Coleman, first journal entry, one week after the passing of his father, Royce Coleman, January 1983~

Life changed in a moment.

This was not what I expected—it's not the place I want to be. Yet, here we are. Suddenly I'm in charge of all of the Coleman holdings, and the privilege of it and the responsibility make my fingers tremble as I write this.

You made it look so simple, Da. Never a thing you couldn't do, and now you're gone, and hell if I know how to fill your boots.

Why didn't you say something—

No. I know exactly why you didn't mention feeling sick. You were always strong. Always the first one up and caring for the family, making the tough decisions and working until you dropped. You didn't want us to know because you didn't want to admit to yourself that you weren't strong enough to fight sorrow and death. Damn stubborn fool.

It was clear you'd been a little lost the last couple of years, ever since Mom died. That wasn't a fault, you know. Caring so much that it broke your heart once she was gone. You taught us a lot with how much you loved.

I'm so glad I had you as a father, but I sure as hell wish I'd been watching closer to see exactly how you made it look so easy. I'm not ashamed to admit I'm going to miss you even as I move forward, one foot after another. No use trying to solve problems that haven't even shown their faces yet.

Thank God for Marion, though, or I'd be in one hell of a mess. She's the one who got us through the funeral and the rest of it. Even hauling baby Matthew around with her, nothing slowed her down. Blake stuck by my side most of the time, the little tyke wide-eyed and with his lip quivering, because even at not yet three, he knows his Grampa is gone.

And now I don't even know who I'm writing this for. You, the family...my sons?

Yet I know you journaled all the time. Somehow it feels right to pick up this part of your legacy. Can the act of copying something you did push me in the right direction?

Maybe it's wishful thinking to hope that, in putting pen to paper, I'll be able to work through troubled times. Maybe it'll let me savour the good times better.

Or perhaps somewhere between the two extremes of grief and joy, I can build a world that makes the Colemans rich. Not as in money overflowing from our pockets, but as in a family that's rock-solid far into the future. That's my goal.

Always did have more gusto than brains, but we'll see.

1

———

December, present day, Six Pack ranch, Alberta

Darkness filtered to the edges of the room, the cool of the early December morning leaving the air outside the quilt crisp.

But the warmth in his arms told Blake Coleman everything he needed to know. Jaxi lay curled against him, face pressed to his chest, legs tangled with his. Skin on skin, the sweet scent of her filled his head and made his heart swell.

How he had this miracle in his life day after day—no idea. No damn idea what he'd done to deserve the goodness in his world.

She moved, head tilting back as her blue eyes opened the narrowest bit. Sleepy warmth and contentment all but dripped from her expression.

"Morning," she whispered.

Blake pressed his mouth to hers, a smile curling his lips. "You're not rocketing out of bed like your panties are on fire."

She hummed, a secretive hush. "You're the one with the lighter. If there's going to be any panty bonfires—"

"Mama? Daddy?"

They both went silent.

It was a long shot. The chance to lay in bed late, with neither of them needing to rush away for chores, was rare in the first place. Add in five kids, and Blake could count on one hand the number of mornings in the last month they'd had the room to themselves past five a.m..

When the quiet persisted, Blake began to relax.

Curled up against him, Jaxi pressed her lips against the side of his neck, easing her legs on either side of his. A throaty moan escaped her, and Blake wanted to both laugh and curse as he realized his hand no longer rested innocently on her hip. Nope. He'd full-on cupped her ass and was even now in the process of dragging her on top of his body.

"Looking for trouble—" Jaxi began.

"*Maaaaama.*" The doorknob rattled as PJ's voice rang against the door. "Daaaaaadeeeee."

Absolutely adorable even as their four-year-old's timing made Blake groan. "Invasion?" he asked Jaxi.

She pressed a quick kiss to his lips before carefully crawling off. "I'll get him. You deal with—*things.*"

With a slightly wicked pat of her hand against his belly, Jaxi swung away before he could grab her, hips wiggling saucily as she headed toward the door.

Blake rolled, adjusting his hard-on to a more comfortable position that was slightly protected in case their oldest son decided to launch his way onto the mattress like he usually did.

"Yes? We didn't order any pizza," Jaxi said as she knelt beside the door.

Around her, PJ's expression went utterly serious as he shook his head. "Not peeza. Cuddles."

"Well, that's totally different." Jaxi scooped him up then closed the door and returned to the bed. "Look, Daddy, we have an early morning delivery of cuddles."

"One of my favourite things," Blake said sincerely, opening his arms.

PJ snuggled in, and Blake felt that pulse deep inside his heart again. The one that ached even as it brought a smile to his face.

Jaxi sat on the edge of the bed, her expression filled with wonder. "I love you."

She said the words so simply, but it was clear the message was meant for him, not their son. Although she totally loved their kids to pieces, this thing between *them* wasn't getting any smaller. After eight years of marriage, it seemed to simply grow, expanding to fill every single bit of room, not just in Blake's heart, but in their home.

Even as he draped an arm around their son, he patted the mattress beside him. "Climb in. It's cold out there."

She smiled wryly. "I will. But I figured I'd wait to let the rest of them in first."

"Who?"

He shouldn't have bothered asking. He knew the answer.

"Daddy?" A chorus of little girls.

Jaxi blew him a kiss before sneaking from the room. By the time she got back with two-year-old Justin in her arms, the seven-year-old blonde-haired twins, Rebecca and Rachel, had settled on either side of six-year-old Lana.

Lana sighed contentedly. "I like sleepovers."

"Not a sleepover when it's Mommy and Daddy's bed..." Becca explained seriously.

"...it's family cuddles," Rae finished.

"Shove over there, kids," Jaxi said with amusement. "Make room for your brother."

Shockingly, ten minutes later the bed was silent. The girls had curled up in a heap like puppies and fallen back asleep almost immediately. Against Blake's chest, PJ's blondish hair spread in a tangled mess. He'd snuck his thumb in his mouth, his little chest moving easily.

Justin was sprawled on top of Jaxi, contented baby snores rising from him.

And Blake and Jaxi were teetering on opposite edges of the mattress.

She was smiling, though. "Are you sure you don't want a king-size bed?"

Blake kept his chuckle soft to avoid waking anyone. "We had any more room in here, we'd be able to fit a couple of the dogs and a small horse."

She snapped a finger to her lips. "*Shh.* Do not suggest that, or the twins will try to sneak them in for a test run."

"The dogs? Or the horse?"

"Both. Either. *All* of them," Jaxi said, lips curling with amusement. Her gaze drifted over the family between them then back to Blake's eyes. "You need to take an extra-long lunch break."

He was lost for a moment before comprehension drifted in. While adult entertainment was out of the question this morning, it appeared there might be hope for later. "If you can find a bit of spare time in your day."

Her gaze grew heated. "Ashley and I are doing baby swaps this week. And it doesn't need to be a *bit*. Unless a *bit* means a couple of hours."

Reaching across the mass of children between them meant risking waking one or two. Blake satisfied himself with his best attempt at a smolder. "I'll be home by noon. We'll see what we can cook up together."

The delight on his woman's face was as sweet as the family that lay between them and as heated as the plans that lay before them.

They stared at each other in silence, smiles on their faces, love pooling around them for another hour until it was time to head into the day.

The chaos of breakfast followed. Then backpacks and getting

three little girls off to the school bus, all of them bundled up in their snow suits.

Jaxi kissed Blake sweetly before grabbing PJ's hand. Justin peeked out of the backpack contraption she wore. "We're headed over to Ashley's. I promised I'd watch the kids this morning so she can paint."

Blake shook his head in amazement. Ashley, Cassidy, and Travis already had three kids—the youngest born only three months ago. "Five kids under the age of four. You're a glutton for punishment."

"She'll have them this afternoon, starting at lunch," Jaxi reminded him, eyes brightening. "Besides. It's nice to hold a teeny baby again."

Her idea of a good time was far too exhausting for him. "See you at noon," he promised.

They were well enough set up these days at the Six Pack ranch. By sharing land and sharing responsibilities between all the Coleman clans, the sense of urgency they'd all faced years before had lessened. The struggle to provide for all the family had been dealt with. While there were still moments of uncertainty, because nothing about ranching could be predicted to go smoothly, having the holdings back together had begun to create some wonderful opportunities.

Everyone's expertise got used where it was most valuable. It meant no longer juggling to find enough grazing land or seed land or feed.

Although he did miss having his cousin Karen from the Whiskey Creek side of the family around, with the way she had with horses. She and her sisters had settled about a three-hour drive to the south of Rocky, which always struck Blake as odd.

He couldn't think of *any* reason family would want to leave. Still, she seemed happy enough. Maybe when she came to visit this weekend for their early Christmas gathering, he could bend her ear for a while. Get some ideas of where she thought the Colemans should go with their horse-breeding plans.

He'd barely finished his morning paperwork when Jesse stuck his head in the door of the office. "This is where you're hiding."

Blake pushed the chair in then joined his brothers in the main barn. He nodded at Travis before turning back to Jesse. "Wasn't hiding, but getting up to date. Looks as if *you* need to hit the books for a bit. Took a peek at your project and it doesn't look as if you're done."

Jesse made a face. "One more push should do it. The last time I tried to finish up, we had that power outage, and I lost about three hours of data entry."

He was using a state-of-the-art genetics program to help amalgamate the Coleman ranch more fully, but old wiring in creaky barns was hell on modern technology.

Blake shook his head. "Shit. Didn't know that."

Jesse shrugged. "Pain in the ass, but it happens. Sorry I'm a little slow. If you need the information right away, I can stay late tonight. I don't mind if it takes longer to get it done."

Well.

Blake eyed him sideways. That was just so not Jesse that both Blake and Travis caught it.

His little brother was no longer a lazy butt or the type to try to wiggle out of work. He also had a wife he was head over heels about and a kid he adored, *plus* his twin brother and family lived right next door. Jesse and Joel were as tight as anything once again.

Jesse deliberately volunteering to be late getting home?

Nope.

Travis obviously had gone through the same thought process. He raised a brow. "Dare kick you out?"

"No," Jesse snapped, but then he looked just about as guilty as Rae had the day before when she'd been caught with her fingers in the cookie jar right before supper. "Not really. Sort of."

"Ha." Travis was grinning way too hard. "And if you want to work late, that means you're also in shit with Joel, because otherwise you'd go hang out with him until Dare wants to see your ugly mug again."

A heavy sigh escaped Jesse. "They're *all* pissed at me."

Joel, his wife, Vicki, *and* Dare? "That's quite the accomplishment." Somehow Blake kept his expression from twisting into a smile. "You deserve it?"

"Probably." Jesse flashed a grin. "It'll be okay. I'll let Dare cuss me out a few times, and then I'll work all the kinks out between us with some makeup sex."

"You can get out of the doghouse that fast?" Travis shook his head. "You need to fight a little harder. I mean, makeup sex is good and all, but they need to be really lit on fire for it to be extra fun."

"The man who has two spouses to get mad at him at the same time thinks fighting is fun?" Blake shook his head. "There's a name for people like you."

Travis actually sputtered for a second before grinning broadly.

Jesse rolled his eyes dramatically then confessed the truth.

"Because *that* conversation is going places I don't want to talk about, it was just a misunderstanding. And yeah, Dare was right —I stuck my nose in where it didn't belong." Jesse leaned back on the wall behind him, folding his arms over his chest. "I walked in on Vicki and Joel having what I thought was a full-out, drag-down fight. I waded into the middle because I knew they'd be upset if they actually tossed bullshit at each other that hard. But it turns out they were reciting some damn movie, and Dare was there, and so all three of them gave me hell."

Travis snorted. "A *movie*? For fucks sake, can't you guys even fight about something that's not comical?"

"Screw you, asshole."

"Diva."

"Loser."

"Jerk."

"Ahhh, brotherly love." Blake slapped a hand at the side of Travis's head, dodging out of the way before his brother's instant roundhouse could connect. "Stop your jawing, and let's get to work."

The entire morning was filled with the goodness of hard, honest labour, followed by a sweet, dirty interlude that left Blake grinning for most of the afternoon.

He thought about all the blessings in his world and wondered—

A sense of foreboding hung over him. Like everything was *too* good to be true. Something was going to rush in and shake things up in a way he couldn't anticipate.

Totally superstitious nonsense, but it felt so real. He paused before leaving the barn to head back to Jaxi and his family, stopping to rap his knuckles against the sturdy wooden frame of the man door for luck.

What they had was priceless—was precious. He didn't want anything to change.

2

———

$\mathcal{T}$he time it took to drive to his home in the middle of the Six Pack land wasn't long enough to give Jesse a solution to his problem.

The concern, he could honestly admit, wasn't the fact the three people he cared most about in the world had been mad at him before he left the house that morning. Travis had been right —it was a silly thing to fight about, and Dare had been justified in calling him on sticking his nose where it wasn't needed. That misdeed had probably been forgiven before his truck had even left the driveway.

Nope, if there was one thing he was absolutely certain about —Dare loved him unconditionally, even when he was an ignorant bastard. And both Joel and Vicki cared enough to call him on his bullshit.

It was like being wrapped in a warm blanket on this icy-cold December day to have that kind of gut-deep assurance in his world.

His problem—

Jesse stuck his hand in the pocket of his sheepskin-lined jacket and worried the envelope again. Half a dozen times that day he'd considered pulling it out of his pocket and showing it to Blake, but he knew better. Even as tangled as the out-of-the-blue offer made his brain, it was Dare he needed to talk to first.

And obviously, ignoring the proposal he'd received wasn't the way to go. He thought he could put it off until the new year, but the information kept buzzing at the back of his brain, distracting him and screwing with his concentration.

Hell. Jesse knew better than to get between his brother and his wife, for more reasons than most.

What was worse, there was no reason to sit there suffering. No reason why he *wasn't* telling Dare exactly what was bothering him.

The final approach up the road to Sunset Ridge added to both the deep sense of contentment and the concern dredging through every part of his body.

Nearly identical houses sat silhouetted against the skyline, showcasing the comfortable yet compact homes where he and his twin were raising their families. It was everything he'd ever dreamed of—to be living next to his best friend, head over heels in love with a wonderful woman who was more than his equal. A beautiful little boy and the excitement of discovering their family would be growing—Dare was expecting in July.

Jesse's fingers tightened instinctively around the envelope, and he cursed. The urge to throw the letter away, or burn it, was so damn strong. Yet he couldn't.

He pulled into the parking space next to Joel's truck, a grin coming unbidden as he glanced over to find his brother sitting behind the wheel waiting for him.

They both got out, meeting at the shoveled walkway that led toward the houses.

Joel eyed him with amusement. "Well, that's disappointing."

Confusion hit. "What?"

"I asked Blake to make you shovel shit all day. Doesn't look like I got my wish."

Jesse used his middle finger to scratch the bridge of his nose. "Hope you had fun on lost-sheep duty. Find them all, Bo Peep?"

"Ass." Only Joel was grinning. "Cassidy and Matt called in the Moonshine clan. We got the entire flock back into the lower pasture, plus all the fences fixed and gates shut. The rest of the season is going to be a piece of cake."

That was good news. "I really like this business of working with the entire family," Jesse shared honestly.

"It's damn handy," Joel agreed. "Although it's going to take a couple of years to get all the cows onto the same season. I'm not looking forward to them dropping all the way from February till May."

"One thing at a time," Jesse said. It was one of the things he was working on with his programming. He met his brother's gaze straight on. "I said it this morning, but I'll say it again. I'm sorry. I butt in where it wasn't my right. I'm glad you told me to fuck off."

Joel nodded once. "Vicki and I were more pissed that you thought we would say such crappy things to each other."

"That's the part that threw me," Jesse insisted. "You and Vicki —if anything, you're way too sweet and gushy. You don't toss words like knives."

"Good to know we've got you fooled." His brother shrugged. "Don't kid yourself. We still screw up, and words get heated. But we don't let it stick. I swear Vicki's been taking lessons from Mom—"

A laugh escaped before Jesse could stop it. "Jeez, you too?"

Joel dipped his chin "The last time I was ticked off about something, she plopped down on the footstool by my chair and waited."

"Which means you have to talk about it. Or you have to admit, 'I'm pissed off and don't want to talk to you right now,' which is okay some of the time, but mostly sounds as if I'm about eight years old and pitching a fit."

They both chuckled before Joel let out a long, slow sigh. "This is probably why Mom and Dad's fights are virtually nonexistent."

"Because he knows he can't win?" Jesse teased.

"Can we?"

"More importantly, do we want to?" Jesse winked before turning toward the path that led to his house. "We're on shift together tomorrow?"

"Six a.m. You drive. Vicki needs the truck to pick up supplies for the Christmas party this weekend."

Another thing Jesse had forgotten about in his distracted haze. "It'll be good to see the Whiskey Creek girls again."

After a final solid thump on the shoulder, Joel turned away and headed whistling toward his home.

Jesse did the same.

Inside, golden light shone onto the wintry landscape and reflected off the walls to fill the cozy space. Both the heat and the scent of dinner welcomed him in.

"*Daddy.*" Enough noise for a platoon of kids rushed toward him. His son, wearing a teeny pair of cowboy boots and riding a stick horse across the hardwood floor.

"Hey, Buckaroo." Jesse swooped down and nabbed Joey, horse and all. "Where's your mama?"

"'puter."

"Ah. She's still working?"

"She's done." Dare rounded the corner, and here was the true welcome. She squeezed up against him, Joey cradled between them. "Hey. I didn't expect you for another half hour."

"Blake sent me home. Told me I needed to come apologize before you decided I had to sleep in the barn."

"Horsies," Joey exclaimed.

"Yes. The horses live in the barn. Daddy lives with *us*, even when he's being—" Dare paused.

"Go on," Jesse encouraged. "I not only want to hear what you say, but I want to know how you're going to say it in a Buckaroo-approved matter."

Her eyes flashed, but he thought it was with amusement. "Even when he's being a buttinski."

Joey's little face curled up in a frown. "Daddy buttski?"

Laughter escaped.

"Yes," Dare agreed, squeezing Jesse and lifting her lips for a kiss.

"Don't blame me when that kid says things we'd rather he didn't in front of Grandma," Jesse warned with a whisper in her ear.

"We'll blame Grandpa."

Worked for him. Jesse pulled her tight. "Hello, love. I missed you today."

Then he kissed her. A sweet moment that made being apart bearable because he knew this was the reward waiting. The coming back together was not just fire and heat—although they had plenty of that between them.

After nearly three years, the *quiet* moments were growing richer. The conversations and the searching for the next adventure to share were being built on a firm foundation.

Jesse was damn grateful.

Her lips on his, the heat of her body and the swells of her breasts pressed against him were also something to be thankful for. Joey squirmed, and Jesse put the boy back on the ground.

Catching Dare's hand, Jesse held her in place when she would've taken off to the kitchen. "I apologized to Joel, and now it's your turn. I was out of line this morning. Thanks for giving me hell. I was distracted, but that's not an excuse."

Dare lowered her chin slowly. "Okay."

Then she waited.

For one moment, Jesse wanted to burst into laughter, because it was exactly what he and Joel had just talked about. "You're not going to let me leave it at that, are you?"

She winked then headed toward the back of the house. "Of course, I am. For now. Go. Grab a shower, and I'll finish supper. I can wait until later to poke you to find out what's wrong."

It wasn't until Joey was fast asleep in bed that Jesse brought it up. Taking Dare by the hand, he led her into the living room and in front of the fire he'd lit in the airtight stove.

Dare sat beside him, arms wrapped around her legs. "This looks serious."

"I guess it is." All evening his admission to Joel had been echoing in his head. The part about how much he enjoyed working with his family. With all of the Coleman clan. Jesse pulled the letter out of his pocket, running his hand over it in a futile effort to straighten some of the wrinkles before passing it over. "I got this in the mail a couple of days ago."

She examined the envelope. "University of Alberta." A small furrow formed between her brows. "There's a problem with your school records? But, *wait*. You went to Old's College, not the university."

Jesse pointed at the letter. "One of my profs moved. It's all kind of technical, but I guess the program he taught us to use was experimental. Somebody with a bunch of money wanted to invest in agricultural technology, and I was one of the guinea pigs."

She nodded. "Go on."

This was the part where it got a little unreal. "Dr. Wadia asked students who used the program to send him periodic updates. For data analysis—that kind of thing."

"I remember that. I remember you asked my brother for permission to share after you did some programming for them down at Silver Stone." Dare no longer looked worried but very curious. "Caleb said both he and Luke really appreciated your help."

"They weren't the only ones." Jesse took a deep breath. "There's more, but long story short—Dr. Wadia's got a research grant that starts in September of next year. They're going to run a five-year program, including regular travel to other countries to help them set up their own systems."

Dare went very still. "He didn't write just to tell you his exciting news, did he?"

Jesse shook his head. "He wants me to join him. He wants me to be one of the main programmers on the project, including teaching and travelling."

Dare sat back, sprawled on her arms as she gazed at him. "Jesse. That's a huge compliment. It's amazing."

It was—and the mere thought of it tangled his insides into a thousand knots. "I don't know what to do."

She was too far away. Jesse pulled Dare into his lap. He circled her with his arms and buried his face against her neck. Her rich auburn hair fell around him like a curtain, blocking out everything except the two of them. The warmth of her body melded against his, the heated brush of her breath ghosted past his ear.

"We'd have to move away from your family and farther from mine." Dare's words were barely a whisper. "Away from Vicki and Joel."

"Away from all of them, yes." Jesse took a deep breath and straightened slightly, cupping her cheek. "My first instinct is to say no, but there's a hefty salary involved. And I do mean *hefty*— the corporation that's funding the research has deep pockets. We need to think seriously about this."

"When do you have to decide by?"

"There's no rush," Jesse said. "Dr. Wadia says he's getting the first steps of the process in place but wanted to give me a heads-up. He should know it's a go for sure by the end of April. The absolute deadline for my decision is August first."

"Wow."

Silence reigned again for a while before Dare nodded decisively. "Well, I can see why you were distracted. But the fact that we've got a long time to make a decision means you have to try to not worry right now. Especially if he won't know until the end of April if there's actually a job for you."

It was good advice, but Jesse knew he would still think about it a lot more than was good for him.

He went for a topic change. "You're not mad at me anymore?"

"Nothing to be mad about," she insisted.

"I'm a little pissed that you're being so understanding," Jesse confessed. "I could use a little arguing."

Dare rolled her eyes. "Yeah, because throwing dishes and shouting is so much more fun."

He rolled her to the carpet, pinning her under his body. "It's not the shouting that's fun, it's what comes after."

"Oh, *that's* the part you're missing." Her gaze shifted to his lips. "We can probably come up with a reason why we need to have some angry sex. It is angry sex that you're looking for, right?"

"Angry. Hot. Heavy." He jammed a hand under her shirt and slid it upward until her breast filled his palm. "I want to take you hard."

Instead of telling him he was an ass or yawning in his face, both responses he would've completely understood, Dare proved once again she was his absolutely perfect partner.

She grinned. "I think we can manage that."

Unexpectedly, she twisted. With a hand on his shoulder, she got enough torque to flip him onto his back. An instant later, she'd crawled over him, peeling her shirt up and over her head to toss it aside.

Jesse hummed in approval. He curled up far enough to undo her bra and then sent it flying after her shirt. "Your tits are always stunning, but pregnant? There should be an entire wing in some museum to pay homage to them."

"They're big enough to fill an entire wing by themselves," Dare teased before moaning. "God, Jesse. *Yes.*"

He didn't know what to do next. He wanted it all. His hands, his mouth, his teeth all over her skin. He dropped his hands to her waistline, rolling her under him as he shred away her pants and undies.

Dare stripped his shirt away, and fabric tore. They were all hands and heat and dirty delicious noises—far too long, yet it was only moments later, he dipped his fingers between her legs and found her ready and wet for him.

"Do it." Dare made the words a challenge, a gasp following as he hauled her over his legs and notched himself against her heat.

One inch of movement. One thrust and they were joined.

Their foreheads met. "You are my everything," Jesse confessed.

Her face lit up like sunshine. "Good. Now fuck me."

With pleasure. For both of them.

He rocked into her hard and dirty, soaking in the sensations streaking over his skin like wildfire. Aching with the extreme pleasure of the tight fist of her body surrounding him. Dare's heels dug into his ass as she rocked to meet his demands with her own vibrant enthusiasm.

He paused for a moment to lick his thumb then reached between their bodies to slide over her clit.

Dare arched, her breasts pressing against his naked chest. Head falling back, her hair slid over his arm supporting her back. Sweaty and hot with every bit of pleasure centered on his cock as she squeezed him, Jesse took as hard as he gave.

A moment later her nails raked across his shoulders, and she let out a cry. He lost it, the connection between them fire and passion.

They clung to each other, chests heaving. Coming down while still connected. Bodies, souls. Hearts.

Dare sighed happily. "I love you. We'll figure it out."

"I love you too," he agreed. "And we will."

Jesse just hoped the right answer wouldn't require tearing his heart in two.

SP Ranch Journal
~Michael Coleman, January 1984~

Still trying to figure out where the hell the past twelve months flew to.

With the successful year we've had, it's time. I know Da intended to someday divide the land into six sections, one for each of us boys to be able to take charge of and find our way.

I'm in total agreement. Just because I had to take over when I did doesn't mean I'm the best man for all the tasks. Plus, I know our hearts lie in different areas. If I have to listen to George wax poetically about his damn horses for another three straight hours...

He's got interesting plans, and I bet they work, but as far as I'm concerned, a horse is part of a working ranch and not a pretty work of art to be pranced around an arena.

Like I said—different paths, neither right nor wrong.

It's clear, though, that John's never going to fully take charge of his section. We'll deal with it easily enough, and he'll never want. He's a fantastic worker—when things are going well. I've done everything I can to get him to see a doctor or a therapist, but he's stubborn. Like all us Colemans, so I guess I'm not surprised. But the land will be his, and when he's up to it, we chat about his ideas, but mostly, he hangs out with Mark and works beside his twin.

I've asked Mark if he's okay with that, and he insists he is. If it ever changes—

Well, I'm keeping an eye on it.

Three of us are married now—myself, Ben, and Randy. George and Sally got engaged over the holidays and plan to get married the summer after next. Not sure why they're waiting so long on the wedding because George told me they already plan to move in together into the house he's working on as soon as it's done. Again—different paths.

I keep hoping Mark will find someone he's interested in. Even sent him to the Stampede and on as many buying and selling trips as I could wrangle in the hopes someone from outside Rocky would catch his eye, but so far, no luck.

His business is his own, but I've made sure he knows he's welcome to bring anyone home, no matter who he falls in love with. Colemans are smart enough to accept a person for who they are, not anything else.

In other news, Marion had an idea. Said we're all getting to the point that our individual families need to build some of their own traditions, even as we spend time together. Christmas Day is for families, Boxing Day for the entire Coleman clan. She has spoken—and I'm not about to argue, because she's right. As usual.

Still, we don't want to leave anyone out. Since they don't have extended families yet, Mark and John were invited over to Ben and Dana's for Christmas Day. For some reason, Mark ended up here instead. Said he promised Blake he'd take him tobogganing. No idea what's going on there. Maybe he and Ben had another fight—oil and water those two at times—but I didn't mind having my kid bro around. Marion just rolled her eyes, set another place at the table, then made him wash the dishes.

The party on Boxing Day was just what we needed. Adults all caught up with each other, the four kids tangled happily like pigs in a pen.

I'm going to suggest we do it all over again later this year—maybe Canada Day. While we get together often, putting those dates aside could make it extra special. Family gatherings are important. I can see them getting even more so as the Coleman clan continues to grow.

3

---

*J*axi pulled the final batch of cookies from the pantry where she'd stashed them and handed the container to her mother-in-law. "I think that's it for us at the main house. Ashley's got everything ready over at the Peter's house for the guys."

Marion glanced around the home that had once been where she raised her six boys. "You did the place up nice."

"Not much different than usual," Jaxi insisted. "Although the poinsettias you and Mike got us really brighten up the room. Thanks for that. Makes it look extra festive in here."

Marion picked her coffee off the table and gestured toward the easy chairs. "Come sit for a minute. Chaos will arrive soon enough."

Jaxi grabbed her own drink, happy to have a moment alone with the older woman. She paused to peek into the playpen to check if Justin was still covered up. "What are the chances he'll try and stay awake the entire time people are here?"

"There'll be enough hands that all the babies will get passed around just fine," Marion assured her. She took a sip of her coffee and smiled contentedly. "I kind of like that we're holding an extra holiday get-together for the Colemans this year." She glanced at Jaxi. "Of course, I can say that because *I'm* not the one who did all the extra organizing."

"It made sense. I've missed seeing the Whiskey Creek girls since they moved away. When they said they wouldn't be coming north for Boxing Day, it made sense to put in a little extra effort."

"Still, thank you. And I know your Uncle George is grateful. It's about time we got a chance to meet that new daughter of his."

Which seemed to Jaxi like one of those fairy-tale moments. "Poor girl. I can't imagine what it must feel like to first walk into a family gathering of this size."

"She's a Coleman by blood. She'll have the guts to handle it." Marion nodded firmly. "Besides, she'll have her sisters."

Which was true, yet Jaxi made a mental note to ask a couple of the quieter Coleman ladies to keep an eye on Julia when she arrived. It didn't matter how brave somebody was, getting tossed into a gathering of strangers you wanted to impress was never going to be a walk in the park.

Jaxi's oldest sister-in-law, Beth, could calm a raging storm. Partly it was her teacher training, and partly the woman just oozed Zen-like vibes. Jaxi appreciated her for many reasons but was especially grateful one of their more immediate family members had no problem being the peacefulness to counter Jaxi's admittedly high-energy leanings.

She caught herself smiling. Her sister-in-law Ashley, who lived next door, was possibly an equal match in enthusiasm and energy. Jaxi had never imagined back when Travis had first brought his partners home that his wife would be so much fun to be around.

Ashley was the master of everything crafty, with an artistic flair that left Jaxi in awe. Most recently, the other woman had designed a snugly cloth to swaddle her babies that could be done up with one hand—a miracle in any mother's books. Add in that the blankets were sinfully soft and made of the brightest, happiest fabric their sister-in-law Hope could bring into her quilting store, and everyone in the community wanted one.

Sitting in the cozy living room, Jaxi gazed around at the comfortable home she'd made with Blake. The signs of children were everywhere, and while the furniture might be a little worn, it was still bright and pretty.

"It's a wonderful place," Marion said firmly.

Jaxi glanced up, amused. "Can you read my face that clearly?"

"Probably because I've seen that expression on my own face so many times," Marion returned. "We've had things good overall, haven't we?"

"Better than good. Pretty much everything I've ever hoped for." Jaxi played with the cup in her hands. It was true, but there'd been one thing twisting inside her over the last while that she'd been wondering about, hard.

After Justin had been born, she'd told Blake they were done having babies. It wasn't until Ashley's most recent had arrived in September that something had changed. Holding their newest nephew had woken up a part of Jaxi that she'd thought was ready to be done.

But that was a conversation to put aside until at least after the party this weekend.

It wasn't until the afternoon that the gathering officially started. The family met in the front yard of Blake and Jaxi's then broke into two. The men scooped up the older kids and hauled them across the coulee to Ashley, Travis, and Cassidy's place.

Blake came and gave Jaxi a final hug, a trio of little blond girls and one four-year-old boy bouncing around his legs like jumping beans. He leaned in. "Have fun making mischief."

Jaxi pressed a hand to her chest. "Us? A choir of angels couldn't be more innocent."

Becca tugged on Jaxi's leg. "We're going tobogganing. Uncle Jesse said he once slid down the hill in the coulee and..."

"...went right over the river and up the other side," Rae finished.

Jaxi's gaze snapped to Blake's face. "Uncle Jesse sometimes has a problem remembering the rules."

"We're going to the *other* tobogganing hill," Blake informed the girls firmly before offering Jaxi a quick wink. "The one that Uncle Jesse doesn't know how to slide down nearly as well as you guys. You'll probably have to teach him."

"Uncle Jesse is silly," Lana pronounced with the wisdom of a six-year-old. "We'll teach him the right way."

"Wight way," PJ agreed.

"You do that," Jaxi encouraged.

Happiness bubbled in her chest as Blake gave her another quick kiss. "I promise they'll return with all body parts intact."

"You as well. I like all your body parts," she said with an utterly straight face. "*Ohh*." She slapped a hand over the spot on her butt where he'd pinched her.

Then she hurried over to greet Ashley and take the car seat from her. "Ready to share your babies?"

Ashley grinned, twisting to the side to display one-year-old River peeking over the side of the backpack. He blinked huge dark eyes as he clutched strands of Ashley's hair as if they were reins on a pony. "Anyone who can get this kid to let go of me for more than thirty seconds is welcome to try."

Blonde-haired Daisy toddled over to Jaxi, her riotous curls poking out from underneath her knitted toque.

"Auntie J., up," she ordered, arms held out demandingly. With three adults in her house willing to offer hugs at the drop of a hat, the little sweetie was a wee bit of a tyrant.

Jaxi got the two-year-old balanced on her hip, then, between her and Ashley, carried the car seat about five feet before Trevor and Becky from the Moonshine clan showed up.

"I've got him," Trevor insisted, pulling the car seat away and peeking inside. "Hey, dude. You want to come hang out with the big boys?"

"Sure, Trev. Just remember Forest will need to be burped and probably changed. After you nurse him, that is," Ashley teased.

Trevor made a face. "Too bad, little guy. Tell you what. This time you keep an eye on your mom and your cousin-to-be."

He stood, carrying the car seat in one hand and wrapping the other arm around Becky to stabilize her. "Come on, Rodeo. Let's get you inside where it's warm."

Becky's smile was patient. "I'm plenty warm, Trevor. I have this internal heat system helping." She glanced at Jaxi. "I don't know how anybody stands being pregnant in the summertime."

Then they were in the house and coats were being pulled off. Trevor actually got Forest out of his car seat and was cradling the three-month-old with a far more experienced air than Jaxi had expected.

He grinned when he caught her staring. "With my little brother and his wife having two kids rapid-fire style, the entire Moonshine clan has gotten a lot of practice lately holding babies."

Everyone moved into the living space, and once the dust settled, Becky cradled Forest, staring down at his dark hair with a secretive smile on her lips. Ashley still held River, and everywhere else, Jaxi's sisters-in-law and the women of the other Coleman clans were settling into chairs and beginning to catch up.

The Whiskey Creek Coleman girls entered the house to loud hellos. The newest member of the family, Julia, stood beside them, her cheerful grin shining out.

Lisa gestured toward their group. "I'm pleased to present the now complete Whiskeyteer four-pack. Everybody, this is Julia. Julia"—Lisa swung her hand as if she were a game show host—"this is everybody."

Julia wiggled her fingers. "I don't see any name tags."

"Just call us Ms. Coleman, and you'll be mostly right," Marion said dryly as laughter bloomed again.

The next hour passed in sweet pleasure as everyone visited for a while then rotated and moved to a new group of family. Babies were passed around with joy and love.

Rachel from the Moonshine clan sank back on the couch with a contented sigh as she breast-fed two-month-old Ava and watched her one-year-old, Liam, take toddling steps toward Lisa. "There's something in the water, isn't there?"

Jaxi glanced around the room. "We've been blessed, yeah."

Rachel snickered. "The Coleman family is funding Doctor Kincaid's retirement all by ourselves."

"He has delivered just about all of our babies, hasn't he?"

"Here's an opening if I ever heard one." Dare got to her feet. She grinned as she checked around the room, little Joey playing some game with stacking blocks with two of his cousins. "Becky here is on the calendar for a March baby. Melody and Anna are using June for a second round of 'let's have our babies on the same day and give them incredibly similar nicknames.'"

"I had Jay picked out for a long time," Melody insisted.

"Kay was born first. That's all I'm saying." Anna folded her arms over her chest. "You're such a copycat."

Melody proved she was one hundred percent Coleman at this stage of the game. She stuck out her tongue at her sister-in-law.

"So far you're only telling us things we already know," Jaxi pointed out. "Unless you're ready to add to that list?"

Dare grinned. "We've booked a mid-July appointment. This time it wasn't an *oops*."

The laughter and congratulations had barely begun when Vicki stood, her smile brilliant. "Joel and I are excited to let you all know baby number two is on the way, also expecting mid-July."

Dare's jaw dropped. "No way."

"Way." Vicki threw her arms around Dare and squeezed tight. "I'm so happy we get to do it together this time."

"Because synchronized vomiting is such a good thing to share." But her obvious excitement was clear. Dare pulled away and offered a wink. "I can't think of anyone I'd prefer to share that experience with."

"*Awwww.*"

As the room quieted, Auntie Kate got to her feet and turned to the rest of the older generation. "I'm going to take a wander over to the other house," she announced. "Marion? Dana? Want to take a peek and see if the guys are holding it together?"

"We might need to stop in the office for a few minutes," Marion said with a smile. "I know where Mike hides the good hootch."

"I'm all for that," Auntie Dana said. She pointed a finger at her daughter-in-law, Laurel. "You're my designated driver, right?"

The blonde-haired woman grinned. "Because you're always such a party animal? Go on. Drink away."

Jaxi waited until the door was firmly closed behind her mother-in-law and aunts before turning to the group and rubbing her hands together. "Okay, ladies, put your thinking caps on. I've got an idea."

A chorus of groans mixed with a lot of snickering greeted her announcement.

"Why does it sound as if I should be worried?" Julia asked quietly from where she'd settled between Beth and Becky.

"Because you have good instincts. Jaxi's been itching to do something grandiose ever since last year with Marion and Mike's fortieth anniversary." Beth glanced at Jaxi over the top of her teacup. "I don't think you've recovered from that disappointment yet."

Jaxi threw her hands in the air. "It's not fair. It would've been a perfect time to do something up, family-wise."

Beth turned to the newcomer in the room "Jaxi likes to organize things."

"This is true."

"Gospel truth."

"Not a word of lie in it."

The words echoed on the air without anyone taking credit for calling out the quick phrases.

Well, now.

Jaxi folded her arms over her chest then took the mature route. It was *her* turn to stick out her tongue at the gathered women.

Beth continued her explanation, amusement tingeing her voice. "Only Marion said that she wanted their fortieth to be about where they were now, not what had been, so all of Jaxi's plans to put together some kind of family history were dashed because—well, you just don't give somebody a present they don't want."

"That makes sense." Julia still looked a little wide-eyed, glancing around the room that was filled with Colemans and kids. "Also, wouldn't that have only been the Six Pack history? And there are four families, right?"

"Actually, there were six brothers. One passed away, four still live here in Rocky, plus Uncle Mark, who's sort of like my guardian angel," Becky said. She turned her gaze on Jaxi. "I'm on your side if your idea is to make some sort of overall family record."

"Only, it's got to be something that the next generation will actually want. Straight-up journals are boring." This from Rachel, who was cradling her sleeping daughter. "Think about who will want this fifty years from now."

Dare was nodding slowly. She'd run a successful blog for years at that point, and Jaxi was curious what she'd suggest to make this idea better. "Turn the spotlight on *any* event. It doesn't have to be only the big occasions like weddings or that kind of stuff. It's more important the events have solid *memories* attached. Happy, or sad, or something that changes you."

"So, you're saying we need...the feelings?" Laurel wrinkled her nose. "Pictures aren't enough?"

"I'm saying it's got to have context. Baby pictures are great *if* we know who they are, but the background is important. The *'why I took this picture'* background." Dare smiled. "For example, Marion gave me a shot of Jesse as a toddler making a terrible face. It's funny on its own, but it's even better when she told me that was the first time Jesse tried ice cream, and he *hated* it. He refused to try any again for years."

"Really?" Jaxi laughed. "I didn't know that."

Dare grinned. "The picture triggered the memory. Stories make it special."

Lisa chuckled, just loud enough to have all the heads in the room swinging in her direction. "This one is easy. Get the uncles into one room and pass around some pictures. Then record what they say. Trust me, you'll get the stories."

"You know what, that's *it*." Jaxi snapped a finger at Lisa. "But not just the uncles, *all* of us. *Everybody's* memories—at least one from each family member—the good ones, the ones that are real, even the bad things."

"The ones that involve food, which means mostly good, *especially* if I'm involved." Vicki offered a wink as laughter rippled around the room. "Well, it's true."

"If you include recipes, I can guarantee the guys will crack the family history open," Dare said with a nod.

"A joint family memory book," Jaxi said. "With pictures, but more importantly, the stories and the recipes that go with them." She glanced around the room, excitement rising as a ton of ideas rushed into her head. "What do you guys think? We could take our time on it, but if everyone helped, we could put it together in digital format for us and print for the older generation."

"Take our time?" Ashley grinned. "So, like, you want our

essays of what we did over the holidays on your desk January fifth?"

"Of course not." Jaxi rolled her eyes dramatically before teasing back. "You can have until the beginning of February."

"Ha. How about you set up some guidelines, and we'll just keep going at it until we're done. *No* deadlines." Ashley winked. "It took a while to make the memories. We may as well enjoy stirring them up."

It was a good idea, because there were too many people to simply herd in the right direction quickly. Jaxi nodded. "This should be fun, not something we dread, so taking our time is important."

"And if we want everyone to share, we need to let them consider what they *want* to share. Especially the older stuff." Laurel was thinking hard. "There are all kinds of random old boxes in the attic at Angel ranch."

"At the Peter's place as well," Ashley agreed.

"I can help go through things. And I'll get Trevor to write to Uncle Mark and let him know what's going on." Becky smiled, her hands resting gently on her belly as she met Jaxi's gaze. "They keep in touch. I'm so glad."

The conversation drifted to holiday activities and food, and between the laughter and the occasional burst of crying from the little ones, the house was full of life and happiness.

And a goal. Jaxi soaked in the sensation of family and considered the question herself.

Of her many memories, which was the most important? Something about becoming a part of the Coleman family? About falling in love? It wasn't as if she could only contribute one thing, but she didn't want to miss the chance to share a truth that would become a part of the forever history of the clan.

This was going to take time, and she planned to enjoy every minute of it.

4

Christmas letter from Trevor Coleman to Uncle Mark,
current day

Considering I write to you about every two weeks, it sure seems there's a lot to catch up on.

First off—you should admire the Christmas card. Ashley (from the Six Pack side of things) made an entire set using pictures the little kids in the clan drew. I think this one is supposed to be the reindeer pulling Santa's sled, but my nephew Jay is only two and a half, and apparently any artistic talent he inherited will involve music, not art. Or Jay thinks reindeer and elephants are related, in which case, he drew them very well.

Another holiday adventure since I wrote: you know how the ladies like to take control of our lives? It appears last week we left them alone for too long, and they came up with this wild idea of putting together a Coleman memory book. We've been told we all have to contribute.

I guess it's supposed to be something a little less dry than just a family history and what days who did what, so I'm in favour of it.

Especially since Vicki (also Six Pack) has agreed to pony up a few of her recipes that she's been keeping under lock and key. Good food that's easy to make? Always a hit in my books.

I wanted to be sure that we get your story as well. It doesn't have to be much, but whatever you want included. Jaxi and Dare—that's Blake's wife and Jesse's wife, if you don't have your Coleman playlist with you—volunteered to interview anybody who didn't want to write stuff up. If you want to do it the easy way, I can get you a phone number.

I suppose I could even help write whatever you want, although I'm not much of a word guy. Becky says the fact I've kept writing to you makes her happy, and since you haven't yet told me that you burn the letters or anything, you're stuck with me keeping in touch and keeping you up to date.

Which means there are a couple of other things to mention. Becky's due date is getting closer—sort of. It's still a few months off, but damn close all the same. I'm scared shitless half the time, and the other half I feel like I'm floating about a foot off the ground. I'm so damn proud, and I barely did anything. She's feeling good, but the bigger her belly gets, the more I have to fight to keep from picking her up and acting as a bodyguard twenty-four/seven. March can't get here soon enough as far as I'm concerned. Still can't believe I'm going to be a daddy.

Last time I wrote I'd mentioned all the Whiskey Creek girls have moved away from Rocky to Heart Falls. Saw them last weekend, and they're all doing really good. Turns out the sister they found last spring is also going to stick around Heart Falls—Julia got married out of the blue the same day Karen did. Becky was trying to explain something to me about it, but it's pretty tangled as far as I can tell.

All I know for sure is when the subject of long-lost siblings came up at our family dinner last Monday, my mom told my dad that she was never missing for long enough to produce any additional Moonshine family members, and hell if she thought that he'd had time to go and plant seeds anywhere else.

Dad made some comment about never straying far from her fields, and it was a really awkward dinner conversation, which I think was their goal, because Dad laughed so hard.

Six Pack ranch is hosting the Boxing Day gathering. Swear they've got enough people for a full hockey team roster, and that's without putting skates on all the babies. Although I suppose I shouldn't throw stones considering how many Moonshine kidlets there will be soon, with more on the way.

My favourite part about the Christmas gathering, other than the food and the bonfire, is the snowball fight. Daniel's boys are old enough now to make great teammates. It's funny to have three teenagers wandering with the under-ten-years-old club, but they don't seem to mind.

Lots of plans for the new year. I've been working with the Angel Coleman clan, dreaming up ideas of what to do with the grazing land on your parcel come the spring. Gabe is a good man to work alongside. Rafe as well, but I see him less. He and Laurel have been busy helping Auntie Dana in their spare time. Word is she's been talking about building a house. Something about setting down new roots for a new year. I guess that makes sense. Rafe and Laurel moved in with her not long after Uncle Ben died. It seems the three of them get along fine, but I know if it were me, after nearly three years, I'd want some privacy.

Anyway, I've rambled way more than usual.

Merry Christmas to you, Uncle Mark. I never think about you without getting a smile on my face and a lot of gratefulness in my heart. As always, thank you for being there for Becky. May this coming year give you what you truly desire.

Let me know what you decide about the history stuff. If you ever want to stop in, the door is always open.

Love from Trevor, Becky, and the bun in the oven.

MARK PUT down the letter and the card and stared into the fireplace.

Thoughts swirled—

Trevor's letters had felt like a taunt at the beginning, but eventually Mark had faced the truth. Even a little news from home was like air into his lungs, giving him life. Giving him hope.

Flames flickered before his gaze, slightly out of focus. So many memories came to mind. Time with his brothers, time when the SP and Whiskey Creek and Moonshine labels were just being applied to the families.

He'd left before the Angel Colemans had gotten their name—Gabriel followed by Michael was too much for the townsfolk to resist.

So many memories he didn't have because he couldn't stand being there watching her—

Temptation called, and Mark gave in, pulling out his wallet and the worn photograph he kept hidden away. Every time he looked at it, he felt slightly wrong. Still, there'd been no stopping his heart from wanting.

He gazed down at her picture. Blonde hair blown by the wind, staring at the camera with a shy smile curling her lips. The only woman he'd ever wanted to be his.

A new year. A new chance. *New roots*—

An old love.

It was damn time. It was *past* time.

Mark shot to his feet and looked around. There was so much to do that he couldn't up and go this very minute, but fuck waiting any longer. He would take what he needed. He would give and become who *she* truly deserved.

It was going to be a wild ride and probably take every bit of sweet talk he could manage, but by the time he was done, Mark Coleman was determined—Dana would finally be his.

SP Ranch Journal

~Michael Coleman, July 1984~

Was in town today and overheard someone mention the Whiskey Creek Colemans. Turns out that's George's piece of land. Makes sense, with the way the creek meanders through most of their section.

Took a bit of chat time and paying for a few cups of coffee, but a few other names finally dropped. I live on the SP ranch, and Randy is on Moonshine land, which cracks me up.

Did Grandpa Stan and Great Uncle Peter ever regret the times they got tipsy on the moonshine they made? Or just mad about the fact they hid the jars on each other? Randy said he finds a stash every few months or so. I wonder how long that will continue.

No nicknames for Ben's or Mark's sections yet, but it's amusing to think that will come eventually.

5

———

*A*shley glanced around the room and wondered at the magic.

It was a brief moment of calm in what had continued to be a very active household. She'd just finished nursing the baby, and he was lying contentedly in the bassinet on the couch. River and Daisy were miraculously still napping, and Ashley had even gotten in a forty-five-minute snooze before Forest had woken up hungry.

How had it come to this? She'd come back to Rocky five years ago, looking for a place to settle down and hopefully find some quiet happiness. What she'd found were two strong and devoted men who had given her more than just a place to set down roots. They'd given her a future and a family and so much more.

Cassidy? He was her endless joy.

Travis had brought her into the Coleman clan and grafted her onto strong, sturdy stock. He'd also twisted his way into her heart, some sharp barbs gripping tight yet protectively guarding her as well.

Love had tangled his, and hers, and Cassidy's lives into something that made her think of a beautiful Celtic knot.

Together, yet each strand independent and strong. That she knew there was always someone ready to stand at her side was a type of magic.

They both made her heart sing. They made her body ache *and* fly.

Two strong arms curled around her from behind, and a scruffy cheek brushed hers. "You've been standing there like a statue for nearly five minutes. Being inspired by your muse?"

"Something like that." She twisted, looking into Cassidy's face, his green eyes shining at her with amusement. "Counting my blessings."

"Me too. One." He leaned close and kissed her. His arms tightened, and suddenly she was airborne. Ashley wrapped her legs around his hips instinctively, fingers thrust into his hair. As he deepened the kiss, she found herself pressed against the nearest wall.

"You're not counting very high." Travis's rougher tone was filled with amusement.

"I'm taking my time," Cassidy said against her lips. Eyes fixed on hers. "I suppose he can be number two."

"I suppose," Ashley agreed, tilting her head to peek over Cassidy's shoulder. "Oops. I think he heard us."

Travis caged them both with his body, pinning them in place as he leaned over Cassidy's shoulder to kiss Ashley. He pulled back just slightly, and Cassidy sucked in a breath.

A hand had slid between Ashley's body and Cassidy's, and she hummed her approval. "I like it when you guys show up in the middle of the afternoon."

"It's a brief stop, tempting as it is to make it longer," Travis growled, scraping his teeth along Cassidy's jaw before stepping back. "We should grab the kids, Cass. Daniel's expecting us."

Slightly disappointed, Ashley voiced her curiosity. "You stealing them away to Daniel's?"

Cassidy carried her to the nearest chair, settling with her on his lap, legs draped to one side. "T is right. As much as we'd like to continue this, you have the girls coming over, yes?"

She'd found a treasure trove of boxes hidden in the attic of the old Peter's house where they now lived. In the ongoing quest for Coleman memory book information, she'd convinced one sister-in-law and a few cousins-in-law to come make an afternoon of it. "They'll be here in half an hour."

"Daniel asked for help boxing some furniture orders he needs to ship before the end of the year. Between his boys and us, we'll keep the babies safe," Travis promised. "You have Forest, though."

The one thing Ashley never worried about in the Coleman family was their protective instincts around children. "Okay. Have fun."

Cassidy cupped the back of her neck. "We'll have more fun when we get back tonight," he promised before searing her lips with a red-hot kiss.

And when Travis joined in, taking control before she'd had much of a chance to gasp for air, Ashley realized it might not be magic but a good old-fashioned lack of oxygen making the room sparkle with a million twinkling lights.

Dangerously sexy, seriously committed. Impulsively, Ashley wrapped an arm around both their necks and gave a huge squeeze before letting go.

Travis's lips twisted up. "What was that about?"

"Just making sure I reset the magic button. I like what we've got," she admitted. "I *love* what we've got. I want to recognize how blessed I am. How loved. How much I love you both."

"Here I was going to make some smartass quip about your *magic button*, then you had to go and be all heart-achingly sweet," Cassidy complained. "Love you too."

Travis didn't say the words but pulled her against him again for a brief, intense hug before briefly vanishing upstairs with Cassidy.

Her guys and oldest babies were out the door a few minutes

later. Ashley sighed happily and slid into the kitchen to get the kettle going. She was still pumping on happy endorphins when her expected company showed up, all four of them.

Jaxi from next door arrived first. Ashley had been spending more and more time with her, much to both their amusement.

Melody and Allison crowded into the house next, laughing as they hung up coats and marched into the kitchen. They were not only cousins-in-law but had been good friends for many years before becoming related by marriage.

Add in Laurel, the youngest and newest Angel Coleman, and the kitchen was suddenly very full.

Melody looked at the stack of boxes lined up beside the sturdy kitchen table with something near to dismay. "You're kidding. When you said you'd found some boxes, I thought maybe half a dozen. Have you been using these to insulate the walls?"

"I don't understand why they're still here," Allison teased. "You're supposed to nest *before* the babies arrive, not after."

"She didn't have time to nest." Jaxi stole Forest from Ashley and cradled the teeny baby against her chest, sighing contentedly. "Now it's not nesting but organizing. Admit it. You want these things out so you can have more room for art supplies."

Ashley raised a hand in the air. "Nope. I confess. I have decided to become a clothes hound. I need way more closet space for all the shoes I plan to buy."

Laurel snickered so hard she ended up gasping for air. Ashley helpfully patted her on the back until the younger woman wiggled away with a laugh. "See, if you'd said rubber boots, I *might've* believed you."

It took a couple more minutes to get set up, Allison ordering Melody around. "Put the damn box down, pregnant lady. Jeez. You need to stop with the heavy lifting."

"I'm pregnant, not broken," Melody complained, but she settled and offered Ashley a wink.

"You'll be tied up and duct-taped to a chair in your house if you go out on another vet visit," Laurel said slyly. "Or so I heard Steve threaten after your little adventure the other day."

Melody rolled her eyes. "I helped deliver kittens. It was not physically demanding."

Allison patted her arm gently. "It's hard to stop when you love your job. But go near anything bigger than a kitten, and the entire clan will intervene."

"I know." Melody rubbed her small baby bump. "I promise I'll be good, kiddo, and it'll be worth it."

Boxes were opened, and Jaxi began passing out the contents. "Sort into garbage or history first, and later we can create family piles to deal with."

Conversation continued, quiet and full of everyday things, including lots of discussion of the eclectic mix of items in the stash before them.

"Do we need a grocery list from sometime in the 1960s?" Laurel asked.

"Does it have the prices listed next to it? Because that would be cool, although it would probably break my brain and make me sad at the same time." Melody leaned over her shoulder. "Nah. It's just a list."

"A lot of beans," Laurel pointed out.

"Dangerous," Jaxi said, and they all hummed in agreement, which caused laughter to start all over again.

An aged envelope slipped from between the pages of a journal. "Oh look, Canada Post has arrived—" Ashley pulled out a single, torn-edged paper and read quickly. "Oh, dear."

She got an awful lot of attention with that small, quiet phrase. Four sets of eyes were on her instantly, waiting.

"I take it it's better than a list of butter and beans?" Melody asked.

"I'm not sure..." Ashley hesitated then turned to Jaxi. "You read it and decide if it's for public consumption."

"Oh. It's one of *those* kinds of letters." Allison glanced at Laurel. "Cover your ears, sweetie. We don't want to corrupt you."

Laurel lifted a hand and very carefully raised her middle finger at her sister-in-law even as she blinked innocently.

Meanwhile, Jaxi had been examining the note. "It's not a dirty message. But it's definitely intriguing." She glanced around. "Family secrets stay family secrets, right?"

Melody drew an X over her heart. "Now you've got me curious."

Jaxi laid the note on the table, pressing it flat, and they all leaned in to read it themselves.

I never knew it was possible to be so happy and so confused at the same time. I'm not sure why I'm torn. I know I love him, completely and thoroughly, which means having any kind of feelings toward his brother is wrong.

A soft whistle escaped Laurel's lips. "*Oh dear* is right."

"Well, that's a bit of an unexpected twist." Ashley glanced at the pile she'd been digging through. She lifted her gaze to Jaxi's. "There's a whole lot of Six Pack ranch pictures in here."

"Marion?" Jaxi shook her head briskly then paused, confusion slipping into her eyes. "Nah. It couldn't be Marion."

"Well, given that we're going through boxes of Coleman memorabilia, it's one of the aunts."

"Or a great-aunt," Laurel pointed out. "You know how everybody gets handed the bits and pieces from past family. They tend to shove it all together then ignore it."

Allison was nodding. "That makes more sense considering it's just a loose page all by itself. It's not the kind of thing someone would leave lying around. Maybe they tore it out of a journal and planned on destroying it."

The mysterious note was put aside when Melody hit the jackpot and discovered a huge collection of pictures in another box. "Somebody made notes on the back, which I know is terrible for archive quality, but thank goodness for our sake, because otherwise it's like a million pictures of Uncle Mike and nobody else."

"Ha—they do all look like Uncle Mike back then." Laurel examined the pile of pictures she was handed. "Oh, that's the Angel ranch. I recognize the roofline." She flipped through the pictures. "It's before they added the deck, and look—"

Ashley leaned in and whistled. "Auntie Dana. Look at the hottie."

She snickered as Jaxi absently smacked her on the shoulder. "Stop objectifying our aunt."

"Just saying." Ashley stole the pictures and fanned them out on the table. "Hubba-Hubba."

"You're *terrible*," Laurel complained. "I want to give these to my mother-in-law, but now the entire time I'll be thinking about how you would've hit on her."

"Whoever took the pictures was definitely hitting on her, and she didn't mind one bit," Ashley offered gleefully. "That is a very *I'm thinking dirty thoughts about you* look in her eyes."

Laurel put her hands over her ears. "*La la la la la la la.*"

Laughter burst free. Jaxi laid a hand on Laurel's shoulder. "Ashley promises to behave herself and not be a terrible sex fiend anymore."

"Maybe only for the next half-hour or so. I don't want her to break anything," Laurel said as she took the pictures back. "These were taken on the rise behind the main house. That crocus field has been there forever, and every spring, it goes wild."

"I wonder where the wild roses are, though," Allison said. She picked another picture and waved it. "I like this one even better. Auntie Dana is surrounded by a sea of pink. It's beautiful."

Laurel nodded thoughtfully. "You know—her signature perfume is wild roses."

"That's neat," Ashley said. She frowned. "How come I don't have a signature perfume?"

"Sure, you do," Melody said. She kept working on the stack in front of her, but her grin slowly widened. "Eau de Testosterone. Aftereffects from those two cavemen you hang out with."

Which wasn't all bad, although Ashley was going to give some more serious consideration to real alternative. Something that was a little more floral and less dirt, sweat and sex appeal.

Not that she had a problem with *that* combination...

She turned back to the women and the task at hand and let the sweet goodness of life wash over her in continuing waves. Mysterious Coleman histories would be chatted about with her guys when they got home.

Keeping a secret in this family, where everyone knew everyone else's business? The fact it had held for this long was a miracle. No chance the truth wasn't going to come out eventually.

6

Blake pushed back from the table, stomach protesting with how stuffed he was. Even though the holidays were over and they'd headed into the new year, there was no such thing as a small meal ever offered at his mother's. "Ma, you and Jaxi outdid yourself tonight."

"Still haven't figured out how to cook for just two," his mom said with a laugh as she eyed the mostly full bowls lining the table. "Your kids need to hurry up and get bigger so they eat more."

"Dear Lord, there's a reason why the garden keeps getting bigger every year," Jaxi said with a wink. She leaned over and pressed a kiss to Marion's cheek. "My thanks as well. It was delicious."

"It was really yummy, Gramma," Lana agreed.

"We like your meatloaf better than Mommy's..."

"... because she sneaks carrots into hers."

A snort escaped before Blake could stop it. He schooled himself and turned a stern expression on the twins. "You seem to eat an awful lot of that meatloaf, even with the carrots."

"Mommy's is good," Becca agreed.

"...only, Gramma's is even better. No carrots," Rae said slowly, as if explaining something to a small child.

"I think you're just digging yourself a deeper hole, Blake." Jaxi clapped her hands. "Okay, dishes time. We'll have conversations about the why of meatloaf ingredients when you get a little older."

Blake helped clear, but then his mom and Jaxi both shooed him from the kitchen area. "I can take the boys—"

"We got it this time," his mom insisted, gesturing to the mass of kids milling around in organized chaos. They even had little Justin perched on a tall stool at the counter, smacking his hands into the soapy dishwater as bubbles flew upward. "Go play crib or relax or whatever."

"And show your Dad that picture I found," Jaxi reminded him before vanishing behind the kitchen door.

Right. Blake reached into the breast pocket of his shirt before rejoining his dad at the now-empty table. "Jaxi and the girls were going through some boxes and found this. I've never seen it before."

He handed it to Mike, who clicked his tongue in amazement. A gentle shake of his head followed as he gazed at the slightly yellowed four-by-five photo.

It was a collection of four Coleman men, all at different stages of their lives. They were seated on hay bales, a small baby settled in the lap of one. Canadian flags and red and white streamers hung in the background.

"Well, I'll be. That was taken on Canada Day the year you were born." Mike pointed. "Grandpa Stan, I mean, your *Great*-Grandpa. My dad, Royce. Me and you. You would've been not even two months old."

"Four generations of Colemans." Blake stared over his dad's shoulder. "That's pretty neat."

Mike nodded slowly. "Great-Grandpa Stan passed away later

that summer, so this is probably one of the only pictures with all of us together."

Blake racked his memory, but he was coming up blank. "I've been thinking ever since Jaxi showed it to me, and I figured it was you and me, but I don't have any memories of when Grandpa Royce was around, either."

"Makes sense. You were still young when he died."

Mike stared at the photo for a little while as womanly laughter and the sound of childish shrieking echoed from the kitchen.

His dad tilted his head then gestured for Blake to join him outside. "Let's go for a walk."

It was brisk outside, the January air cool against their skin. Their breath formed fog clouds around their heads as they strolled the path between the trailer his parents had moved into and a small barn/workshop. They'd built it last summer so Mike had somewhere to work on projects without going to the main barn across the road at the Six Pack land.

Something was obviously on his father's mind, but Blake paced silently beside him and let the older man take the time he needed.

They were inside the barn, the golden lights overhead reflecting off the wooden walls. Mike stoked the coals in the airtight stove and placed another log on them before stepping back and brushing his hands clean.

He sat at the small table along the sidewall and gestured to the seat opposite him. "Was thinking now that it's a new year, we should head to the bank and finish up some paperwork."

Blake eyed his father. "You need extra money for something?"

Which, if he did, wasn't a problem. Nothing his Ma and Dad needed would go unanswered if Blake had anything to say about it.

Mike shook his head. "We've been moving this way for a

while. I want you to keep taking on more responsibility, and I want it official."

"Retirement." Blake grinned. "You deserve it. No need to do anything on paper, though. None of us mind if you take extra time to go fishing or don't do early chores anymore."

He'd expected his father to chuckle, but instead, the man took a deep breath then proceeded to very earnestly mess with Blake's mind. "The picture reminded me. You don't remember, as both your grandpa and great-grandpa passed on before you were anywhere near old enough to understand, but there's a bunch of stuff I want in place before it's too late."

His dad was being far too serious, and it shook the amusement right out of Blake. He leaned forward, elbows resting on the table. "There something wrong that you haven't been telling me about?"

Mike shook his head. "Healthy as a horse, last time I went to the doctor. Only, the truth is, I don't expect that to stay the truth."

"Everybody gets old, Dad."

"Unless they go young, like my father. He was only sixty-four when he died. He'd been broken up bad in the logging accident he had when he was in his twenties. That man lived with pain every day of his life, yet you never would've known it." Mike was staring off into the distance now, rocking his chair slowly. "Didn't complain, but I knew it hurt something inside that his strength wouldn't be enough to get him through to old age."

"From what you and my uncles have said about him, he was an incredibly hard worker and a good man."

Mike nodded decisively. "The best. He taught me a lot." He looked firmly at Blake. "And he taught me to do what's right, even if it means planning ahead. Great-Grandpa Stan lived a lot longer —all the way to ninety—but the last twenty years of his life, he wasn't really there. He lost himself. I suppose it was Alzheimer's or some kind of dementia."

That was a surprise. "I didn't know that."

"Wasn't a thing we usually talked about. It came on fast, and then he took a lot of caring for." Mike met Blake's eyes. "None of us begrudged the effort it took, and I'll straight-up say it. I know if I go the same way, none of you will be sitting there cussing me out for forgetting what day it is."

Holy shit. "You think this is going to happen to you?"

Mike nodded. "It's possible. It's *very* possible, and while I'll tell you right now, I don't want it and the thought scares me to death, even in the midst of fighting to do everything I can to keep my brain rolling the way it should for as long as I can, I am going to do the *other* thing my dad taught me. That's make sure my family is ready."

Blake collapsed back in his chair. "I don't know what to say."

"Nothing to say," Mike returned dryly before shrugging. "Who knows. Maybe I'm wrong. Maybe I'll live to a hundred and beat you at crib until my dying day."

"I look forward to that."

"But if that's not what happens, we're going to be prepared. And that means *you* need to be ready." Mike caught his hand. "You have been doing so much to make sure the Coleman ranches are successful. This is just a little more official. Ensuring you can make all the decisions you need to, not just for the Six Pack ranch, but when dealing with your uncles and cousins. And so you can take care of Marion and make sure she's got everything she needs."

Blake was floored. "You know I'll do whatever it takes. Of course we can take care of this. Also, if you want to have nothing to do with the daily tasks, you can spend your days between the grandkids and going for rides—"

Mike laughed, a loud, hardy burst of noise. "Jesus, you really think I'm looking for a life of leisure?"

It was Blake's turn to shrug. "Just saying. I've got a whole lot of stalls that need rebuilding that I planned to put your name beside, but maybe you and the uncles want to go on an extended fishing trip instead."

His father shook his head. "Other than getting things in place legally, just in case, for the rest of it, you treat me the same as you've been. I like working, and I love working beside my boys. Nothing in the world gives me more joy than being with my family. As good as it is to sit still every now and then, it wouldn't feel right to be lazing about."

Blake nodded. "Okay, okay."

A soft chuckle escaped his dad. "I'm not looking to stop, but I'm preparing you. Ask questions, think forward. I want you to be ready and feel you have this under control and not have to scramble in the future."

"I can do that," Blake assured him. "But you make sure you tell me if you want things to change."

"Use your judgment. Chances are, at some point, you'll have to give me made-up chores like I used to give you when you were a little tyke, tagging along at my heels and wanting so hard to help." Mike sat quietly for a while then dipped his chin. "But we'll deal with that day when it comes."

Blake's head was whirling. "I love you, Dad."

Mike paused for a second in the middle of rising to his feet then caught Blake up in a huge hug and squeezed him tight, pounding him on the back. "I love you too." He took a step back. "Almost forgot. There's one more thing I'm going to turn over to you."

He pushed over the hardcover book that had been on the table. It was neatly labelled *SP Ranch Journal* with the current year.

Blake's fingers jerked to a stop unbidden. "That's your diary."

"Hush. Men don't have diaries," his father said dryly. "Or so your grandpa informed me when I caught him writing in his."

They grinned as they met each other's eyes. But Blake had to take a deep breath before he continued. "Why are you giving it to me?"

His dad looked thoughtful for a moment. "Okay, maybe I'm not *giving* it to you. I'm going to keep journaling myself, but this is a tradition that's been in our family for a long time. It's not just the records of what crops or how many animals or that sort of thing. I wasn't even quite sure what the hell it was for when I started, but it's been useful. Making notes about what I see, what I feel. What I hope for, or what's been disappointing and needs to change."

Blake considered. "Not something I've ever given much thought to—keeping a journal."

"And maybe it won't be something for you, but I'd appreciate if you gave it a shot." Mike coughed as he scooped the book off the table and pressed it into Blake's hands. "I bet you Marion's looking for us. Probably got the teapot going and ready to catch us up on everything amazing your kids have done since we left."

Blake was still reeling a little when he and Jaxi got home. After all the kids had been tucked into bed, he sat in his big easy chair and pulled Jaxi into his lap.

She held the journal, tracing a finger around the label. "That's a pretty big change for Mike to make."

"He's seventy," Blake reminded her. "Seventy-one this year."

She nodded. "He just always seems so invincible. Both your parents." Her nose wrinkled for a moment. "My mom and dad have been out of the picture for so long, I don't have any connection with them. Marion and Mike are mine as much as they're yours."

Blake had never understood Jaxi's folks. They'd moved away from Rocky shortly after he and Jaxi got married. They'd paid a couple of visits and sent a few congratulation cards when the babies had arrived, but there'd been no real connection.

He wrapped his arms around her. "Ma and Dad *are* your parents in all the ways that count. We'll just keep doing what we're doing. Loving them and appreciating them and being there for them, whatever that means."

Jaxi put the journal on the side table, wrapped her arms around his neck, and squeezed tight. Holding on to him as if she could somehow soak up the sadness inside and take it away.

"Blake?"

"Darlin'?"

She sighed. "I love you."

Nice try. Blake slid his fingers into her hair and tightened so he could pull her back far enough to meet her gaze. "What are you not telling me? Because the difference between that *Blake* and your *I love you* were about hundred and eighty degrees in tone."

Her brow furrowed. "It's bad timing."

"It's bad timing for you to have something you want to talk about and then *not* talk to me." Blake gave her a warning look. "Let's try again. Darlin'?"

She closed her eyes and spoke softly in a huge rush of words. "I know I kinda said before that I was done with having babies, but I've been thinking about it a lot, ever since the fall, and I would really like to see if we could have one more."

Okay. That was a change of topic. Blake focused in on the main point. "You want to have another baby?"

"I don't think I'm good to try for the six boys you always poked me about, but—" She nodded. "You want some time to think about it?"

"Yep. I need some time."

She was in the middle of nodding when he jerked to his feet, still cradling her in his arms. Jaxi's arms tightened around his neck as he stepped quietly down the hallway to their bedroom. He laid her on the mattress then followed an instant later, her body soft and welcoming under his.

"There. I thought about it. I would *love* to bring another

beautiful baby into this world to fill our home with even more joy."

Her eyes danced with happiness. "Oh, good answer."

This part never got old. The chance to unwrap her, one piece of clothing at a time. From the very first occasion until now, he loved the privilege of it. The way she shared so enthusiastically, arching against his hands as he pulled away the fabric and bared her skin to his lips. His tongue. His gaze.

He pressed a kiss directly over her heart. "I love every inch of you."

"You do love every inch—oh, *yes. There.*" Jaxi breathed in deep before letting the air out in a low, lingering moan. He teased his tongue around her nipple and sucked again.

It took a long time to move from her breasts to her belly. To ease between her thighs and find the sweet heat of her sex already wet for him. Every taste, every nip, every suckling kiss made him harder and yet somehow eased the tightness in his heart.

Loving Jaxi was right and perfect. Them being together was perfect and familiar. He knew exactly how to please her. How to please himself as he slid a finger into her sex and stroked until she shattered under him.

Moving to notch his cock against her, Blake slid in before the waves were done. The pulse of pleasure wrapped him in a tight embrace, and he groaned out his own happiness.

Gazing into her eyes, he drew back then plunged deep.

This was love. Complete acceptance, complete trust. Jaxi dragged her hands over his shoulders as fire lit in his heart. They fell a moment later, the sheets tangled under them, chests heaving as their bodies trembled with sweet, dirty connection.

No matter what the future held, this much was true; he and Jaxi would face it together.

SP Ranch Journal
~Michael Coleman, November 1984~

There's a hole in the heart of this family that's never going to be filled. Not with Mark run off to who the hell knows where, and John—

Never knew my soul could hurt this bad.

Mark leaving last month was somewhat expected. He was growing more and more unhappy, but he wouldn't talk about what was wrong. I didn't know it was serious enough to have him simply pack up and leave.

John was still living in the house they shared, and he seemed okay with it for the first weeks.

Until he wasn't okay. I can't believe that John's gone.

And to top it off, I can't get a hold of Mark. No matter which numbers I call, I can't track him down. He's going to be devastated to know his twin is—goddammit, I can't even fucking write the words.

He's dead. John's dead, and I didn't help him.

What could I have done differently? What did I miss? Why didn't I see?

[halfway down the page, a different set of handwriting.]

My darling love.

I know I've said it to you a dozen times now, and I'll say it a dozen more. I thought maybe sneaking into your journal and putting it front and center for you to see might help remind you—

This wasn't your fault. You can't see all, do all, be all. You are a good father, a good husband, a good brother.

A man—fallible and yet trying.

Don't punish yourself for others' choices.

At some age, our boys are going to do things we don't want. They'll be stubborn, and rude, and maybe break a heart or two along the way.

And there's a fine line between caring and interfering, and we'll have to walk it.

Your brothers are family, and in our hearts, but ultimately, they're not your responsibility. You can't make choices for them. You can't lead them in any way other than stepping forward each day and trying your best to be your best.

I love you so much. Please, please, let the guilt go. Be sad, be mad, be furious, but not guilty.

We must live our own lives and stand accountable for our own actions. I will stand with you, but I will kick your ass if I have to...

But I'd prefer to love you and hold you and wipe away your tears, so we can step into tomorrow and try to find something that makes us happy.

We can't fall into bitterness. We can't live in unending sorrow. We need to live for our children, each other.

Ourselves.

That's not being selfish—that's protecting the garden we've planted. We need to ensure it grows strong, starting with our sons. With us.

We can do it.

Together.

~Marion

7

Travis caught himself whistling as he hung up the final saddle he'd polished. It'd been a quiet task and not one that he usually did, but today it had been a welcome opportunity to use his hands and let his mind wander.

The whole family memory book had been teasing at him. Trying to come up with a good idea of what he should share hadn't been nearly as simple as he thought it would be.

For so many years, he'd loved his family and yet hesitated to truly be himself around them. Not just the sexual identity part, but the deeper, less civilized needs he felt. It had made him feel separated, in spite of how much he knew that especially Mike and Marion loved him.

Linking up with Ashley and Cassidy had been the answer to so many unanswered threads. And now that they had started a family—dear God, *three* babies in the house—he understood a little more about how his parents had loved him *in spite of* not totally understanding what he needed.

Ashley was his motivating light, always willing to poke her bear. And Cassidy was a solid, quiet pool, with more strength than Travis could ever muster. The three of them together were something unique and beautiful, and somehow, he had to find a way to put that into words?

Sure. No problem there.

He was still chuckling as he rounded the corner and nearly walked into his oldest nephew. "Whoa. Sorry."

Lance stepped to the side, shaking his head. "My fault." His youthful expression went from severe concentration to a wry smile instantly. "I was somehow looking for you *and* not paying attention to where I was going at the same time."

"Got a problem with chores?" Travis asked, pausing to look the kid up and down. Although, he supposed he should admit *kid* was the wrong word. Lance was seventeen and closing in on graduation this year.

They'd gotten so used to having Daniel's boys around the barns that their growing older had snuck up on them all.

The fidgeting was unusual, though. Lance didn't seem to know what to do with his hands before shoving them in his pockets and firmly lifting his gaze to meet Travis's. "All done with my chores, but I did want to talk to you. I mean, my best friend does, and I kind of already told him that I didn't think you'd mind."

With how tangled up his own brain was, Travis was having a bit of a problem following this conversation. "Your friend?" He thought for a second before finding the name. "Jeremy, right?"

"He's waiting outside. He actually helped me with my chores, but when I said I was going to go track you down, he said he'd hang out by the creek in case you didn't want to..." Lance paused and took a deep breath. "It's kind of a personal topic, but I said you would be somebody good to talk to."

Aw, hell. Travis could sense which way this one was going from a mile away. "Personal, huh?"

Lance nodded.

"Which means it's about sex."

His nephew grinned. "You look awfully uncomfortable right now, Uncle Travis."

"You're an evil creature," Travis told him dryly. "My kids are years away from having to have the birds and bees talk, and you want me to have to start already?"

"Please. We don't need the basic sex talk. We've got the Internet," Lance informed him before making a face. "And we've got my dad, who I will tell you is *way* too blunt."

Somehow that bit of information about Daniel made Travis extremely happy. And totally confused. "Then it's not about sex?"

"Oh, no. It's totally about sex." Lance's smirk faded a little. "Honest, it's nothing terrible, and we kind of already know the answer, but I think it would be good if Jeremy told you what's up."

This had all sorts of trouble written all over it, but there wasn't much that Travis wouldn't do for his family, and that included his nephews.

Still, he was going to be careful. "You're going to be there, yes?"

Lance peeled himself off the stall wall and tilted his head toward the east where the coulee lay. "Yep."

Wandering outside and down the trail was a bit of a shock as they left the warmth of the barns and the sweet scent of the animals behind. And yet it was fresh, crisp, and clear. The path between the house where Blake and Jaxi were raising their family and the one where Travis, Cassidy, and Ashley were raising theirs was well-packed.

Not only was it the route he and Cassidy took to get to work most mornings, Ashley and Jaxi pranced back and forth most days as well with the kids. Which was all kinds of mental fuckery when he stopped to think about the history of it. His wife and *Jaxi* as damn near besties. The girl next door who he'd once thought might save him, and the woman who truly had.

It was pretty much the most perfect thing, truth be told.

Down at the bottom where a bridge crossed the frozen water,

another tall, lanky youngster twisted toward them. Jeremy's gaze skipped over Lance and landed on Travis. Worry and hope clung to his expression.

What the hell. He was a teenager. Travis could deal with this.

He lifted his chin at the kid. "Jeremy. Heard you helped Lance get through his chores."

The kid was all arms and legs with a hint of muscle coming on. He dipped his chin and flashed a quick smile. "Chores at my house mean dishes. I like working with the animals better."

Interesting. "Well, next time we need to hire some help, we'll see if you're available."

His green eyes lit up like Travis had plugged him into a high-voltage battery. "Yes, sir."

Lance laughed then moved into position next to his friend. He nudged him with a shoulder. "Okay. Uncle Travis is here, so spit it out."

A soft swear rose from the kid—young man, considering he too was in grade twelve.

Jeremy looked Travis straight in the eyes. "I'm ace."

Okay. Not the opener Travis had expected, considering he figured the kid was going to pull something out of his hat about liking both guys and girls. "That's cool."

Jeremy nodded. "It was a bit of relief to figure it out, actually. I thought for a while I was broken because nothing seemed to turn me on."

A little tidbit Travis was looking forward to sharing with Ashley. "My wife teases that people get real hung up on naming stuff, but at the same time, if it makes things easier, having a label for how you feel is a good thing."

"That's not the part I need—" Jeremy glanced quickly at Lance.

His nephew sighed dramatically. "You want to finish this before summer? I already told you it was okay to share."

"So, yeah. I figured out that I was ace, because it didn't matter what the guys showed me on the Internet or in books, I didn't get turned on by any of it. But then Lance and I got to be friends, and now..." Jeremy stared determinedly down at his feet. "And I know he doesn't feel that way about me, but it sucks that the first time I actually get turned on is with somebody who doesn't want me."

Damn, this plot just got more and more tangled. Although, Travis caught himself smiling. "Dude. You're getting all tangled in knots because you now feel sexually attracted to someone you can't have?"

Lance frowned. "It's not funny."

"Nope," Travis agreed. "But it *is* pretty much life."

Jeremy's eyes snapped up to meet his. "What?"

Travis shrugged. "I'm sure, with the Internet, you've probably figured out—if you want a label for this one—that you're still ace, but you're probably demi-sexual. You don't get turned on until you have an emotional connection with somebody."

Lance slapped the back of his hand against Jeremy's chest. "See. I *told* you."

Jeremy rubbed his palm over where he'd been hit. "So fucked up."

"No, it's not," Lance insisted. He turned his gaze back on Travis. "I really care about Jeremy, and he's my best friend, but I don't have *those* kinds of feelings for him. And he got all tangled up because I told him that, and he was saying some bullshit about us not being able to be friends anymore, and I think that's crap. It does suck that he wants me that way and I don't, but that's not going to change."

Travis was grinning now. He was no longer quite sure why he was in this conversation because his nephew and friend were pretty much right on track. "Yes, no, maybe. Sometimes the way we feel *does* change, but the two big things I see here—if you want me to tell you what I think's most important?"

Jeremy nodded rapidly.

Travis stepped forward and met Jeremy's gaze square on. "The cool thing about being demi-sexual? I mean, sex can be a lot of fun, but for most of us, it's *more* than just fun with somebody you care about. Which means when you do find somebody, *and* things work out to the place that you end up having sex, it's going to be way better than the average guy's first time. Or second, or the rest of it."

Both the boys stopped.

"I never thought about that," Lance admitted. He raised a brow. "Good for you, J."

Jeremy rolled his eyes. Then he looked back at Travis. "And what's the second thing?"

Travis kept his body language casual. "It's not fucked up for you and Lance to stay good friends. Truth is, most of us become attracted to someone inappropriate at different points in our lives. You just need to deal with it, Jeremy."

He seemed to have shocked them again.

"But it's not Jeremy's fault that he feels like that." Lance was frowning now.

"Nope. But it's also not *your* responsibility to do anything about how he feels." Travis went for the killing blow, considering he knew Lance had been seeing the same girl for the last three years. "You ever get turned on when Kim's not around? You know, watching a show or while chatting with some other girl in your class?"

His nephew's face went beet red, and he stumbled for a moment, mouth opening and closing until he straightened up. "I've never done anything about it, but yeah. It's happened."

"Of course you didn't do anything about it, because you respect Kim, and the other bits are just physical reaction. It would be wrong for you to act on it, just like it would be wrong for Jeremy to hit on you when you're with someone else. Plus, you've said you weren't interested. So that's it." Travis slipped his hands in his pockets. "But there's no reason why you guys can't be friends."

"That's what I told you, dumbass," Lance said sternly to Jeremy.

"Of course, that means you need to be a little smarter about not being a tease, Lance," Travis finished.

His nephew blinked in surprise. "Tease?"

"If one of those girls that you accidentally got turned on around kept doing stuff even though she realized it was driving you wild, what would you do?"

"Walk away." Lance said it instantly. "My dad says it's not the girl's fault if what she's wearing or how she's acting makes me hot. I'm responsible for me."

"Right. So dealing with how he feels is going to be up to Jeremy, but as a friend, you need to not act like a dick and make things tougher for him. If he needs to walk away so he can be respectful of what you want, then you need to let him."

Lance looked a whole lot more miserable than he had a few minutes earlier. He glanced over at Jeremy. "Well, shit. This is more complicated than I thought."

His friend shrugged. "Fucking sucks. Don't worry, I think we can figure it out." He glanced up at Travis. "You know, that made a lot of sense. That whole comparing it to Lance not getting to fool around with all the girls that he's ever had a hard-on for. That makes it relatable. Because there's been a lot of them."

"You're such a jerk," Lance complained, but he was smiling again.

"Thanks, Travis," Jeremy held up a fist, and Travis bumped his knuckles before reaching over and grabbing his nephew for a tight squeeze.

And then because Jeremy looked as if he needed one as well, Travis opened his arms and gave him the option. "Free hugs, offer expires in five seconds."

He ended up with the stuffing being squeezed out of him by two teenage boys before they exploded away from him, racing back up the hill to where the ancient truck Lance drove was waiting.

"Thanks, Uncle T.," Lance called over his shoulder.

Travis stood there for a moment at the bottom of the coulee, the quiet of the February evening surrounding him. Life was damn weird at times, but he wouldn't change a minute of it.

8

———

*P*reparation for Valentine's Day was turning out to be a
lot more hands-on than grabbing a box of chocolate
and a bunch of flowers from the store.

Joel adjusted the apron strings around his waist before
turning his attention back on the activity at the kitchen island.
"You guys done stirring?"

At not yet two, little Jessica didn't have the fine motor skills
necessary for more delicate tasks, but she was stubborn. So damn
stubborn that in spite of the mixture under her spoon being far
too thick for her strength, she'd come up with her own solution.

Which meant Jess and her cousin Joey were wrist-deep in the
cookie dough, squeezing the thick mass through their fingers
while they giggled and chatted in the semiprivate dialect they'd
begun using after spending so much time together.

In a way, it reminded Joel of the semi-secret communication
between he and Jesse, his twin, during their growing up years.

"Good thing they're not making a mess." The amusement in
his brother's voice rang loud and clear as he stepped up to the
counter and reached around to tug his son's fingers away from his
mouth. "Joey. Let's bake the cookies before you eat them. Or at

least *some* of them—remember these are supposed to be for Mama."

"Auntie Kee too," Joey insisted, looking up to meet Joel's eyes. "Auntie Kee gets val'ntine cookies too."

"Of course, Vicki gets cookies." Joel plopped a cookie sheet in front of them, breaking off a chunk of cookie dough for each of the kids. "How about you try making cookies this size?"

He rolled a chunk of batter into the size of a golf ball and put it on the pan in front of them.

The two kids glanced at each other before little Jess's nose wrinkled up. "Too little."

Big Jesse chuckled. "Gotta say it, the kid's got an eye for sweets."

Amusement rising, Joel motioned his brother away. "The cookies will get bigger when we put them in the oven," he promised his daughter. "Better get working, or your mamas will be back before their surprise is ready."

Which initiated a flurry of activity. Cookie batter was hurriedly shoved into shapes nowhere near round. Some of them bigger, some of them smaller, but all of them made with one hundred percent of the children's love.

The cookies finally in the oven, hands scrubbed, their kids toddled off to the bucket of toys in the corner of the room. Jesse and Joel stood side by side, looking into the living room.

"Ever feel like it's not real?" Jesse asked. "This whole being a dad thing. Being married? Hell, being a grown-up?"

"Every damn day," Joel confessed, twisting toward his brother as he settled on a tall stool by the island. "Some nights I catch myself expecting Mom and Dad to march through the door and ask why I'm still up."

A low chuckle escaped Jesse. "I expect them to come marching in when Dare and I are fooling around in the living room, and I start looking for things to hide behind while I jerk on clothes."

Joel snorted. "Yeah, well, some trauma takes a long time to forget." He glanced at his brother and took the opportunity to change the topic completely. "You've been quiet lately. Something on your mind?"

He hadn't been positive, but Jesse's reaction said his guess was right. His brother slowed then stared across the room to where the kids were playing. "Yeah, but it's nothing bad. And it's nothing I want to talk about yet."

"Everything okay with you and Dare?"

Jesse blinked in shock, straightening up. "Hell, yeah."

"Everything okay with the baby?"

Dammit if Jesse didn't jerk again. But his answer was clear and firm. "Everything's going well with the pregnancy, Dare and I are rock-solid, and before you ask, everything's fine with the rest of the family too."

Joel folded his arms over his chest. "Okay."

His brother narrowed his gaze. "No. The ladies get away with it, but I am not letting you start doing this *go quiet until Jesse spills all the beans* bullshit."

"Not bullshit if it works," Joel pointed out. The timer on the oven went off, and he turned to grab oven mitts. "Stay back, kiddos," he warned as the children raced over to join them.

Jesse scooped the children up, pretending to be a bear. He growled and nibbled as their kids shrieked with laughter, allowing Joel to safely deal with the hot pans and close the oven.

It was only after the cookies were all baked and glasses of milk consumed, after everyone bundled up in snowsuits to go out to greet Vicki and Dare, who were expected to return soon, that Joel realized he'd never returned to the conversation with Jesse. Never found out what was bothering his brother.

He considered as they walked outside, laughter ringing around them and the beautiful setting of their homes a joy inside his gut.

Not knowing was okay.

Jesse *knew* he could tell him anything, but it wasn't Joel's responsibility to tease out the trouble. Jesse had Dare to confide in, to celebrate with, plan and even worry with. Joel had Vicki for all those same things. That was right, and it was good.

The bond between them as brothers was as strong as ever, but they no longer had to be everything for each other.

Joel held his daughter's hand, walked beside his twin, and stared out over the land to where his wife and unborn child were riding slowly toward him.

This? Yeah, it might feel unreal at times, but it was exactly where he needed to be.

DARE TOOK another deep breath of the crisp February air, letting it out slowly as their horses began the final slow ascent to the houses silhouetted against the winter sky. "I'm so glad we went riding today."

Vicki grabbed hold of the saddle horn and let out an enormous sigh as she all but sprawled on the back of her mount. "Me too. Don't think I'll be riding for too much longer, and I'll miss it." She glanced over at Dare, eyeing her also blooming belly. "Your days are limited as well."

"Truth." Dare examined her sister-in-law and how relaxed she sat on the back of the horse. "I have to admit it's rather amusing to know that the idea of *not* getting out on the big, stinky beasts is making you sad."

"Shut up," Vicki said, but she smiled.

It was neat to have been a part of each other's lives for long enough now that even stories from when they hadn't been friends were well enough known to be shared and teased about.

Vicki's past fear of horses had been the catalyst for her getting together with Joel. Dare's sadness over the loss of her family had triggered the one-night stand that resulted in both Buckaroo and Jesse changing her world forever.

Vicki knew the stories. Dare knew the stories. They were sisters by choice in a way that made each day special.

Which meant teasing was very necessary.

"We could put some horse manure in a bucket," Dare offered. "We'll stick it in the back of the crew cab, and then you can drive down the road with the windows open and have that same sensation—"

"You're terrible." Vicki sat a little straighter, but she patted a hand against her horse's withers. "You're not stinky. Nope. You're a pretty girl."

"Still think it's funny."

This time, when her sister-in-law glanced toward her, Vicki's expression was more serious. Thoughtful. "Yeah, it is funny, but in all the right ways. I mean, it feels like a long time ago I made that confession to Joel. And back then, the idea of getting up on a horse was enough to make me want to get sick."

Dare stayed silent, but again her gaze drifted over the other woman who had become a friend as well as family. There was no hesitation as she moved in an easy cadence with the solid beast under her. Vicki's hands on the reins were competent, nearly as relaxed as Dare's, and Dare had grown up on a ranch and been around animals her entire life.

Vicki continued, her voice growing clearer by the moment. "There's a lot of things we think when we're young. There's a lot of—call it baggage—we have to go through. And I know we're still young in many ways," she said, meeting Dare's eyes. "But we've got each other. We've got Jesse and Joel, *and* all the rest of their family supporting us... It's like the things that scare me now are so fleeting, because I know there's a whole mess of people willing to help me with problem-solving. To help me find my way through."

It was a simple but profound truth, and Dare found herself

nodding. She considered her own past, with the pain of having lost her family and yet being surrounded by the love of chosen family, both here in Rocky Mountain House and in Heart Falls, where she'd grown up.

These were people who would help her and Jesse, no matter what.

They finished the ride in peaceful silence, their men meeting them in the small shared barn that sat across from their houses. Jesse and Joel took care of their mounts while the children caught them by the hand and tugged them back toward the house.

"Val'ntine surprise is ready," Joey insisted, glancing for a moment at Jesse. "Right, Daddy?"

"Right, Buckaroo. You and Jess take your mamas to the house. We'll be in right away." Jesse offered Dare a wink. "Valentine's Day refuses to wait any longer."

The house smelled amazing, but both she and Vicki laughed as they reached the table where childish Valentine's cards were propped up in front of two plates, each with a single cookie on them.

Vicki leaned in and murmured softly, "You did spot the cookie crumbs in my daughter's hair, yes?"

"I was kind of distracted by all the cookie crumbs decorating my son's mouth and the front of his shirt, but now that you mention it..."

Dare and Vicki grinned at each other.

The guys came in, and they gathered in the living room to talk and share stories and just be together. Jesse pulled Dare into his arms, and she settled against him easily, his warmth perfect on the chilly day.

She hummed with happiness at the touch of his fingers on her jaw as he turned her face toward him and kissed her right then, right there, just because he wanted to.

Laughing when he let her go, they turned back to the room to discover little Jess and Joey lined up at the edge of the couch, waiting for their own kisses.

Valentine's Day was no longer just about romantic love but about enduring love, giving love. Laughing and teasing and connection beyond imagining.

Cookie crumbs and sweet kisses filled her heart to overflowing.

SP Ranch Journal
~Michael Coleman, August 1985 ~

This summer—God, what a year.

The boys all arrived in June. Yes, all boys.

Randy and Kate added Trevor to the Moonshine clan. Dana had Michael, and before the day was out, that nickname I expected was making its way through the hospital. I guess that's what happens when you give two kids specifically biblical names. The Angel Colemans are all doing well.

And our Daniel arrived right before the month finished. Marion told me she might be willing to do it one more time but to not get my heart set on six boys like Ma & Da had. I'm not set on it. Still have this sneaking suspicion that it's going to happen.

(Marion, I'm just kidding. Don't skin me.)

Daniel's a sweetheart of a kid. Marion says she can feel peace pouring off him, which is good, because there's been a hell of a lot...

I'm getting ahead of myself.

Or behind myself—between the babies and George and Sally's wedding last weekend and the rest of the work around here, I've fallen out of journaling. Need to get back to it, though.

Truth is, I learn a lot when I'm taking the time to write out my thoughts. Told Marion I needed her help to keep me on the straight and narrow when it comes to journaling. She's agreed to pick up and read what I've written. I don't have secrets from her, anyway, and knowing that she'll poke me if too many days go by without an entry is the motivation I need right now.

I want a record of all the things that need remembering so I can fix what goes wrong.

And it's a doozy this time. Mark finally showed up yesterday. We were all gathered in the barn, and he just walked in as if he hadn't been gone for almost a year.

God, just seeing his face made something break inside me all over *again, because I instinctively looked behind him, expecting to see John step in any second as well.*

So, the bad and the ugly—it wasn't a good meeting. I mean, I get it. I'm disappointed in so many ways that Mark left without a word then simply showed up out of the blue.

But Randy was pissed, and George was rude, and Ben—

God, no matter what I said, there was no way to counter the toxic bullshit that flew.

This time I don't blame Mark for leaving. I'm broken up all over again that what could have been a stepping-stone toward healing became a total breaking point for our family.

This time, I'm going to do exactly what Marion reminded me of. I'm not responsible for my brothers. They have to make their own choices. I'll still intervene if they ever step over a line, and I'll always help if they ask.

But my focus is now on my own family. On Marion, Blake, Matt, and Daniel (and any others that show up in the future.) If I can somehow be a father and husband who makes a difference to those who are mine to shape, then I will count my job as complete.

And I will always, always leave the door open for Mark to return.

Because while the choices he's making right now aren't the ones I'd make, I don't know the entire story. I can't imagine his heartbreak or his struggles.

I feel the weight of my own struggles, and I know they're made that much easier to bear because Marion is by my side. Love her with everything in me, even more than I did when we started this ride.

Since I know you're reading this—love you, darling.

[halfway down the page, a different set of handwriting.]

Love you too. So, so much. And our family will grow strong into the future, because these boys have the most caring and thoughtful daddy they could hope for.

And I have a thoughtful, caring, sexy husband who makes me smile, and gets me riled up in all the right ways.

Don't be too late coming to bed tonight.

~Marion

(But I'm NOT going through three more pregnancies. Just saying.)

PART II

Tell me, what is the present hour?
'A green and flowery spray
Where a young bird sits gathering its power
To mount and fly away.'

Past, Present, Future
Emily Brontë

9

It had taken a couple of months to put thought into action, but by the first week of March, Mark had sold his house, loaded up the remaining things he wanted to keep into his rig, and headed north.

Hours later, he pulled into the yard outside Rocky Mountain House and stared at the house that had once been where he lived. It had been a lot of years since he and John had shared the place, and for a moment, memories swapped in so hard and fast, he had to clutch the wheel to keep himself steady.

I miss you, bro. So damn much.

The confession came every single day, because that's what it meant to have lost a twin. Add in the way that he'd lost John—

Mark took a deep breath then straightened. That was the past, and now it was time to move into the future. Which meant dealing with the present moment.

John had been the one to push him forward. Which was strange in a way, because his twin was the last one any of them considered a risk-taker or go-getter. But the truth was John had been solidly at Mark's back all their growing up years. Not the one to step in front, but damn eager to follow behind as closely as possible into whatever sort of trouble they could find.

And trouble they found. John always insisted he was only there to try and keep his brother safe. Most people bought his innocent act, except their parents.

The memory of being disciplined for good ideas gone bad turned the churning in Mark's gut into a memory that made him smile.

He'd had a reason to leave, but there'd been a lot of good times here on the Coleman land. Maybe while he was stepping forward, those were the bits he needed to focus on. Kind of like Trevor's letter had said—putting together the good memories along with the bad, but focusing on the positive.

The other part of why he was back was to build *new* memories.

He pushed open his rig door and got out, wondering what Trevor would say when he realized Mark had finally responded to his oft-repeated invitation.

He stopped on the front porch, admiring the clean, welcoming area, with its fresh coat of paint and a pretty little flag hanging under the protected eaves. He put his knuckles to the door after there was no response to the doorbell.

Testing the doorknob, he found it turned easily. He was grinning pretty hard as he cracked the door opened and shouted, "Hello. Anybody home?"

Complete silence.

He closed the door firmly and headed back to his rig. Seemed he was going to have to do a little tracking to find his nephew. And while he could've gone over to Mike's or one of his other brothers' places, somehow it seemed right to deal with Trevor first.

The kid deserved it, if only for how obnoxiously tenacious he'd been over the past years with those damn letters.

Mark pulled out his phone and, for the first time ever, used the number Trevor had given him so many years ago.

"Uncle Mark?"

Yep. That was definitely a Coleman on the other end of the line. "I could swear I was talking to Randy. Yeah, this is Mark. I assume you're Trevor."

"Hell, yeah. It's good to hear from you." There was a momentary pause, other voices in the background. "Or at least, I hope it's good to hear from you. Everything okay? You need something?"

That was a fairly open-ended question. "Took you up on your offer. Decided to come to Rocky, and thought I should stop in and say hello."

"Great news. You know when you might be in town?"

Mark glanced around, noting the changes and improvements to the barn and fences since he dropped Becky off a couple years earlier. The whole place was in excellent shape—not that he expected anything different from one of Randy's kids. "Truth be told, I'm standing in your yard right now."

Trevor chuckled. "Well, you don't do things by halves. Guess you figured out I'm not there right now. Want to come into town? I took Becky out to the café. We're about to have lunch. We'd love to have you join us."

Which was probably a better idea than storming into their personal space right off the bat. Should've thought of it sooner. "I can be there in about fifteen minutes," Mark told him. "Go ahead and order without me."

He was experienced enough that it only took five minutes to unload his one-ton truck from the trailer, which meant, barely ten minutes later, he was walking through the doors into the same café he used to visit back in the day.

It hadn't changed much. The booths had been updated a little, but the long counter still stretched in an L shape around the kitchen. Coffee pots lined the counter, and the scent of bacon grease hung heavy on the air.

This was where they'd gone for burgers and fries during school hours and invaded in the evening while out on dates and spending time with friends.

"Uncle Mark." The tall, dark-haired man marching toward him with his hand outstretched could've stepped out of the pages of Mark's memory.

"Damn. It's like looking at your father thirty years ago." Mark shook the young man's hand firmly. He glanced beyond to the familiar face of the sweet, strong woman he'd first found standing alone at the side of the highway in pitch-black darkness. "Becky."

She wiggled her way off of the bench, her belly stretching forward in an obvious soon-to-be-mom proclamation.

Then she pushed right past the hand he offered and slid against his chest, squeezing her arms around him as she burst into tears.

Shit. Mark wasn't quite sure what to do for a moment, but Trevor was there, one hand on Becky's back while the other rested on Mark's shoulder. Calm and reassuring. Making it clear that if what Becky wanted was a hug, that's what Becky got.

So, Mark cradled the girl, patting her softly as she cried. Oblivious to the attention they were drawing from curious onlookers.

Trevor leaned in and lowered his voice. "Rodeo, you're gonna have to let the man go so we can actually say hello."

She nodded briskly, stepping back and wiping at her tears. She met Mark's gaze with big brown eyes filled with emotion. "Sorry about that. I'm glad you're here."

"Me too." And as they settled back down at the table, Mark checked himself and realized it was true.

None of this was going to be easy, but it would be worth it. *This* was where he was supposed to be. It hadn't happened before because the time hadn't been right, but everything felt different now.

Trevor draped an arm around Becky's shoulders and kept her

tucked up tight against him. He met Mark's gaze firmly. "I sure the hell never expected this, but like Becky, I'm glad you're here."

Mark glanced across at Becky, who was smiling even as she worked to pull herself back together. "I got your Christmas letter, and it got me thinking. We can talk about that more later. For now, I wanted to say hello to you first and see how things were going."

"You going to be in town for long?" Trevor asked. "We've got room in the house if you want it."

Mark had considered it, but settling back into Rocky was another thing he needed to do right. He shook his head. "I want plenty of talking time with Becky, and with you, but the house is yours the same as always. I'm not here to change that."

Becky tilted her head, wonder shining out of her eyes. "Sounds as if you're here for more than a visit."

He nodded slowly. "Still working on my final plans, but yeah. I hope to stay."

Trevor looked a little dazed. "Wow."

"I think that's—" Becky's eyes widened. "Oh, shit."

Mark had *never* heard the girl swear. Not even once during the months that he'd taken care of her while she recovered after running away from a terrible situation.

And from Trevor's instant reaction, spine stiffening, head snapping to attention, her cussing still wasn't a common thing. "Rodeo?"

Becky caught hold of Trevor's hand. "My water broke. I am so sorry. Can you get me a towel or something—?"

Trevor was out of the seat, darting two steps toward the door, then two steps back. "Screw the towel. You need the hospital. Uncle Mark—" Trevor didn't finish the sentence. He ran five steps toward the door this time before returning. "I'm starting the truck. I'll be right back."

It appeared his nephew was going to be one of *those* type of fathers.

Mark glanced across the table at Becky. "You feeling any contractions?"

Becky shrugged, wiggling her way toward the edge of the bench seat. "Some. Nothing too dire."

"Okay. Then we'll get Trevor to drive you to the hospital."

He offered a hand, and she took it, standing up easily. She glanced over her shoulder then back at him. "I feel terrible about the mess."

"Not any worse than someone accidentally tipping over a pop." He pushed a few napkins off the table and onto the bench. "That's why they make the place wash and wear, sweetheart. Come on."

He'd barely had time to wrap an arm gently around Becky's waist, when the door of the café flew open, the bells going off as if being shaken by a tornado.

Trevor stood in the doorway, his eyes wild. "*Someone took my truck.*"

Unexpected, a snicker escaped Becky. "Really? I wonder how that happened."

"They're not supposed to take my truck *today*." Trevor all but shouted the words. "That's not how this works. I have to get you to the hospital."

A dozen set of keys were lifted in the air from all of the excited onlookers in the café.

"You can use mine, Trev."

"Mine's parked right outside."

"Don't even need to gas her up when you're done," someone else offered.

Becky was full-on laughing at this point, even as Trevor came to take over, his arm sliding around her waist. She lifted bright eyes to meet Mark's gaze. "Could I bother you for another ride?"

The beauty of the moment just about floored him. "I would be honoured."

10

———

ecky walked the hall with her fingers tangled with Trevor's. Inside, she was so filled with emotion that it was difficult to keep from bouncing. Of course, when a moment later tears threatened to burst free, it wasn't quite as much fun.

Glancing at Trevor's concerned face, she tried to explain. "I'm like a yo-yo right now. Scared, then thrilled, sad then delighted, all at the same time."

Trevor pulled her into his arms, one hand cradling the back of her head as he held her. "I'm right there with you."

Seeing Mark had brought back sad memories, but oddly that wasn't the part affecting her the hardest. "When I ran away from Paradise Colony, I had no idea where I was going. What I would do."

A shiver shook him, and his arms momentarily curled tighter around her. Trevor pressed a kiss to her temple. "You're safe, Rodeo. Nothing from there can touch you."

She shook her head, peeling back far enough to be held yet meet his eyes. "I know. I know that to the complete innermost part of me. It's just, thinking back to how Mark took me in that day? He gave me a ride then took care of me. Not knowing who I really was, he trusted me and ended up giving me a future."

A contraction hit, and she paused, hands braced on her knees in the middle of the hallway they'd been pacing. Trevor rubbed her back and breathed with her until she was able to stand again.

This time she knew what she wanted to say. Becky cupped Trevor's face in her hands. "Mark gave me a future where I found you. Falling in love with you and having you love me back has been beyond anything I could've ever imagined when I was living in Paradise."

Trevor leaned in and kissed her. Sweet and intense. "We live somewhere better than paradise. We have a home." He slipped a hand over her belly. "We're building a family."

"We are, and I'm so glad." It'd taken a while, but between therapy and Trevor being his sweet, unendingly patient self, their physical relationship had changed. Sex no longer traumatized her. It was something that—*with Trevor*—made her hot and ache and truly feel alive to the center of her being.

Just the thought of getting tangled up with Trevor in bed sometime in the future made her heart skip a beat.

Trevor grinned. "You're blushing. Thinking dirty thoughts?"

"Hush." She tapped him on the chest and pushed back, offering a wink.

They walked another while, dealt with more contractions, before Becky pulled the conversation back to what she needed to share. "When I lived with Mark, before he dropped me off at the house here in Rocky? We talked a bunch. You know that. But while he shared some information about his home, it always seemed as if something about what happened here with his family was missing. I want to help him if he needs it. I want *him* to be happy."

Trevor nodded. "Of course we will. He's a good man, and he's family."

"He was family to me before I ever met you." Becky's throat was tight. "I need him to know that."

Trevor squeezed her fingers. "We'll make sure he does."

Not long after, Rachel showed up. Her sister-in-law was nearly ten years older, but she'd become more than family. She was pretty much Becky's best friend.

"Too bad I'm not working any longer. I could've come straight with you from the café," she teased.

"Where are your babies?" Becky asked. Rachel and Lee's children had come ten months apart from each other, which meant Liam had just turned one, and Ava was barely two months old.

"Mom and Dad have them," Lee said as he patted Trevor firmly on the shoulder. He waited for Rachel and Becky to untangle themselves from their massive hug then swooped in and squeezed Becky tight. "You've got this. We're here for you, and Rachel's ready to give you tips."

"Since you've practiced a couple of times already," Becky teased before adding, "You should get pregnant again soon, so you don't forget how it's done."

Rachel visibly shuddered. "No. Please no. I love the babies, but that would be too soon."

"Didn't Ashley almost do that?" Trevor asked.

"She waited a full three months between starting the next baby," Lee said before adding dryly, "I'm surprised it took that long since she's got *two* guys to deal with."

Becky had to stop snickering to breathe through a contraction.

The wonder of it hit. So much had changed over the past years. What she had lived through in the cult and their strange sexual norms had *nothing* to do with the loving relationship that Travis, Cassidy, and Ashley shared. Knowing that to be an absolute truth was amazing.

Love was love, and it could shine out in many different ways. Without love, nothing was right.

The distraction of having Rachel and Lee there was good, but when push came to shove, literally, it was just Trevor in the room with her. The nurse practitioner helped, the doctor arriving barely in time. Moments later, Dr. Kinkaid laid a sweet, squirming little girl on Becky's chest.

A few precious moments of quiet followed after the baby was cleaned up, her little pink mouth moving in a bow as she attempted to latch on and nurse.

The physical tug at Becky's breast was nothing compared to the one squeezing around her heart. Seeing the precious life she and Trevor had made—Becky felt as if *she'd* been reborn.

She glanced up to discover tears trickling down Trevor's face. Softly, Becky touched a fingertip to one.

He caught her by the wrist and brought her hand to his lips, tenderly kissing the moisture away. Even as he stared at the baby, he gave a small shake of his head and spoke with his heart in his voice. "I love you so much, Rodeo. That was one hell of a thing. Seeing you bring our baby into the world—damn. I always believed you were strong, but now I know you can move mountains."

Becky swallowed hard. "Love you."

They both lowered their eyes to the sweet wonder of life. "You ready to share her name?"

Of all the joyful blessings, it was one Becky had never imagined she would get to experience. "I think so." She gestured toward the door. "You want to go let Rachel in?"

Trevor laughed heartily. "I'll also see if the *rest* of my family might be out there."

His amusement was entertaining, yet the truth was another part of the perfect joy Becky let surround her in that moment. "Nope. Not even going to apologize. Rachel's *especially* mine."

Trevor stood, pausing to give Becky a kiss. Then he leaned a little lower, pressing his lips to the baby's temple. "You better get ready for some loving, little lioness."

The joy inside Becky's heart was pouring over the edges so hard, not even the room could contain it.

And as all of the people she had come to know as immediate family filed into the room, her gaze touched on each of them. Marking them as blessings beyond anything she could've imagined.

Rachel hurried to her side, baby Ava cradled in her arms. But she still had room to reach in and brush her fingers against the newborn's cheek before leaning down and kissing Becky on the forehead. "I am so glad you have your beautiful little girl."

Becky blinked back tears. "I didn't want to cry anymore," she complained.

Lee was there, infant son braced on his arm. He also offered a kiss to both the baby and Becky. "I don't see any tears," he assured her. "Look, Liam. Another pretty baby."

Liam twisted his head, looking at the newborn and at his baby sister in his mom's arms. "B'bies?"

"Yes. This one is Auntie Becky and Uncle Trevor's."

Pudgy little fingers reached forward before jerking back partway. "Gen'tle."

Laughter swelled as more people joined them.

"Yes. We have to be gentle with babies." Becky looked up to see her mother-in-law, Kate, paused beside the edge of the bed with one hand pressed over her chest. "Look at you. Look at this precious little bit of perfection."

Trevor's dad, Randy, stepped into view behind her, arm sliding around her shoulders. "You grow good crops when you start with good seed. *Ouch.*"

Kate shook out her fingers after having slapped his arm, but she twisted with a smile. "Hold off with your ranch parables. This is *all* Trevor and Becky's doing."

"All Becky." Trevor was there, easing beside her. He rested on the edge of the bed as he tucked his arm around her and laid a hand over their little girl's body. His hand was so big, fingers callused from years of hard labour, yet Becky knew that he would never be anything but gentle with their child.

He was never anything but gentle with *her*, and Becky's heart filled.

The room grew busier as the oldest children of the Moonshine clan arrived. Steve with two-year-old Jason in his arms. Melody's baby belly was bigger than the last time Becky had seen her.

Trevor's only sister, Anna, her belly a near match for Melody's, leaned back against her husband, Mitch, their two-year-old girl, Kasey, resting easily on her hip. "So. We're all here and suitably delighted with your little girl's arrival."

Lee spoke softly. "Trev? You going to let us know what you're calling her?"

Becky met Trevor's gaze. This man had been her savior in spite of herself. A man who had never thought himself worthy or able to be anyone's hero, but who had turned out to be the only one who was absolutely everything she needed. "Her name is Arabella."

"Beautiful lioness," Trevor added, his gaze falling to their daughter. "Because we'll teach her to be beautiful inside and out —it'll probably come naturally because she'll take after her mama. But she's also going to be strong like a lion. Able to take on the world and care for herself and everyone around her." Then he lowered his voice, just for Becky's ears. "Also like her mama."

That was it. The fight against tears was a battle she could no longer win. "I love you," she choked out before burying her face against his neck.

The family reacted like usual, going on about their business as if there wasn't a blubbering woman in their midst. It gave Becky time to pull herself together.

Somewhere in there, Arabella got passed around to be

greeted by everyone in the family. Kisses from cousins, aunts and uncles, and her adoring Grandma and Grampa, Kate snapping pictures.

Becky thought about the Coleman memory book that was being put together and wondered how to wrap up something as rich and full as what she felt at that moment and put it into words.

Impossible.

And yet, out there, waiting for more conversation, was a man she had known for a brief time who had impacted her world beyond imagining. Mark was a memory, but so much more.

Maybe family memories weren't only a snapshot of this moment or that. Perhaps it was somehow about how each tiny bit of family built on what had come before.

Becky's gaze met Trevor's across the room as he finished taking Arabella back from his father.

The bed dipped beside her, and Becky glanced over to discover Rachel resting on an elbow, smiling like the Cheshire cat. "You done good, sweetie. I'm looking forward to raising our babies together."

Becky nodded, smiling through the tears. "That's the best part of this. The love's just going to keep growing and growing, isn't it?"

Rachel blinked back a few tears of her own. "Pretty much. And we wouldn't want it any other way."

Coleman Memory Book
~Lee & Rachel (Moonshine) Coleman~
~Lee~

Winter in Alberta triggers a million memories all by itself. Snow caves, ATVs stuck in the drifts. Freezing cold fingers. Hot Chinook winds that unexpectedly melted the snow base and left our skidoos stranded. It took forever to walk home, our feet soggy messes by the end of it. The Coleman land is pretty big, and there's a lot of nooks and crannies to get lost in.

But the winter memory that hits the deepest is from when I was about ten. Mom had made us drinks, and all of us sat by the fire, the wind howling outside the windows. We were trapped for three days. Other than chores in the nearest barn, we didn't leave the house. Didn't see or hear from anyone.

Trevor cheated at Monopoly every time Anna didn't watch close enough. Steve practiced the same damn song over and over on the guitar. I'm sure I did something annoying in retaliation.

Mom and Dad sat in the love seat and held hands as they stared at the storm whirling outside. They were so connected that, as a kid, it made me feel safe. The world might disappear, but they would never change or leave us.

I learned a lot watching them. I'm still learning from them.

[Images of snowy winter scenes. A snow drift piled higher than the man door of the barn. Four children in snowsuits, grinning. Three lopsided snowmen with two adults standing between them and pretending to also be snowmen. The man wore a top hat, the woman a scarf, both with arms held out as if they were branches, carrots poking forward from their mouths.]

~Rachel~

I guess I have a winter memory as well.

Getting stuck in a cabin with Lee was a game changer. It's funny, because I went there alone to put aside a bunch of sadness in my life, but if I'd had that cabin all to myself, I don't think it really would've happened.

I learned that sad memories aren't things that you can burn up, or drink away, or shove aside and not deal with. Sometimes you need to face them, but I think mostly you need to have something new to fill the aching hole in your soul.

That's the biggest memory I have regarding coming into the Coleman family. Sometimes love comes when you don't expect, from the direction you least expect.

From whom you least expect.

11

They'd made good time. Dana Coleman smiled as her daughter-in-law Laurel pulled into the yard outside Becky and Trevor's house.

"There's a big truck in the yard," Laurel noted. "But not Trevor's. I wonder if he's home?"

Dana laughed. "You know that doesn't mean anything. That boy still offers his truck to everyone and anyone."

"True."

Dana pointed toward the open spot with a cleared path through the snow to the front door. "If Becky's here, she can tell us where to put things. If she's not, we'll do what we can to unpack the groceries we brought her so things are out of the way."

"If you get the door, I'll grab the first bags," Laurel offered.

It was slick underfoot, but Dana made her way to the front porch with no problem. Her other daughter-in-law, Allison, had given her a new pair of boots with some magical material on the sole that made her footing solid enough Dana could skip over ice if she wanted to.

Not that she wanted to. In fact, this year's winter could be over sooner than later, Dana decided. Although she knew better than to voice that opinion out loud, in March, in Alberta. If history was anything to go by, they could have snow all the way up until June, especially if anybody complained that it had been a long, hard winter.

She cracked open the door and offered a cheery hello, not really expecting a response. "Becky? It's Auntie Dana. We've got the stuff you asked for from the Costco run."

When nothing but silence echoed back, Dana slipped off her boots and got ready to transfer the bags from the front door into the kitchen.

"Dana?"

She jerked to attention so hard, one sock-covered foot slid to the side, sending her off-balance.

A moment later, strong arms caught her before she could lose her dignity and land on the floor in a heap. Strong, *masculine* arms—not ones that belonged to her nephew.

She glanced up into blue eyes, and the world stuttered to a stop.

An older man cradled her carefully, her age or thereabouts, his features declaring he was Coleman plain as day. Each of the brothers had the unique twist of them. Kate had always teased it was their personalities coming out—

Mike was serious yet kind. The type of man you willingly told your troubles to, and if he couldn't solve them immediately, he'd sympathize and do his damnedest to make things right.

Randy was the Coleman peacemaker, with laugh lines at the corners of his eyes and scars on his knuckles, because if he couldn't jokingly convince others he was right, he'd pick a fight and convince them that way.

Ben—the Coleman brother who'd been hers—had been grumpy around everyone else, but in the early days, he'd had a sharp wit and a clever eye and a wry way of saying things that always made her laugh.

The man standing in front of her now, the brother she hadn't seen in too many years to count, was the one with mystery in his expression. Even when they'd been friends at school, he'd always seemed to have something he wasn't quite saying.

"*Mark?*"

He was tall—taller than she remembered to be honest. The years that had passed had written themselves onto his face the same as changes had come to her. Lines at the corners of his eyes, but still a strong jaw, firm lips.

Strong muscles flexed under his shirt as he helped her find her balance then stepped away.

Good grief, she'd been draped there in his arms like some damsel in distress the entire time she'd been ogling him. Still, her brain hadn't quite come online yet.

"What're you doing here?" If the words came out a little harsh, he didn't seem to notice.

"I've come home."

His gaze was eating her up, and a wicked flutter kicked into gear in her gut that made her feel far too light-headed to be safe.

"This isn't your home." Dana slapped a hand over her mouth before meeting his eyes and adjusting her tone. "I'm sorry. That was terribly rude, but you surprised me."

"No. You're right. I might own the house, but this isn't my home."

The door swung open behind her, cold air rushing into the front hall. Laurel jerked to a stop, shopping bags dangling from her fingers. "Oh. Hello."

Dana pulled herself together rapidly. "I'll take them from here. You go and get the rest," she ordered without giving Laurel time to do so much as blink as she scooped the bags from her hands.

Her daughter-in-law glanced at her before slowly heading back outside.

Dana turned, intending to ignore Mark and get on with the

job. "I need to put a few things away. You can tell Becky that I was here."

"She and Trevor are at the hospital," Mark informed her.

Delight bubbled up, and Dana paused, forgetting herself and grinning at Mark. "The baby?"

"Haven't heard anything yet, but I imagine the Coleman gossip chain will deliver news as there's any to share."

The fact he knew that—

Mark was such a part of the family, and yet he hadn't been here.

Anger rushed in hard on the heels of the other rioting emotions and unanswered questions she had. Just because he *hadn't* been there didn't mean he hadn't been the topic of conversation more times than she could remember. Which had been wonderful and terrible and downright confusing. "So, you've come to say hello to the baby? When are you leaving?"

"Trying to get rid of me?"

Dana made room in the fridge for a block of cheese, which allowed her to keep her back toward Mark. "None of my business if you come or go. Just making conversation."

The front door opened, and Laurel's call cut off anything Mark was going to say. "One more load to grab, Mom. You got everything under control here?"

Mark took a step toward the front hall.

Dear God, don't let Mark say anything in front of her daughter-in-law. Not until—

Dana all but sprinted to cut him off, slowing the instant she was past him. "I'm good. This won't take long."

Laurel took another inquisitive glance between her and Mark before reluctantly disappearing outside the door one last time.

Moving as quickly as she could, Dana unloaded the next two bags of groceries before Mark stepped closer. "Dana. Tell me I can turn back the hands of the clock. Tell me how to make up for not being here all those years."

Dana looked at him. Really looked.

He was handsome, but sadness also marked his face, something that had rarely been there when they'd been friends so long ago. He'd been full of laughter and excitement during the years they'd shared at school.

But it *had* been years, and he *had* left—and while he'd been gone, the Coleman family had dealt with many things. So much sadness, so much loss.

Dana choked back the pain swirling inside and stuck to the basics. "You're family. You should've been here, but you weren't. That was your choice. But if you want to be here now, I suppose you'll have to put in the time. Eventually people will get used to you being around again. I don't know for sure."

Her own heart had been broken more than once, and to have this reminder from her past waltzing in—

She was simultaneously curious and angry and sad and flustered, and *none* of it made sense.

She must've been staring, because he was suddenly there, right in her space. He tucked his fingers under her chin and lifted until her eyes met his. "Tell me I have a chance."

Confusion swept in. "A chance...at what?"

"Forever. With the woman I love."

What? A sharp laugh burst from her. "*Love*? What are you talking about? Who?"

"You, Dana. I want to be with you. I've loved you forever."

Never in a million years could she have imagined this. Speaking instead of simply sputtering was almost impossible. "We were never more than friends. It's been ages since we've even seen each other. I was married! You can't just go tossing off words like that—"

"It's what I feel, and I refuse to call it anything else." Mark stepped back, his hand falling to his side. "I took the coward's way once, walking away because it was the only option I had. But I won't leave again. And you can correct my words all you want, but you can't change what's inside my heart."

"*Mark.*" Dana hadn't felt this conflicted in forever.

She'd loved Ben, and then she'd hated what life had turned him into. But even during the toughest times toward the end, she'd still felt deep emotion for the man he had once been.

Maybe Mark did feel something, in spite of it having been so long since they'd even seen each other. But for him to come marching in and toss around a word like *love*—

It was too much, and too soon, and *way* too unexpected. She shook her head. "I can't deal with this. I need time. I need to think, and I need to—"

"Of course, you do," Mark agreed. "I'll give it to you. Time, at least a bit more. But I *am* back in Rocky, Dana. I've come to rejoin the family. I know that's going to take more than a little work, but I'm ready for it."

Incredible.

His smile grew, and her heart began pounding.

He spoke again, and there was laughter in his words. "I learned a lot during my years away about working hard and being successful. Just so you know, I totally plan to find a way to win you to my side."

It was his amusement that got her back up. "*If* I decide I want to see you as anything other than a distant family member, I'll tell you." Her shock was bubbling now into a nice hot rage. "I can't believe you expected to come in here and order me around. I'm not some submissive little thing. I'm still figuring out exactly what I want—"

"That's going to be me," Mark promised. "The *what you want* part."

Her cheeks had to be bright red, they were so flaming hot. "That's pretty cocky talk."

"Confidence. I seem to remember you liked that in a man."

He stepped around her and took the final package from Laurel as she raced through the front door.

The young woman had obviously been running. Now she glanced back and forth between the two of them. "Anything I need to do?"

"We're done," Dana told her. "See you around, Mark."

"See you," he echoed, but there seemed to be volumes of warning in that comment.

It was only a short drive back to the house Dana shared with her son and daughter-in-law. Laurel's gaze darted to the side over and over, and in spite of the mass of confusion, anger, and everything else Mark's arrival had triggered, Dana found herself amused enough to hide a smile. Her daughter-in-law had to be wildly curious at the moment but was stifling her million questions rather handily.

Or mostly stifling them.

"That's the missing uncle? The one who left all those years ago?"

"Mark. Yes. I guess Becky's having her baby, and he's come out to..." Dana lost the flow of her thought for a moment.

He's come for me wasn't remotely on the list of things she was about to say. But that's what he said he was there to do.

Dear Lord.

She forced herself to smile at her daughter-in-law. "He's come for a visit. Which is going to be interesting."

"Sounds kind of like that Chinese curse—*may you live in interesting times*," Laurel said dryly.

Oh, boy. "Pretty much exactly like that," Dana agreed.

What was a woman supposed to do with the knowledge that, after thirty-five years, one of her classmates and the younger brother of the man she'd been married to for ages, claimed to love her?

Good thing she had enough chores to distract herself until

the evening. Somehow, she'd find a way to wrap her brain around this.

Mark was home. He said that he loved her.

Dana shook her head and fell into distractions like a gladiator heading into the ring.

12

———

After nearly three years of living with her mother-in-law, Laurel knew better than to poke when Dana pulled on her stone face.

Colemans knew how to keep secrets.

But after nearly three years of living full time with two Colemans and being totally immersed in Coleman-landia, not to mention all the years growing up as best friend to Rafe, Laurel also knew there were ways of getting results that didn't involve trying to move unmovable stones.

As quickly as possible, she grabbed the couple of items that needed to go to her sister-in-law's house. "I'm going to run these over to Allison. Need me to take anything else?"

A slightly dazed and distracted Dana shook her head. "I'll get supper started while you're gone."

The only reason Laurel didn't spin out of the driveway was because too much snow packed down the gravel. After fishtailing onto the secondary highway, she slowed enough to stay out of the ditch, because that would make all of her plans far more complicated.

Even while she drove, though, she used Bluetooth to put through a call in search of the first answers.

"Hey, Ms. Coleman, how are things on Angel land?" Jaxi teased.

"I need intel, stat." Laurel got straight to the point. "Uncle Mark. Why would he and my mother-in-law be acting all awkward around each other?"

A split second of silence hung on the air before Jaxi gasped. "You *saw* him?"

"In Becky's house, and Dana has never been so flustered." Laurel slowed and checked the three-way stop before illegally rolling through the intersection. No one drove these roads but Colemans in the first place, but it was probably a good thing that cousin Anna no longer delighted in handing out tickets to her family like Halloween candy. "I know he's been gone forever, but I didn't think there was any really bad blood between the brothers. And I certainly didn't know of anything that would make my mother-in-law rattled enough to be anything other than a bit surprised."

"My father-in-law has talked about it. After Mark left, there were a few hot tempers the first time he came for a visit, but it's been years. Mike's been in contact with him off and on. Everything I've heard or seen since makes me suspect Mark would be welcomed back with open arms. Especially after everything he did for Becky."

"That's what I thought, but Dana never once mentioned that part. Which is strange, which is why I'm calling you." Laurel took the turn onto Allison and Gabe's driveway. "Okay, keep this quiet for now. I'll let you know if I figure out anything else. Oh, and Becky's at the hospital. You heard anything yet?"

"Nothing, but I bet I can get an update."

"Text me," Laurel said. "I'm at Allison's."

"Later, sweetie."

Talking to the source of all information Coleman-related had been simultaneously useful and piqued Laurel's curiosity even further.

Why had Dana acted so strangely? Especially considering the most recent thing Mark had done was give Becky a fresh start after escaping a bad situation.

Laurel marched in Allison's front door, kicked off her boots, and headed straight to the kitchen. "I got your stuff, and I want to gossip."

Her sister-in-law's dark eyes sparkled with mischief as she rose from where she'd been sitting on the couch, baby in her lap and four-year-old Micah stacking toys on the coffee table. "It's good to know you've finally been totally corrupted."

"Ha. If you think this is a recent event, you obviously weren't paying attention back when Rafe and I were constantly seated outside the principal's office." Allison went to put Ariel in the playpen at the edge of the kitchen, but Laurel held out her arms. "Here. Give her to me. Auntie needs some lovin'."

The little girl's blondish curls stuck up every direction, and Laurel settled the one-year-old in her lap and smoothed her fingers through the soft tangles.

Allison went to unpack the groceries. "Who's the topic of gossip?"

"Mom. *Our* mom—Dana. Oops." Her phone buzzed in her pocket, and Laurel wiggled to grab it. "That should be an update from Jaxi."

Allison had her phone out as well. "I got it. Baby girl for Becky and Trevor. I'm so glad for them."

"Me too." A small knot inside her tightened, but Laurel pushed the feelings aside, squeezing Ariel a little closer and concentrating on how good the news was. "Becky deserves all the joy possible."

"Agreed." Allison put her fists on her hips. "Now, take a step back. You want to gossip about *Mom*? What did she do? You *never* gossip about Dana, which I figured meant you've got the constitution of a saint, considering you live together."

"She doesn't usually do anything that's gossip-worthy," Laurel admitted. "She's wonderful, and I love her to pieces. Which is why I want to find out—has she ever mentioned Mark Coleman to you?"

"Becky's Uncle Mark? I mean, Gabe's uncle, but the one who helped Becky out?" Allison shrugged. "Sure. I mean his name came up in conversations even before he dropped Becky off at his place. And what with the Colemans working together now, we're planning on using a bunch of his territory that met the organic standards to expand operations. Gabe tried to get in touch with him a bunch of times, but he's been sending all correspondence through Trevor. And Trevor said Mark basically told us to do anything we want, he's okay with it."

Which was not remotely the direction Laurel wanted this gossip to go. "But has she ever mentioned Uncle Mark *outside* of owning Coleman land? Like some reason that she would have to blush around him?"

Allison jerked to a stop, the bag of nuts in her hands sliding to the counter with a crash. She turned, all her attention fully on Laurel. "Okay, so this wasn't a hypothetical question. You saw Uncle Mark and Mom, and Mom was *blushing*?"

"Over at Becky's. Mom kept trying to keep me out of the way, and the instant we were done, she scooted out of there like her pants were on fire. And she didn't do more than give me his name."

Her sister-in-law blinked in surprise. "No *hello, how are you doing, so good to see you, when are you coming over for dinner* spiel?"

"None of it." Laurel dipped her chin firmly. "That's the part that made me suspicious."

"I hear you, but there's not much else I can say," Allison admitted. She thought hard for a moment then shrugged. "Uncle

Mark didn't live in Rocky at all while I've been here. If Mom knows him, it's something from the distant past."

Which meant if Laurel wanted to know more, she had to talk to her mother-in-law.

Or...

Ariel squirmed in Laurel's arms. She caught hold of a strand of Laurel's hair and tugged. "Pre'dy."

"Careful, baby." Laurel detached the death grip, gently easing herself free and moving Ariel far enough back she wouldn't get tugged again. A moment later, Micah was there, holding a truck for Laurel to admire.

She spent the next half hour playing with her niece and nephew and chatting with Allison, but when she slipped away, that sense of concern had grown so strong, Laurel needed to do something with it.

It was interfering—

No. Not interfering. In a way, she was only being friendly.

Justification firmly in place, Laurel headed back to Becky and Trevor's house on the off chance she would catch Uncle Mark there.

He was coming out the front door as she drove into the yard. He paused, confusion on his face until his eyes brightened when she met him on the front stairs. "Hello, again."

Laurel stuck out her hand. "Didn't get to introduce myself before—Laurel Coleman." She made a face as he laughed. "Yeah, you probably could've guessed that last part."

"At this point, I plan to assume half the people I meet are somehow related, and I won't go far wrong." Mark examined her empty hands. "Did you forget to drop something off?"

Laurel paused. What was her excuse? Oh, right. "No. I thought I'd make sure there was something easy for the family to heat for supper, depending on when they get home from the hospital. Did you hear? About the baby?"

"I did. Trevor took about five messages to get all the details to me. He was so excited, he kept hitting *Send* before he was done typing." Mark's grin bloomed, and suddenly Laurel saw in him an image of what her Rafe would look like in thirty years. A handsome man, strong, yet with kindness in his eyes.

Another thought whirled by rapidly—that's not at all what Rafe's father *Ben* had looked like before he passed.

"And you don't have to worry about dinner," Mark went on. "I figured I had the time, so I made up lasagna and left it in the fridge."

Another unexpected jolt. "Well, that's nice of you."

Mark stood there, silent.

This was the moment when, given the excuse she'd offered, she should say goodbye, turn around and go home. Only—

"What did you say to Dana?" The words blurted free. Laurel kind of wanted to take them back, but now that she'd made a partial fool of herself, she figured she may as well jump with both feet and humiliate herself all the way. "After she talked to you, she was kind of upset."

His face folded into a frown. "Well, *shit*."

Honesty prevailed. "She didn't say anything to me. And she wasn't upset like you'd scared her or she was angry, but as if something had made her confused."

The corner of his lips curled upward briefly. Rafe wore the same expression when he was trying not to laugh at her. "Sounds as if you know Dana pretty well to be able to pick that much up from her *not* saying anything."

"There're a lot of times ladies don't say things because we can't, so yeah. Maybe I can read another woman even without them using words." Laurel wanted to stare at her toes, but she forced herself to meet Mark's gaze. "Sorry. I'm a little outspoken at times, but if you want the honest truth, yes. I *do* know Dana pretty well, and I love her very much. After the hell she's gone through, she doesn't need anybody making her life harder just when she's finally getting to spread her wings again."

It was such a weird conversation, the cool weather of March barely warmed by the sun as they stood outside on the porch as if it were a summer day.

Mark's expression changed again, no longer amusement but sheer confusion. "What are you talking about? What hell did she go through?"

Her snort was definitely rude, but Laurel no longer cared. All the warning signs she'd picked up earlier were ringing loud and clear.

This man might have been the cause of a wonderful change in Becky's world, but that didn't mean he had carte blanche to wade in and interfere in anyone else's life. Not when he seemed so clueless.

Laurel's mother-in-law deserved to be protected.

"Oh, I don't know. The bit where she lost a son or where she lost her husband. Frankly, she lost him years before he even died and had to put up with a man who didn't appreciate her and didn't treat her the way he should've."

For the first time she saw an echo of Rafe's father, Ben, glaring at her as if she were the cause of his troubles. The sheer disgust the man had felt even talking to her had always shone in his eyes.

But when Mark spoke, the anger wasn't against her. "I had no idea."

Laurel took a deep breath and let her own anger, frustration, and confusion slide away as much as possible before she spoke again. "I'm sorry. Maybe I shouldn't have said anything."

"No," he said quickly. "I'm glad you did."

He seemed sincere. Laurel got ready to head home, pausing to give one final unasked for bit of advice. "I'm glad you're here, for Becky's sake, but please—you've been gone a long time. You need to tread carefully. The Coleman clan is wonderful, and collectively, they're a force of nature. But sometimes the individual people need a little careful handling."

"Thank you." He paused for a moment before his expression

hardened. "I'll think about what you said. I'm truly glad you told me."

A little embarrassed now that the heat of the moment had passed, Laurel was still flushed when she made it back to the house. She slipped in the side door to access the part of the house she shared with Rafe without bumping into her mother-in-law.

She'd barely finished washing her face and was staring out the window, taking deep breaths, when a door opened behind her.

"Sitko? What are you hiding in here for?" Rafe crossed the room in three big steps and pulled her into his arms. His tone dropped a notch, hot enough to make her skin tingle. "Not that I mind finding you in our bedroom in the afternoon."

Coming on three years together, and no matter how often she teased, he still called her by her old nickname.

She curled her arms around his neck and eased her body against his. "Maybe I knew you'd be home early and wanted to surprise you."

He raised a brow, gaze dancing over her cheeks, which felt a lot hotter than they should've. "That's as close to a lie as you can get without lighting up like a candle. What's up?"

It took about ten minutes to share the whole story—Laurel talked fast—and at the end of it, Rafe looked as confused as Laurel felt.

"I'm not going to even try to figure out what's going on at this point." Rafe stroked his fingers through her hair, leaning in to brush his lips over hers. "My mom is strong, and she's smart. And if there's something she needs help with, we have to trust that she'll ask."

"That's not how we do things in the Coleman family," Laurel complained. "The Coleman way is to run in, scoop people up, and help them whether they want it or not."

"You've been hanging out with Jaxi too much," Rafe said with a grin as he backed Laurel to the wall. "In the meantime, I thought maybe I could distract my wife. Considering it *is* the afternoon, and we both *happen* to be home."

A wall of muscle pressed against her, heat rising between them.

"Your mom was in the kitchen when I got home," Laurel whispered.

"I passed her as I came into the house. She was headed to the barn for at least an hour," he whispered back.

Because the one bad part about sharing a house with her mother-in-law was sex. As in, being quiet during.

Laurel hurriedly undid Rafe's shirt, sliding her fingers over the warm planes of his muscular chest. "Someday I'd like to have sex on the kitchen table," she murmured. "Our *own* kitchen table, when I'm not worried about anybody interrupting us."

"Someday," Rafe promised. He pushed her pants to the ground then stood and ripped her top over her head. His gaze heated as he examined her hungrily. "But for now, I'm just so thankful I get to do this."

He dropped to his knees in front of her, one strong arm pinning her in place. Laurel leaned against the wall and let sensation rush over her as he pressed kisses along the edge of her panties.

"When did you get these?" His question was midway between a growl and a moan. He cupped her intimately, leaning back far enough to meet her eyes. "Silky purple. I like them."

She wasn't about to interrupt what was happening with a lengthy reminder she'd gone on another shopping trip that Ashley had been party to. No one came home without at least one naughty purchase when the woman was around.

Laurel offered the sexiest smile possible as she whispered, "Take them off me."

"Soon." Rafe slid his hand back and forth, gliding the sinfully soft fabric over skin that had grown hot and needy. His fingers pushed the panties gently between the folds of her sex as his thumb came down with deadly accuracy over her clit.

Somehow, she remained vertical. Maybe it was by grounding her fingers in his thick, coarse hair, the strands cool against her heated palms. Maybe it was the unyielding pressure of his forearm over her hips.

Or maybe it was the sheer electric energy that zipped through her limbs as Rafe tugged the gusset of her panties aside and put his talented mouth on her.

Tongue teasing over sensitive skin, he stole her breath away with each slow, deliberate stroke. And when he slid his fingers in and pumped lazily, Laurel gasped and moaned and rocked toward him.

A low chuckle rose even as he continued the sensual assault, and pleasure struck in one unending wave. Laurel attempted to loosen her fingers, her grip in his hair too tight, too rough. He didn't seem to mind, though, his hands now cupping her butt. Rafe pressed his mouth even tighter against her sensitive skin and pushed her orgasm into overdrive.

The echo of blood pounding in her ears still remained when she opened her eyes to discover she was flat on her back in their bed. Rafe grinned from where he lay beside her. One hand possessively cupped her breast as he leaned up on the other elbow and stared into her eyes.

"Wow." Laurel took a deep breath and let it out slowly. "That was wild."

"We're just getting started." His words came out rough, needy, and when he rolled over her, Laurel welcomed him. Opening her thighs to cradle him closer. She wrapped her legs around his lean, muscular hips, rocking his rigid cock against her sex.

She tugged his shoulders until he moved toward her, close enough to join their lips together and kiss him with everything in her.

Being loved by Rafe was everything she'd ever wanted. Loving Rafe back was the thing that gave her the most pleasure.

As she moved under him, teasing and touching until he couldn't wait any longer and joined them together in the most intimate way possible, her heart swelled with happiness.

This was home. Not the physical house, but where her heart lived. With Rafe. Always and forever.

Coleman Memory Book
~Tamara (Whiskey Creek) Stone~

I remember the talking. The out-of-the-blue conversations that sometimes made life turn on a dime.

We talked while on horseback, and in trucks, and on porches. Talked over cake and way too many cups of tea at Auntie Dana's and Auntie Kate's houses.

We talked late at night while coyote howls carried on the air all over Whiskey Creek ranch. Even though I don't live there anymore, I can close my eyes and picture clear as day the horses racing over the land, the Rockies in the distance, my sisters' voices and their laughter ringing around me.

We talked the wrong way at times. Raised voices. Shouts. Or silence, while we also refused to listen. Or, as in my case, refused to speak and turned away instead of trying to make it better. That's a hard confession considering how radically I insisted on doing what's right in other ways.

But the good memories are growing again, and that's what I want to share as my part of this memory book. Families are sometimes hard, but they're precious. They're worth fighting for.

A lot of times we screwed up in spite of trying to be there for each other. But if we listen harder and speak the truth with love, we can slowly change to a better way.

[Images: tea cups on rustic wood table, sliced cake on plate. A faded photo of a trio of young girls on horseback. A brightly-coloured new photo of George Coleman surrounded by his grown daughters and grandchildren, a slightly shocked yet pleased expression on his face.]

13

Mark's conversation with Laurel had been the strangest and most unexpected conversation ever. Not to mention the most infuriating.

Still, he had things to accomplish that couldn't be put off any longer. He bundled up all his frustration and headed over to Whiskey Creek.

He hadn't expected to stay at the house with Trevor and Becky. And while all he had were a few bits of contact, the one letter George had sent him not even a month ago had been enough to make this the right decision.

It wasn't late enough in the day to be sure his brother would be home, but as Mark drove into the parking area outside the horse barn, George stepped into the sunshine. He glanced over and examined Mark's truck with interest before striding toward him.

Mark took a deep breath, opened the door, and slipped to the ground beside his vehicle.

Three steps away, George nearly tripped over his own feet, shooting upright. "Mark?"

"Sorry I didn't call first—"

That was all he got out before being trapped in a hug so tight, he could barely breathe.

George squeezed the living daylights out of him, finally releasing his grip only to catch hold of Mark's shoulders. "You're here. You're actually here."

It was too amusing to keep a straight face. "I'm actually here," Mark agreed.

George nodded decisively. "I'm glad."

Which was one of the best things Mark had heard, ever.

His brother gestured to someone outside the barn. The man joining them was clearly one of the nephews. A very large, very solid specimen—broader than Trevor and possibly a few years older.

George reintroduced him. "Since you both look a little different than the last time you saw each other, let me. This is Blake, Mike's oldest. He's been helping me understand the paperwork his brother put together—" He waved a hand in the air as if erasing the topic he'd been diving into. "Never mind that. Blake, this is your Uncle Mark."

The young man's handshake was firm without being obnoxiously overwhelming, and the smile he offered was honest. "It's good to meet you again. My dad talks about you a lot. He know you're in town?"

Mark shook his head. "I meant to get in touch with people before I arrived, but then it just seemed as if it might be easier to simply show up."

"Makes sense to me." George gave his shoulder one final squeeze before dropping his hand and gesturing toward the barn. "Why don't—" He paused and shook his head, a wry smile twisting his lips as he turned toward the house instead. "I bet you'd appreciate a bite to eat."

"And time to talk, yeah. That'd be good," Mark agreed.

Blake gestured toward the parking area. "I'm expected at

home, but I'll see you both soon. Uncle Mark, we'd love to have you over. Whenever it works."

"I'd like that," Mark said honestly. "I'll let you know as soon as I get in touch with your Dad. Maybe we can do something with the whole SP ranch."

His nephew's grin flashed. "Been a long time since I heard somebody use the real initials. We'll talk soon."

It was a small comment, but for some reason the innocently said words were a loud echo of what the little spitfire Laurel had said. That Mark had been gone a long time. That he needed to tread carefully.

He would, because it was true, and yet there were some things that he was not going to back down on. He was staying in Rocky, and whatever it took to find his way back into the Coleman family, he would make it happen.

And while he would be a lot more patient, he was going to find a way to put sunshine back in Dana's eyes.

He didn't bother to bring anything into the house. That could wait until he and George had a chance to talk.

They were barely in the door when George pointed to the kitchen table. "Beer?"

"I could drink."

Minutes later, George settled at the table kitty-corner to him, playing with the open beer bottle in front of him without tasting the drink. "I'm sorry."

Mark hesitated. "For what?"

George stopped fidgeting with the bottle and put his hands flat on the table before meeting Mark's gaze. "You came back once, and I was a shit. I didn't treat you right. I figure that was a lot of the reason why you stayed away for so many years. I'm sorry, because it was wrong."

For a moment, Mark felt like examining his beer. "I don't think either of us have had enough to drink for this kind of a conversation yet."

His brother's lips twitched. "It's not a drunken confession. It's something I've been wanting to say for a long time. I hope you got my letter, and I meant every word I wrote. You *are* welcome here. I want you to feel like this is your home, no matter what it takes to get us there."

Well, shit. Drink abandoned on the table, Mark rose then caught his brother by the shoulders. It was his turn to squeeze the stuffing out of him. "I'm sorry too. I shouldn't have stayed away so long, but—hell, I had my reasons. But looking back, none of it seems as if it was the right choice."

"You don't need to justify yourself." George wiped at his eyes and then coughed, straightening slightly as he pulled himself together then resettled at the table. "You're here. There's so much I need to tell you, but this is the biggest one. We all make mistakes. Sometimes we make damn *big* mistakes, and there's no coming back from those. But mostly there's a way to find something good in the here and now."

George said it as if it was a hard-learned lesson.

"You made a mistake?" Mark asked quietly. "Not because I want to gloat over you being a ridiculous ass like I was, but because it sounds as if you're on the other side of that blunder."

"Don't know if I'm quite at the top of the hill and on the downward slide, but I'm working on it," George confessed. "I've got four girls I didn't say *I love you* to often enough. Not with my words or my actions. I'm just damn grateful they're still willing to let me try and make a change."

One part of that Mark had heard from Trevor via the letters over the past year. "Four girls, not three. Damn, bro. That must've been a hell of a surprise, finding out you had another daughter."

George finally took a sip of his beer then stared at the label. "A surprise, but also a blessing. And I'm working my ass off trying to be a worthwhile dad in her life instead of a hindrance."

So many years. So many wasted opportunities, and yet it seemed Mark wasn't the only one.

Mark clapped his hands on the table. "How about I start working on getting supper together? If you're truly good with me camping out with you for a bit."

His brother was on his feet. "Let me help grab stuff from your truck."

The second lasagna that Mark had put together while over at Becky and Trevor's was popped in the oven, then George found him a place in one of the empty rooms.

The house was familiar in the way that an old melody scratched and teased. Mark had helped build this house. He and John, and the rest of the brothers. The year before he left. The year before John died.

If the house wasn't full of memories, his head was.

They hadn't quite put the food on the table when George paused. "You talk to Mike yet?"

Mark shook his head.

"Why don't you give him a call?" George suggested before offering a wry smile. "As my daughter Tamara pointedly reminds me, putting off something painful doesn't make it less painful when you actually do it."

"You think Randy wants to come out tonight? With the new grandbaby and all?" Mark offered a grin. "Because I'd like to do it all at once, like ripping off a Band-Aid. Which works well with your less-painful analogy."

"Give them a shout."

Which is how, before seven p.m., Mark found this unending day of activity finishing up with what would be the make-it-or-break-it moment.

Standing in George's living room, he faced his three surviving older brothers.

It had been clear from the moment they walked into the room, though, that this wasn't going to be about holding old grudges. Not on their side at least.

Mike gave him a hug and a back pounding. Randy nearly

shook his hand off his arm before going in for his own rib-creaking squeeze.

George just grinned.

Mark stared at the floor for a moment to find his balance. "I didn't expect this." He lifted his gaze to meet each of theirs in turn. "I told George, but I'll tell you all again. I'm sorry. And I missed you. And I'm sorry I missed so damn much over the years."

Randy rocked back in his easy chair, stretching uncomfortably before offering a smile. "I hope you don't expect us to catch you up on everything that happened while you were gone, because my list of complaints would take a good three months to go through, and ain't nobody got time for that."

"Really? You're going to complain about something?" Mike tilted his head with a grin. "I'll let Blake know."

Randy immediately straightened. "Hell. Don't you dare."

Mark thought it through quickly and put two and two together. He turned to Mike with a laugh. "I met your oldest boy this afternoon. Is Blake doing all the work scheduling these days?"

"Yup." His oldest brother eased back and put his feet up on the coffee table, damn near gloating as he glanced across at Randy. "Trained that one up right. He follows our da's example of sweating the complaints right out of a man."

It was such a flashback to their growing up years. Their father, Royce, had been a man with endless energy in spite of his pain. He never made any of them suffer to the point of physical danger, but he did encourage his sons to keep a positive attitude and their butts in gear. Any complaints were met with a chore list guaranteed to make a man sleep solid. "Trevor said having the ranch back together is working well."

Mike nodded, his expression going thoughtful. "I guess I messed up on that one."

"Nah," Randy said. "When you divided things up, it worked. And when it stopped working, we put it back together."

"Thanks." Quiet, but obviously sincere. Mike looked around the room. "Mom would've love this. Seeing us together again."

"She'd be heartbroken George isn't winding her clock," Randy offered, dodging the pillow George tossed at him. "What? She loved that thing. It's supposed to be *cuckooing* and ticking and making such a racket that a man can't sleep past five a.m. even on the coldest, darkest morning in the middle of winter."

"Which is why I don't wind it anymore," George said dryly. "Consider it wall art, not practical. That should help your delicate sensitivities."

"I think the unending racket was the only reason Mom actually kept the clock," Mike said. "I think it amused her."

"Something about it made her happy, and that was the most important thing to Da." George was staring at the clock now. "He kept that thing going religiously the two years after she died before he passed away."

"Coleman men love hard," Mike said.

"Ben didn't." The words snapped out of Mark, and while he regretted breaking the fragile peace, he didn't regret having let it slip.

Especially when silence swept in like a tangible thing.

He peered at his brother's faces, seeing guilt on Mike's, regret on Randy's. In that moment, Mark was immensely grateful that Laurel had said something. He wanted answers. Wanted to know why.

"Is it true what I heard? That Ben was far less loving than he should've been?"

George was the one who shocked them all. He shook his head, sadness etched on his face. "Ben loved so hard, he broke."

The shock of it made Mark inhale sharply, air cutting like a knife. "What?"

"When he lost his son." George spoke softly but clearly.

"When that happened, something snapped, and he never went back to being right. No matter that he saw he was on the wrong path, he couldn't get his feet under him enough to make a change."

Some of the bluster Mark had inside was smothered in a cloud of sorrow. He'd been ready to lift fists and make George see sense like they'd done too many times when they were teens.

But his brother lifted his head, gaze fixed at a point somewhere by the familiar cuckoo clock that had hung on the wall in their family kitchen growing up. The acorns on the winding mechanism hung low, the hands stilled. George spoke again in a quiet, earnest tone. "When I lost Sally, I did the same thing in a way. I stopped listening to what was right there in front of me. I let the fear that swept in take charge, and it tied me up nearly as hard as Ben's sorrow."

"Not the same," Randy assured him. "You were never anything like Ben."

"You see my girls here in Rocky? You see them working at my side, happy to be under my roof?" George shook his head. "This isn't about me, but at the same time, you all need to know. I screwed up big time with my kids because I was so damn afraid to lose them. I'm the one who loved them so hard, I damn well broke our relationship to try and keep them safe."

Mike spoke then, softly, his voice filled with regret. "Ben did break. And he made wrong choices. And so did Randy, and George, and me. All in our own ways. Just like you, Mark."

"But my mistake hurt nobody but me. Can you say the same for Ben?"

Randy shook his head. "Leaving must've hurt like hell, but don't kid yourself. *We* felt it. For years, it was like an aching spot right in the middle of our hearts. The empty places at the table were wrong, so don't go thinking you were the only one who felt the pain when you left. We felt it too."

Before Mark could pull the topic back to Dana, Mike took it there.

"Every time I spoke to Ben to try and get him to see what was happening, I warned him there was a line he couldn't ever come back from. He never crossed it." Mike met Mark's gaze straight on. "But the truth was, when things started to go wrong, Dana came to me first. Said she had made a promise, and she meant to keep it. She had to keep hoping that the man she married would find his way back."

Mark could just imagine her. Sweet, stubborn optimist. "I've already told her this, but I'm here for Dana."

His brothers blinked at the sudden change of topic.

It was Randy who smiled first, his amusement overpowering the shock. "Knew you liked her."

"Dear God, this is going to devolve into one of those conversations that my granddaughters have, isn't it? But does he *like her,* like her?" George rolled his eyes. "You're serious about this?"

"Dead serious."

Only Mike hesitated.

"You don't think I should go after her?" Mark asked even as he planned to ignore his brother's protests.

Mike shrugged. "I'm more concerned about the bit where you already told Dana you plan on making a play. With a Coleman woman, sometimes it's best to have the advantage of surprise. Not to mention, if you told her, it's likely that by now at least a half dozen of our daughters-in-law know, which means you're either going to be chaperoned to the eyeballs every time you try and make a move, or if they decide you're not worthy in the first place, you can kiss your idea goodbye."

"Well, shit." Mark *had* been gone for too long. He'd forgotten how much sway the ladies held in this kind of situation. Add in that the female population had blossomed in the years he'd been gone, and he'd just lit a bonfire in the middle of a field of grass.

Good thing he loved a challenge.

In the meantime, though, tonight had been one solid foundation block in his return to not just Rocky but to the family. He looked around the room as general conversation resumed and let hope sweep in.

Hope and the deep-seated need for connection he'd missed so much without ever wanting to admit it.

14

---

*I*f Blake wandered a little slower than usual from where the tractors were neatly parked outside the main barn, he'd blame it on too little sleep rather than too much on the brain.

They were having a bumper crop of calves this year, and while that was a thing to celebrate, not even a full Coleman crew could keep up. Plus, rather than make anyone else do extra shifts, Blake had taken to dealing with the emergencies the family called in by himself.

March was going out like a lion, storm clouds brewing on the horizon. He wasn't about to send Trevor out somewhere remote on the possibility his cousin got trapped and couldn't make it back to Becky and his barely three-week-old baby for a few days.

Which also put the rest of the Moonshine clan off the list. Blake wasn't about to be the one to blame in case Anna or Melody went into labour early, and then there was Lee and Rachel with their babies—

He caught himself snickering. "Isn't just the damn cattle having a bumper year. The Coleman breeding program is overproducing kids too."

"You say that anywhere near one of the Coleman women, and you'll be relegated to hot dogs with the kids for a year instead of enjoying steak." Matt joined him, brushing his hands together before tucking them under his armpits. "Jeez, it's gotten nasty cold."

"Uncle Randy said the weatherman predicts a huge snowfall sometime in the next three to four days," Blake warned.

"Lovely. And how many more of the cows we've got on Mark's grazing land plan to hide their babies just for shits and giggles?"

"All of them." Blake ducked his brother's half-hearted swing. "Damn, you're getting slow."

"It's the lack of beauty sleep." But Matt said it without any serious complaint. Just the comment of a man who knew this was par for the course at this time of the year.

By the time calving season was done, they'd all be so tired, they'd be sleepwalking. Eventually the seasons would change, and spring would arrive, and they'd get to do the next thing. Preferably after a good solid week of sleep.

Blake clapped a hand on Matt's shoulder. "Good thing you started out prettier than the rest of us."

Matt snorted. He pointed ahead. "That Uncle Mark's truck?"

The vehicle was becoming more familiar.

For the first couple weeks after he'd arrived in town, Uncle Mark had mostly stayed over at the Whiskey Creek place. He'd come to visit Blake's Ma and Dad, and Blake had heard that he'd been over at Randy and Kate's as well. The visits had been slow, though. A trickle instead of a full-out assault on becoming involved with the family.

Which was definitely not what Blake had expected after Jaxi had given him the lowdown from Laurel that very first day.

Just this week Mark had shown up a few more times in places where Blake was. Usually tagging along with George, helping out with whatever tasks his uncle was assigned to.

"What'd you think of him?" Matt wasn't the type to want to discuss the topic for no good reason.

Blake turned and gave him a little more attention. "Specifically?"

"Oh, don't give me your sphinx face. You know as well as I do the girls have been chatting this up all over text and the phone lines. You think him being interested in Auntie Dana is a good thing?"

"Interesting question, coming from you." Blake held up a hand. "And I don't mean that in a shitty way. I mean it—"

"You mean it took a hell of a long time to figure out which family member was the one worth spending time with. It's true. Everything that I dreamed of having with Helen ended up coming true with Hope." Matt stared at their uncle's truck thoughtfully. "I think this is different. My case was being too distracted by expectations. Helen and I were boyfriend and girlfriend, therefore we should do the next thing, then do the next thing. I never stopped to open my eyes wide enough to realize I was following tradition rather than being with the person who wanted to be with me."

"You think Auntie Dana and Uncle Ben were right together?"

"Dad said they were. At least at first." Mark shrugged. "I think it took a hell of a lot of guts for Uncle Mark to come back here, and the last few weeks have shown he's not an overbearing asshole. Or at least not right out in public, he isn't."

"That's a pretty low bar to start approval at," Blake said with a chuckle.

Matt grinned. "I guess my point is, I changed, and that's what made me the right person for Hope. Maybe it's taken this many years for Mark to become the right person to be a part of this family in more ways than one."

The man they were discussing popped out of the barn. He spotted them and gave a wave, marching forward with a steady gait that spoke of a strong body and a clear conscience.

"He did a damn good thing helping Becky," Blake said quietly. "And he did it when there was no possible reward for his actions. To be honest, that says more to me about his character than anything he's done recently."

Matt met his gaze. "You're right. You're absolutely right."

"It happens sometimes," Blake said dryly. He turned to his uncle and offered a greeting. "We're wandering slowly. Need help with something?"

Mark shook his head. "I was hoping that I could help you."

Jaxi passed the final plate to Becca to place on the table before lifting her gaze to Blake's. She spoke softly so that the children rushing around to get the dinner table ready couldn't hear. "So, Uncle Mark wants to be added to the work schedule? As in, he's planning on going back to taking a full draw from the family finances?"

"He's always taken a partial amount for the parts of the land that were co-owned by all the Colemans. But no." Blake caught her by the wrist and hauled her against him for a moment, soothing his own concerns in the way that she instantly nestled against him, a perfect fit. "He said he's here and he wants to work. He said we'd figure out the financial part in an official meeting in a month or so, but that he's got no dastardly plans for any of us to worry about."

"Oh, that's reassuring," Jaxi said dryly. "I'm so glad he says he has no dastardly plans."

Blake snickered, tilting her chin up so he could press a kiss to her lips. She relaxed, the tension draining out of her as he took what he needed at that moment.

"Mooooommy. Daaaaaddy. We're *hungry*."

"And you're kissing again."

Jaxi's lips curled into a smile under his. "We have very observant children."

"I noticed that," Blake said with a tease, glancing toward the kitchen door. "Is the table set?"

"Yes. Except we need pickles." Lana marched past them to the refrigerator, jerking the door open and reaching inside with an experienced air. She glanced back at them then waved a little hand imperiously. "I got this. You can ring the bell."

"Why, thank you, princess," Blake said politely. He winked at Jaxi then led her into the dining area. "Who's my bell ringer tonight?"

Rae pointed as Becca said, "Justin."

Blake scooped his son out of the playpen and with great delight handed him the metal stick that went with the dinner bell. "Ring away."

Justin went to town, squeezing his eyes tight as he whaled on the triangle that had called so many Colemans to share sustenance at this table.

And not just food, Blake realized all over again, but the feeding of the deepest kind of need a man could have. Lust was a hunger, pride as well. But this was bigger.

This was food for the soul.

PJ marched to his chair, both hands plastered over his ears. Becca held the door for her sister as Lana carried in a glass bowl filled to heaping with sliced pickles. Rae pulled out the chair for Jaxi like the queen that she was.

The absolute monarch of this love-filled place.

Matt's question came to mind again. What did Blake think of Mark pursuing a relationship with Auntie Dana?

Maybe it didn't matter so much what Blake thought. Did he understand *why* the man wanted it? He glanced around the table that was surrounded with his children and covered with food that had been prepared with love. He looked into Jaxi's eyes and saw amusement and strength and so much connection—

What Blake couldn't understand was why Mark had walked away in the first place.

But then again, maybe leaving hadn't been Mark's idea.

Blake finished the meal, gave Jaxi a kiss of thanks, then helped wash the dishes. Rae and Becca chattered the entire time they worked at his side, but his earlier thoughts distracted him enough, he figured he may as well follow through.

He waited until after homework was done, and after the kids were tucked into bed, before scooping Jaxi up and giving her a tight squeeze. "I'm going out for a little bit. Want to stop in and chat with Rafe for a while."

Jaxi nodded, but she seemed a little distracted. "Trouble?"

"Not at all," Blake assured her.

"Okay." She went up on her toes and pressed her hands to his chest, leaning in and nuzzling against him like a cat. "I'll be here when you get home."

That was the kind of promise he liked. "I won't be late."

"Even better." She headed off to the computer station at the side of the room. "Got some stuff I wanted to look up, anyway."

She was already focused on the screen before he had enough layers on to be willing to face the winter's chill.

He didn't even feel guilty for the partial lie that he'd just told. He knew damn well that Rafe and Laurel were out tonight and that pulling into the Angel homestead meant he should find his aunt by herself.

Maybe he was out of line, but ever since his da had basically passed the baton back in January, Blake had been struggling to figure out what it meant. What he was supposed to do.

Uncle Mark showing up had been a doozy of a puzzle, but this small moment seemed clear. He had to find out from Auntie Dana if she wanted some extra protecting.

The Angel homestead always had a cozy glow to it, but the place was worn at the edges. Rafe and Laurel had worked hard to try and turn things around, but the years of neglect by Uncle Ben meant some things could only be temporarily patched until they could be rebuilt.

Blake grabbed the package he'd brought as an excuse off the seat beside him and made his way to the door.

Auntie Dana opened it almost immediately, surprise in her eyes. "Blake? Something wrong?"

He shook his head, stepping in as she backed away to let him enter before too much warmth escaped into the bitter chill. "Jaxi found a few more things you might like. I thought I'd bring them to you."

His aunt looked him over, her gaze going suspicious. "Well. That's very considerate."

Drat. Jaxi had seen Laurel earlier that day. This was probably the *second* package Dana had received.

Being sneaky was not Blake's forte.

He took a deep breath and decided to lay it on the line. "I wanted to let you know I heard about Uncle Mark's...intentions. If you have any problems...with him... Or if there's ever anything else that I can do—just let me know."

Auntie Dana's cheeks flushed fire-engine red as if she'd been standing in front of an open stove for a good hour. "Well."

She opened her mouth to say more when suddenly, to Blake's horror, another voice rang out.

"Blake Coleman. Did you just stick your nose into your aunt's business without her asking you to?" It was his mother, Marion.

"I'm pretty sure I heard it too." His aunt Kate said, amusement ringing in her voice. "Dana, did you put out an ad for a knight in shining armour and not tell us?"

Dana lifted her gaze skyward for a moment before stepping back far enough, Blake spotted his mother and other aunt settled at the kitchen table. They had cups of tea in front of them as well as a cake, and it was very clear he had interrupted one of their hen parties.

Hell, no getting out of this without feeling like he was twelve years old. He grinned. "The offer stands. And now I'll go mind my own business."

"That would probably be a good idea," Auntie Dana said with a nod. "Give my love to Jaxi."

"*Blake*." His mother again.

He paused with one foot out the door. "Yes, Ma?"

"Tell your father I'll be home by ten."

Which was, as he figured out later, Marion's way of getting revenge on him. Because when he pulled into the yard at his father's to offer the quick message, he found Uncle Randy there as well, the two of them playing cards.

His dad looked him over. "And your mom *gave* you this message to pass on to me?"

"Yes, sir." Blake really did feel twelve years old and getting sent to a timeout.

"Which means you saw your mom tonight," Randy pointed out, his grin widening. "Which means you were over at Dana's."

His dad tilted his head to the side and looked almost sympathetic. "Oh, Blake. Tell me you didn't do something I'm going to hear about for the next umpteen days."

"I didn't do something..." Blake began to repeat dryly before caving into a sheepish smile. "The Coleman ladies are scary. They barely look at you, yet they know exactly what you've done."

"Both generations," Randy said with a nod. Then he held up a hand and raised an additional finger. "Three generations. Heck, four if you count back to the original matriarch, who I bet never let Stan get away with a single thing either."

Mike raised his glass in the air. "To the all-powerful Coleman women."

Blake was still chuckling when he made his way home. He pulled Jaxi away from the computer to enjoy a celebration with his own wonderful Coleman woman.

15

Gabe had spent a lot of years being called an angel, but he'd known it wasn't true. He was just as prone to anger as the next man, but he'd worked hard to still those urges when the time hadn't been right.

If he was going to get himself a label, he wanted it to be *patient*.

Then Allison wandered around the corner of the barn, her bright eyes glancing up to meet his, and he knew the right word was *blessed*.

He hadn't deserved her. Hadn't deserved any of the good things that had come over the past years, but he would take them whether they were his by rights or not.

Allison slipped in next to him, curling under his arm as he pressed a kiss to her temple. "This is a nice surprise."

"I'm only here for a minute." She pulled the baby monitor out of her pocket and shook it in the air. "We have a miracle happening. They're both down for a nap at the same time."

"Why are you wasting it on me?" he demanded. "Go sleep."

She squeezed him quickly then held out his phone "You forgot this in the house at lunch. I was trying to message you."

Well, damn. "I'm sorry."

"It's April. We're all a little sleep-deprived," she said with a laugh. "I couldn't figure out why the coffee table was vibrating."

He slipped the phone in his pocket. "Do I need to read the text?"

She shook her head. "Just remind Rafe he's having supper with us. Laurel and Dana have something at the church tonight, so I figured he may as well stay and help eat stale leftovers."

Which was a bunch of nonsense. Allison's family might use a talented chef at their local restaurant, but she had her own recipes that knocked his socks off. Plus, she liked cooking, so it was a good thing he had plenty of hard physical labour to keep him in shape. "Will do."

She went to give him a quick kiss, but Gabe wasn't having any of that. He caught her tight and lingered over the connection. The sweet, giving way she lifted up on her toes and enthusiastically gave back set his heart pounding and pushed away the cold.

He enjoyed the moment, and the next as she stepped away, his gaze pinned to her swaying hips. Even somewhat hidden under the layers, he couldn't keep his eyes off.

One contented sigh later, he headed back to work and the strange tangle of discomfort he needed to deal with.

Discomfort caused by working alongside his uncle.

Gabe couldn't fault Blake for the scheduling—he'd tried his own hand at it once and knew it was complicated as all get out to keep everyone lined up and working efficiently.

But it sure seemed as if Uncle Mark had been on Angel land a lot over the past couple weeks.

First, though, Gabe got a hold of Rafe on the phone, trying to push away the uneasy edge poking at him. "What time do you think you'll be done?"

A nicker of a complaint rang in the background before Rafe

answered. "Another couple of hours for sure. Add in a good forty-five minutes to get back to your place. That okay?"

"Definitely. Allison wanted to remind you you're sticking around here. She's got a liver-and-lima-bean casserole she wants to feed you."

"If Allison made it, I'll eat it." Rafe chuckled. "Honestly, right now, if *you* made it, I'd eat it. I'm starving. What is it about the cold weather that makes my appetite triple?"

"It's your growth spurt," Gabe teased his little brother. "When you finally get out of adolescence—"

"Shut up." But Rafe said it with a laugh before going a little more serious. "What's Uncle Mark up to today? Do you think Blake's deliberately putting him out at our place? What do you think of him?"

"He's dealing with supplies. Yes. And I'm not sure yet." Gabe hesitated and then expanded on that last one. "Okay, that's not quite true. I like him, Rafe. He is a damn hard worker. I mean we've worked around Uncle Mike and Uncle Randy for years, but it's kicking my butt to keep up with Mark."

Rafe chuckled. "That's because younger brothers have *way* more energy."

"Asshole."

"Jerk." Someone shouted in the background. "We can continue this scintillating conversation over dinner. Tell Allison I love her, and I will be there with my lima-bean-eating fork at the ready."

Gabe was still laughing as he worked his way over to his final task of the day.

He paused before diving in, though, tucked around the corner far enough back that Mark couldn't see him. Gabe stood and watched while something increasingly uncomfortable built in his chest.

Mark was hauling sacks of feed off a pallet, carrying them across and stacking them in a dry, secure location. Each one he picked up just emphasized his strength—and Gabe was struck with a contrasting image of his own father before he passed on.

Ben had been old. Crooked in his soul, crooked in his body. He hadn't been able to lift a heavy weight like that for years, but Gabe would never have held that against him if it hadn't been for the bitterness in his heart.

Heck, Uncle Mike was older. And while he didn't try to outlift his sons anymore, he also didn't complain, or scold, or blame.

Watching Mark move made Gabe have to come face-to-face with a part inside him that regretted his relationship with his father. Nothing he could've done to fix it—the break had been on Ben's side—but that didn't reduce the pain.

To add to his burden, Gabe had heard the rumours from the girls regarding some incident involving his mother and uncle. Allison had told him to mind his own business when he had wanted to march over and demand to know exactly what Mark had done. Her cooler head had prevailed, and now he was glad.

Uncle Mark had been around Rocky for over a month, and judging the man by his day-to-day action made it easier for Gabe to admit that maybe having him there was a good thing.

As Gabe joined him, Mark offered a brief smile and head tilt. "Hoped to have this done before you showed up."

"You're gonna make me look like a slacker," Gabe offered dryly, stepping aside to let the other man pass with his burden before joining in the queue. "I don't mind a little weightlifting on a cold day. Gets the blood pumping."

"Ha." The bag smacked into position on top of the others, and Mark turned back with a grin. "Your grandfather used to say that about a lot of things. *Gets the blood pumping.* He used it on cold days, on hot days, on boring days—"

"Boring days?"

Mark hefted another bag onto his shoulder. "You know, the twenty-third pass of the field in the spring when you're finally able to stop until the first cut? He'd tell us 'quiet contemplation is good for a man. Gets the blood pumping to ponder for a while about all the things he can accomplish'."

There was another twinge of remorse. Gabe loved hearing stories about his grandfather, but it was usually Uncle Mike or Uncle Randy who shared them. Gabe had wondered if there'd been a bit of judicious editing going on.

"Did my dad get along with Grampa Royce?" The question surprised Gabe as much as Mark.

The other man lowered the bag on his shoulder a little less vigorously, seemingly lost in thought. "They didn't *not* get along," he said slowly. As if he was choosing his words carefully. "Ben liked to do things his own way. That didn't always fit well with your grandpa."

Gabe worked silently for a moment before Mark spoke again.

"Your grandfather, like all of us Coleman men, wasn't always right. Some of the times, what Ben wanted wasn't out of line."

It was the fairest, kindest thing Gabe had heard anybody say about his father in a long time. He met Mark's gaze. "Thank you for that."

Mark looked uncomfortable. And Gabe really didn't want to start in on another conversation that would make *him* uncomfortable as well, so he changed the topic. "Want to stay for supper?"

"I'd like that. Thanks." The sheer happiness on the other man's face made Gabe feel bad for not having issued an invitation sooner.

When it was time to call it a day, Gabe gestured to the shower room they'd added when they'd built the new barn. "You can get cleaned up in there. Side cupboard will hold some T-shirts that should fit you. The cousins have left clothes here over the years, so it's a bit of a free-for-all. I can grab you a shirt once you come in the house."

"Will do." Mark held out his hand.

It wasn't the usual end-of-the-day ritual, but at the same time it made sense. Gabe reached out and offered a solid handshake. "It was good working with you."

Once again Mark's appreciation shone through. "I'm glad. Me too."

Gabe wandered over to the house, a little bit of nostalgia messing with the *what if*'s in his brain.

Which meant he was all the way into his and Allison's bedroom, headed for the shower, when he paused, turned around, and went back to look. "Allison? I was going to ask if you could set the table for one more, but you've already set it for five."

She whirled from the stove where she was stirring something that smelled amazing. "Laurel and Dana's thing got cancelled, so I told them to join us."

"Oh, shit."

Allison's eyes widened. Both of them glanced over at Micah, who was tossing toys back into the playpen as Ariel happily threw them out.

"Sorry. Both for the swear and the fact that I invited Uncle Mark to join us for dinner."

"Oh, shit."

Allison slapped a hand over her mouth. Gabe snickered.

Then she shrugged. "It was going to happen sometime. At least this is a safe setting." She gave him a quick glance. "Still, shower fast. I do not want to deal with this by myself, and Laurel said they'd be here in under ten minutes."

The temptation to linger under the hot water was there, only Gabe wouldn't do that to Allison or to his mom. He was dressed and ready to greet them when they arrived.

Dana accepted his hug then headed for the most important people in the room, scooping Ariel out of her playpen and pressing kisses all over her face.

Rafe grinned as he caught Laurel against him. "Nice surprise."

Her cheeks were flushed when he brought her back to

vertical.

Gabe was about to warn them all about the final guest when a knock sounded on the door.

"I'll get it." Laurel danced over, pulling it open. "Oh. It's you."

It was only because Gabe was watching that he saw his sister-in-law blush beet red, which was a thing he only saw when she'd been caught in a lie.

Uncle Mark's deep chuckle sounded. "Mind if I come in? It's a little cold to let the breeze in."

Laurel snapped to attention. She glanced over her shoulder as if looking for assistance. Her gaze darted over Dana then landed on Gabe.

He took pity on her, marching forward and holding out a hand. "Uncle Mark. Come in. We've got a few more for dinner than I expected, but Allison always cooks enough for an army, so we'll be okay."

"Good to know." His gaze had shot straight to Dana, but he spoke to Allison. "Smells wonderful in here."

"Lima beans and liver, or so Gabe claims," Rafe said as he came forward and shook Mark's hand as well. "Can I get you a drink?"

"Just water." Mark knelt to say hello to Micah, who had made his way over and was tugging at his jeans. "Hello, young man."

Micah lifted his arms, and as if it was the most natural thing in the world, Mark picked him up. He held the toddler with an easy confidence.

Meanwhile, Gabe had been sneaking peeks at his mom. After the initial widening of her eyes, she had turned to absolute calm. A kind of peacefulness that said nothing could touch her.

He hated it with everything in him. That was how she had reacted when Ben had been acting out. She'd gone cold. Not icy as if annoyed, but silent like a lifeless winter day. Making sure she didn't draw any attention to herself, to ensure whatever it was that had set Ben off didn't get repeated.

Gabe went straight to her and took her hands, speaking quietly. "If this doesn't work for you, tell me. Because family or not, this is your place first."

Dana lost some of her quiet, her lips curling upward and her head tilting slightly. She raised a hand and patted his cheek as if he were no bigger than Micah. "You really are my angel boy, aren't you?"

"I can be the devil if that's what you need," he promised.

But she smiled, shaking her head. "I was surprised, but this is not wrong. You said it. Mark's family, and he deserves a chance to find where he fits."

By the time everything was on the table and all the chairs were occupied, including the highchair that somehow found its way beside Laurel, some of the tension in the room had faded.

Rafe shared a story about their cousin-in-law Cassidy being distracted enough that they'd found him surrounded by an entire nest of kittens. Allison mentioned something that happened with her brother down at the restaurant, which led to Gabe bringing up an item to put on the agenda for growing come the spring.

It was an easy conversation, family-filled and bright.

Dana turned to Mark. "Tell us a bit about your time away. My boys say you're back on the schedule, but you never wanted to ranch."

"Did a lot while I was gone. Some of it was fun, some of it was sheer work." Their uncle wiped a napkin over his mouth and considered. "Truth is, when I said I didn't want to ranch anymore, it was for a lot of reasons, but none of them were really about the work itself."

"You drove a truck for a while." Laurel was making faces the way people do when feeding babies. She waited until Ariel had a mouthful, caught the overspill, and fed it to her again before lifting her gaze to Mark's. "When you found Becky."

"That was pretty much the last job I did, yeah." He stared at the ceiling for a minute. "Driving was a quiet trade. Just one man, although I listened to a lot of radio and audio. Took some online classes even. A librarian at one of the places I lived put together some courses for me one time. It wasn't anything that gave me a degree to hang on the wall, but I know a little about a lot of things."

"What was your favourite job?" Allison asked.

"Worked in a nursery," he said instantly.

Rafe frowned. "Like a greenhouse?"

Mark laughed. "Like in a place with a whole bunch of these little varmints." He caught Micah, who was in the process of wiggling off his chair, headed for the ground. He put Gabe's son back in place then handed him his fork. "Your mama said beans first."

"Shit," Micah said politely, then poked his fork into his beans, and filled his mouth.

Gabe and Allison bit their lips and tried not to howl with laughter as Dana shook her head and stared at the ceiling as if looking for strength. Thankfully, the moment passed without further comment.

"How did you get a job in a nursery?" Dana asked in a quiet voice.

"Went to school. I've got an early childhood teacher's certificate." He looked across at Ariel. "They're precious—kids. Teaching seemed like a way to make a difference."

Then he asked Allison a specific question about the organic market and what stage Angel land and the combined Coleman holdings were at, and the conversation turned.

But the teaser had been enough to make Gabe curious. And watching his mother, it was clear that she too had more questions than she was ready to admit.

They weren't anywhere near solving the puzzle of where Uncle Mark fit, but he was stepping slowly, so Gabe was willing to wait and watch.

16

———

The scene in front of him was too perfect to ignore. Cassidy paused in the doorway of the kitchen to stare into the living room and soak in the view.

While Cassidy had been doing the dishes, Travis and Ashley had settled on the couch. Ashley was partially supported as she leaned against her husband's strong body. She had the scoop of her blouse pulled down and her breast exposed, six-month-old Forest latched on and enjoying his dinner. Her face as she stared at the baby was as awestruck as if examining a priceless work of art.

Forest had a hand resting on top of the heavy swell of her breast, and that part of the picture was like a perfect Madonna and Child.

The other side of the couch held Travis, with River and Daisy balanced on his lap as he read them a book. One and a half and two and a half seemed too young to be as fascinated as they were with the pages before them.

River tilted his head and rested his cheek against Travis's as he used pudgy fingers to stab the page. "W'ale."

"Humpback," Daisy added with a brisk nod.

"In the waters of the Pacific, yes." Travis glanced up and caught Cassidy staring. He kept their eyes locked together as he recited from the book without hesitation. "The whales dance, the seabirds sing, the earth rolls, the sunlight beams."

"*Shhhhhh.*" River and Daisy both pressed fingers over their lips and made the childish sound as Travis turned the page.

"It's nighttime," Daisy said in a whisper, leaning higher to talk to River. "Have to be quiet now."

River squeezed his lips together and pressed his fingers tighter over them.

Travis continued reading. The slow, melodious pace of his voice as he finished the children's favourite story got even little live-wire Daisy to snuggle in tight against his chest as he read about the animals falling asleep all across Canada.

Cassidy glanced at Ashley to find her eyes locked on him, a secretive smile twisting her lips as she lifted Forest onto her shoulder and burped him gently. She pursed her lips and blew a kiss toward the door. Cassidy instinctively reached up as if to catch it in midflight, pressing it against his chest.

The room was filled with love. He'd never dreamed of experiencing such deep and precious connectedness.

It took a surprisingly short time to bundle the babies off to their room. He took Daisy from Travis, the little blonde sweetheart cupping Cassidy's face in her hands and pressing kisses all over him the entire ride up the stairs and into the bathroom, where he helped brush her teeth.

Tucking her in was sweetness and joy. "I love you, Daddy," she said, kissing him fiercely before peeking around his shoulder. "I love you, Papa."

"Love you too, flower," Travis said quietly as he laid a sleeping River on the mattress beside her. Then he leaned over to accept his minty-fresh kiss.

"Papa loves Daddy too," Daisy added as she snuggled in next to her brother. "Kiss."

"Little dictator," Travis whispered in Cassidy's ear before he pulled back far enough to tap Daisy on the nose. "Yes, Papa loves Daddy and Mama. There's always enough kisses to go around."

Then he caught Cassidy around the back of his neck, pressing their lips together in a brief but firm kiss. They would never dream of hiding the honest affection and connection between them.

Daisy sighed contentedly, her eyes closing in the sleep of the innocent.

They left the room and caught up with Ashley, who was just leaving her room, where Forest's bassinet was positioned beside her bed for easy nighttime access.

They'd barely made it into the living room when Ashley accosted him, tugging Cassidy onto the couch before she crawled over him. "You."

"Me?" Cassidy glanced to the side as the couch dipped, Travis's weight settling tight against him. "How come it looks as if you guys are ganging up on me?"

Travis didn't answer. Instead, he pulled out his phone and flipped it open. When he held up an image in a text, Cassidy groaned.

His head hit the back of the couch. "I'm going to kill Rafe."

"I don't know, he did a pretty good job balancing the composition of the shot. What do you think, Ash?" Travis twisted the picture toward her.

She put a finger against her cheek as if analyzing. "The dark to light ratio might be a bit off, but overall, the harmony works. Cassidy, that far off-look in his eyes as if he's been put into a trance. The—how many are there, twelve, thirteen?—kittens draped over him as if he were the ultimate climbing tree."

"Climbing tree is good," Travis murmured before tucking the phone aside. He twisted slightly, elbow leaning on the couch back. "As cute as the picture is, that isn't the first time you've gone off to la-la land in the middle of doing something recently."

"Which makes us think you have something on your mind." Ashley stroked her fingers up Cassidy's cheek, humming as his five o'clock shadow rasped her skin. "What's wrong, baby? Is there anything we can do to help?"

"Nothing's wrong," Cassidy began.

He stopped. His fingers were linked with Travis's, the other man's strong grip holding tight. Ashley's warm butt rested on his thighs, and she continued to drag her fingers through his hair and down the side of his neck as if petting him would make him feel better.

Papa loves Daddy and Mama.

There was love in this house, and *that* was the thing that kept overwhelming him.

"I'm not lying," Cassidy insisted. "It's the fact that something's so right that keeps knocking me off-kilter."

The two of them didn't interrupt. The unique, thorough connection that they had was buzzing slowly. Because the relationship wasn't just between him and Travis, or him and Ashley, but somehow with the three of them, life was richer and simply *more* than he had ever expected to experience.

"When the Coleman memory book project started, I thought it was a good idea, because I was curious about the history. You know I like your family," he said, meeting Travis's eyes. "Your parents are rock solid. I love working with your brothers, and I feel confident that every one of your cousins would step up the instant we asked for help." He snorted. "Hell, they probably wouldn't even wait for us to ask."

"God's truth in that one." Ashley dipped her head in agreement. "I came home the other day from shopping to find Laurel had stopped in. Since I wasn't here, she just *happened* to wash the floor, do the dishes I'd left in the sink, and left a pot of soup in the crockpot."

"I like her," Travis admitted. "Not just because the soup was damn good."

"We all like her," Cassidy agreed. "She's the type of person I think about when hearing somebody say they've got a good heart. For all her churchgoing, never once have I felt as if she's judging us. Or that she's praying for us—you know, the way people act all concerned when they think you're going to hell."

"She prays for you plenty, you and Travis. But that's because she's heard me complaining and knows you need divine intervention to get back in my good books." Ashley blinked dramatically.

Travis nudged her with his shoulder before turning his attention back on Cassidy. "So if everything is all right, why do you keep going off into this haze?"

"Because I didn't have a family, and now I do." The confession came out a little ragged at the edges. "I can't think back on my years growing up without it hurting, so the reminder that everybody's looking back makes me relive that sadness."

"Oh, Cass." Ashley cradled his face in both her palms. Her big expressive eyes filled with tears. "I'm sorry."

"Don't be," he insisted, leaning forward to kiss her. Wrapping his arms around her and pulling her lush body flush against his. He spoke past her ear, allowing the embrace to wrap him up with sweet tenderness. "Because every time I feel that sadness, it gets stomped on so damn hard and fast because the beautiful truth of what we've got now hits like a bale dropping from the hayloft."

Travis's strong arms wrapped around them both. "This is real, and it's ours, and we're not ever giving it up."

"Damn right," Ashley agreed. Then she wiggled and broke the embrace between the three of them, sheer mischief on her face. "Well, now that we know what's causing your distraction, we need to set up the counter-distraction. Because, sweetie, you just can't go off like that at the drop of a hat. It's not safe."

"I agree." Travis looked Cassidy over, heat rising in his eyes.

Oh, hell. "What do you have in mind?"

"Giving you something else to think about when those sad thoughts try to sneak in." Ashley held out her hand.

It wasn't a decision that needed much thought. Cassidy got to his feet willingly, following the two people who were his lovers into the largest bedroom. The one with a lock on the door that they shared when they needed privacy and space to play.

His partners. His husband and his wife, no matter what the names were on any legal papers.

It didn't matter how many times the three of them had fooled around over the years, it was still a fresh miracle every time.

Travis took control, naturally, catching Cassidy's hand and pulling him tight to his torso. The strong, masculine lines of his body contrasted sharply with lush softness as Ashley pressed against Cassidy on the other side.

"Take off his clothes," Travis said.

"Oh, boy." Ashley's eagerness was clear, not just in how she popped up in front of Cassidy but in the way she moved to obey. She grinned. "His bossiness is feeling extra bossy tonight."

"And once you're done with him, take off your own," Travis added, clearly amused.

"How about I help with that?" Cassidy said. "Since this is supposed to be about making good memories for me, and all." He met Travis's gaze. "I like unwrapping things."

"You'll be too busy," Travis informed him. Before Cassidy could ask what that meant, he was being kissed.

The press of Travis's lips against his was wild. Hungry and raw, one step up from animalistic. The sweet kiss in front of their children earlier had been about connection and a gentle, eternal type of love.

This kiss was all fire, and Cassidy dove in with hungry eagerness. Teeth bumping, hands digging into Travis's muscles, bracing himself to enjoy the assault. Clothes were tugged away, but it was the sharp nip of teeth on his lower lip and the demanding thrust of Travis's tongue that kept Cassidy's attention.

A moment later, naked breasts pressed against his back. Ashley's soft hand slipped between them to wrap around his cock. Cassidy swore, but it wasn't to make her stop. And while Travis backed up just far enough to rid himself of his own clothing, Cassidy soaked it all in.

A memory? Hell, this night was being burned on every bit of him. His retinas, his skin, his taste buds as Ashley curled herself around him and took up the kiss. Her hands continued to move in a wicked, dangerous tease over his cock.

Sometimes, when they made love, it would go on for hours. Between the two of them, he and Travis could switch off and work over Ashley, or each other, multiple times. But tonight wasn't about leisurely pleasure. It was about taking and being taken, and moments later, Cassidy found himself flat on his back, Ashley straddling his thighs and rocking her wet heat over his aching erection.

"Now, sweetheart," Travis encouraged, gripping her hips and lining them up. Taking control of even this as Cassidy and Ashley sighed with satisfaction as they joined.

Ashley's eyes fluttered shut. "That feels so good."

Cassidy thrust up into her, pleasure spiking as she dragged her fingernails over his chest. "Fuck."

"Roll over," Travis ordered, and the next instant, when Cassidy found himself over Ashley, staring into her bright-blue eyes, he realized they were only halfway there.

Taking and being taken—

Travis covered his body from the back, lips pressed against the side of Cassidy's neck briefly in a far-too-tender kiss for the heat of the moment. "I love you," he said.

Calm kisses, but Travis's hands were doing dangerous things, sliding over Cassidy's body, preparing him. And when Travis pressed his cock into Cassidy and the three of them were connected in their own unique, dirty-sweet, and passionate embrace, it was perfect.

"Oh my *God*, this is—" Cassidy fell silent. There really were no words for it. The extreme pleasure of feeling Ashley under him and Travis deep and hard inside him...

"*Move*." The order came from Ashley, her hands extending around Cassidy's shoulders to scratch Travis. "All of us, together."

Slow at first then harder. Cassidy stared into Ashley's eyes and saw a reflection in them. Just like the black and white art that hung on the wall over the bed, they were one. Surrounding each other, the painting Ashley had made so many years ago remained a reflection of their life together. Not just the sex, not just the creating of a family, but every day.

Wrapped around each other, watching out for each other, loving each other.

After Ashley had dragged her nails down Cassidy's arms hard enough to leave marks. After Travis had come, and Cassidy as well, stars floating in front of his eyes—

After the physical act was done, the emotional connection pulsed between them like a live wire, raw and energetic. Powerful, potentially dangerous, yet for them, the only possible way.

Cassidy held his hearts close. He kissed Ashley's temple then wiggled until Travis was included in the embrace. "Good memories," he said softly.

Travis grinned. "The best."

Coleman Memory Book
~Kate (Moonshine) Coleman~

For me, memories come in small, medium, and big packages.

My time as a Coleman started when I fell in love with Randy. Finding our way as a twosome was magical and sweet as well as frustrating and annoying. Because, as we like to joke, if two people in a relationship always get along, then you don't need one of them.

Overall, our twosome is a unit, and we work together to get things done and enjoy life. Play as well as work. Still learning that at times.

The medium package is the Moonshine family. Which admittedly is growing, with grandbabies for me to adore, but in the beginning, it was a two plus four, and that meant finding new ways to balance happiness, play and work with extra bodies. I'm so grateful that my children have all grown up to be adults I'm not just proud of but want to spend time around. People I can have easy conversations with yet be challenged and supported by.

Which means the big package is the entire Coleman clan. And that's where the memory I want to share comes from, because otherwise I'll just gush about my grandkids. Which is good and right, but not what this is about.

When we started the family gatherings on Boxing Day and Canada Day, it made life simpler. Every other year would be our turn to host, once in summer, once in winter. But the year Trevor was born in June, there were two other new babies as well, so Sally said Whiskey Creek would host.

Their house was mostly built by that time, her kitchen a little chaotic and not yet sorted because they were getting married in August and still working on things. Myself and the other sisters-in-law came over early to help each other finish cooking before the actual gathering.

I had offered to make lemon pudding pies. The crusts I'd done ahead of time, so with little Trevor being taken care of in the other room, Sally and I whirled into action, scooping up sugar and mixing vigorously. As soon as the custard started to set, we poured it into the piecrusts and then admired how pretty they looked, all creamy, yellow perfection.

Until Sally decided to lick the spoon.

Her face—*dear, Lord*—I can picture it now. The sheer horror and the way her mouth puckered before she raced to the sink and spit and spit and spit.

I'd used salt instead of sugar.

Once we figured that out, and Sally had rinsed her mouth and was no longer gagging, that's when the giggles hit. For the next umpteen minutes, we laughed so hard, we ended up on the floor, stomachs aching.

Sally suggested we scrape the terrible pudding out of the crusts and start again, and in the end, it worked. But to this day, I can't give that recipe to anyone without enjoying a small snicker.

I learned three important lessons:

1. Sometimes mistakes are the way to learn (i.e., always check that the white, crystal-like substance *is* sugar).

2. Sometimes we need a bit of laughter to ease past our mistakes.

3. And family is a good place to find both laughter and good advice. Whether you open a small, medium, or large package of Coleman.

[Images: lemon pies. Family gathered around a fire. Big laughing group. Hugging couple.]

PART III

And what is the future, happy one?
'A sea beneath a cloudless sun;
A mighty, glorious, dazzling sea
Stretching into infinity.'

Past, Present, Future
Emily Brontë

17

———————

*H*ope turned the sign on the front door from *open* to *closed* but left it unlocked. Then she wandered back into the Stitching Post, deep satisfaction rising as she gazed around her neat shop, admiring the sample quilts hung along every available surface above the well-stocked fabric shelves.

After nearly seven years, she could honestly say she was no longer afraid of failing. She had loyal customers and experienced teachers and a place she loved to go every day.

Thumping from the back stairs behind the shop brought a smile to her lips. She moved toward the door and welcomed Colton in with a hug. "Hey, big guy. How did your afternoon go?" This question was directed partly toward her three-year-old son, and partly his caregiver, Mandy, who was now passing over one-year-old Cameron.

"Good," Colton said even as he made a beeline for the play area Hope had set up for kids in the shop. He stopped, hands snapping to a position behind his back. "Can I play?"

With the daycare Mandy operated out of the room she rented from Hope directly above the quilt shop, Colton didn't need to spend that much time in the actual store. Which meant the shop toys were a special treat.

Hope grinned. "Sure, kiddo. Your Auntie Becky will be here soon, so you get extra play time today."

Colton was gone in a flash.

Cameron tugged on Hope's ears to get her attention.

"Just a minute, sweetie," Hope said as she grinned at Mandy. "You got the rest of them off early?"

"You know how it is on early dismissal day. Most moms give up and grab the little ones before even heading to school." Mandy tilted her chin toward Cameron. "That one only had about half an hour to nap, so apologies if he's cranky."

"Not a problem. Have a good evening."

While it wasn't exactly what her sisters-in-law were doing, Hope and Matt had discussed it a lot. The quilt store was more than just a way to make money—it was something Hope had dreamed about for years. And while raising a family was also a dream, she and Matt were finding a way to make both dreams work.

When Mandy had rented the apartment upstairs from Hope and then asked for permission to do some childcare, it'd been a perfect solution. And if it occasionally sounded as if there was a herd of elephants running around above them, no one in the quilt shop minded. Most of them were moms or grandmas, and the noise just brought amusement.

Colton and Cameron were around other children the few days of the week that Hope and Matt's work schedule overlapped. A few more days right now since Becky was no longer able to fill in gaps in the schedule.

Hope paused in front of the quilt she'd temporarily hung in the shop. It wasn't the Six Pack family quilt—the one that Matt had sweet-talked his brothers into helping him sew. That one had been shown off a few times over the years and was well known in the community, considering Matt had attached her engagement ring to it.

No, this quilt was the one that had taken her forever to design. She had finally figured out how to incorporate everything she wanted. Staring up at it, her smile widened into a grin.

It wasn't a pattern anyone else would ever want to imitate, but for her and Matt, the snowflakes falling against an icy-cold Alberta sky were a reminder of where they started. Below the flakes, a clawfoot bathtub—Hope snickered—was surrounded by reflective pieces of fabric that made the edges glitter like a mirror.

Quilts said a lot to the people who knew how to read them, but this one was readable only to her and Matt. A sweet, intimate reminder of important moments in becoming who they were to each other.

The warning bell at the front door rang, and she turned to see Becky come in, baby seat cradled in front of her. Arabella's thin baby cry trembled on the air.

Hope hurried to help. "Trevor drop you off?"

"Uncle Mark did. We had a late lunch, but he's headed back to work. Will you be able to take me home later?"

"Of course."

It was comfortable and easy, spending time together. Becky had worked in the shop until Arabella had arrived. Hope had missed seeing the other woman the past couple of months.

Becky pulled her crying baby out of the car seat, sheer joy on her face. "Sweet princess. Yes, I know, you've been very patient."

Arabella cried again, the sound bringing Colt running to see what was wrong as Becky unwrapped her little girl then put her into position to nurse. Colt rested a hand on Becky's arm before very carefully touching the back of Arabella's head. "Baby 'ella's hungry."

"Very hungry," Becky agreed. "Hello, Colt. Did you have a good time at preschool today?"

"Yup." He glanced at Hope. "I'm hungry too."

Cameron wiggled in Hope's arms. "Hu'gry too," her other son agreed.

"Snack time it is."

She'd barely gotten her boys settled when the door rang again, and she shot to her feet.

"Sorry, I forgot to lock the door after me," Becky murmured.

But instead of a wayward customer, it was Auntie Dana coming into the shop. "I forgot it was early closing day," she said apologetically.

"Twist the lock," Hope instructed her aunt, "Then come and join us. We're about to have a snack. Unless you need me to grab you some material?"

Dana took off her layers and settled on the couch beside Becky. "No snack, and no material." She took a deep breath. "I need advice."

Hope and Becky exchanged glances. "Okay."

"I don't want to ask Allison or Laurel because I think it might get a little awkward." Dana shook her head. "Not that talking to you is any less awkward, but anyway…"

Hope's amusement grew. "We don't mind embarrassing conversations, do we, Becky?"

"Embarrassing is what we do best." Becky said it with an absolutely straight face.

"I'm thinking about dating Mark."

The words gushed out of Dana like water bursting from a broken pipe.

All of the cousins knew—and had known since the day he'd arrived—that something had gone down back at the beginning of March. But since nothing more had happened except for Mark beginning to work with the rest of the family, living quietly with Uncle George at the Whiskey Creek ranch, everyone had gone into wait-and-see mode.

Becky looked delighted. "Oh, really?"

Dana frowned. "You sound as if I just announced I won a lottery."

"As far as I'm concerned, you kind of did." Becky offered a smile, the soft, kind, and caring one that seemed to well up out of her like magic. "You've had a lot of sadness in your life, Auntie Dana. I was there once—not in the same way, but I do know what it's like to feel lost. Uncle Mark was in the right place at the right time for me, but he was also the right man. Because no matter how scared I was, he seemed to know what to do."

"Do you *want* to date him? Or anyone?" Hope asked her aunt. "I mean, putting aside the fact that I also think Uncle Mark is a pretty cool guy, and quite the hottie—"

"*Hope*." Dana sounded slightly scandalized.

"Oh, please." Becky this time. "I am perhaps not as well-versed in categorizing hotties as Hope is, but I think you'd call him a *silver fox*."

Aunt Dana's cheeks were bright red. "He's pleasant enough to look at."

Hope snorted then covered it up by reaching for her drink. "Pleasant is good."

Becky grinned.

Hope returned to her original question. "I mean it. Are you looking for someone to date? Because you don't have to if that's not something you're interested in."

Dana looked down at her fingers for a moment before nodding decisively. "I had considered it was time to find company I like to do things with. I don't want my children to feel as if they have to be constantly entertaining me. And I love spending time with my sisters-in-law, but it's the same thing there. They have their own circles and husbands, and that's healthy and good."

"So you want someone to spend time with?"

Dana nodded.

"Someone to..." Becky looked at Hope as if trying to figure out which way to steer the conversation. "Go for rides with? Help weed the garden? Deal with spiders?"

Dana's lips curled upward. "I can do the spider part on my own, thank you, but, yes. Someone to talk to at the end of the day."

"Do you have a problem with Mark being your brother-in-law?" Hope had to ask. "I'm allowed to ask about that, considering my husband dated my sister at one point."

"I don't think…" Dana hesitated then spoke clearly. "It doesn't bother me. Mark was my friend in high school before I fell in love with his older brother. And Mark's been away from Rocky for so long, it's not as if— Well, honestly, it feels as if he's a bit of a stranger come to town, and I'm curious about him."

Hope leaned forward and spoke softly. "Did you actually have a question, Auntie Dana? Because it sounds like you're interested, but you're worried someone will react badly to what you're considering."

Dana nodded slowly. "Do you think that's silly? I'm sixty years old, with grown children and grandchildren and plenty of things to occupy my time. I've had a husband—I don't know that I want another one."

"Sixty years old is still young enough to want a good, close friend you like spending time with." Hope said it with a decisive nod.

"And if you don't want another husband, you don't have to marry him." Becky shrugged. "Date him. You can even fool around—we won't tell."

Hope snickered. "You are so bad."

"Well, speaking bluntly, I plan to be having sex with Trevor when *I'm* sixty years old. I don't see any reason why Auntie Dana shouldn't have somebody nice in her world to enjoy *that* with." Becky's cheeks were also flaming red, but the sentiment was sincere.

"And on that note, we've officially gone well into the area

where my daughters-in-law would have never dared venture, so thank you," Dana said with her own embarrassed smile. "You're right, on all counts. Now I'll ask you to forget that this conversation ever took place. Especially the last part."

"Already forgotten, although I'm very glad you came to us and didn't go to Jaxi or Ashley for advice."

Becky laughed loud enough Arabella's arms shot out in surprise. "No, they would've been a little more blunt."

"Oh, dear."

Amusement danced in the room, the three of them from such different backgrounds, with different sadness in their pasts and yet sweet happiness in their current lives.

And for one, hopeful potential hovering so close.

Whatever it was that Auntie Dana was looking for, Hope wished her nothing but joy.

18

The past two months had felt like an eternity.

Dana had spent every minute of it with her mind whirling through questions and possibilities. To say that Mark's arrival had been a shock was an understatement.

Back in March, she had only begun to ease toward the bigger changes she needed to make. Ben had been dead for over three years, and while sadness rushed in at times, she refused to lie to herself. There were moments when she was grateful he was gone. The man she'd fallen in love with had been missing for a long time. Not her fault, and not what she wanted, but it was real.

She'd grieved long before she'd watched his casket lowered into the ground.

And now, nearly two months after she'd stumbled into Mark at Becky's house, it was time to admit another truth.

Dana picked up the phone and called him.

"Hello?"

"Hi. It's Dana."

It was a soft curse, a pause, then a loud clatter that had her jerking the phone away from her ear.

When he came back on the line, Mark sounded slightly

breathless. "Sorry. Dropped the phone. Good to hear from you. Everything okay with the kids?"

Dana held in her amusement. "Since you're probably working with Gabe, I'm sure you got apprised this morning about exactly how everyone's doing."

"I haven't seen Gabe today." Then Mark chuckled. "Although Rafe left about half an hour ago, so yeah. I'm up to date."

"Why are you working for the ranch?" It was the one point Dana had gotten hung up on over and over again and still not been able to figure out. "You left Rocky because you didn't want to work the ranch anymore."

"It was a little more complicated than that, Dana."

"Then uncomplicate it." It might be an unreasonable request, but she no longer cared.

"It's not a conversation I'm willing to have over the phone," he returned.

Dana took a deep breath for courage and pushed ahead. "Then I guess you need to have a private conversation with me in person sometime soon."

That was as bold as she could get. Even knowing she wanted to explore these feelings inside, she simply couldn't—

Thankfully, Mark picked up the reins and ran with it. "Tonight. Dinner in town."

"Darts at the pub," she countered. If she was going to do this, it wasn't going to be at a quiet dinner table the first go-round. That would be too intimate. "Drinks, if you still drink."

A long, low chuckle carried over the line. "Traders? That's fine by me. And once we've done some talking, we can try a round or two on the dance floor. I promise I won't step on your toes too much."

"You were the only one in our class who *didn't* step on my toes," Dana admitted. "Dear God, high school phys ed classes were a long time ago."

"Don't look that direction," Mark ordered. "Our date is five hours from now, which is way too long, but thankfully getting closer by the second."

Dana hesitated.

"This *is* a date," Mark repeated. "Which means I'll pick you up at the house. Six-thirty?"

She was a teenager again, with everything from the flutter in her stomach to the goose bumps rising on her skin. "Six-thirty."

After hitting the end of the call, Dana stared out the window for a good half hour before she had herself together enough to be able to go on with her day.

Neither Rafe nor Laurel seemed to suspect anything, even though she rushed through dinner and dishes in order to slip back into her room to get ready.

When she came out, the living space was empty, both her son and daughter-in-law having vanished. Good for them. They'd probably appreciate her not being around for an evening.

Her living situation dilemma struck again. It was more than time to move on in that area as well—this house was old and too filled with memories, good and bad. She didn't want to live there anymore. But she didn't want Rafe and Laurel to feel they had to, either. If anyone deserved a fresh start, it was her kids.

She was so deep in thought, the knock on the door made her pull up sharply.

Mark stood on the front porch, a paper bag in one hand and a grin on his face that said he was very pleased to be there. "Hey."

She gestured the man in. "I need my coat."

"Trade you," he said holding forward the bag and taking her coat from where it was draped over the chair by the door. "I made you cookies. Chocolate chip with macadamia nuts."

Dana peeked in the package, somewhat shocked. "You made them?"

"With my own little hands," Mark agreed as she put them carefully on the side table near the door. Then he held out her coat, and she slipped it on, intensely aware of how near he was.

The feel of him nearly wrapping his arms around her as he settled the shoulders in place.

Then he stepped back and politely waited until she'd done everything up and slipped her shoes on.

The trip to Traders passed quicker than she'd imagined. Mark asked what she'd been up to, but when she answered with a typical "worked around the house," and figured that would be enough, he clicked his tongue.

"Didn't ask out of politeness," he said softly. "I asked because I'm honestly interested."

"I don't know that how I spent my day *is* honestly interesting," she returned.

"Sometimes the stuff we do isn't fascinating but still needs to be done." He glanced over. "After you called, I had to finish the task list that Blake put me on over at Whiskey Creek. But I was thinking about you a lot, and that's when I figured I wanted to have something to bring with me. So I ran into the house and got a batch of cookies going, then ran out and did some more of my chores, then ran back in when the timer on my watch went off."

She laughed. "George must've thought you were out of your mind."

"George thought I had a hankering for cookies, and since I left him a dozen, he wasn't about to complain." Mark glanced to the side again. "Now your turn. After you called, what were you working on?"

She wasn't going to tell him about the daydreaming, the thought of his voice combined with the memory of how good he looked in that T-shirt stretching over his broad shoulders the evening he'd stopped in at dinner unexpectedly at Allison's house—

The man was built in all the right ways.

"I spent a couple of hours going over information for Allison. She needed an update on garden produce harvest times from the past few years so she can give it to their chef for plotting out menus." After that her day got really boring. "Then I made dinner. Laurel's working at the library, and Rafe you see all over the place helping with the Coleman spread. So I told them while we were sharing a home, I didn't mind being chief cook and bottle washer. Laurel does most of the groceries, and Rafe washes up more times than not, but it's only right that I do my part."

"How does it work, sharing a house with your kids?"

She'd answered this one more than a few times over the past years. "It's not ideal, but I say that more for their sake than mine. Laurel is wonderful, and she never makes it feel as if I'm intruding in her home. It's been sweet to see them grow from best friends into a solid couple."

"They were friends in school?"

So many stories he didn't know. Dana glanced over, examining his profile. "From kindergarten on. Those two got in so much trouble together over the years, I kind of figured they got married to keep on making mischief more conveniently."

"Gabe said he and Allison also went to school together." His smile was visible even as he focused straight ahead at the road in front of them. Wildly hinting that having been friends in school should lead to more...?

She focused back on his earlier question. "I'm trying to figure out the house thing. After Ben died, I was glad I didn't have to be alone. But I think this might be a good time to make a move. At some point, Rafe and Laurel need a place of their own."

"You want to move out?" He pulled into Traders, the place full enough that they had to park at the far end of the lot. "Hang on until I'm there."

Dana paused in the middle of opening her door, wondering at the bubbles popping in her gut.

Up until now, it had been a slightly awkward yet normal exchange, but as Mark opened her door and helped her down, these were most definitely *date* feelings she was experiencing.

Mark held out his elbow, and she wrapped her fingers around

his biceps, the position closing the gap between them as he led her across the parking lot. He picked up the conversation again. "So, are you house hunting?"

She shook her head. "I considered building a small place, sort of like Gabe made himself at the start. You can see where they've added on to his original cabin. But then I think about it harder, and if anyone should have a new house, it should be Laurel and Rafe."

"Why not both? You and them?"

Dana laughed. "Because that doesn't fit the budget."

He pulled open the pub door. She walked in ahead of him, this side of the pub with multiple tables and seating areas, the pool tables at the back of the room. The volume was a low buzz instead of the high roar found on the dance hall side, so the sudden swell of voices was unexpected.

"Well, damn." Mark tugged her little closer, helping her catch her balance when she realized the entire middle section of Traders was filled with Colemans.

Dana glanced at him. "I didn't tell anyone."

He shook his head. "Not me. Damn Coleman hive mind."

An instant later, his oldest brother stood in front of them. Mike grinned as he glanced between them. "What can I get you to drink?"

It was not at all what she had expected, but after that initial panic-induced moment when she realized there would be no keeping any secrets from the family, Dana discovered she appreciated the interference.

Mark brought her to the table and sat next to her, the pair side by side as friendly banter swirled around them. Mike and Marion, Randy and Kate. George chatted with Daniel and Beth Coleman from the Six Pack side, while Mike's twins and their wives circled around the activity. The girls drank pop while Jesse and Joel hovered protectively, hands resting on pregnant bellies every now and then.

It was relaxing, except that every time Mark moved, his thigh nudged against hers and shivers slid up Dana's spine. That same thrill hadn't gone away just because she'd gotten older.

And when he leaned close, his whisker-roughened cheek brushing past hers as he whispered, "Would you like to dance?" in her ear, literal goose bumps hit.

Maybe the family thought they'd been interfering, but the short interlude of being absolutely surrounded and supported had been exactly what she needed. The perfect dose of connection to shake away the fear and uncertainty.

She wanted this. So she should take it.

Clearly to his utter shock, Dana caught Mark's hand then tugged him to his feet before turning to the rest of them. "We're going dancing. We don't need chaperones."

A lot of masculine chuckling followed her comment.

Dana ignored them all, keeping a tight grip on Mark's hand. He followed her willingly across the room into the opposite side of the pub and onto the dance floor.

That first moment when he twisted her toward him and brought his arms around her—

She could barely breathe. Didn't really want to. It was like opening a fresh page on a brand-new journal, with so many pristine, blank opportunities going forward. Part of her was afraid of making a mark, of doing something that would mar the experience.

He moved her against his body, swaying in time to the music, and it was so strangely familiar and right that fear slipped away, and happiness warmed her, inside and out. She wasn't going to worry if she made a few mistakes. Hope had said it—Dana was allowed to want a good, close friend in her life who wasn't family or someone who had been around forever.

Unfortunately, that also reminded her of the other comment made that day in the quilt shop. The bit about how she was also free to fool around, *and more*, if she wanted.

Her fingers rested on his firm shoulders, his hand on her waist. It was intimate, and yet when the next song dropped a pace, Mark's low, rumbling laugh made the tingles strike harder.

He settled her the slightest bit closer, lips brushing her ear. "Relax, darlin'."

"I thought I was," she said, happy none of her current lustful thoughts snuck into her voice. "I'm not doing chores."

He had both hands on her hips, sliding them down slightly until the ends of his long fingers rested against the upper swell of her butt. "Looks as if we need to practice a little more. Mr. Stevens would be very disappointed right now. You're not applying yourself adequately, Ms. Tetrenko."

The reminder of their high school gym teacher's favourite phrase made her laugh. Her maiden name sounded odd after so many years. She chose to push aside both amusement and uneasiness and simply savour the moment. "Quiet. I need to count the beats."

It was his turn to snicker, because that had been *his* comment back in the day. The fact that she'd remembered put a smile on her face.

It felt good to be in his arms. Truth be told, it felt better than she wanted it to feel, because for one strange, inexplicable moment, guilt slipped in.

That useless emotion was pushed away rapidly. She wasn't doing anything wrong. Her husband was dead, and she didn't need to be faithful to a memory. She was alive and deserved to live.

They were almost all the way home before she realized the whole reason she had given him for the evening out still had not been answered.

They were on the porch steps when she twisted toward him. "You said you would tell me why you're ranching again when you left Rocky to avoid it."

"Right." He adjusted the collar of her coat, smoothing the

lapels as he stared at her lips. "I was drawn to you, all those years ago. I didn't move fast enough, though, so when you and Ben fell in love, I couldn't say anything. It wasn't your fault, and it wasn't your responsibility, but I couldn't stay and watch you build a life together."

His words took a moment to sink in. To register. Then the shock of it hit, hard and quick. "You left because of me?"

Strong shoulders lifted in a gentle shrug. "I left because it was the right thing to do, for you *and* for Ben. It wasn't the ranching I was running from," he confessed.

She didn't know what to say.

They stood, separated by mere inches, staring at each other. It had been a wonderful evening, more wonderful than Dana had hoped. His confession was a piano falling out of the sky and striking the ground with huge impact.

He had hold of one of her hands. "I want to kiss you."

"Maybe I'm not the type to kiss on the first date." She tried for lighthearted, but her pulse pounded in her throat.

His lips curled upward as he leaned toward her. "I've dreamed about this day for so long, it doesn't count as a first date anymore."

And then he was kissing her. Fingers strong under her chin, holding her steady as he brushed his lips over hers once, twice. A soft kiss followed, slowly deepening as his hand slid over her cheek and into her hair, cradling the back of her neck as he pulled their bodies tighter.

It had been forever since she'd been kissed with that kind of passion, that kind of gentleness. That kind of need.

Dana tangled her arms around his neck and jumped in with two feet. Accepting the worship he gave. Moaning as his tongue dipped between her lips, shivering as he pressed a hand against her lower back, and even through the layers, his arousal was clear. Every bit of him hard, a solid and unyielding man—

Who had taken time out of his day to make her cookies.

A man who even now was pulling back, breathing heavily, with fire in his eyes and yearning on his face as he put space between them.

"I'll call you," he promised.

Before she could say anything else, he was gone.

19

———

*B*y the time Blake got out of bed for the second time, the sun was high in the sky and the house was quiet. He'd missed the entire rush and rumble of the kids headed off to school.

The sound of singing lured him out to the big vegetable garden area beyond the back door on a beautiful spring morning.

Jaxi was planting. Blake had turned over the garden the previous day, and now the fresh scent of sunshine on dirt rose on the air like a promise.

PJ walked beside an open row, a bucket in his hand and sheer delight on his face. Jaxi pointed to the ground, and he dropped to his knees to push in a couple of seeds. Together, they were singing the alphabet song loud enough to echo off the house.

It took another moment to spot Justin. The little dude had both arms wrapped around Jaxi's leg, clinging like a leech. He laughed every time she moved, his eyes squeezed shut as if he were on the wildest, most exciting ride at the Stampede.

Jaxi's smile stayed constant, no matter how off the mark PJ's planting efforts went.

Blake was struck with a memory. One of the garden the

summer after he and Jaxi had gotten married. The twins had been born in May, but Jaxi had still planted, the newborns tucked into the double stroller in the shade while they slept. The rows of corn and beets and carrots had been ruler straight and picture perfect. Delicious to boot.

Contrasting that was a memory of last year's crop. The rows had meandered like a drunk man had planted them—or a mom with a one-, three-, and five-year-old helping, since Lana had only been at kindergarten on alternate days. The garden had been a lush, disorderly jungle, the yellow heads of sunflowers randomly rising skyward like tall, happy-go-lucky sentinels. It had still produced delicious food for their table.

Jaxi knew growing up straight and tall happened inside babies and that sometimes messy gardens made the magic happen.

Blake marched into the dirt and dropped to his knees in front of her. She barely had time to blink before he was attacked by two little boys, but his hands went to Jaxi first, pulling her in for a sweet, tender kiss.

For one moment, quiet surrounded them, or as much quiet as they could get on a ranch in the springtime with two children laughing and the birds turning the air into a symphony of joy.

Blake rose and brushed the dirt off his knees. "I'll be in the office if you need me."

"Always need you," she said with a wink. Which was true, even though Jaxi was the most independent and capable woman, bar none, Blake had ever met.

He walked into the office they'd fixed up in the main barn and stopped in surprise. "Daniel."

His brother glanced away from the maps pinned to the wall. "Hey, lazybones."

"Bullshit on that," Blake said dryly. "Or has it been long enough you forgot what calving season is like?"

"Time and therapy are beginning to knock off the edges,"

Daniel said before marching forward and giving him a quick hug. "Got a minute to talk?"

"Always." Blake headed to the side of the room where they'd put in a new-fangled coffee maker. He'd thought it an extravagant luxury, but moments like this, he was very appreciative of the one-cup wonder. "Can I get you a coffee?"

Five minutes later they sat in the hard-backed chairs, leaning back and relaxed.

"I'll get straight to the point. Lance graduates in June. Beth gave Jaxi all the details about the ceremony, but I wanted you to know that Lance *specifically* asked to make sure you and Travis are there. And at the barbecue afterward. Seems you two are his favourites." Daniel's grin said so much.

The three boys Daniel had adopted had turned all of their lives upside down at different stages of the game, but Blake's younger brother being a dad to teenagers well ahead of the rest of them all—

Priceless and educational.

"Of course, we'll be there. I can't believe he's graduating already."

"Going to be like clockwork the next two years, with Nathan and Rob so evenly spaced in age," Daniel said proudly. "The other thing is, Beth and I would like to give Lance a horse as a graduation present. I've already been in contact with Karen, and she's got a good possibility lined up, but are you okay if the beast boards here? Lance seems to do most of the work you schedule out of the Six Pack stables."

"I schedule him here because I like seeing the kid," Blake admitted. "Plus, it gives Dad a kick to have a grown-up grandson hanging around, worshiping him."

Daniel laughed. "Yeah, we get a lot of 'and Grandpa said' at the dinner table."

Which made Blake happy and sad at the same time, the thoughts of his father's confession never too far away. If he could help build a few more good memories for both grandfather and grandson, it was a good thing.

"Of course the horse can stable here." Blake glanced at his brother. "You okay with me offering Lance full-time work once high school is officially done?"

"You can offer, but he's headed to university at the end of summer. He's keen about getting his bachelor's degree in sustainable agricultural systems."

Blake blinked. "Right. The conservation stuff he was telling me about."

Daniel smiled. "Yeah, that's pretty much what I said too. But once he's done, I know he wants to come back and rejoin the family."

"And he'll be welcome," Blake assured him, twisting as a knock on the open doorframe echoed off the walls.

"So this is how the other half lives." Jesse wandered in and eyed their coffee cups. "At least you're not munching down cake or doughnuts."

"I can help with that." Another voice sounded, and Jesse moved aside to allow Uncle Mark to join them. "Good to see you again, boys."

He placed a full box of doughnuts on the table, popping the lid open and helping himself to one before pointing at Jesse. "You don't need to make yourself sound so hard done by. I saw the size of that sandwich you were eating in your truck."

Jesse paused in the middle of reaching for a chocolate Bismarck. "Jeez, you spying on me, Uncle Mark?"

"You were parked at the side of the road," Mark said dryly.

Blake's brother grinned then nabbed his target. "Vicki makes Joel's lunches. The woman must think Joel's got a tapeworm, because there is always more than enough for both of us to have second breakfasts."

The room was getting crowded. Blake caught hold of the

rolling chair behind the desk and moved it out. "Jesse, grab a chair from the hallway."

"Don't bother," Daniel said as he rose to his feet. "I need to get back to the shop." He said his goodbyes all around, grabbed a doughnut with a wink, and headed out.

Jesse eyed Uncle Mark. "So."

Their uncle raised a brow.

"If the Coleman genes bred true, you're here to ask a favour. Basing this on the fact that you showed up with bribe material." Jesse grinned.

Mark leaned forward, elbow resting on his knee as he met Jesse's gaze evenly. "If the Coleman genes bred true, then you'd know a man doesn't need to bribe anyone to succeed. You've obviously had to connive your way out of a mess of trouble far too many times in your life."

Blake rubbed a hand across his mouth to hide his smile.

Jesse leaned back, but if anything, his grin got only bigger. "I like you. You're nearly as cocky as me."

This time Blake couldn't control himself. He laughed, the sound escaping like a donkey bray. He shook a finger at Jesse before turning his attention to the older man. "Uncle Mark, what can I do for you? And thank you for the doughnuts—it's a treat."

"You're welcome." Mark spoke to Blake, but his gaze lingered on Jesse. "I wondered what the procedure was for building on Coleman land. I know this one and his twin have fairly new homes on SP land."

Blake had wondered when this might come up and had even discussed it with Mike recently, to be prepared. "Until the amalgamation, it was up to the individual families. Now, I'd suggest you build on your own personal land, but somewhere it makes sense so as to not limit our future land uses."

"So no dropping a place in the middle of prime grazing land?"

Jesse grinned, licking chocolate from his fingers. "Oh, you can build there, but you're going to have mooing neighbours up close and personal off and on throughout the year as we move the herds around."

Blake crumpled up a piece of paper off his desk and threw it at Jesse's head. "Hush," he ordered before nodding at Uncle Mark. "If you're thinking of building, one spot would be somewhere close to the rental—I mean your original house, where Becky and Trevor are, or…"

He got to his feet. Mark joined him, and they walked over to the maps to examine the entire Coleman holdings.

Jesse joined them there as well. He tapped his finger on the corner near the junction of four ranches. "This spot would work. Gabe's new place is *here*. I've heard that Lee and Rachel are thinking about building sometime soon as well, and there's a great building site on this Moonshine corner. You'd end up with houses close to each other but not on top of each other, spread between Angel, Moonshine, and…whatever we're going to call your land, Uncle Mark."

Mark's chin dipped slowly, his mouth curving into a smile. "That's not a bad idea."

"I'll put out feelers, make sure nobody objects, but I don't think anyone will." Blake eased back, examining his uncle a little closer. "Feeling good about staying around, then? Good enough to think about building?"

"Lots of things going well," Mark agreed, still staring at the map. "If I don't use Coleman money, is there any objection to me getting started sooner than later?"

Blake shook his head. "Like I said, give me a few days, but it's your land."

"And so far, you're not an asshole." Jesse danced out of the way before Blake could land a solid punch on his shoulder. "We're all thinking it."

"You're such a jerk," Blake offered.

"Dick."

Mark snickered, jamming his hat back on his head offering a

chin dip. "On that note, I'll be off. Give me a shout if you do have any concerns, Blake, and otherwise I'll let you know once I've made a decision on the building site."

Then he was gone, and Blake was down to just Jesse, who was going through the doughnuts as if he hadn't eaten for days.

Blake gave him a deliberate knock on the head as he marched past. "You were right on the edge of tipping past outspoken into rude," he warned.

Jesse lost his grin. "Shit. I'm sorry. I honestly didn't mean to."

Huh. Blake folded his arms over his chest. "What's wrong?"

His younger brother dropped into a chair, legs sprawled in front of him as he glared at the nearly empty doughnut box. "That easy to read?"

"Sometimes," Blake said softly.

This was one of the hard-learned lessons from the past years. When Jesse had left, it had nearly broken his parents. Blake had known something was wrong with his little brother. Hell, all of them had figured something was up, but none of them had known exactly what or how bad.

It had been luck in a way that had brought Jesse back, and Blake never wanted to rely on luck again.

He leaned forward, elbows on the desk. "I keep an eye on you," he admitted. "Not in a creepy way, but I don't want you to ever feel like we're not listening. I don't want you to ever feel you need to leave because you're not being heard."

Once again, Jesse blinked. "Jeez. You serious?"

Blake lifted his shoulders. "We're a big family, Jesse. There's an awful lot of sound and bother going on all the time. But you're an important part of it, you and Dare, and we want you to *stay* a part of it. This is your home, here with your family. So, yeah. I'm trying to be a little more alert—although hell if I know if I'm succeeding half the time."

Jesse swallowed hard. "Well, *shit*."

Confusion struck. "Why does that sound like you're even more upset than when you came in?"

Then the words poured out of Jesse. The job offer, the possibility of moving away from Rocky Mountain House—away from the Coleman family.

Ah, hell. Emphasizing the importance of staying in town had not been the way to go. Blake was batting a thousand when it came to poor timing. He tried his best to do a one-eighty without it feeling forced. "It sounds like an amazing opportunity."

Jesse sighed heavily. "It is. It's an honour and a compliment, and accepting should be a total no-brainer." He looked up and met Blake's eyes. "But what you said is also true. We *are* family, and this is our home. How can I give that up?"

"You wouldn't be giving it up," Blake said. "Dare, Joey, and the new baby—they'd be right there with you. You'd only be about three hours away from us, which means you'd have people invading all the time."

But he wouldn't be living next to his best friend and twin. He wouldn't be dropping into the office and making Blake smile with his asinine jokes.

He wouldn't be around for the little moments. The day-to-day connections.

Blake stood, pushing the pain in his gut back and desperately trying to come up with some wise words to share. "You don't have to decide right now, so try not to worry about it yet. The answer will come."

Jesse snickered. "That's what Dare keeps saying, but it's hanging over me. I can feel the muscles in the back of my neck tightening up every time I remember, and I remember a hell of a lot. It's driving me up the wall."

"Stop it," Blake said sharply, frowning at his little brother. "I get it. It's a huge decision, but it's not life-and-death. You don't have to decide until the summer, so let it rest a couple more months. In the meantime, think about how you'll feel five years from now if you don't take the opportunity. And think about what you can do if you decide to go and then change your mind. Because this *isn't* irrevocable. You'd be moving three hours away, not three thousand, and you've always got a home to come back to."

An instant later, Blake found himself wrapped in a bro hug, Jesse smacking him hard enough on the back to make his bones creak. "You're right. You're right."

Blake wondered why everybody always seemed so surprised when they said that.

He laid a hand on Jesse's back and squeezed before breaking the hug and pushing Jesse toward the door. "Now go and take the doughnuts with you."

20

———

*L*aurel stepped into the kitchen and jerked to a halt. "Oh. Hello."

Uncle Mark went to rise to his feet, but Laurel waved him down, slightly uncomfortable at his ultra-politeness, especially considering her greeting had been as perky as leftover dishwater.

"I'm so sorry, sweetheart," her mother-in-law said as she began fussing at the papers on the table. "I don't have lunch anywhere near ready."

"Both of you, relax." Laurel put as much teasing as possible into her voice. "I'm home early, Mom. I don't mind pulling the meal together so you can keep on with what you're doing. Mark, are you joining us?"

"Yes, please."

He'd been around more often over the past two weeks. Still, there was nothing about his behaviour that Laurel could fault, and he seemed to be extraordinarily considerate around her mother-in-law.

The glow of happiness in Dana's eyes was all too easy to read.

No way was Laurel going to do a single thing to crush that development.

So she worked on putting aside her own problems and focusing on what seemed to be a mass of floor plans covering every inch of the table. "Are you finally ready to move ahead with your building plans, Mom?"

"No."

"Dana," Mark scolded.

"Maybe," Dana said reluctantly." She glanced at Laurel. "Mark was telling me about someone he knows who keeps an eye out for abandoned packages. You know, the ones that are custom-built and then the people can't afford them."

"That's how Jesse and Joel ended up with their places."

It was a great way to get at least the framing of the house for a fraction of the regular cost.

"And you know somebody who has contacts?" Laurel directed the question at Mark, who nodded firmly.

"Only there's no sense looking at every one of them if you already know some won't meet your needs. I'm trying to help Dana square away a few of her wish-list items." He leaned back in the chair and stretched his long legs out in front of him. "What about you and Rafe? If you were getting a home built, what would be the things that you must have?"

"A family room with lots of bookshelves, a fireplace, and a big porch looking toward the mountains," Laurel said instantly.

Mark held a hand out to Dana as if Laurel's words had been proof of something.

Dana folded her arms over her chest. "It's not that simple," she insisted. "Laurel just said a couple of things, but she didn't mention a word about what type of kitchen she wants, or how many bedrooms, because if you're going to build an imaginary house, there's no use in skimping on the bedrooms you'll need down the road."

Something tightened inside, but Laurel kept her smile firmly in place. "Imaginary houses can expand as necessary."

She moved to start lunch prep, more as a way to keep her hands busy and her back toward her mother-in-law so that her expression wouldn't give her away.

"It really is about the *concepts* of what you want," Mark said. "Rooms can be rearranged, porches and balconies added. But the kind of ceiling and windows are little more set in stone."

"Well, since my budget is also set in stone—as in, I don't have one—I can take as long as I want to figure this out," Dana said clearly. Papers rustled, and when Laurel turned, Dana had two floor plans pulled forward. "These are the prettiest. I don't even know why I like them, though, so don't ask," she said with a laugh as Mark leaned forward.

"If you like them, you don't need a reason why." Mark nodded, though, as he peered at them more closely before tapping one. "This is a really good design for around here. I like the great room with the fireplace. It would be cozy on cold nights but open enough to have lots of family visit."

Laurel was too curious to stay away. She moved in to look the design over. "Oh, that is pretty." She laughed. "Want to know where I think you should build it?"

Dana glanced at her in surprise. "You're going to offer advice on building sites?"

"Why not? If it's all imaginary." She smiled, attempting to make up for her earlier downhearted attitude. Not their fault that she was grumpy. "I'll take you after lunch."

Which is how she found herself a third wheel to her mother-in-law and Mark, guiding him up a narrow dirt road off the secondary road between Angel land and his own.

He paused the truck at a gate, and Laurel hurried to open it. "Not too much farther," she assured him.

When they were through and she'd closed the gate behind them and rejoined them in the truck, Dana leaned over the seat to look into the back of the crew cab. "What on earth were you doing up here?"

Laurel hesitated. She and Rafe had discovered the spot two summers ago and had been using it ever since to enjoy privacy to fool around. Which meant there was no way she could answer without her cheeks going red, either from telling the truth *or* lying.

"Oh, look, that's where I want to show you. Just to the left," she ordered, ignoring the question.

Mark pulled to a stop and stared over the land in amazement. "I had forgotten there was a rise this high on the parcel."

"Wow." Dana was out the door, Laurel hard on her heels. Together they walked to the level place, a slight rise at their backs.

It really was an amazing spot. Laurel gestured to the west. "Can you imagine that view every morning while you're drinking coffee?"

Dana slipped an arm around her waist. "It's almost the same view as at home, but wow, elevation makes a huge difference."

"The driveway would be a little bit of an adventure in the winter," Mark said with a grin even as he joined them, shaking his head slightly. "But you're right. This is an amazing location."

Uncle Mark's land spread before them all the way to the foothills. If Laurel twisted to the right, she could spot the Angel property, and just at the eastern edge, a thin trail of smoke rose from Gabe and Allison's home. Farther to the right lay Whiskey Creek, with its rolling landscape, a herd of horses even now appearing over the top of one hill. Straight to the east was Moonshine land, mature trees visible along the meandering river, but the rest of it was pasture and crops.

"Well, this is pretty much perfect," Mark said, sneaking a hand onto her shoulder to squeeze lightly. "Thank you."

"It's your land," she said. "You would have found it eventually."

Dana laughed, a hand extended farther to the south. "Look."

They joined her, and Laurel suddenly realized that the entire side of the hill to the south of where they stood was covered in bushes, some of them big enough to be called trees. "Are those all wild roses?"

Her mother-in-law nodded happily. "I *adore* wild roses."

Dana wandered along a deer trail, happiness written all over her face as she examined the bushes. Sunshine danced over her, the gentle wind lifting her hair and making golden highlights dance.

Laurel was close enough to Uncle Mark to hear his sudden intake of breath.

She turned to him and spoke softly. "You okay?"

He'd been staring at Dana. He turned slowly back toward Laurel, his eyes full of longing, but he twisted his lips into a smile and nodded briskly. When he spoke, it was a secret, shared just with Laurel. "I would do anything to make her happy."

His heart in the words. Truth. Laurel felt it to the core of her being.

Dana laughed again, and this time as she turned, her eyes met Mark's and something new was there. Laurel felt less in the way and more honoured at having witnessed something so pure and sweet and right.

But continuing to eavesdrop wasn't on her agenda. No lingering, not now. Fortunately, the perfect distraction had been offered right at hand. "I think I solved a problem," Laurel announced boldly.

"The issue of where to build the house?" Mark offered.

She shook her head. "The issue of what to call *Mark's land*. It's obvious." She held out a hand and gestured, pointing to the mass of greenery that would eventually be covered with pale-pink, fragrant flowers.

"Oh, yes. That's perfect," Dana said. She turned to Mark and grabbed his hands, eager and giddy and not even aware of how broad his smile went because she'd touched him. "Welcome to the Wild Rose ranch."

If she hadn't been there, Laurel bet that Uncle Mark would've kissed—

Well, that was a problem easily solved. Laurel deliberately turned her back and walked down the rise, as if eager to explore.

More eager to leave the two of them alone, at least briefly, because if she couldn't see them, they couldn't see her, and she was one hundred percent sure that Mark was capable of taking advantage of the presented opportunity.

In the quiet of their room that night, Laurel told Rafe about having given up their tryst spot.

His expression turned thoughtful as she shared witnessing the kiss—or at least the aftereffects of it, because Dana's cheeks had glowed the entire trip back to the Angel homestead.

Rafe nodded slowly. "I need to adjust my brain. Mark seems to be a good man, and if anyone deserves to be happy, it's Mom."

Laurel agreed. She'd come to that conclusion a while ago. Now she cuddled in against his side. "I was feeling sad today," she confessed.

Rafe curled his arm around her and pressed a kiss to her temple. "Anything I can do?"

She shook her head. "Thinking about kids. With all the cousins constantly popping out babies, the question keeps getting brought up. When do we plan to have some? Today Mom was asking how many rooms we'd want in a new house. You know, planning for the hoard of children we'll raise."

He hummed softly, rolling toward her until he'd pinned her in place with his strong body. "You still want to wait a little longer before we start trying, or have you changed your mind?"

"I'm not ready for kids, but part of me worries," she admitted. "What if we can't? What if things don't work for us that way?"

Rafe stroked his cheek against hers, kissing her softly. "Then we'll find a different way to build a family. I like kids, but I figure the raising of them is more important than the birthing. I'm a guy, though, so I could be missing the point."

"I agree with you in principle." She curled her arms around his neck and tugged until he came over her, a warm, secure weight guarding and keeping her safe. "Like I said, I was just feeling sad and wanted you to know why. You don't need to try and fix it. Just love me."

"Always." His tone dropped a notch as he made a dirty offer. "Can I try and distract you?"

"I'm pretty focused right now," Laurel teased. "You'll have to try really hard."

Which he did, thoroughly but quietly.

21

Kissing Dana had become an addiction.

Mark had known quick enough that every privilege she offered would mean no turning back. And while they'd only had a couple of official dates, he'd taken to stopping at the house in his free time and between work shifts with the Coleman clan.

Laurel's suggested nickname for his parcel had caught on instantly with the rest of the family. Now to make sure that Wild Rose ranch was a new start in all the ways that Mark needed.

Although, getting to begin by kissing Dana while laughter shone in her eyes, the sunlight dancing around them on the spot where Mark intended to build their home—

Okay, that was jumping the gun a little, but he couldn't help himself. Spending time with her had made it clear all his memories weren't built up or unrealistic. Dana was sweet and gentle and giving, and he couldn't wait to be able to give to her in return.

The warning that Laurel had issued, though, echoed loudly in Mark's mind. That Ben had been changed so hard—

Mark couldn't imagine what it did to a woman to have her trust in a man completely broken.

So he needed to be cautious, but at the same time, he kept being distracted by the kisses and the urge in his gut that told him to press forward faster than his head thought wise.

Yup. That kiss up on the ridge a week ago had been a whole lot of perfect.

Blake had given him the go-ahead, so when Mark heard from his building contact, the news was too exciting to wait to share.

He hurried to the Angel ranch, pausing on the main road before entering the driveway. Rafe was running the harrows over the gravel to remove the ruts caused by winter freeze and snow removal.

Rafe gave him a wave but kept on with his task as Mark parked then strode rapidly toward the ranch house.

Dana bolted upright in surprise when he marched through the door and into the living room. She had a load of laundry in a basket on the chair, neatly folded piles organized on the couch.

"Mark. Gabe said you were working with him this morning."

"I am," Mark said, sliding in close and breathing in her sweet scent. A familiar floral aroma wrapped around him and mixed with the comforting smells of food and fresh laundry that were the epitome of home. "Coffee break. Thought I'd come to see how you're doing."

She flushed. "That's sweet."

"Sweet enough to give me a kiss?" he teased.

When she instantly tipped her face toward him, his heart leapt. He cupped her chin, leaning in to enjoy the innocent brush of their lips together.

Then her tongue snuck out and stroked against his.

Sweetness vanished as heat rose between them. His body hardened, and for a brief moment, they clung to each other, the kiss growing deeper. Dirtier. Somehow, he kept a handle on it, breaking contact and stepping back far enough to give her space.

Dana lifted a hand to her kiss-swollen lips. "You are far too tempting," she said softly.

"That's my line." Mark took a deep breath then changed the topic before he suggested they go test her mattress springs. "I have some good news."

She tilted her head toward the kitchen. "Coffee? Since you're on a coffee break?"

"Sure."

He made it to the kettle before she did, filling it at the tap and letting her take care of the other details. It was good, working together in the small space. Not only because this wasn't the first time they'd done it and they were already finding a joint rhythm in the routine—which made Mark smile.

He had to admit the small size of the kitchen also allowed for ample opportunities to bump into her, which didn't suck.

Dana laughed after he had once again *accidentally* brushed past, grabbing her hips to stabilize himself. "Sit down," she ordered, an amused smile on her lips. "You're as handsy as a teenager."

Not much to do in response to that except grin and enjoy watching her.

The rumble of the tractor in the background cut off, and the room grew quieter. Mark waited until she had the cups on the table, and slices of banana bread as well. "I heard from my building contact. He's got a package for me."

Dana's eyes lit up. "For your house? Already?"

He wasn't about to mention that he hadn't bothered to wait for a sale package to appear. He had no problem footing the bill for a custom build which would be exactly what they wanted down the road. "He's given me a delivery date of August first, which means I've got until then to get the site prepped. Which, with all of June and July ahead of us, is doable."

"And you're definitely building up on the ridge? That's going to be a pretty spot," Dana said with approval.

"Won't even have to take out the trees," he told her. "The place will be surrounded with wild roses."

"Even better, considering that's what your ranch is now called." Dana took a sip of her coffee, a smile of approval warming her expression. "I'm happy for you. I'm glad you're getting the chance to set down roots here, close to your brothers."

"It's been good to reconnect with them," Mark admitted. "Living with George is an adventure, though. He's been the only guy in the house for a long time. I think every time he sees me, he's a bit surprised."

"If you put up the frame in August, that means you can get to lock up before the snow flies." Dana made a face. "You'll still be bunking with George for the winter."

"I think I can fast-track the interior. Maybe not by Thanksgiving, but by Christmas. Or at least that's what I hope."

"That is exciting." Dana caught his fingers and gave them a squeeze. "That would be a lovely Christmas present."

He sure thought so. Being there with Dana would make for an extraordinary holiday season.

Mark flipped his hand over and trapped her fingers in his. "That means next year we can put some money into fixing up this place. Build that wall of bookshelves that Laurel wants and fix the porch. Exterior stuff is easy to do."

Confusion slid into her eyes. "I suppose it is, but we don't really need any improvements right now. I still need to figure out whether I should get a little place to myself or help build the kids a new home—"

"Dana. That problem is already solved," he said earnestly. "Really, the bones of this place are good. If we fix it up for the kids, the place will work out fine."

She went still.

"Wait." Her frown grew deeper. "Mark, before I jump to any conclusions, let me ask a question. While *we're* fixing up this place for the kids, exactly where do you think I'm going to live?"

He lifted her hand to his lips and kissed her knuckles softly. "With me. In the home I'm building for you."

If he'd expected her to smile sweetly or throw her arms around him gratefully—

Dana jerked her fingers from his and rose to her feet, fury sweeping in. "Why, you arrogant *asshole*."

Not the response he had expected.

You jumped the gun, his brain warned even as the door from the porch swung open. Rafe stood in the doorway, eyes wide with shock.

Dana was just getting warmed up. Fists planted against her hips, she shook her head in disbelief. "I told you I was willing to date you. That didn't mean I agreed to move in with you, that didn't mean I agreed you could make decisions about what my children or I do. That *didn't* mean you get to assume anything about me or what I want or need."

"I know it's not a given," he began before she cut him off.

"Shut up." She looked slightly shocked at her own words then took a deep breath and lifted her chin resolutely. "I am so disappointed in you right now. I think you should leave."

"Dana, sweetheart—"

"No," she snapped. "I am *not* your sweetheart. Not yet. And if you don't talk to me and ask my opinions *before* making decisions for both of us, I will never be your sweetheart." She snapped up a finger toward the door. "Now get out."

Slipping out of the house, Mark felt a little as if he were a dog skulking away with his tail between his legs.

That had gone well. *Not.*

His pride thoroughly chastised, Mark glanced over to discover Rafe pacing beside him. "Really? You plan to escort me to my truck or follow me all the way until I'm off Angel land?"

"Mom asked you to leave, so I making sure you do."

Holding back a growl of frustration was tough, but somehow Mark managed. The last thing he needed was to get into another fight today, although—dammit—he'd meant well in the first place.

Stupid misunderstanding. Stupid moving too fast.

But then again, he'd been upfront about his intentions since the start.

They walked in silence for a moment, then Rafe cleared his throat. "You've got the day off tomorrow, don't you?"

"Yeah."

"Me too." The young man tilted his head toward the old barn. "Got any plans? Bunch of stuff in there that I could use some help sorting through."

The question was unexpected enough to make Mark stumble to a stop. He stared at his nephew for a moment, but even after repeating the comment a few times in his head, it didn't make sense. "What are you doing?"

Rafe looked at him seriously then offered a light lift of his shoulders. "You pissed Mom off but good, which takes a hell of a lot of energy. Or something else." His lips twitched. "I've heard her swear maybe twice in my entire life. It's that rare, and she's had a lot more reason to curse than most. Which means something about you hit hard. But since she's willing to speak her mind about you riling her up, and she didn't close the door on a relationship with you completely, I'm going to assume this is a good thing."

Hope rose suddenly. "Which is why you want to give me a job to do?"

"One that might put you in close proximity to my mom a lot sooner than if you hit the road and stay away like she suggested? Yeah," Rafe confessed before lifting blue eyes filled with laughter to Mark's. "Although, if you mention that specific reasoning in front of her, I will deny it."

A silent assist was better than no assist at all.

Mark took a moment to look Rafe over. Traces of his brother Ben were there, but more importantly, he had a firm confidence that seemed surprisingly strong in a man of his young years.

Getting to be with Dana meant being in this man's life.

And in Laurel's, and Gabe and Allison's.

The realization was a bolt of lightning. Dear God, he wasn't just getting involved with Dana, he was running full-out at an entire family.

The seriousness of this thing struck him like icy lightning, but the overall sensation was good. He wanted this—*all* of this.

He thrust a hand toward Rafe. "Thank you. And I swear, I want nothing but the best for your mom."

Rafe offered a firm handshake in return, that amused smile flitting around his lips again. "So do we. Still stands to be seen if *you're* what's best."

Coleman Memory Book
~Becca (Six Pack) Coleman~

I like being a Coleman. I like being part of something big. Uncle Joel says you can't build anything with one piece of Lego, and he's right. We've got lots and lots of Legos in the Coleman family, and we like to do things together.

Family is many arms to hold me tight. My sister always by my side. Mommy and Daddy dancing in the kitchen.

We live in the same house that Daddy grew up in. And Grandpa. There's a doorway in the kitchen that's all beat up, but when Mommy painted the walls last year, she was real careful not to paint over the marks on it.

She said that's a piece of history, all the little pencil lines showing how tall my uncles were when they were little like me.

I'm going to be as tall as my daddy someday, but Mommy says even if I'm not, I can still be the best Coleman possible. Because we've got love in our hearts and love in our heads.

I think it's because there's a lot of love in our house, and it's like a battery. Every night when we sleep, we get all charged up so we can shine real bright on everyone.

That's what love is. That's what being a Coleman is like. Shiny and bright.

[Images: of a doorjamb with dozens of pencil marks, showing names and ages. Outside picture of the SP homestead taken at night, with golden light shining out of the windows. Two little girls holding hands as they stand beside a haybale.]

22

A podium and seating area had been constructed outside of the high school gym. The same school Daniel had attended, with the same kind of setup in place for his own graduation, and those of his brothers from the Six Pack ranch.

He might possibly be more nervous now than he'd been all those years ago.

Beth stepped in front of him, straightening his tie and smoothing it over his shirt before fixing his lapels. "You can stop fidgeting any time," she teased.

"I don't know why I'm so jittery," he complained.

"Because your son is graduating, and you're excited."

He caught her against him and gave her a half twirl, her dark curls flying wildly, before leaning their foreheads together and looking into her eyes. "Miss Beth, *your* son is graduating, and you're excited, yet you don't look like you've got ants in your pants."

Her smile widened, and she trailed her fingers through his hair. "I'm wearing a skirt."

He snorted, pulling her back to vertical before tugging her

close to steal another hug. "You've done good. Congratulations on reaching this point. Lance can be proud."

"We did it together." She breathed in deep, wrapping herself tighter against him and murmuring softly, "I love the way you smell."

Electric need slid up his spine, clear and strong. It didn't matter how many years they'd spent together, the simplest touch of Beth's hand sent Daniel skyrocketing every time. "Hold that thought for a private celebration tonight," he ordered.

A bit of milling about was happening as the graduating class —albeit small—gathered to the side of the podium and only partially out of sight.

As ordered, Blake was there, coming forward to solemnly shake Daniel's hand and give Beth a hug. Travis arrived as well, while the rest of their families gathered in the seating area, taking up a lot of room.

Daniel grinned. "Good thing the organizing committee knew to prepare for a Coleman onslaught."

"They took out twice as many chairs as last year," Beth informed him. She wrapped her arms around him and squeezed tight. "I love that your family is here. All the second cousins and twice removed or whatever."

All Daniel's uncles and aunts and cousins had come to celebrate. Lance had worked with most of them at the various ranches, which meant it was extra special since they weren't here because he was a Coleman but because he had put in the time.

Lance had become someone they all knew and liked because of who he was, and Daniel was so proud of him.

"Uncle Mark's here." Daniel and Beth's youngest, who had now insisted his name be shortened to the more mature Rob, slid up and leaned on Daniel's arm before lowering his voice. "He must still be in trouble, because Auntie Dana is here too, but she's sitting over *there*."

He gestured with his head to the opposite side of the gathering, next to Rafe and Laurel.

Beth folded her arms over her chest. "Robbie," she said disapprovingly.

Rob held his hands up and attempted an innocent look. "What? I can't help it if the aunties were talking about it in the yard. He really likes her. I don't know why she got so mad. *I* wouldn't get mad if somebody wanted to build me a house. I feel bad for him."

Laughter began to bubble in Daniel's chest, but he wrapped an arm around his youngest son's shoulders and guided him toward the chairs they'd staked out for their immediate family. "Remember our ongoing conversation about girls being confusing?"

"Yeah?"

"That doesn't ever change, no matter how old we, or they, get," Daniel said dryly before patting Rob on the back and aiming him at his chair. "Stop gossiping, and get ready to cheer for your brother."

Only when they sat and Beth leaned her head against Daniel's shoulder, amusement tinged his voice as he whispered in her ear, "I hope they get that straightened out soon, or Rob is going to be upset all summer. I wouldn't be surprised if he tried matchmaking."

A snicker escaped from Beth. "Don't start me giggling."

The ceremony began with all the usual pomp and circumstance. The principal made a short speech. Teachers presented a few awards. Then suddenly—

"I'd like to ask the class valedictorian to come forward, please. Lance Coleman."

Shocked silence for a moment before cheers rang out, and Lance made his way up the stairs at the side of the stage, headed to the podium.

Daniel wasn't sure if he was coming or going. "Did you know he was valedictorian?" he whispered to his wife.

Beth's eyes shone as she shook her head.

Lance appeared a lot more comfortable behind the podium than Daniel would've been. When his son's gaze flickered over the crowd before landing on Beth then meeting Daniel's eyes, though, Daniel smiled in encouragement.

Ahh. His son was hiding it well, but he was nervous as all get out.

Lance cleared his throat then began, glancing over the audience with youthful exuberance and a grin on his lips.

"People say graduation is a turning point. We're supposed to consider the past years of learning as a base, and now it's time to leave behind childish things and move into a world where what we do matters. Which makes sense, but also seems confusing. What if there are childish truths we need to hold on to?"

He turned slightly, gaze locking on his grandfather, Mike, and grandmother, Marion. "I'm lucky because I not only have a great family around me, I've got a large extended family. The bad part of that means I can never get into trouble without *somebody* finding out."

Laughter trickled from the gathered audience as Lance twisted, facing his classmates. "That big extended family of mine has been working on a project over the last while. When I first heard about the memory book, I figured it was kind of like those scrapbooks my mom's got. The ones with me and my brothers as little kids. There are a lot of pictures in there that are embarrassing, and yet I secretly go through them when she's not around. We don't have a lot of them—baby books. And some of you in my graduating class have the same thing, for different reasons.

"Sometimes our parents were divorced. That meant shuffling from one house to another, a week at a time, so not everything got recorded or not everything got put in the book.

"Sometimes—if we're honest—there weren't many good memories to record."

A few heads dipped in agreement, not just amongst the youth, but the gathered parents and grandparents. It was a sad yet relatable truth.

Lance turned to where the teachers were seated. "When I mentioned what my family was up to, my friends and I got to talking and realized that's where school steps in and fills a need. Teachers. People who make an impact on us and build memories with us *in spite* of having to be there. The assignments they insist we do, the deadlines we have to meet. The time we spend together. So, thank you to the teachers who stepped in and became our parental figures when we needed it most."

A spattering of applause grew into a solid rumble. It was clear by the grins on the teachers' faces that Lance's acknowledgement was appreciated.

Fingers tightening on the edges of the podium, he took a deep breath and started again.

"But for my memory page, when I look back at the years here in Rocky—when I think about the time with my family and my friends, the one person who stands out is somebody who *didn't* have to be there, but *chose* to be there."

Beth's fingers tightened on Daniel's thigh, and he went very still as Lance deliberately met his gaze across the gathering.

"The first time I saw Daniel Coleman, he gently gave myself and my brothers hell for swimming unsupervised in the coulee below our rental house. And when I say gently, I mean he somehow convinced three strange boys that he wasn't a danger *and* that it would be the most fun ever to get out of the deep water and into a section where we were less likely to drown."

The memory was there for Daniel as well. Sharp and sweet, because it had been the beginning.

Lance continued, gaze drifting over the audience that

included the rest of his extended family. "That first chance meeting was followed by more official swimming sessions and then babysitting, but even when I figured out that he was interested in my mom, I never felt as if he wasn't interested in me. Spending time with me was not a means to an end, but because he thought I was a pretty cool guy.

"Since then, in the childish moments where I felt the world was cruel or unjust, there was somebody who *chose* to be there, to tell me he didn't understand why either, but that somehow we'd get through it. Or the childish moments of joy, when everything went right, he chose to be there as well, joining in the laughter and the praise. Those are moments I never want to let go of."

A subtle silence had fallen over the gathering, heads once again nodding as they all considered the truth of Lance's words.

He turned again to the graduating class.

"And while this is my world, I know it's true for each of you, my classmates. In the future, there will be times we'll be disappointed. There will be times the struggle will be hard, and what we'll need is someone in our lives who chooses to be there for all the right reasons. Maybe we'll have to go looking for them. Maybe they're already there.

"Or maybe the biggest gift we need to give the world we're stepping into is to be that person for someone else.

"Let's hold on to the lessons of childhood and make a difference. Let's do this right. Let's choose to be the change."

A round of applause and cheers rose from the audience, but Daniel was already moving, Beth's hand on his shoulder pushing him toward the aisle.

Lance marched across the stage, not toward the side where he was supposed to wait with the rest of his class but toward the makeshift stairs at the front on a direct trajectory for where his family stood.

They met, Lance damn near running the final steps to throw

himself into Daniel's arms, the tall, strong young man just about bowling Daniel over.

He didn't care that they were right out there in public, and obviously neither did Lance, because he squeezed Daniel tight, letting go only enough to reach out and grab his mother and pull Beth into the mix as well.

"I love you." Lance made it a declaration as if it were the final line of his speech. As if nothing was complete without this. "I am so proud to be your son."

Joy bubbled up, chasing away the tears that were there and the emotion that was strangling Daniel's throat so tight, he couldn't speak. Because he needed to speak. He desperately needed to share this truth.

He looked his son in the face. "It has been my privilege to be in your life, and you have no idea how much it changed me for the better. Getting to be your dad—?" Daniel shook his head. "I love you."

Lance grinned then turned and squeezed Beth as well. "Thanks for picking him."

Beth laughed. "I did it just for you."

Lance tucked himself under Daniel's arm, still holding Beth on the other side, and the three of them made their way back to the family seats only slightly embarrassed to discover the entire ceremony had paused until they sat down.

Lance slid in far enough to accept hugs from his brothers, giving Robbie a noogie as he settled between them. Beth and Daniel once again next to each other.

In the row behind them, Blake leaned forward and laid his hand on Daniel's shoulder briefly and squeezed.

Beth hung on tight to Daniel's right hand, his left arm around her waist. Connected. Together. Daniel had no idea what happened for the next half hour of the ceremony because he was in his own little glowing circle of happiness with his wife and his children. His sons—the ones he'd never expected to have, yet who were his to his very core.

He glanced over and found his father's eyes on him. Mike's expression was twisted tight, and Daniel worried for a moment until he realized his father's eyes were full of tears and he was trying not to cry.

Ah, shit. Daniel leaned forward and pinched the bridge of his nose, desperately fighting to regain control before he lost it again.

Thankfully, by the time the rest of the ceremony was done, his emotional level was no longer riding on teary but happy enthusiasm. The entire clan gathered around, taking turns to shake Lance's hand as laughter swelled around them.

A sharp tug on his sleeve brought Daniel's attention back to his middle boy, Nathan, who was grinning from ear to ear.

"How come you look like trouble?" Daniel asked softly.

Teeth flashed white. "Not me," Nathan insisted before leaning against Daniel's side, comfortable his affection would be accepted and reciprocated. He lifted a hand and pointed to the other side of the gathering. "Just thought you might be interested in watching this."

Rob was talking earnestly with Auntie Dana.

"Aw, *shit.*" It wasn't right that Daniel's first impulse was to laugh. "Your brother has no idea that he's dealing with dynamite, does he?"

"Not a clue," Nathan agreed. Then he shrugged. "Truth is, he gets away with murder when it comes to girls. That whole innocent 'but I just wanted you to have this pretty flower' spiel works for him far too often."

Oh boy. Something to be worried about on a day in the future that was not today.

Daniel and Nathan watched as Auntie Dana listened intently to Rob's rapid words that were accompanied by much hand swinging. She tilted her head slightly as if not quite believing her grandnephew's argument. But then she laughed, and Rob gave her a quick hug before turning and sauntering away, hands shoved in his pockets and a pleased expression on his face.

"I really wish I could read lips," Nathan complained.

"It would be entertaining." Daniel wrapped an arm around Nathan's shoulder, ready to pull him back toward the family.

"Wait."

Auntie Dana was on the move. It wasn't as if she was on a mission, but more on a focused meander that sooner than later brought her into the path of Uncle Mark. They didn't meet for long, but there was clearly a moment of pleasant conversation before Dana continued on her way, Mark staring after her, his bemused grin growing steadily wider.

"Son of a gun," Daniel whispered.

Nathan snorted. "See? Robbie's terrible. And good."

This time Daniel laughed, tugging his son with him and pointedly ignoring whatever was going on between certain older family members. "He's a busybody. He got lucky this time."

"He gets lucky a lot," Nathan said before jerking upright and blinking hard. "That came out wrong. I didn't mean it the way it sounded."

They were nearly at where Beth, Lance, and Robbie were waiting, but Daniel couldn't resist. He stopped and tugged Nathan into a huge hug, the two of them chuckling the entire time.

Daniel patted Nathan firmly on the shoulder. "I love you."

"I love you too, Dad," Nathan said as easy as anything, the words flowing freely in their family. "Can we go? I'm starving. I can't wait for the barbecue."

Daniel took Beth's fingers, holding hands as they walked back to the car. Their three boys milled around them, nearly as active as they'd been eight years ago when he'd first started seeing her.

Her eyes shone brightly as he paused to open her car door. "I love you, Mr. Coleman."

"Love you too, Miss Beth." Daniel stepped against her, pulling her into his arms to kiss her. The sweet rightness of her there, his family, his sons, who were all making smooching noises and laughing...

It was where he had chosen to be, and he couldn't be more grateful for what he'd been given.

23

———

Dana hated to admit it, but she missed Mark. It might've been only a short time since he'd returned to Rocky, but for the past month she'd woken each morning wondering what he would do that day to make her smile.

But even as well as things had been going, him assuming they would be together down the road? Him *assuming* anything—

That was a no go. She was actually kind of proud of herself for having spoken up the way she had.

Since she'd kicked him out, however, there'd been constant reminders of how much their days had become tangled. Every time she looked into her yard, it seemed he was there. Working with Rafe outside the barn. Delivering animals from Gabe and Allison's—Dana's oldest son and Mark riding confidently into the yard with the ranch dogs barking enthusiastically as they helped herd sheep into the summer pens.

Mark, stripping off his sweaty and dirty shirt as he stopped at the old hand-pump outside her garden plot. His lean yet muscular body far too mesmerizing as he soaked his head and torso then casually dried off.

She was torn between giving Blake a stern talking to for

scheduling Mark near her or baking her nephew a cake for keeping the man close enough to ogle.

Add in her grandnephew's meddling—still, Robbie had been the only one bold enough to come out and say what the entire clan seemed to be thinking. Give the man another chance.

It's what she truly wanted. But she would bend, not fold.

So a couple of days after Lance's graduation, Dana sat in the local coffee shop and waited for Mark to arrive. They needed a solid conversation on neutral territory to get things straightened out.

As she fidgeted with her coffee cup, other thoughts whirled. While she wanted this relationship to work, she was still afraid. That wasn't his fault, but if she couldn't move beyond hesitant friendship, she needed to let him know sooner than later.

Someone slid onto the bench seat across from her. Dana glanced up with a welcoming smile to discover her brother-in-law George. "Oh."

His lips twitched. "I know. Wrong brother."

It wasn't right her cheeks flushed so hot, so quickly. "George. It's always good to see you," she said honestly.

"You too," he said, waving off the waitress who had come forward to offer a mug and the coffee carafe. "I won't stay long. I know Mark's on his way. He had to stop at the seed mill to pick up something for Blake."

She eyed George. "What're you doing here?"

He placed both palms flat on the table and took a deep breath. "At the risk of being told to mind my own business—"

"Oh, dear. Conversations that start that way rarely end well," she warned.

His nervousness vanished as his grin widened. "Right? Sally would've told me to stay out of it. But then again, afterward she would've slipped in behind my back and come to you on the sly."

George's wife had been gone for over twenty-five years, but Dana could picture it plain as day.

Dana eyed her brother-in-law closer. He too had experienced sadness and loss over the years. He'd ended up raising three girls by himself. He'd had help from his sisters-in-law, but he'd been fiercely independent for the most part.

"I still miss her," Dana admitted.

"Me too," George agreed. "I'm finally working to be the dad to our girls Sally would've wanted me to be. I get to see all four of them regularly—you heard that Lisa is expecting in October?"

Dana nodded.

George made a face. "Okay, getting to the point, I think you deserve to be happy."

Well, that was easy to agree to. "Thank you."

"I think Mark can make you happy."

She wanted to laugh. "He has a lot of champions," she informed George. "From my grandnephew, to my sisters-in-law, to my children, to you."

George looked pleased. "Good. That means I'm not the only one in your targets, then."

This time she did laugh before leaning forward and lowering her voice. "Why do you feel you have to tell me this?" she asked in all seriousness. "Do you all think I'm not able to figure out what's right for myself?"

George reached across the table and took hold of her hand. Like a brother, like a friend. His words were a low rumble full of concern and caring. "I think you spent a lot of years doing what was right *in spite* of how much it hurt. I want you to be able to do what's right and have it result in happiness. But knowing what that feels like might be hard after so many years of being brave."

A shiver went through her, and she sighed heavily. "I hear you. It was hard," she confessed, "but I don't regret staying with Ben."

"We all regret not helping him more, and that's on us," George said seriously. He nodded and gave her hand a final squeeze. "We won't interfere unless you ask, but we all hope the path forward is nothing but sunshine for you."

"You never see a rainbow if it never rains," Dana pointed out. "But thank you. See you at the Canada Day celebrations?"

"I'll be there with flags on," George promised.

He was walking out the door when his brother walked in, the two men pausing for a brief hello before Mark sauntered toward the table.

Looking the man over was enough to give Dana a thrill. Mark wore faded Wranglers over well-worn cowboy boots, his strong thigh muscles pressing against the fabric. A hint of a black T-shirt peeked out from under his red flannel shirt, and as he sat opposite her, he placed his cowboy hat on the seat then dragged a hand through his hair to straighten it.

She caught herself smiling in admiration. He was easy on the eyes. He was, in fact, the hottie that Hope had told her—

Oh, dear.

A sharp *zing* darted up her spine, and Dana played with her empty cup to hide how much she was feeling at that moment. Correction—how much not *we should only be friends* she was feeling.

"You all coffee'd out?" he asked.

"You haven't had a cup yet," she pointed out, thankful for something specific to answer to instead of continuing to drool over his sexy forearms and the firm cut of his jawline.

The jawline on a face that had gone sheepish. "I want to apologize properly, and I don't want to do it here."

Dana considered then nodded, leaving money on the table for her own drink.

They walked quietly down the sidewalk side by side before Dana gestured toward the empty playground with strategically placed benches around the perimeter. "Want to sit there?"

"Sure."

They settled then twisted to face each other. Mark caught her hand, cradling her fingers gently. "You're right. I was an ass, but—"

"Is this an apology?" Dana interrupted. "Because usually when my kids used the word *but,* it meant they were about to explain why they had done the thing they weren't supposed to do that they weren't *really* sorry for doing in the first place."

"I have thought about you for so long." Mark's amused tone was also honest and deep, a rumble sliding over her and making her warm to her very core. "In fact, I have been thinking about you being mine for longer than I should've, which means I pushed way too hard."

She couldn't fathom what he was talking about, even though he had admitted it from the first moment. "You are light years ahead of me," she pointed out. "I like you. I even—"

She bit back that particular confession, because it wasn't what was needed right now. Instead, Dana shook her head and focused. "But you need to be patient, because what you want and what I want *could* be the same thing, but you've got to give me time to get there."

"I know, and I'm sorry. Not for the *building our house* thing, but for not giving you the time to know that building our house is the right thing."

A laugh escaped in spite of herself. "You are absolutely terrible at this, aren't you?"

His grin widened, all sweet mischief as if they were about to sneak off behind the barn and he couldn't wait. "I'm being very patient in some ways," he pointed out, the innuendo in his deep voice unmistakable.

Oh, boy. The shiver that went through her body was intense and sharp, edgy with need.

Stick to the point. "You need to be patient," she repeated. "But the other thing you have to understand..."

Her throat closed tight. Just the thought of this confession seemed so wrong.

Mark instantly wrapped an arm around her. "*Shhh*. It's okay."

She shook her head. She spoke quietly, barely above a whisper because it was all she could manage. "I spent a lot of years hoping Ben would find his way back. At times he'd be better, but there were moments that I didn't do what I wanted, didn't say what I needed, all in the hopes that—"

She pressed her face against Mark's chest and let the tears come.

Over the years there'd been plenty of times when things had gotten rough. When Ben had been hard to handle or loud and belligerent. She'd rarely cried.

Crying wouldn't have changed anything.

When she finally got herself under control and wiped up, Mark's expression was a lot more solemn than she'd seen until then. "I think I hear what you're saying. That's the part that set you off. The not listening. Not giving you a chance to voice yourself."

"*Yes*. Because even if it's to be able to say you're going too fast, I need to be respected enough for you to hear me. And then we can argue about what speed we go—I have no problems with a good, honest argument," she said, the words still shaky. "Because fighting means we both get to say what we want. We can come to a compromise if that's what's best."

Mark tipped his chin slowly. "Okay. You know I'm already there, waiting for you to catch up. I'll also screw up because patience isn't one of my superpowers." He pressed his fingers under her chin and stroked his thumb over her cheek, wiping away a final tear. "But I will listen to you. I promise."

His words were exactly what she needed.

Dana caught him by the shoulders and pulled him forward, their lips meeting in a sweet kiss that heated up far too quickly.

She draped her arms around his neck, stroking her fingers through his hair. His hat tumbled off, unminded. He nibbled on her lips, tongue teasing, their breaths mingling.

When he caught her by the hips and lifted her across his lap, Dana went willingly. The heat of his body lined up with hers as she rested on his strong thighs, kneeling over him.

He nibbled along her jawline and up to her ear, tugging on her earlobe briefly and sending shivers through her. "I can't wait to speed this part up. I can't wait to touch you. To make you feel good."

He adjusted her slightly, and Dana sucked in a quick breath. The hard length under her lay dangerously close to intimate positioning.

Was she ready for more on this level? Her body was one hundred percent ready. Her mind needed a little bit more time. Not to mention—

"*Ahem.*" A solid cough sounded.

Dana and Mark jumped apart as if they'd been hit with a cattle prod. Sliding to separate positions on the bench, Dana quickly straightened herself while Mark rescued his hat and laid it strategically over his lap.

Standing next to the bench, grinning wildly, was Anna Thompson, the only daughter of the Moonshine clan and local RCMP now on maternity leave. She pushed a double stroller, her two-year-old daughter bouncing with excitement to be released and her newborn baby son swaddled up and sleeping in the back section.

"Auntie Dana. Uncle Mark." Anna said their names in her best cop voice, before reaching down to let Kasey free.

Dana's cheeks were on fire. "Um."

"Do you know how many Coleman family members I have caught parked at Heartbreak Ridge? Never mind, you don't want to know." Anna continued, her amusement shining clear. "But this is the first time I have ever caught one of *your* generation fooling around in a public place."

"Because our generation usually knows how to have a good

time without getting caught?" Mark said without a hint of apology.

"Dear God," Anna said in a long-suffering voice before lowering her volume and speaking like a conspirator. "You might want to move this to a more appropriate location, considering a whole bunch of the clan will be arriving in the next half hour to use the playground."

Dana rose to her feet, stifling the urge to giggle as Mark stepped behind her and held onto her hips, obviously hiding his erection. "Well, I hope you all have a good time."

"You too."

Anna's laughter drifted over them as Mark caught Dana by the hand and marched them back toward Main Street.

They grinned at each other, but amusing as getting caught was, a major glitch in going forward had just revealed itself.

Mark was living with George. Dana lived with her son and daughter-in-law.

Where could they go if they wanted to take the physical part of this relationship farther?

24

The truck rumbled, engine revving hard as Blake threw her into four-wheel drive and drove cautiously over the rutted road leading to their destination.

"Hell of a good idea," Travis said from where he was sprawled in the back seat of the crew cab.

Cassidy slapped a hand on Blake's shoulder and squeezed in approval. "Agreed. And man, did you pick the day right, or what?"

"I'll take credit for that," Mike said from where he was riding shotgun. "Blake here doesn't seem to believe in checking the weather forecast too often."

"Don't see the need with the way you and all the uncles spend your day constantly checking for updates." Blake grinned at his brother and brother-in-law in the rearview mirror. "The instant a cloud appears on the horizon, a text arrives from Uncle Randy, and I know exactly what he's going to tell me."

Travis chuckled. "Well, give thanks to the weather gods, because a day off fishing deserves this kind of blue sky."

"I don't even care how hot the fishing is, the day off is a win. Plus, it'll be good to see everyone," Cassidy added.

"Only a couple of days until Canada Day. The entire clan will be together then," Mike pointed out.

"Yeah, but this is special because it's just Six Pack." Travis bumped a shoulder against Cassidy. "And this import."

"Cassidy is one hundred percent Six Pack." Blake met Cassidy's eyes in the mirror and winked. "Maybe a hundred and ten, considering you put up with Travis's bullshit all the time. That makes you extra Coleman, or something like that."

Travis snorted but didn't dispute the *bullshit* comment.

The chatter in the truck remained light and entertaining until Blake pulled to a stop beside three familiar vehicles.

Daniel was there, Lance as well, the kid pleased as punch at having been invited to the grown-up gathering. Matt stepped forward, poking Joel over his shoulder about something.

Jesse had lawn chairs set around a fire pit, three coolers lined up at the side of the open space.

"You plan on even getting a line wet?" Travis teased. "Or are you going to sit with your feet up and drink all day?"

"Joel and I can't decide. Fishing is fun, but catching a nap might be a better use of our morning, considering our days are numbered before the next kids drop." Jesse settled in a lawn chair, fiddled with something underneath it then leaned back, turning the contraption into a lounger. "*God*, this is nice."

Joel snickered. "That was just mean. Now I have to decide if I should tell Dare that you referred to the baby's due date like a cow birth."

"She doesn't care. At this point, all Dare wants is to be done."

"Don't blame her. This summer is going to be a hot one," Mike said, grinning as he turned to Blake. "At least, according to the Weather Channel."

Blake caught himself chuckling as he headed to the back of the truck and pulled out his fishing gear.

For the next two hours, he simply enjoyed time with his brothers, his father, and his nephew. An old dock extended into the lake, and a well-defined trail meandered around the perimeter, giving plenty of places for them to shuffle off, usually two at a time so they could cast lines into the water and then chat. Or cast lines into the water then reel in silently, the sheer connection of being together enough.

The morning gave Blake time to appreciate once again how far they'd come. The brothers comfortable with each other, teasing Lance and Mike, although that last one was always done respectfully.

Some things never changed.

Blake was grateful to be able to see how tight the bonds were between them all. It gave him an assurance that if what his father feared most came to be, it wouldn't only be Blake who would step in and help.

And watching Lance good-naturedly steal his grandfather's line so he could tie a minuscule fly at the end of the tippet said something about how the next generation would also be there for Mike, no matter what.

One lingering fear came crashing to a head when, just before he broke for lunch, Jesse gave him a shout. "I volunteered you to help me get things ready."

Blake might have told Jesse to not worry and that the right decision regarding his job opportunity would eventually become clear. He hadn't realized he'd have his own share of sleepless nights after hearing about the possibility of his brother leaving again.

Whatever Jesse and Dare had decided, Blake swore he would make it work. He'd find a way that his brother and Dare and their kids felt connected and a part of everything happening back in Rocky.

"Wanted to let you know something." Jesse popped up a portable table and began pulling lunch fixings out of the cooler.

"About the job?"

"Yeah." Jesse stopped, shaking his head. "Toughest damn decision we've ever had to make, and yet in the end, so simple."

Everything in Blake tightened. "Oh?"

Before Jesse could speak, his phone went off. He blinked in surprise, hauling it out of his pocket even as he glanced up at the sky. "We have reception up here?"

Joel's phone went off as well, and suddenly Blake had a bad feeling.

Or maybe a good one because Jesse's eyes were widening as he took the call. Joel had abandoned his fishing gear beside Matt and was running hell-bent for leather toward where their picnic was arranged.

Jesse hung up, eyes a little on the wild side, but a huge grin in place. "Dare's in labour. I gotta go."

Panting heavily, Joel arrived. "Vicki just called. Dare's—"

"We heard." Blake went to aim them both toward Jesse's truck then paused. "Either of you capable of driving without going off a cliff?"

"Where are my keys?" Jesse demanded, hands digging in his pockets frantically. "And hell yes, I can drive. Now where are my *goddamn keys*?" he shouted.

Joel swung the key ring in question on a finger as he winked at Blake. "I stole them when we got here. We'll be okay." He danced away from Jesse, who made a quick grab at his hand. "Nothing doing. Dare made me promise to take care of you. Said something about how she doubted you could keep it together this time. Let's go."

By the time the twins were driving away, the rest of the family had gathered 'round, shouting good wishes after them.

"Isn't it early for the baby to arrive?" Lance asked with a hint of worry.

"Babies usually arrive when they're ready," Blake reassured him. "Except if it's really inconvenient. Then they'll come early or late, depending on what causes the most chaos."

Lance blinked. "Babies don't really do that."

"No, they can't *deliberately* do it. But in any family, there's at least a couple stories like that." Mike turned his grandson toward the lunch. "Your aunt had one of those *oops* babies. Lisa, from Whiskey Creek."

"Tamara," Matt corrected him. "Lisa's still expecting."

"Right. Tamara." Mike nodded then grabbed a plate and pushed it at his grandson. "Either way, we'll hear soon enough from Jesse and Dare. In the meantime, we should carry on with our day. There's extra fish to catch now that Joel and Jesse aren't tangling up our lines."

They still had a big group with the seven of them. They laughed and shared stories, and Blake treasured time with his immediate family.

But having the twins gone only emphasized that knot in Blake's gut. He wanted Jesse to do what was right for him and Dare, but what he wanted even more was for Jesse to stay close.

Jesse and Joel had been gone for four hours. The rest of the Six Pack fishermen were closing in on the time to pack it up and head home. The picnic had been tucked away, and the group was out on the dock casting a few final times.

The instant his phone buzzed with a text message, Blake hauled it out. They must've all been on high alert, because every other Coleman standing with him did the same, peering down eagerly to read the announcement.

Jesse: *Dare is doing great. We are very excited to announce the arrival of a healthy baby boy. Ryan will be ready for visitors tomorrow morning.*

Tension slipped away, at least part of it. "Good to hear," Blake said sincerely. "Although I hope, for his sake, he offers a little more detail when he messages the ladies."

"Bigger than a breadbox doesn't cut it?" Matt grinned.

"Dear God, don't say things like that in reference to the size of babies. It makes *me* hurt," Mike said with a groan.

They were nearly packed up, headed for their doors, when their phones went off again.

"Here come the details," Daniel suggested.

Only the message made them all stop before shouts rang out, echoing against the mountain behind the lake.

Jesse: *Dare is still doing great. We are very excited to announce the arrival of another healthy baby boy. Royce would very much like his Grandpa to drop in to say hello. He'll see the rest of you tomorrow.*

Blake casually slipped an arm around his father's shoulders, because it was clear that his dad was getting choked up. "Well, then, Grampa. Looks like you and me have somewhere we need to go."

Mike nodded briskly, even as he blinked hard. "Twins. Damn, I had no idea."

And judging from the expression on Dare's face when Blake led his father into the hospital room an hour later, joining Marion and Jaxi, who were already there, his sister-in-law was pretty damn proud of having kept the secret.

"You Colemans are a dangerous lot," Dare said with mock seriousness. "Twins. He got me pregnant with *twins*. That's it. He's cut off."

Jesse was cuddled up beside her, a baby cradled in his arm, but he paused to kiss her cheek. "You've just gone through a traumatic event, so I'll forgive your poor choice of words. I don't think you really want to *cut off* anything."

She tilted her head and eyed him. "I just pushed out two six-pound footballs. You really want to get into an argument about semantics?"

Jesse winked then curled himself upright and marched toward his father. "I hope you don't mind we borrowed Grandpa's name for this one. Figured with my genes and Dare's, he needed something to give him some solid roots."

Mike took the baby from his son with a grin of delight. "Your genes are solid," he insisted. "And your roots as well. Never doubt that."

Jesse watched his father for a moment, gaze dropping to his son then sliding over to meet Blake's eyes. "Those roots are important. I know that, and so does Dare. But the best way to grow strong is to be planted in the right spot. We've got that here in Rocky."

They were staying. Blake got the message loud and clear.

Even as his concern vanished on one level, another level of truth arrived. It wasn't worry but a clear, concise understanding.

His brother staying required as much of a commitment on Blake's part. All the things he would've done if Jesse and Dare had chosen to live hours away would be so much easier to do with them close.

Those family-connecting things still needed to happen. He still needed to make the time.

Blake dipped his head at Jesse before sliding around to where Jaxi waited for her turn to take little Ryan from Marion. Slipping an arm around Jaxi was the most natural thing in the world.

She squeezed him tight. "Have fun fishing?"

"Yep." He held on as she leaned in closer, head resting on his chest. He whispered, careful to make sure no one else overheard, "You a little bit sad?"

She shrugged but then shook her head. "If it's right for us to have another, we will. I'm not worried one way or the other."

"But you're gonna cuddle everybody else's babies as much is possible, ain'tcha?"

Her eyes danced with laughter. "Of course." She leaned in and bumped their noses together. "Same way I catch you sneaking baby cuddles every chance you get. You big old softy."

Blake couldn't deny it. He had no objection at all to baby

cuddles, toddler cuddles, or the rest of it. Although, dear God, they were going to be heading into the teen years eventually, and that was going to be an adventure.

Although Daniel had managed it, and so had his parents. Somewhere amongst those roots and branches, he figured there was enough wisdom in the Coleman clan to get them out the other side intact.

Still, as he watched Jaxi cradle little Ryan, the look in her eyes made him want to give her everything she wanted. Or at least the things he had some control over.

Maybe it was time to do a little plotting of his own.

25

———————

There were people everywhere. Far more than Mark expected even if he counted up the number of people in the Coleman clan.

He caught Mike grinning at him, his oldest brother stepping forward to offer a cheery hello. "Don't worry. There's a horde, but we've got enough food to feed two hordes."

"Did you import people from Red Deer?" Mark asked as he glanced around.

Mike considered then shrugged. "Not impossible." He caught Mark in a tight hug then aimed him toward the nearest circle of people. "Canada Day started small, but now it's a free-for-all. Just wait. Once you build your place, we'll add you to the list so you can host."

Mark tried to picture this many people swarming around what was now a concrete foundation on the top of the rise. He shook his head. "Sounds like a plan. I can put them all to work, yes?"

His brother laughed then introduced him to the pastor at Dana's church, who also happened to be Laurel's dad.

Fortunately, it wasn't that uncomfortable of a conversation considering churchgoing wasn't Mark's thing.

When Dana arrived, though, he was grateful that after a short time, she took him by the hand and led him farther onto Moonshine land.

"I shouldn't steal you away," she said. "This is a good chance for you to get to know everyone."

"We'll wander," Mark offered. "You say hi to everyone, and that will let me get a chance to make sure I've got all the names and faces right."

Her lips twitched. "I don't think anyone expects you to remember all of us this quickly."

"It's been four months," he offered dryly before inspiration struck. He leaned in closer. "What do I get if I can name everyone we meet? I mean family only, no random strangers included in the bet."

Her chin rose in a bit of bravado. "What do you want?"

The answer to that would take far too long. Mark stepped back far enough to look her over.

Her blonde hair hung to her shoulders, her ever-present curls bigger as if she'd deliberately puffed them up. Her bright eyes shone, and she wore a sundress of pale green with embroidery along the hemline. The vee dipping over her breasts stopped high enough to be modest, but the curves under it were full and tempting.

She wore half boots instead of sandals, which was a great idea for a party being held at a ranch. There was a straw cowboy hat in her hand that she put firmly on her head as she offered a cocky grin. "Cat got your tongue?"

"Just thinking about what I want to do to you," he confessed. His voice came out kind of breathless. He stepped closer. "Just thinking about what I want to do *with* you."

She looked at him from under her lashes. "Let's hope you're very good with names."

For the next hour, they wandered. Mark knew the lay of the land well enough. He'd helped build this house as well as the one at Whiskey Creek, when Kate and Randy had decided to set up a home away from where Mike and Marion lived.

He supposed it was like kids stretching their wings, the very thing he wanted for Rafe and Laurel—

Okay, his motivation wasn't all altruistic. He wanted Dana to be with him.

They said hello to Becky and Trevor again. Mark visited with them on a fairly regular basis, stopping in at the house to see how things were going. The kids—meaning Rafe and Laurel, and wasn't it odd to be thinking of them as *his kids*—were with Rachel and Lee. Rachel eyed him speculatively before winking, as if offering her approval.

The newest babies were all there as well. Anna, the RCMP who'd busted him and Dana in the park, wiggled her fingers at them then adjusted baby Ethan in her arms. The veterinarian married to Steve Coleman held her baby girl, Raine.

The gathering also flowed around Jesse and his wife, Dare, each of them carefully holding a small, blue-wrapped bundle.

Dana pulled Mark forward. "I did not expect to see you out of the hospital yet," she said as she slipped up to squeeze Dare carefully. "Congratulations. And you're sneaky."

Jesse grinned. "Had to follow my big brother's example," he said.

"Yeah, because your *big brother* totally carried twins and never said a word," Dare drawled before lifting her shining face toward Dana and Mark. "This one is Royce, and Jesse's got Ryan."

"They're as adorable as any three-day old," Mark said honestly.

Dana slapped the back of her hand against his chest, but Jesse offered a wink. "Want to hold Ryan?"

If anything, Mark figured Dana was dying to hold one of the

babies, so he sat, and a minute later, both of them were being passed teeny bundles.

Mark looked into the little scrunched-up face, amused and pleased to be able to be a part of his family in this way after so many years of not getting to share the celebrations. "Okay, I lied. This one at least is cuter than most three-day-olds."

He stayed and chatted for a while, but eventually they rose, heading to grab some food.

En route, they were waylaid by Travis. "Can I talk to you for a minute, Uncle Mark?"

"I'll grab us places at the table," Dana offered.

Mark watched her walk away, admiring the sway of her hips. He might've been watching a little too closely, because when he turned toward his nephew, the other man was grinning very hard.

"That is one hell of a fine woman," Mark said firmly, not a hint of embarrassment at having been caught gawking.

"Ashley wanted me to pass on a message," Travis said, ignoring Mark's comment. "She's been working on a painting you might be interested in."

Mark paused. "Ashley does good work. I'll be needing art for the house."

His nephew's grin grew wider. "This one might be perfect."

He vanished before Mark could dig any more information out of him.

Then he and Dana caught up with Mike and Marion for a while, but as they ate, the most curious sensation poked at Mark.

Dana sat against him, comfortable and easy, his hand around her waist. She'd placed her hand on his thigh and was rubbing her knuckles up and down, almost as if she wasn't aware of the motion.

Only when she wrapped her hand a little farther around his thigh, rising a little higher than usual, Mark barely caught himself before a growl escaped.

She kept on talking, the face of an absolute innocent, and not at all as if she were damn near stroking him right in front of their family.

Mark was willing to take the pain, but when Rafe and Laurel walked past, plates full of food as they headed to join a set of their cousins, sudden inspiration struck.

He leaned in close, fingers sliding over Dana's hip as he whispered in her ear. "You do realize your house is empty right now."

She stiffened slightly, her fingers freezing in mid-tease.

"And I seem to remember having gotten all the names right for everyone we met. Which means I get a reward, yes?"

Dana wiped her mouth with a napkin then grabbed hers and Mark's plates, stacking them and smiling across the table at her brother and sister-in-law.

"We'll catch up with you later," she said sweetly, somehow dragging Mark away without *looking* as if she was hauling him along as fast as she could.

He made it to the truck before giving in to temptation. He whirled her against him, backing her up against the vehicle and pinning her in place with his body. "Please tell me yes."

"You might need to be more specific," she teased during the split second before his mouth covered hers.

The kiss was wild enough to get his blood pounding and his entire body tightening with need. When he did pull back, it was to damn near growl, hips pressed tight against her. "I want to take you home. I want to take off your clothes and kiss you everywhere. I want to make you scream my name."

He eased back, putting enough space between them to see her eyes had gone dark, pupils wide.

"Dana," he whispered. "I want you."

Her head bobbed, a small movement but rapid. "Yes."

Good answer.

Somehow, they both made it into the cab of his truck, Dana

sitting beside him in the middle of the bench seat. Both of them got their seat belts on before he cautiously manoeuvred out of the crowded parking area and headed down the gravel road the couple of miles toward the Angel homestead.

Only once they made it to her house, his attempts to stay slow and in control failed.

It didn't help that as soon as they walked into the kitchen, she turned and caught the hem of her sundress, stripping it over her head and dropping it over the back of the chair.

"Sweet fuck." Mark nearly tripped over his own feet as he stopped to stare.

Her chin rose again as if she were gathering courage. "I'm no spring chicken. What you see is what you get."

"Then I'm a lucky, lucky man," Mark said, closing the space between them. He trickled a hand over the sweep of her waist and up her side to where her pretty green bra covered her breasts. "Dana, I'm the same age as you and have done far more miles. The map might not be quite as fresh as it once was, but the picture's all the richer for the details the time has brought."

He stepped forward, stripping away the layers over his torso and tossing them on top of her dress.

He brought her against him and got ready to listen in a whole new way.

DANA HAD GIVEN this moment a great deal of thought over the past months. She was sensible enough to guess the opportunity for sex would eventually arrive. Hopeful enough the event would be something she could truly enjoy.

What she hadn't wanted was a series of comparisons or thoughts about what had been. Which meant taking charge in any way she could.

Time, place. The man.

It became very clear very quickly that controlling that last one was futile. Mark seemed intent on putting every bit of preplanning she'd done to waste.

His torso against hers was scalding hot and not nearly enough. Skin on skin, he continued to kiss her as sensations spiraled upward with each touch, each tease on her senses.

He kissed his way along her neck, sliding his hands down her back until he cupped her butt, dragging her closer. The firm length of his erection pressed against her stomach for a moment before he lifted her, placing her on the table.

He slid his hands over her thighs, fingers teasing the inside of her legs as he opened her wider until he was able to rock directly against her core.

None of this was on the agenda, but Dana was quite happy with the change in plans.

"I like this," she whispered, stroking her fingers through his hair, loving the cool tease against her fingertips. Loving that she could drag her hands over his shoulders and trace the muscles there.

"You smell so good," he said with a groan, hips flexing as she scratched her nails down his back. "God, *yes*."

Then his hands were at the clasp of her bra, sliding the straps from her shoulders as he watched the cups fall away.

She refused to hide. Refused to be embarrassed about anything regarding her body.

A soft curse escaped his lips, then his hand rose, brushing knuckles over her nipple as it tightened from—being exposed? From being so close to the man she desperately wanted?

From being licked, his tongue teasing a moment before Mark wrapped his lips around the peak and sucked.

No use in trying to categorize any of it. It felt good, and she didn't need to know *why* other than he looked mesmerized and his body had reacted positively.

He held her, hands cupped on either side of her breasts. "I have dreamed about this." He lifted his gaze, thumbs moving over her in a soft caress. "I have dreamed about this and so much more."

More turned out to be stripping away her panties and pulling her hips to the very edge of the table as he dropped to his knees.

An instant later his tongue was teasing at her sex, hands drifting over her thighs, brushing over her hips, then returning in a circle.

Dana sat on her kitchen table, stark naked, sexual pleasure rising like a storm as her boyfriend—time to make it official—proved his patience was more than adequate to bring her to the very edge and over faster than she thought possible.

"*Mark.*"

Her fingers had ended up buried in his hair, and she jerked unwittingly. He leaned back far enough to show off a wide grin, his now familiar cocky expression back in place.

His gaze drifted to meet hers with great satisfaction. "That was fun."

Oh no. Well, yes, it had been, but if he thought this was where they were stopping?

She tugged on his hair again. "Are we having sex here or in my bedroom?"

He hesitated for a minute. "I don't want to push. I meant what I said—I want you, but I don't—"

She caught him by the hips, undoing the button on his jeans and pushing at the zipper, the backs of her heels wrapped around his thighs, trapping him in place.

"*Listen.* I said yes." She was pushing away the fabric when she hesitated and worked on listening back. Was she pushing *him* too fast? "I want you too. But only if *you're* ready."

Mark swore, shoving at his jeans and underwear, hopping to try and strip them away. They were both laughing when he picked her up, settling in the nearest kitchen chair and lifting her over him.

"Very ready."

She rocked a few times over his hard length. She was wet from her orgasm but still not one hundred percent sure how this would go.

Dammit, it was worthwhile making sure everything went better than *okay*. "Come with me."

Both of them naked as jaybirds, she pulled him down the hallway into her bedroom. She grabbed the container of lube and a condom from beside her bed where she'd placed them after having a blunt conversation with her sister-in-law a few weeks earlier.

Mark grinned as she put a hand on his chest and pushed him back into a seated position on the edge of the bed. "Prepared."

"Once a Girl Scout, always a Girl Scout." Her heart was racing, but she wanted to return to where they'd been a moment earlier. Connected. Ready to become one.

She slowed, opening the tube and coating her fingers while he slipped on the condom. Then she wrapped her hand around his erection and pumped. Soft and strong. Silky and iron hard.

Mark's head fell back, and he swore. "So good."

Touching him. Seeing him—this beautiful man who cared about her and who wanted her...

A special kind of magic filled the room.

Dana crawled onto the bed, straddling his thighs, bodies once again touching. Mark cupped her face with his hands and kissed her, deep and long and sweet before his hands dropped to tease her body. Pinching her breasts, taking hold of her hips and rocking her, slowly, slowly, pause—

The head of his cock notched against her. She pulled back to look into his eyes as he guided her down, the sweet stretch teasing in a wonderful way.

His face crinkled into a terrible scowl. "Oh, *hell*."

Dana froze. "Mark?"

"It's good, it's good," he said hurriedly. "It's *too* damn good."

Dana found her lips turning up in a smile, and she impulsively hugged him tight, laughter escaping. "I'm so glad. I'm so glad it's good, and I'm so glad you're here," she confessed.

The little moment seemed to be what he needed to regain his control, because when she met his eyes again, there was both laughter and rising fire. He kept hold of her hips and rocked her, up and down, over and over again until they were both gasping for air.

Then he reached between them and pressed his fingers over her clit, rubbing even as he kept thrusting.

She didn't care if anything else happened, but for a man who had seemed on the verge of losing control, Mark pulled in energy from somewhere. The pressure building inside her was nearly at the peak when he pulled her closer, her breasts brushing against the silver-laced hair on his chest. "Dana. Oh, *yes*—"

He kept going, tipping her over the edge, the muscles in his back bunching as she held him, body tightening around his thick length.

She was nearly finished when he cursed, pressing her down as hard as possible and locking her there as his body shook with release.

The slightly sweaty, slightly sticky pleasure was followed by kisses as Mark rolled her onto the mattress and covered her body with his. He kept coming back to her mouth over and over, whispering sweet things until her grin was so wide, Dana was pretty sure her cheeks would hurt in the morning.

She ran her fingers through his hair as he rolled to his side and they lay there, still tangled together. "Want to grab a shower?"

"That depends." He brushed his knuckles over her shoulder and down her arm, *accidentally* making contact with her breast. "Is there room for two?"

Easy question to answer. "Just barely. We might have to stay really close."

"I can do that." Mark's expression went more serious. "Thank you. Thank you for sharing with me, trusting me."

There was nothing to say in follow-up, not yet, so she pressed her lips to his then pulled him off the bed and into the shower.

Coleman Memory Book
~*Marion (Six Pack) Coleman*~

Memories are funny things.

When I think back over the years, I can picture so many moments I'd like to share that were important. Then I remember I've already told that story to my children or laughed over it with my sisters-in-law.

Or there are the times where Mike and I try to tell each other the same story we've told a dozen times before—about something that we were both there for when it happened.

Does it matter if memories get repeated? Maybe it means that moment is even more precious because we want to share it again.

But here's a memory I don't think I've ever told anyone.

There's a lot of waiting involved in life. Waiting for that special someone to call you. Waiting for a wedding. Waiting for a child to decide to arrive. Waiting for the garden to grow, the calves to drop, the storm to pass.

One night just over a year into our marriage, Mike was out in one of those storms, and I was scared for him. So very scared that something had gone wrong because it was dark and cold, and we didn't have a way to be in touch in those days—although even now cell phones don't always work.

I stood in front of the window, staring into the darkness, with nothing to do but wait.

As I waited, I finally noticed it wasn't just the dark storm in front of me, the pale yard light on the barn flickering as driving snow blew past it—I could also see myself and the room where I stood. My reflection, the window a perfect mirror.

While my mind raced, imagining all sorts of terrible things, my body was completely motionless. When the snow swirled outside, it looked as if it swirled around me, but my body was still, and warm, and seemingly peaceful.

Right then, I knew. I needed to reverse the image.

I needed my thoughts to be peaceful *in spite* of the whirling storm. I needed to trust that Mike was doing what he could in order to come home safe. I had to find something to think about right then that would be good and positive and make me enjoy the moment—even enjoy the storm.

Which meant my body had to do the moving and let out the restlessness.

I went to the kitchen and made a pot of tea then started a batch of cookies. The whole time I worked, I thought about what Mike would like most once he got home from his cold, hard trip. How I could show how grateful I was for his work and his caring.

How I could show him love with my hands instead of standing there, frozen with fear, and rushing to him so he had to wipe my tears when he did finally make it home, cold and hungry.

While my revelation might not be the answer for everyone and every situation, it's given me somewhere to aim my heart. Every morning I get up and think, "What can I do today to show I care? Is my mind calm and are my hands busy with good things?"

I can do this because all the while I know that Mike is doing the exact same thing—thinking of me. Working to make my life better and to show his love. It's a two-way street, and it works.

And I suppose my story just proves that a mother can turn even a memory page into a life lesson.

Love you all.

[Images: A face reflected in a window. Warm meal on a table. Wrinkled hands busy knitting.]

26

July turned out to be hotter and muggier than any in recent record.

With all the kids home from school, and the house and the garden chores to be done, the days were filled to the brim. Jaxi was very grateful for an air-conditioned minivan to get the lot of them over to visit with family on a regular basis.

The third week of July, she stopped in at Dare's. Jaxi had brought a number of prepared meals but mostly just wanted to spend time with her sister-in-law.

Dare's foster sister greeted her at the door, the dark-haired woman grinning widely. "Hey, you. Need help with the munchkins?" Ginny asked.

"Hi, Auntie Ginny," Rae and Becca shouted as they pushed past her into the house, one of them holding Lana's hand, the other guiding PJ.

Jaxi adjusted Justin on her hip, holding out a package for Ginny to take. "Cabbage rolls. Marion and I made a big batch. You can pop them in the freezer and deal with them later."

Ginny's dark eyes widened with amusement, but she tossed

her shoulder-length hair back over her shoulder then took the bag. "Efficient as always."

"Never underestimate the power of a well-written to-do list," Jaxi quipped back. "How're you doing?"

"Learning about the wonders of sleep deprivation," Ginny said over her shoulder as she headed to the kitchen and put the food away.

"Oh, please." Dare rolled her eyes from where she sat on the couch, pillows strategically lined up to help support the babies as she nursed them.

Ginny grinned. "What? I'm not a parent. I don't have any parent genes, so not getting to sleep from when I want to go to bed until when I want to wake up is a hard thing."

Vicki was there as well, sunk deep into a chair with one hand resting on the top of her baby-full belly. She gave Ginny a disbelieving look. "Honey, you live on a ranch. Or you did, and you will again. And on a ranch, thanks to animals, there is no such thing as going to bed when you want *and* waking up when you want, not unless Silver Stone is some sort of magical unicorn, in which case, can I move there?"

"Can you move, period?" Dare teased before turning to Jaxi and grinning evilly, all of her teeth showing. "It's kind of fun that Vicki is just as immobile as I am right now, albeit for a totally different reason."

"It is utterly unfair that we were due on the same day," Vicki complained. "I feel like a defective turkey. The basting button's popped, but nothing else is happening."

Ginny chuckled, which was a braver thing to do than Jaxi would chance at the moment. Women who went *over* nine months pregnant were not known to be entirely rational. "This is the universe balancing out. Dare was two weeks early, ergo that means you will be—"

Vicki flung a pillow hard enough it hit Ginny square in the

face then rebounded. "You shut your mouth," Vicki said, but she was laughing.

The children had found their cousins, Joey and Jess, and the pile of toys in the corner of the room. Ginny helped organize the lot of them, stealing Justin from Jaxi's arms. "Hang out. Chat. I do get more of that sleep thing than you guys."

Which meant the three of them—Jaxi, Dare, and Vicki—fell into sweet conversation. Ginny joined in at times, and the children came back and forth between them, looking for attention as well as the occasional kiss for new boo-boos.

"I've got just about all the memory pages from the aunts and uncles," Jaxi told Dare. "I'm glad Lisa suggested a way this could become an ongoing project."

Dare nodded. "Agreed. It's fun to think about adding pages as milestones occur. Having stuff online makes it even easier to enjoy."

"How did you do with the pictures?" Jaxi hesitated then grinned. "I mean, before you stopped everything because of Ryan and Royce. I do *not* expect you to spend time on it now."

"Well, it's a good thing that I also agree that one should never underestimate a well-written to-do list," Dare said with a sparkle in her eyes. "I finished scanning all the pictures before Thing One and Thing Two arrived."

They both ignored Ginny's exaggerated groan in the background.

"Everything's in the Dropbox we set up. When you have time, you can get the families to spruce up their sections." Dare lifted Royce from her breast, wordlessly handing him to Jaxi. A moment later Dare finished adjusting Ryan into position then blinked before offering an exasperated sigh. "Well, that was terrible. Jaxi, would you *like* to burp my baby? He's extra spitty these days," she warned.

Jaxi had already grabbed a receiving blanket off the table and placed it over her shoulder. Patting Royce lightly on the back, she pressed her nose against his little baby head and sniffed, soaking the new baby smell into her very soul. "You're family, Dare. Assuming that we're going to love on your babies is *not* being rude."

Dare went speechless for a moment, looking down and fussing with Ryan.

It was Ginny who crossed the room to where Jaxi sat, dropping to her knees, a bit of moisture in her eyes. "I love you Colemans so much. I'm glad Dare found you."

She hug-attacked Jaxi, carefully, working around the baby.

"We love her too," Jaxi said honestly. "And you, by association. Are you planning to stick around for a while so we can enjoy your company?"

"Since Miss 'I can do anything anybody else does' decided to pop out twins in imitation of you—" Ginny began.

"Not my fault," Dare insisted. "Besides, two boys means this is all on Jesse."

Ginny folded her arms and stared at her sister. "Hush. Grown-ups talking."

Jaxi snickered.

"I'm going to stay and help Dare for at least a couple of months. There's no rush to get back to Silver Stone. At least not until the snow flies."

"You've been gone for a couple of years, haven't you?"

Ginny nodded, sliding over to help one of the little ones who had dropped crayons off the table. "It'll be an adjustment to be home, so no use in going until I'm ready to settle down."

"If you want to stay in Rocky, I'm sure we could figure something out," Jaxi offered. "There's a number of trailers empty. We could even move one out here to Sunset Ridge if you wanted to stay close to your sister."

Dare and Ginny exchanged glances, and laughter rose so quickly, Jaxi wondered what she'd said.

But when Ginny pulled out a twenty-dollar bill and tucked it under Dare's feet on the table, Jaxi sighed. "Have you been taking lessons from Lisa? She's the one always making bets."

"Kelli does it as well, out at Silver Stone ranch. I figured it was a given that at some point you would offer to adopt Ginny." Dare puckered up her lips and blew Jaxi a kiss. "Love ya."

A few minutes later, Jaxi realized Vicki had grown astonishingly quiet over the past while. She glanced at her sister-in-law to discover the woman's cheeks were no longer flushed red but shockingly white. "Vicki? Sweetie? You okay?"

The young woman met her gaze across the room, glancing for a moment at the children before turning back and shaking her head slightly. "I don't feel too good," she whispered.

Dare swore. "Really?"

Vicki gave a sheepish grin. "The baby's coming. I don't think there's time for an ambulance."

Jaxi was already moving, popping a sleeping Royce and Ryan into the bassinets at the edge of the room. Then she and Ginny rounded up the rest of the little ones and herded them into the basement where there were toys and electronics to help entertain them.

Ginny pushed Jaxi back toward the stairs. "The kids I can handle. That?" She pointed upstairs. "Not my territory."

Jaxi made it upstairs in time to find Dare guiding Vicki to a comfortable spot in the kitchen.

"You promised me you wouldn't do this again," Dare scolded with a tease. "No having babies in the living room."

"Hey, I promised not to have a kid in *my* house. This is your place." Vicki sucked in a sharp breath. "Hey, Jaxi. We called the guys and the ambulance, but just in case, did you bring your catching mitt?"

"I'm usually the one pitching," Jaxi said with a soft laugh, "but I think we can figure it out. Don't worry. Everything's going to be fine.

Not even forty-five minutes later, when the front door burst open, Joel rushing in with Jesse hard on his heels, Vicki was on the couch, her baby wrapped comfortably in her arms.

Dare had one of her twins, and Jaxi held the other, and Ginny was riding herd on the rest of the children. It was the finest of chaos in Jaxi's opinion.

Joel cuddled in next to Vicki and kissed her tenderly before accepting his baby boy into his free arm. "I'm sorry I wasn't here this time."

"It's okay," Vicki reassured him. "You'll be here for the rest of it."

Jaxi was still buzzing with excitement when she got to share the story with Blake that night. "It was probably one of the most exciting things I've ever done," she admitted. "And one of the scariest."

Their children were all asleep, and she and Blake were sitting on the floor in front of the fireplace.

He leaned on one elbow, stroking his fingers down her thigh as she sat cross-legged in front of him. "You were worried about Vicki?"

"And the baby, and just—*everything*." She caught his hand and pulled it up to her mouth so she could kiss his fingers. "You've said it before, but I never quite understood until now how hard it is to be there and *not* be the one having the baby."

She'd been running on sheer adrenaline by the end of it, wanting to take the pain away from Vicki and yet knowing she couldn't. Hoping with every breath that things would be fine, and knowing all she could do was one thing at a time.

Blake dipped his chin. "I know they're very grateful you were there."

Another rush swept through her. "I'm not going to be able to sleep tonight," she exclaimed. "They named the baby after *me*, Blake. Not just because of tonight—they said they always planned to."

Joel and Vicki announcing that their little boy would be

called Jackson in her honour made something magical flutter inside.

Blake curled upright, pulling her against him and surrounding her with his strong arms. "Joel told me a few days ago they planned on it. He said you were the best kind of sister ever. Someone who'd been there from the beginning. Someone who wasn't always perfect, but when you screw up, you apologize then work to make it right. He said they looked up to you even as they feel comfortable telling you anything." She took a shaky breath, and he squeezed her again. "It's quite a compliment, and I agree completely."

Great. Now she had tears as well as adrenaline running her system ragged. "It's quite something to know that my family of choice is far *more* than my family by blood."

It was easy now to let go of any final bitterness from being an afterthought to her parents. Maybe the peace should've snuck in a long time earlier. Maybe in some ways, it had. This moment was the icing on a beautiful cake. A sweet, pretty covering over the deliciousness she'd been enjoying for years.

She squeezed Blake extra hard then pulled back. "So, how was *your* day?"

His grin slid from amusement to heat. "I've got something to show you."

Jaxi snorted. "Excuse me?"

Blake blinked then joined her in laughter. "You've got a dirty mind, Slick."

"You love my dirty mind," she told him with a bit of an attitude.

He scooped her up, rising to his feet as she bit down a shout of surprise. This was definitely not the moment to wake any of the kids.

"My day was pretty good as well," he told her. His strong hands squeezed her butt as he held her against him. Jaxi wrapped her legs around his lean hips, fingers digging into his muscular shoulders as he carried her down the stairs.

They were slightly safer now, since the children were still sharing bedrooms on the main floor for a few more years. Jaxi waited silently until he put her down in the dark corner of what used to be the family ranch office at one point.

"You need my help to balance some ledgers?" she whispered.

A low, dirty chuckle escaped him. "You're going to be a little too busy."

He clicked a switch, and teeny lights went on, strategically arranged around the perimeter of the room. Wall sconces burned as well, and soft country music began playing, almost as if they'd stepped into—

No way. Jaxi twisted to look into Blake's grinning face. "You made us our own version of Traders Pub?"

"Dance with me?"

His voice was lust-filled and smoky, and it sent a shiver racing up Jaxi's spine.

She didn't plan on sleeping anytime soon. Getting to rock against her favourite person in the entire world while he held her, one hand caressing her lower back, fingers teasing the back edge of her butt, was delicious. His other hand slid over her shoulders and through her hair. Trickling down the front of her body, boldly caressing her breasts.

Oh, she could handle a dance or two. If she must.

Hmmm. Nothing said she couldn't make this as much fun for him as it was for her. Jaxi eased a little tighter, took a slightly bigger breath as she arched and savoured the delicious sensation of his hard muscles rubbing fabric over her breasts.

"Jaxi." His groan was already a reward, but when he reached between them and undid the button on her pants, her blood pumped a little faster.

"Is the door locked?" Because this wasn't something she wanted interrupted.

"Yes." He pushed her pants to the floor, taking her panties with them. "There. Much better."

She wanted to laugh, because the shirt she wore was extra-long, and the tails hung over her hips like a dress. "You seem to have an agenda."

"Making good on a promise," he told her. "I'm sorry it's taken this long. I promise I'll make it worth your while."

He flicked another switch, and the back half of the room lit up to reveal—

Shock and amusement hit. "Blake Coleman. Is there a *pool table* in here?"

"They were nearly giving it away. Said they ordered new ones and I could have this one cheap." He backed them up two paces then placed her on the edge of the table. Then he caught hold of her knees and pressed her legs wide before trickling his fingers up the inside of her thighs. Teasing as he slid his fingers past the line between where her leg and her torso connected. Small circles inching closer to her sex. "You're not in a sundress, but this works for me."

He stood there, fingers now cupping her possessively. Waiting.

"Oh, yeah. This works for me, too," she agreed quickly. Gasping when he reacted by sliding his fingers through her folds. "Oh, this so works for me."

Blake teased. Fingers slipping into her sex. One. Two. Just the hint of three before his thumb danced in a series of rapid pulses over her clit. He did it again, and a strong pulse built inside her core.

Her breasts ached. She wanted to tear away the rest of her clothing. Tear away his clothing so they would both be naked, and yet there was something so deliciously dirty about the way he stood guarding her. As if a whole room full of people stood behind him, none of them quite aware of what was going on. None of them able to see the fire in his eyes as he stared at where he worked her sex.

None of them able to see what was on his face when he glanced up and whispered her name, pinching her clit lightly.

Jaxi rocked as the first wave struck. Blake rubbed harder, thrusting her into overdrive. Pushing hard so that pleasure rose, then dipped, then flared higher again. It wasn't until she gasped his name that his hand vanished.

The hard length of his cock took its place.

He leaned his hands on either side of her, staring into her eyes as he pushed into her body. An inch, and another inch. Slow and yet inescapable. Her only option for movement was to arch her back, but all that did was press her tighter against him as he buried himself fully. Filling her.

Loving her.

Jaxi cupped a hand to his face. "*Blake.*"

He grinned. "Promised I'd take you on a pool table sometime."

Then he did. The sweet, gentle, *fulfilling* connection turned down-right dirty. Blake's big hands gripped her hips like iron as his hips sped up. Thrusting hard, pulling back. Driving her toward the heavens again.

It was still lovemaking, but this was perfect and dirty and perfect and hard and just...*perfect*.

It didn't matter how many times they'd come together before; this time was special because it was a promise fulfilled. It was special because it was the same promise he'd fulfilled every time since their very first time.

Love. Dirty, hot sex, but *always* love.

He fucked into her. Jaxi dug her heels into his butt, loving how intensely she and Blake burned, loving every bit about giving to him.

She spiraled, scratching his back without meaning to. Then she buried her face against him and fought to contain her scream.

He made a noise that sounded painful, followed by the most satisfied moan ever.

The two of them stayed there, locked in position, Blake's legs shaking nearly as hard as Jaxi's. Their chests heaved, but their expressions were all satisfaction and smiles as they stared into each other's faces.

Blake leaned down and offered a kiss. "That was a wonderful dance."

She had to agree.

27

As the summer progressed, Dana collected each precious moment and tucked it into her brand-new set of memories.

The collection the Coleman family was putting together had given her a chance to revisit all of the best moments of her high school years, followed by the time dating Ben, and then marriage.

She refused to let the later sadness erase the seasons of good they had enjoyed. She wouldn't have wanted the brothers to have wiped Ben from their childhood reminiscing or from the stories that had been shared about when they had raised *this* barn and who had been involved in building *that* shelter. Ben's hand had touched many things in a positive way, and that's the part she wanted to honour.

But seeing Mark's earnest blue eyes and his firm smile across the table as she shared a coffee with him was a new sweetness washing away years of pain.

As he took her by the hand and they went horseback riding together, or walked beside the river, or joined the children for a picnic dinner, Dana found her feet growing more comfortable on this new path.

He picked her up a few days into August, absolutely giddy as he drove her to the building site to witness the timber frame being lifted into position over the foundation.

Mark had done some building of his own, creating a level platform on the highest ridge to the south side of the future house. Today he put two lawn chairs on it, with a small table to the side and a cooler tucked under a blanket.

"Looks decadent," Dana said with a laugh.

He grinned, opened his mouth and then closed it, looking thoughtful. "I have to be careful what I say." He met her eyes and winked. "I want to share this moment with you. It's a very special moment, for many reasons—and I'll stop there."

He didn't have to say more because Dana could read the words on his face. He wanted her to witness the home he was building going up. The home he wanted them to share.

The home she was very much beginning to want as well.

What she did was give him a hug and a quick kiss before settling in one of the chairs. "It's *very* exciting. I'm glad to be here with you."

It was fascinating to watch the crew fit the long, sturdy pieces into each other one at a time flat on the ground. Then they attached a chain to the topmost point and used a crane to lever the entire wall up at one time, wooden beams rising toward the robin's-egg-blue sky.

A week later the house had framed-in walls and a finished roof, beautiful pine boards shining overhead as Dana stood in what would be the living room and stared upward. "This is happening so fast."

Mark stepped behind her, his arms gentle but possessive as he curled them around her. "You think?"

She turned, sliding against him and lifting her face for his kiss.

Every time they got together, they told stories. What Mark

had done while he'd been gone. What Dana was the proudest of accomplishing over the years.

They touched on joys, and even slipped into sharing sorrows. And maybe that was when Dana began to realize—

Began to acknowledge—

She caught herself staring out the window when he wasn't around, gazing into the distance as if that would help her push past the final bit of worry and admit, at least to herself, that she was falling in love.

They went up to the house often, to enjoy picnics on the floor in what would be the kitchen someday. To dance to music playing on Mark's phone in the living room. Lawn chairs were placed on the porch once it was framed in—a perfect location to watch the sunset over the Rocky Mountains as the day ended, and it would be late, but neither of them wanted to stop talking.

Neither of them wanted the days to truly end.

Tonight he'd moved his chair close enough that their fingers were tangled, hanging between them. Off in the distance, the sound of a hawk's cry rippled over the air.

Mark hummed, soft and low. "Every time he heard that, Dave used to say, 'Hold on to your hat,' and then he'd duck down as if he were hiding."

"You've mentioned him before," Dana said. "Friend of yours from university, right? Where is he now?"

Mark hesitated. "He passed away about eight years ago."

His sadness was so sharp. Dana laid a hand on his arm. "I'm sorry."

"You couldn't have known." He adjusted position, sliding his chair closer to hers so he could rest their joined hands on his thigh. "He was a good friend for many years. We met at university then taught in the same school for over twenty years. He got cancer. It took him pretty quickly."

It struck her then that all of them had lives traced with loss.

Mark, her, her children. So many of them in the Coleman family. "You must've really missed him."

"Still do," he admitted. "I suppose the silver lining, if you want to call it that, was the six months he had at the end were full of one hundred percent *live life to the fullest* attitude. I quit my job, and between his chemo sessions, we took an extended road trip all over Western Canada." He smiled, sad amusement in that gentle curve. "We went into every small-town museum we could find. Gave most of them a thrill to have Dave willing to let them talk about grain elevators and train routes and what all for hours on end."

"I'm glad you got to do that with him."

"Me too. That's when I switched to driving a truck. I needed a change."

Night was falling, and in the midst of the quiet, something changed. Dana wanted to listen to Mark talk for hours, and the truth sank in deep.

He must have felt it too.

Abandoning his chair, he moved in front of her and caught her hand in his. "You know, there're still so many stories to share. It's not as if we can know everything about each other instantly. Or that we have to know everything before we know what's right..."

He let the words trail off, not as if he wasn't sure what came next but as if he was waiting. Trying to be patient.

Failing dismally.

Sweet, happy hope began spiraling upward in Dana's chest.

It was the truth. "You're saying we should probably move in with each other because that would make it easier to catch up?"

He lifted her hand and brushed his lips over her knuckles. "That, and it would make it easier for a lot of *other* things."

She waited to see if he would waggle his eyebrows, but apparently, the man had decided to remain thoughtful.

Which meant the bubbles lighting up her bloodstream were

dangerous, because *she* didn't want to be sober right now. She wanted to pull him to his feet and dance, to laugh as they wandered over the hillside.

She wanted to pull him into bed and dance all night long in a whole different way. To sleep in his arms and know he was there.

Mark. Her caring, cocky, *listening* man.

This wasn't a moment for serious—not that kind, anyway. This was a moment of serious joy.

Before she could say anything, Mark rose to his feet and held out a hand. "I have something to show you. I was going to wait, but I couldn't resist seeing how it looked in its new home."

She walked with him, curiosity rising as he led her across the great room toward the master bedroom.

The cozy, rustic farmhouse where she had lived for over thirty-five years had been built with love. She'd raised her children there. Buried lost ones there. Spent time with her son and daughter-in-law, and began to live again.

This new house set amongst the wild roses, with a view of the mountains, was dreamily perfect. Everything shiny, everything glowing, and the room Mark led her into was nearly the size of the living room in her old place.

Yet what made her lips curl upward wasn't the spectacular luxury but the air mattress on the floor, a quilt and pillows neatly in place. "Mark Coleman. That's the fanciest bed I've ever seen."

He looked confused for a moment then laughed. "Honestly, that's not what I wanted to show you."

She was laughing as well, amusement tickling so hard, she couldn't stop. "Sure."

He spun her as if they were on the dance floor, ending with her back against his chest, arms crossed in front of her as he twisted her toward the wall that divided the bedroom from the master bathroom suite.

An enormous picture hung on the unpainted drywall, and she gasped. "Mark."

"It seems Ashley was inspired. It's one of the most beautiful things I've ever seen," he said, softly pressing a kiss to the side of Dana's neck.

Ashley had painted an eerily familiar scene. A woman stood surrounded by verdant-green bushes, pale-pink roses blooming exuberantly everywhere.

It was her—Dana. Only it wasn't identical to the image that had been in the photographs her daughter-in-law had brought home at the start of the year, sending memories dancing that had hurt and yet been bitterly sweet.

She remembered the day so long ago—the one in the picture. They'd been taking photographs for a family album, and Mark had been there. He'd taken the camera from Ben, supposedly clicking shots of them as a couple, but when the film had been developed, nearly half the roll had been Dana by herself. Dancing in the rose bushes, daydreaming about what the future would bring.

Turning to discover Mark staring at her, a sensation in her gut jumping furiously. He was her friend, *not* her boyfriend. She wasn't supposed to feel *that* way about him.

And so in the end, Dana had pushed the feelings away and focused on what she needed to, convincing herself the emotions had simply been a momentary glitch.

Never once over the years had she done anything she needed to feel guilty about. But this one thing—this one truth? She needed to tell him.

She turned from the image, her heart pounding. "Mark—"

He pressed a finger over her lips. "I have something else to show you."

HER EYES SHONE, and after what she'd jokingly said earlier about moving in with him, he was already hopeful.

But he needed her to know everything.

He pulled his wallet from his pocket and slipped out the picture he'd had for so many years. "You've been with me forever," he said.

She took the tattered photograph, breathing uneasily. "You carried this all those years?"

"I couldn't let go," he confessed.

Dana lifted the photograph toward the painting.

Then it was easy to see how brilliantly Ashley had brought new life to the image. Oh, she'd used a little artistic license when it came to making the rose bushes. Her style leaned toward three-dimensional, paint on paint, that looked a whole lot better when the viewer stood back instead of looking at it from inches away.

But the real magic was she had taken the image of Dana in her twenties and turned it into a current portrait. Just as beautiful, but her smile somehow *more*. The lines of her face, especially at the corners of her eyes and her mouth, showed life had not always been easy, but also that Dana was still young at heart. Still smiling, still hopeful.

She was still dancing.

Vibrant and glowing, the Dana in the painting held her arms out and embraced the beauty around her.

Mark pulled Dana's hand down, turning the woman toward him. "I don't need the photograph anymore," he said softly. "Or even the painting, because I've got you. The real thing."

She nodded, a series of sharp little head bobs that made him smile. Then she glanced back at the painting. "I think *I* needed this," she said clearly. "I needed a reminder that it doesn't matter that there's a little more paint on the canvas, I'm still me."

He laughed, and as she stepped into his arms, he accepted every bit of her. The young woman he'd fallen in love with and had never been able to tell. The mystery woman he'd dreamed of for so many years. And the strong, brave woman who was even now backing him toward the makeshift bed he'd placed in the room that he wanted to share with her forever.

"You are still you," he agreed.

He brought her down to the mattress. Sunset danced as golden and orange rays filtered through the windows and played across their bodies.

Clothing stripped away, he kissed her softly, rolling over her as he breathed in the scent of roses. He kissed her harder, teasing all the places that he'd been learning over the past months. Every time they'd been able to steal away, testing, and taking, and enjoying.

Then he kissed her sweetly as they came together, the sensation so good, he wasn't going to be able to be patient—

Except this was Dana, and for her, he would *always* find a way.

After, they lay tangled, the sheets kicked back because the air around them was heated from the summer day and their bodies.

Dana stroked her fingers through his hair, examining his face. "You look like you did that day when you took the pictures of me."

Mark paused, thinking. "What look is that?"

She laughed. "Like you had some enormous secret, and as if you wanted to eat me up like an ice cream cone."

Mark shrugged. "Pretty accurate."

It was a good thing he was already lying down, because otherwise what she said next would have knocked his feet out from under him.

"I felt it," she said. She took a deep breath. "I mean, I felt it *too*."

His heart rate sped up.

She pressed her fingers over his lips to keep him from speaking. As if she needed to get this confession out. "Mark, I was attracted to you as well. It was a pure, sweet moment of something that wasn't meant to be, not right then. It wasn't wrong, because we never did anything about it, but it was very beautiful. And now I think it's that moment that brought us *here*. It was one of those strange things, almost reverse déjà vu. Maybe something of today magically jumped back in time to that moment, and we felt a hint of what would be."

Oh, *hell*, yes. Mark curled upright, hauling Dana with him. They both sat on the bed naked, grinning at each other. "Dana, I love you. Are you telling me—"

He couldn't breathe.

She stared at the mattress for a moment before deliberately lifting her eyes to meet his. "Part of me isn't ready to say it yet, but part of me has loved you for a long, long time."

The sensation in his heart bloomed bigger and bigger until the entire room was pounding with it. "Does this mean you'll marry me?"

Dana crawled over him, one hand on his chest to angle him back against the mattress. "I would like to move in with you, first," she said clearly. "Because we have all that talking to finish up. Plus, it would be good to let Rafe and Laurel have some time to themselves."

"Good thing I'll soon have a place for you to move into, then," Mark said. "But will you marry me *eventually*?"

Her eyes sparkled. "Eventually, maybe."

She folded her arms over her chest, expression going teasing. He didn't care, not with her perched over him, her naked skin heating his body and his hands on her hips where he could caress soft skin.

"Labour Day? Or maybe Thanksgiving?"

She snorted. "*Eventually* means longer than that..."

He didn't stop. "New Year's? Valentine's?"

Her lips twitched. "You are so not good at the patience thing."

"I know. Canada Day, next year. It'll be the first time that the Wild Rose Colemans host the gathering. We can make it extra special by having the entire family here to witness our vows."

Dana stilled, her expression softening. "You make it very difficult to not be charmed out of my socks."

"You're not wearing any socks," he pointed out before taking control and rolling her under him again. He pressed a sweet kiss to her lips. "I love you, and I want everyone to know. But I will be patient until—"

"Yes," she whispered.

Something deep inside him cracked wide open and happiness spilled out, washing over them both. "Yes, *what*?"

Just to be certain.

"Yes. I'll marry you. July first, here at Wild Rose ranch. But between now and then you have to promise me—"

"Anything. I'll do *anything* for you."

Dana poked him in the ribs, laughter rising up. "Just love me. Promise to keep listening and keep loving. That's all."

"I promise." He said it quietly, but somehow the words echoed in the room and bounced down the hall, slipping into the farthest corners of the house.

The place he would make sure was filled with listening and love. Because it wasn't only a house. It was more.

Mark had truly come home.

28

———————

October, Six Pack ranch

Blake caught Jaxi as she flew past him at high velocity. "Whoa, slow down there, Slick. I need to talk to you."

"I've got two minutes," she warned before wrapping her arms around him and squeezing tight. "Hey, love. Missed you this morning."

"Travis had problems, and I was on call." He slowed her enough to be able to kiss her, deep and lingering by the time he stopped.

She sighed happily. "Okay, you have my attention."

"Anything else you need me to do for the party this coming weekend?" he asked.

Jaxi considered then shook her head. "Jesse and Joel came out yesterday and helped get everything ready in the space we've cleared in the barn." She pressed her fists against her hips and looked annoyed as all get out. "Of course, there's supposed to be a huge snowstorm this weekend, way ahead of normal."

"I don't know that it's early. This is October in Alberta,

sweetheart," he reminded her, "but I'm glad we've got the barn as backup. If you think of anything else you need, let me know."

"I will."

She went to head away, but Blake kept hold of her fingers, tugging her back against him so he could hold her a little longer. "How are you feeling?" he asked softly

Her expression went dreamy. "Really good. *Really.*"

He slid a hand between them, fingers spread over her belly where their baby was growing. "I still can't believe it."

"I guess we needed to have sex on a pool table sooner," she teased.

"Still not telling anyone?"

Jaxi shook her head. "There's a lot of other stuff to celebrate right now. Let's let the rest of the family be the focus."

Which was pretty much what he'd expected her to say. "Agreed. Love you, Slick."

"You're pretty much my favourite guy as well," she agreed, dancing out of reach. "Go. Do big cowboy stuff."

So he did.

He was on his horse and heading out the front gate when he saw another figure sitting tall on horseback across the road. Blake directed Thunder toward where his father sat waiting.

Mike leaned on the saddle horn as he grinned contentedly. "Was going to ride for a bit before that storm decides whether it wants to arrive or not."

"Want some company?" Blake offered.

"Always."

They turned their horses toward the trail along the extreme eastern border of the Coleman land. A little farther from the Rockies, with the knowledge that everything between them and the mountains was Coleman country.

It was an incredible feeling. An incredible rush to have the privilege of being a steward of the land *and* a part of something so much bigger than himself.

Blake stared off into the distance, thinking hard. Trying to figure out what it was that wanted to come to the surface, because the past year…

He'd watched and listened and learned, and there was a truth even bigger than the Coleman land that he needed to share with his father.

"I've been thinking a lot about what you told me at the start of the year." Blake glanced over at Mike. "You know, there's a big difference between what you had to do when your dad passed away and what we're looking at going into the future."

Mike lifted his eyes, surprise there. "You think?"

"Oh, some of the differences are pretty clear. The equipment we have, the technology. The amount of land that the Coleman clan has cleared and is using in different ways. Hell, the number of Colemans, period. All of that's a lot more than you faced." Blake shook his head. "That's not what I'm talking about, though."

Maybe it was a combination of having spent the past year looking through pictures, dredging through memories. Listening to his uncles tell stories about the things they'd dealt with, so often needing a bit of luck and a prayer to try and get through.

Today the wind blew cold, clouds building on the horizon, but where they rode, the sun was still shining, the brown grass of late fall ready to be covered with the pristine white of a fresh, clean winter.

Every month that had passed, every moment Blake had watched as his family had taken a long hard look back, seeing them enjoy the memories then turn to the future with bubbling enthusiasm.

Okay, maybe that last part was mostly Jaxi. His heart.

But here and now, his father needed to hear a powerful message.

"Travis is someone I trust with any part of the ranch. Trust him with my kids, and I like spending time with him." Blake pictured his brother with Ashley and Cassidy, and while what they had wasn't typical, it was totally right and so full of love, only a fool would try to deny it.

"Matt's gone a little quieter over the years, but it's a contented thing. He and Hope are like one of her quilts. Beautiful and yet content to stay at home and enjoy each other. Still, he works his ass off every time we're out in the fields, and I can barely keep up."

Mike was nodding, his smile growing. "Tell me about Daniel."

His father was too smart and too perfect. The man had already clued in to what Blake was doing. "He's my little brother, yet he's already shown me there's a solid path to follow where I'd feared to tread," Blake admitted. "He and Beth have built something amazing, and they're close to sending three mature, productive and caring adults into the world. Plus those boys of theirs are just as much a part of this family as any of the kids being born into it."

Mike leaned forward in the saddle again, lips curled into a full out grin. "What about your little brothers?"

"Still learning. Still making me laugh and making me roll my eyes at times, but they don't give up. Not on each other, never on family." Blake examined his father from top to bottom then shook his head. "You had your brothers, but each of you had your own dreams, and for a short time, they pulled you apart. Plus, you had your troubles, and they were big, but Dad?" Blake paused to gaze out over the Coleman land. Over everything that had been accomplished during the past hundred years. Then he met his father's eyes. "You were one man, and there was no way you could do it all. But you sure the hell tried."

Mike laughed. "I guess I did."

"You succeeded," Blake told him plainly. "You might tell us that you didn't do everything right, but still you somehow got six fiercely independent boys to all see which direction they need to head. You made it clear by the way you treated Ma over the years that she's the number one thing in your life. And then us, and then your extended family, and then the rest of it. Every one of your children-in-law thinks you hung the moon because they know it was *you* who taught us by example how we're supposed to treat our wives, and husband."

Mike was listening, his expression gone a little tighter.

"So really, it doesn't matter one bit if I have to tell you every day from now until you're a hundred and ten how much I love and admire you, I'll do it gladly. So will the rest of your sons. And your brothers. And your grandkids, and everybody else in this town you've made an impact on over the years."

His father took a deep breath. Stared out over the land for a moment before dipping his chin firmly. "Then I guess I did all right after all." He took a peek sideways. "Proud of you. And I'll say it—I love you."

Before Blake could respond, Mike tugged the reins, moving his horse into a little brisker of a walk. Blake followed, wiping at his eyes quickly before catching up and riding beside his father.

He didn't need to take Mike's place someday. No one could take Mike's place. That was kind of the point.

But with their roots gone deep, the tree that was the Coleman family was strong and sturdy. Lots of branches, beautiful foliage. Good fruit.

They would be able to stand strong going forward.

Family, forever.

Coleman Memory book
~Dana (Wild Rose) Coleman~

July first. Canada Day. My wedding day.

The flowers are in full bloom at Wild Rose ranch, and the deck platform Mark built nearly a year ago is completely surrounded by fragrant blossoms. Rafe and Gabe built an arbour, and Allison and Laurel wove it through with extra flowers, and today Mark and I stood under it as we said *I do*.

Which means I became a Coleman for the second time.

The first time, I was a young woman, somewhat a stranger to this family, but I was welcomed in and loved. This time, I'm no longer so young but able to see far more clearly how rich and deep and strong love needs to be to stay true.

All the family was there today. Whiskey Creek, Six Pack, Moonshine, and Angel. Jaxi and Blake showed off their littlest one. At only a week old, Dane is adorable and the entire family was fawning over him. Rafe and Laurel shared with us the wonderful news that they're expecting right around Christmas. I'm so excited for them. Rafe couldn't stop grinning, holding Laurel as if she were precious.

Having the children here at the Wild Rose ranch house—with their children and all the rest of the family as well—was perfect. I've found a place to set down new roots so I can bloom as well.

I'm glad.

That the sadness is over, yes, but not that the sadness ever occurred. Because light and dark are both parts of our world, and while pain hurts, it teaches. The memory of sorrow reminds me to cherish every moment of the sweet goodness I now have.

Also, somewhere along the way, I seem to have lost the thread of what these pages are supposed to be about, and it looks as if I'm sharing a diary update. But Mark (and Laurel, and Jaxi, and Marion!) have all assured me that the idea behind the memory book has changed over the past year. It's become a living memento of what's important. What's happening now, and in the future—it will *all* get recorded in some way.

But for this, my first chance to add to the story, I want to affirm that family is laughter *and* tears. Sometimes you get more of one than the other, but if you hope and pray and dream hard enough, in the end, love wins.

Love wins.

Please turn the page and enjoy all six vignettes in the Six Pack Ranch world:

Making Memories
Never Too Far
Home Building
Rubber Boot Romance
Lights and Secrets
A Daddy's Love

1

———

MAKING MEMORIES

This piece features Jaxi and Blake Coleman. The oldest brother of six, Blake's been enjoying married life and his twin baby girls. He wouldn't change a thing, even though he still teases Jaxi they were supposed to have all boys. Jaxi's more than content—this is what she'd longed for.

Timeline: This scene takes place during the final months of Rocky Mountain Desire, and about eight months before Rocky Mountain Rebel begins.

~

Childish laughter echoed again, the vibrant noise bouncing off the living room walls and warming the room as much as the fire in the old stone hearth. Rebecca peeked out from between her fingers and shrieked even louder as her daddy raised his hands in the air, growling like a bear. The second of the nearly two-year-old twins rushed from behind the couch to come to her sister's defense. Rachel, in her usual outgoing way, threw her arms around Blake's neck and clung tightly while she shouted for her sister to run.

"Where'd those little girls go?" Blake twisted in mock confusion as the twins' shrieks dropped to secretive toddler giggling. "I could have sworn they were here a minute ago."

Jaxi stood in the doorway of the kitchen, and soaked it all in. The gentle affection, the happiness—the *love* that filled her home from morning to night. Her heart filled with pleasure as her husband dropped to his knees to better play with his children.

She'd been in love with Blake forever, but the last two and a half years had been so much richer than she'd ever imagined. He'd been even more than she'd dreamed, this generous man who'd been up long before dawn, who'd put in a full day's work on the ranch, yet still found time to offer his little girls the tender affection of a daddy.

She watched until a wave of sleepiness struck, and she blinked hard to chase away the cobwebs. If she didn't move now Blake would have three to tuck into bed. She hated to put an end to their fun, but it was time.

Jaxi stepped into the room. "Blake, did you lose my babies?"

They turned her way—two tiny, but beautiful blond heads, and a dark-haired one whose expression of admiration and intimate heat made her knees weak and her heart pound, as if she'd been the one being chased.

"I didn't get losted," Rachel reassured her. The little one padded up and curled her flannel PJ clad body around Jaxi's legs.

Rebecca, like the daddy's girl she was, took advantage of his distraction to crawl into Blake's arms. She caught his neck in a one-armed death-grip and stared earnestly at Jaxi. Instinct won out as the little girl slipped her thumb into her mouth, eyelids drooping, as the fight to stay awake grew more intense.

"All my girls ready for bed?" Blake asked.

"Story first," Rachel demanded.

"Of course, story." Jaxi cuddled her close then savoured the evening routine of tucking her precious babies in for the night.

Kisses, stories, and more kisses done, Jaxi found herself

enfolded in strong arms. The fire in the grate had burned low while they'd put the girls to bed, but in Blake's embrace Jaxi didn't notice the chill in the room.

Blake snuck his fingers under her chin and raised her lips to his. A sweet, soft caress that melted away the minor frustrations of her day. Everything put aside except seeking his touch.

"Hmm." Jaxi cupped her palm to his cheek. "That was extra delicious."

"It's a special night." Blake spoke seriously, his dark grey gaze dancing over her face.

Jaxi paused and considered. *Really?* It was the middle of March. Not her birthday, and there were no calendar holidays anytime soon.

She twisted to face him. "Special?"

Blake nodded. His serious expression melted at the edges, and his smile broke free. "What? Don't tell me you don't know what we're celebrating?"

There were no family events, or even remote anniversary dates to commemorate. She shook her head, covering her yawn. "You lost me."

"I was sure—" He paused, then nodded determinedly. "I *am* sure."

March. She racked her brains. The only thing that came to mind was St. Patrick's Day, but green beer didn't usually make him this excited.

"You know, it's kind of fun to know something before you do." He leaned back against the couch, easing his hands behind his head.

Gloating. Definitely gloating.

Jaxi was too mellow to care. A second yawn snuck up and ambushed her.

Blake grinned even harder.

She ignored him. If he wanted to have his fun, she'd let him.

Other things needed saying before she succumbed to slumber's call.

"I love watching you with the twins." Jaxi curled herself beside him, resting her head against his chest and closing her eyes. "You're a good daddy."

"Love those girls so hard. As much as I love their mama."

She must have been doing more than she thought lately—she was simply beat. Between the fire and the lethargy in her limbs, she was done for the day. Still, Jaxi savored his touch, appreciating once again simply being able to lie there and be with him.

He pressed his lips to the top of her head. "You and me, we make pretty babies."

Jaxi trembled on the edge of sleep. Relaxed. Content. She hummed back at him in response because it took less energy than speaking.

"Darlin', you sure you don't have something to tell me?" Blake stroked her shoulder.

"Nope. Nada." She tilted her head back and stared into his loving eyes. "You got me."

His gentle caress continued. "I've heard a rumor, then."

"From who?"

"You." His eyes sparkled.

"Me?" Well, that made no sense at all.

"More specifically, your body."

Jaxi laughed. "Damn gossipy body, then, for talking to you and not to me. What'd it tell you? Is it planning on running away to join the circus?"

Blake tweaked her nose. "We're already running a circus around here. No, it's more that you, my source of endless energy, are tired. Like *crawl in bed at the same time as the girls* tired. Instead of hopping out of bed like your ass is on fire in the morning, I find you cuddled up against me, which I'm not complaining about one bit, mind you."

"I noticed you not complaining." She'd enjoyed the extra minutes together as well—time to savour the physical connection that neither of them had grown tired of. It was never for long enough, though, before either the girls crawled in with them or Blake had to leave for chores.

"Yesterday," he continued, "you pulled this hilarious face at the first taste of your coffee. And you've served macaroni and cheese three nights running, which is number one of your comfort foods."

His list made her laugh. "Bonus points for being observant, but I don't see…"

"And there's these." He cupped her intimately, his big palm gentle against her tender breast—

"Oh, Lordy." Jaxi snapped to vertical, staring at him in shock. Was he saying…? Could she be…?

She might be.

How could she have missed the clues?

Blake snorted. "You should see your face right now."

She could only imagine. "Blake, I had no idea."

"You mean you ain't keeping secrets and waiting for the right moment to share?" He traced a finger over her cheek, completely focused on her response. "I mean, we've been trying to get you pregnant."

The slight embarrassment that had snuck in for being an unobservant twit vanished in an instant. There was no room inside for wasted negative emotion when joy and disbelief were battling for the top billing in her brain. "I'm *pregnant*."

This time he outright laughed. "That would be my guess," he said, opening his arms as she straddled his legs and settled herself tight against him. "Love you, darlin'. Thanks for being willing to do it all over again."

"You just better hope this baby is as sweet as last round," she teased. "Of course, if she takes after her mother, we know she'll be perfect."

A soft chuckle escaped him. "Why're you so insistent it's not a boy this time?"

"Woman's intuition."

"Same intuition that poked me before you about the baby coming? I swear I'm more into your head than you are," he teased.

Jaxi narrowed her gaze. "I hear there's a machine that lets men experience labour. You want me to find one so you can really get into my head?"

His grey eyes widened and he shuddered. Jaxi laughed at his instant reaction.

"You win, hands down. I know damn well I'm not brave enough to go through that." He linked their fingers together. "In the meantime, though, I know there's no use in telling you to take it easier, but if you need extra help, you make sure and let me know."

"I will." Jaxi cupped his face in her hands and took in a deep, satisfied breath. "A baby, Blake! We're gonna have a *baby*."

"Looks that way." He kissed her, soft and slow before heating up and stealing her breath away. She threaded her fingers into his hair and soaked in every moment. Every touch.

It *was* a good night to celebrate, and Blake seemed determined to make it a memorable one. Which was just fine with her.

2

NEVER TOO FAR

This scene features Vicki Hansol and Joel Coleman. The youngest of the six brothers on the Six Pack Ranch, Joel is committed to a summer spent working the family spread. His brand-new fiancée has accepted a position months earlier that had taken her hours away from him to a trail-riding camp. After recently realizing they were in love, having to be apart from each other is turning out to be a challenge.

Timeline: This scene takes place about two weeks following the end of Rocky Mountain Rebel, during the adventures of Rocky Mountain Freedom.

～

The internet flickered.

Vicki jerked upright from where she'd been relaxing against her pillows. "Joel, you still there?"

Her fiancé's answer came through increasing static. "Still here, but I think we're losing our connection. Not only did the video feed go, now I can barely hear you. It's late, anyway. You need to hit the sack so you don't burn breakfast in the morning."

She laughed even as she stifled the yawn she'd been fighting for the past twenty minutes. "Extra early rising tomorrow. We're heading to the nearest big city to pick up supplies again. Two hour trip to civilization."

"Then I won't keep you any longer. I'm glad you're doing well, though. I miss you, darling."

"I miss you too. So much." Vicki clutched the thick quilt wrapped around her shoulders in spite of the fire in the airtight stove. Debated, and then accepted it was the grown up thing to do. "Hey, Joel? You know how you said you'd drive out and visit me this summer?"

"Yeah."

"I don't think you should. I mean, I want to see you so badly, but..." Static picked up again, and Vicki hurried to finish before she lost the line, or lost her nerve. Changing their plans wasn't what she really wanted, but it *was* the mature choice. "I've done the trip from the main highway twice now, and it's a long haul. Add that onto the hours you'd need to drive from Rocky? It's not worth it. And we should be saving our money. I'll be back in late August, and we'll have all kinds of expenses and—"

"Hey, hey, slow down," Joel ordered. "You're moving in with me when you get back, so that's already taken care of. And you'll find a job, maybe take a few classes. We'll be okay."

"It's going to be tight, though. So I think we should stick with Skyping. I know it sucks, but it's only for a few months."

"Four is more than a few." His words broke up. "Damn. There's too much interference to do this tonight. Tell you what— next time we talk, we'll decide, okay?"

"Okay. I love you." Vicki put as much emotion into the simple words as possible.

"Love you, too. Sleep well."

She shut down the internet and closed her computer, this time officially crawling under the covers on her tiny bed in the tiny canvas-sided tent she'd been assigned at Trailblazers.

She was grateful there was internet access this far into the bush. The assistant cook position had been her dream job when she'd been offered it the previous fall, and she was enjoying the cooking.

She just wished she wasn't huddled under the blankets by herself. Not only because of the heated things Joel did to her when they were together, although, *holy moly* had he ever taught her everything she needed to know about sex. No—it was more than the physical pleasure he brought that she missed. The way he listened to her. Believed in her when no one else had. Those things were a huge part of it as well.

Even from miles and miles away, his love wrapped around her as she fell asleep.

Six a.m. came far too early. Vicki sat bleary-eyed in the passenger seat next to her boss, the truck rising farther on every bounce than it would on the return journey when they'd be loaded with supplies. She clutched her travel mug and stole sips of coffee between jolts.

They pulled into the grocery store parking lot minutes before the eight o'clock opening. "I made two lists this time," Ted announced. "You take one, I'll do the other. Once you finish, load your stuff in the truck, and you can have the rest of the day off."

Vicki shook herself awake. "Time off?"

"Yeah. Wander around town. Do some shopping. Whatever." Ted put the truck in park and was out the door, Vicki scrambling to follow him. "I need to do some personal stuff, so meet here at two. That'll get us back in time to fix dinner for the crew."

He handed her a folded paper, grabbed a cart, and took off, leaving her wondering why he was acting so strangely.

Vicki shrugged. The man was a great cook, but a touch eccentric. And... she was going to have to find cheap way to waste time after she was done her part of the shopping. Because, as she'd told Joel the night before, saving cash was a high priority.

First, work.

She unfolded the paper, stepping back in surprise as a couple of twenties fluttered to the floor. Vicki grabbed them before examining the page closer for an explanation.

There was a brief note from Ted: *Lunch is on me.*

Well, that was sweet.

The only other thing on the paper was *4 pallets of bottled water.* Vicki glanced around for her boss, wondering if he'd accidentally given her a draft list. She found no sign of him, even though she peeked down every aisle on her way to the water.

She rounded the final corner and nearly ran someone over with her cart. Vicki jerked to a stop barely in time. "Shit. Sorry."

The solidly built dark-haired man turned, and Vicki's heart just about leapt out of her chest.

She abandoned the cart and threw herself forward, arms spread wide. Joel caught her, wrapping his arms around her as she squealed with happiness. "Oh my God, oh my*God*, you're here. Joel, you're *here.*"

His strong embrace supported her, feet off the floor, as he leaned closer, his bold laughter and his smile just as she remembered. "I'm here. Now, kiss me."

No objections on her part. Middle of Costco, there could have been a million people watching them, and she didn't give a damn. Vicki thrust her fingers into his hair, toppling his cowboy hat to the ground as their lips met.

Kissing him was never going to get old.

Goosebumps arrived as he deepened the kiss farther, his tongue doing wicked things to her. All too soon he pulled away, leaving her lips tingling and the rest of her not far behind. "Come on. Let's get your chores done so we can go elsewhere and do this properly."

"Wait." Vicki blinked at him in confusion. "Okay, first, I'm so glad to see you, but *why* are you here? I said you shouldn't bother making the trip."

Joel laughed as he loaded pallets of water onto her cart, cowboy hat firmly back in place. "And I said we'd decide when we talked next. Which would be now."

Vicki hugged herself, hoping she wasn't dreaming the entire event. "So you decided to drive seven hours anyway?"

"You take seven hours on your bike. I'd take less, plus I found a route that cut it to five and a half. I'd already talked to Ted to check when I could come to the camp, and he'd suggested we meet here and save me two hours driving each way." He linked her fingers in his, using his free hand to push the cart toward the registers. "Your boss is pretty awesome. He said you could have the day off to spend with me."

Vicki was glad Joel was leading because her feet weren't touching the ground. "I can't believe this."

"Believe it." Joel waited at the till while she pulled herself together enough to put the order on the camp bill. He transferred the water into the back of Ted's truck then guided her to his truck in the far corner of the parking lot. "Anywhere in particular you want to go?"

Vicki settled in tight to his side, thighs touching, fingers curled around his biceps. "With you. That's all. I just want to be with you."

He took them just out of town, opening a cattle gate and going four by four to the edge of a lonely bluff overlooking the North Saskatchewan river. The long line of the majestic Rocky Mountains stood as a backdrop, spring flowers dotting the nearby field. Vicki stared out the window for all of two seconds before ignoring the view and crawling into his lap. "I get to look at mountains all day long. I need to see your face."

Joel shifted the steering wheel out of the way as much as possible before resting his hands on her hips. "We could probably find somewhere with a little more room for while you look at me," he teased.

"Don't need more room." Vicki glanced out the window at the wide expanse of field, wondering if he'd think she was crazy, but she didn't want to wait much longer. Not when they had limited time together. "This place looks nice and deserted. Will it stay that way?"

"The land belongs to a friend of mine who moved a few years ago. No one will be by." Joel smoothed a hand up her back, pressing their bodies intimately close. "If you're thinking what I think you're thinking, I have a blanket in the back..."

Vicki had their lips together and her fingers on the buttons of his shirt before he even got the door open, carrying her to the rear of the truck.

A lot of the details from the following moments vanished. Somehow they ended up naked on the blanket surrounded by wild grasses and spring flowers. There was nothing to focus on except how amazing she felt. How right it was to be with Joel, his blue eyes locked with hers as they made love.

Much later they were both grinning pretty damn hard, physical satisfaction obvious as he tucked a flower behind her ear. "Now that I can think straight again, I'll mention I brought a picnic, but if you want to go out to eat, we can."

Vicki shook her head, pushing him to the blanket and straddling him. She pulled on his shirt, the sides still hanging open. "I vote we eat here. Talk. Fool around some more. I don't want to waste a single minute of the time we've got."

Joel drew circles on her skin with his fingertip, the sensation so familiar—so right. "You glad I made the trip?" Teasing in his tone as well as love.

"So glad, although it is crazy far for you to drive."

He curled upward to a sitting position, his abdominal muscles rock-solid under her hands. He caught her chin in his fingers and held her trapped as he whispered, "Whatever it takes to be with you? Is never too much. Never too far. Because that would be putting a limit on how much I love you, and darling?" His gaze burned her with passion. "We've only begun to figure out how much that means. It's gonna take the next sixty to seventy years to even start."

Vicki rejoiced inside, and held on tight as her cowboy rolled her under him and proceeded to prove his point all over again...

3

HOME BUILDING

This piece features Gabe and Allison working on building their new home.

Timeline: 7 months after the end of Rocky Mountain Freedom, and about a month before book seven in the Six Pack Ranch series starts.

~

The ringing of hammers against wood echoed in her ears as Allison Coleman darted out of the path of the approaching tractor.

Her young brother-in-law, Raphael, gave her a sheepish grin as he slowed down the big green beast, lowering the front bucket just slightly to reveal another load of shingles. "Sorry. Didn't see you there."

She resisted making a smart-ass comment about his driving, instead shaking a finger at him before scooping up the buckets she needed to return to the horse lean-to. The excursion took her far enough away that on the return trip she paused to admire the cabin, now clearly visible all at one time.

The area was a beehive of construction. The Coleman clan had come out in full force to help with a modified barnraising—or at least the older boys and their wives were all in attendance. They'd taken a Saturday break from their springtime chores to help her and Gabe add onto the little cabin where they'd been living for just over a year and a half.

The exterior walls had been vertical within an hour of them starting, the roof shortly after that. Now half the crew worked to finish the exterior while others were completing the interior wiring and drywall.

It was astonishing how fast the clan could accomplish something when they set their minds to it.

"Crazy, right?"

Allison swung her head to the side to offer a smile to Jaxi. Her sister-in-law was dressed from head to toe in sturdy work gear, her three-month-old baby snuggled up tight in a fabric contraption strapped to her chest. At her side, eighteen month old Lana clung to Jaxi's hand, her big blue eyes staring up at Allison as she earnestly sucked on her thumb as if it was the most important thing in the entire world.

Temptation was impossible to resist. Allison knelt and opened her arms, her heart fluttering as Lana came forward willingly to be picked up.

As the little blonde bundle of happiness snuggled against her, Allison grinned even wider, answering Jaxi with the only possible response. "It's supposed to be crazy—it's family."

"True." Jaxi pulled off her cowboy hat and ran a hand through her hair before replacing the sturdy straw head-covering. "I made some sandwiches—they're in the kitchen when we need them, because that crazy family is going to be done with the walls and roofing sometime in the next forty-five minutes, and then they'll turn into a ravaging horde."

"Beth brought watermelon and cookies, and Gabe's mom said she'd be over with potato salad once she was done her morning chores." It was one thing she'd learned over the time of being married to Gabe—having family involved was a serious social event in terms of food. It was never just one or two people stopping in for a cup of coffee. And that was just fine by Allison.

There was nothing she liked better than being surrounded by people who loved her.

People like the blond haired man striding his way up the gentle slope toward them, his shirt undone at the neck, fabric stretching over muscular shoulders and the familiar bulge of his biceps. Gabe had his cowboy hat on like usual, and that expression on his face that never got old. The one that said he couldn't believe she was there.

The one that said he was never going to let her go.

"That is one fine man you've got," Jaxi teased. "Just watching him move makes me think about all sorts of naughty things."

"Go on with you." Allison bumped their hips together gently, so as not to wake the baby sleeping in the snuggly. "You got a Coleman of your own. "

"I do indeed. Vintage Coleman from head to toe, but that doesn't mean I can't admire the one you snagged as well." Her satisfied grin flashed so fast Allison couldn't hold back a burst of laughter, which of course set Jaxi off as well.

"I hope you're laughing with me, and not at me," Gabe warned as he came to a stop at Allison's side, slipping his arm around her back to ease her and the little girl she held against his strong chest.

Lana immediately reached up and patted him on the head, setting off the laughter again.

Gabe smiled good-naturedly before tweaking her nose. "That's my own fault for playing doggies with you last time you were over."

"I think you were having just as much fun as she was," Allison taunted.

"Of course I was. I get to be a rancher all the time." Gabe bent down to stare earnestly into Lana's face. "It's only on special occasions that I get to be a doggie."

Lana smiled, showing off her gap-toothed grin.

Gabe straightened up and focused on Jaxi. "Blake asked if you could come—the twins put their handprints in the concrete we poured, which is just fine. But now they want to add foot prints and maybe other body parts. There might be some stripping going on."

"Sweet mercy. Three years old, and they've already got him wrapped around their little fingers so hard he doesn't know up from down." Jaxi took off in a rush, calling over her shoulder. "Lana, you stay with Auntie Allison and be good girl."

Allison didn't even try to hide her amusement. "Blake really cannot say no to those girls, can he?"

"Who could possibly say no to his best girl?" His right hand gently cupped her face as he kissed her softly, Lana cradled between them. "And Blake's got four girls to try and keep happy."

"And one boy. Lordy, that poor child is going to be the most mothered male on the face of the planet." Allison watched as Jaxi disappeared into the construction area, her endless energy inspiring and a little overwhelming. "She never stops, does she?"

"Hmmm?" Gabe brushed his thumb over her cheekbone, staring into her eyes and ignoring everything going on around them. "Forget about Jaxi. How are *you* doing?"

That inner bit of excitement flared again even as she adjusted Lana into a more comfortable position. Every time Allison thought about what was happening, it was like opening a brand-new present. "I feel good. Much better than this morning."

"Hopefully that won't last too much longer. The morning stuff, that is."

She hoped so too. She eased away slightly, slipping her fingers into his as she tilted her head toward the cabin. "By the way, I'm okay with us letting people know."

A deep chuckle escaped him.

"What?"

Gabe helped her over a rough patch of ground, tucking his head beside hers to whisper, "The instant we started talking about adding rooms to the cabin, I think everyone in the clan assumed you were pregnant. I think it's pretty safe to say they know."

He was probably right, but...

"How come they don't say anything?" Allison tugged him to a stop before they reached the actual cabin. "I mean, there's been plenty of opportunties, but no one's asked. Not Jaxi, not even your mom."

His eyes sparkled. "No one would dare take away the fun of us getting to announce it."

She squeezed his fingers before letting them go, rearranging Lana on her hip more comfortably as she headed into the house and he left to rejoin the crew doing something to the windows.

Inside the cabin, her familiar living space was both bigger and brighter. They'd torn down the wall between the small living room area and the new construction, a wide passageway leading off to the two new bedrooms. That would give them a space for the baby and a spot for Rafe to stay with them when he needed to get out of the family house. Thick timber cut on their property had been used in the supports, and the new results fit in perfectly with the cabin Gabe had constructed years earlier.

"Well, that turned out nice."

Allison turned away from admiring the changes to greet her mother-in-law. "It'll be good to have a little extra room."

Dana nodded slowly, her lips twitching as if she were fighting temptation with every bit of her willpower.

It was impossible to resist any longer. "You're just dying to ask, aren't you?"

"I have no idea what you're talking about." The older woman's smile just grew wider. "But if you'd hurry up and share any news you might have, it would make it easier the next time I go to town. Not saying anything is just about killing me."

Gabe was going to gloat so hard about being right.

~

IT WAS impossible to be in more than one place at the same time, but damn if Gabe didn't want to try.

Swinging a hammer and working with his cousins to make the house even more of a home—he had to be in the middle of that. To put a bit of himself into the four walls that would protect his family.

The other part of him just wanted to wrap around Allison and protect her. Not just from feeling sick and miserable, but from the other fears that had crept in along with the joy of finding out about the coming baby. The sadness that struck at not being able to share the thrill with her own mom.

So he did both, best he could, splitting his time between working and poking his head into the cabin to keep an eye on her. Daniel Coleman had taken control of the construction project, offering a knowing wink at Gabe before lining up tasks for all the cousins who'd come out to help. Then he'd given specific jobs to each of his adopted pre-teen sons.

Gabe couldn't think of a more appropriate way for the walls to go up than under the loving hands of family.

As expected, cheers of delight and good-natured teasing accompanied their impromptu announcement over the lunch break. Hours later they sat in their new living room, Allison curled up at his side on the couch as he ran his fingers through her hair.

She sighed happily. "It's like a whirlwind hit our part of the world and left behind the perfect house for us."

"The Coleman clan pretty much is a whirlwind, I have to agree with you there."

He slipped his fingers under her chin and tilted her head back so he could touch their mouths together tenderly.

It never got old. Not the kissing, not the lovemaking. He brushed her lips again, butterfly soft.

She changed position and then crawled into his lap, knees straddling his thighs as she ran her fingers through his hair. "Thank you for making this happen."

"I got the easy part." He dropped his hands to her hips, caressing her carefully. "It took two days to add the extension. It's going to take you a whole lot longer to build the more important part."

The changes in her body were still subtle, but he loved seeing every one of them.

Her expression grew more serious. "Are we ready for this?"

"It's a little late for second thoughts," he teased. "We changed the roof line. If we take it down now, the shingles are gonna look awful funny."

Allsion snorted. "Angel boy, you're nuts."

He leaned their foreheads together, his thumbs rubbing gently on her waistline. "We can do this. I expect we'll make mistakes, and we'll have to learn all sorts of new things, but we're good at that. The learning bit. And we're good together."

She let out a long slow breath, nodding slowly. "It's a huge change. One minute I'm really looking forward to it, and then the next minute it terrifies me."

"Well, we're not having twins, so we don't have to worry about convincing two little people they aren't allowed to put their butt prints in concrete."

"Poor Blake." She covered her mouth with her hand, hiding her laughter. Then she nodded and leaned in to kiss him all over again. Which was just fine by him.

They had a whole new house to fill with memories, and with laughter, and most of all...

With family. Every crazy bit of it.

$$4$$

RUBBER BOOT ROMANCE

This vignette takes place after Rocky Mountain Freedom and about a month before Rocky Mountain Romance begins. Travis, Ashley and Cassidy have been together officially now for nearly nine months. It's the spring after they moved in together, and they're still finding new ways to enjoy making their three-some relationship stronger.

Especially Ashley, who has some mischief up her sleeve...

~

*A*shley spoke quietly as she teased, mindful that they weren't the only ones in the house. "You think you're a smart one, Travis Coleman, but the only thing smart about you right now is your mouth."

"Sticks and stones, darlin'." He leaned closer, his dark-grey eyes peering into hers with far too much amusement as he stole a kiss, the flavor of peppermint toothpaste filling her senses. "You know I'm right."

"Ha. Right off your rocker."

"Fight it all you want," he insisted, checking in the mirror as he smoothed his fingers through his dark hair, taming the tiny bit of bedhead that lingered even after he'd soaked himself down under one of their two massive bathroom sinks. "And if you want proof, just ask Jaxi. My sister-in-law knows everything there is to know about Coleman history ever since she got a bug in her head about the topic, and started digging through the old records."

Ashley paused to consider before making her next move. If Jaxi had spoken, there wasn't much use in fighting Travis's information. "Fine. I'll let you win this time, but I'll remind you that your dad said we could renovate the house as much as we wanted."

"And we did." He grinned as she slipped into his arms, wrapping herself against him and tilting her head back to stare up into his face. "New bathroom, rearranged bedroom spaces— new wiring *and* a new kitchen."

"Old paint," she grumbled.

Confusion flashed in his eyes, interrupting him on the way to kiss her again, which was kind of sad, because she liked his kisses, thank you very much. "New paint. How the heck could we have put on two coats of *old* paint in every room?"

Even in the middle of their debate she couldn't resist running her hands over his broad shoulders, the flannel shirt he'd layered over a T-shirt soft under her fingers. Firm shoulder muscles curved into rock solid biceps, and she sighed happily.

Getting to touch such a fine man anytime she wanted made the start of each day just about perfect, even if it was barely five a.m.

But there was a reason why she'd gotten up with him this morning, and she needed to stick to her agenda. Ashley attempted a small pout—not too much, or he'd know she was pulling a fast one. Just enough to keep him off balance.

"I meant we used old colours. Everything is cream or off-white."

Understanding flooded his expression. He tightened his hold

on her hips and she found herself airborne for a moment before being cradled against his chest. "Ah, now I get it. The artist in your soul is offended by all the blank canvases you see all around you?"

Ashley tightened her legs around his hips, every bit of contact between them so right. But in spite of how wonderful it felt to be in his arms, she didn't want to lose track of the conversation. "You do see the problem."

Travis leaned in and kissed her, pacing out of the bathroom with her wrapped around him. He hummed contentedly, breaking the contact between their lips to whisper, "Don't distract me, woman. I need to get started on chores. It's hard enough to get out of bed and leave you guys in the first place."

Which was why she'd crawled out from under the covers for in the first place. This was the best time to start the wheels turning.

"I just want to find some ways to brighten up the place."

He lowered her to the floor, their bodies still in contact. He cupped his hand around the back of her neck so he could tilt her face toward him. "You brighten up our world all by yourself, darling."

Awww. "Sweet talker."

"It's true. You know Cassidy and I would be lost without you."

He pressed their lips together and she got lost in the kiss. It was nearly a year since she'd returned to Rocky Mountain House, hoping to find something special with Travis. She'd never imagined she could end up with both him and Cassidy in a house full of love.

He reluctantly let her go. "We can talk about this more when I see you later. I've got to run or Blake will kick my butt."

He slapped her on the ass and she glared momentarily, unable to keep her expression from breaking into a smile as he tossed her a wink before taking the stairs two at a time.

The floor was cold underfoot, and Ashley didn't hesitate. She snuck back into their bedroom, her heart beating faster at the sight of the blond haired man nestled under the quilt on their oversized bed. She crawled under the covers, nestling against Cassidy's firm chest.

He groaned softly, but slipped his arm over her, pulling her tight against his warmth. "I thought you two would never stop talking."

Ashley pressed a kiss against his neck. "I'm sorry. Didn't mean to wake you."

Heat slowly wrapped around her, and once again she counted her blessings that she could have such a perfect life. Travis and Cassidy in love with her, and in love with each other, plus a whole bundle of family on the side.

He rearranged her slightly, his lips close by her ear. "What game are you playing with Travis?"

Whoops. "I don't know what you mean."

Cassidy laughed, the deep sound curling around them and filling the room with happiness. "Honey, we've been together for long enough I know when you're pulling a fast one. And I haven't seen you trying anything on me in the last few days, which means whatever it is you want, Travis is the one you think will say no."

She let him see her grin. "That's what I love about you. You're sexy *and* you're smart."

"So I'm right? You're trying to get something out of Travis?"

"Nothing bad," she swore.

"Of course not."

He said it with such droll understatement she was the one to laugh this time. "I mean it—although you're right, my *game* does involve you, but I already know what your answer will be."

"You have my blessing in whatever mischief you are about to undertake," Cassidy assured her as he rolled over her, and suddenly the plot to get the upper hand on Travis was the last thing on her mind as she stared up into his green eyes. "There is, however, a punishment for waking the man who was not on early chores."

She batted her lashes, anticipation rising rapidly. "Oh, please sir, are you going to have your wicked way with me?"

Cassidy answered in the best way possible.

~

THE EARLY SPRING weather was damn nice, and Travis found himself whistling as he worked, ignoring the smirks on his brothers' faces every time he passed them in the yard.

His youngest brother, Joel, finally said something. "I don't know that it's right, seeing you flitting about like a bluebird."

"Would you rather see him pouting and being all dramatic?" Blake shook his head. "Nope, I far prefer working with this ridiculously-in-love version of Travis."

Travis just grinned harder as he grabbed hold of a couple of feed pails and marched off toward the corral. To his delight, Ashley was perched on top of the railing by the gate.

She gave him a thorough up-and-down leer. "Hey, cowboy, you're looking mighty fine."

He glanced over his shoulder, but unfortunately there was family within viewing distance. He faced her, speaking quietly. "You're lucky. I was about two seconds away from ordering you to strip so I could test the rail's strength."

Ashley raised a brow. "I don't know how you think not ordering me to strip makes me lucky. I have no objections—"

It was his damn fault for starting this. "You're a handful of trouble."

"I'm *your* handful of trouble," she pointed out. And then she changed the topic, thank goodness, because he was already going to spend the afternoon daydreaming about dirty sex in the outdoors. "I have a proposition for you."

"Isn't that what we were just talking about?" he teased.

Ashley ignored him. "I want to brighten up things. I'm serious, and I have some really good ideas, but I need you on board."

"Anything you want to do in the house, or the shop. You're in charge," Travis offered. "Heck, you're the one with the artistic eye. It's not like I'm about to argue with you about colour pallets."

She nodded happily, which made something inside him warm and content.

"There are some *outside* things as well," she warned.

Travis hesitated. "You don't want to paint a mural on the outside of the house or something, do you?"

"Oh no, nothing like that. Just a few spots of colour. That's all."

There was something she wasn't saying, but he didn't have time right now to worry it out. "If it's something my dad and mom will approve of for around the yard..."

"I'm pretty sure they'll have no objections,"

"And Cassidy's onboard?" Because that expression in her eyes said he was the last one to know whatever it was she was planning.

He didn't mind one bit.

The past year had been amazing. Being surrounded by love and acceptance had melted all the hard spots in his soul. Not only did he have two people who told him all the time how much he meant to them, he knew he was completely accepted by his extended family. After years of doubting, and being afraid that he would never find happiness, the change in situation made his head spin at times.

He put the pails down and rested his hands on either side of Ashley's hips, staring up at her bold smile. "Okay, mischief-maker. Here's my offer. If whatever it is you're up to—and don't pretend you're not doing something twisted—if you can convince Jaxi and Blake to do whatever it is that's on your mind, then you get my one hundred percent cooperation."

"Promise?"

Travis raised a hand in the air. "I promise."

Her smile shone brighter than the sun. "I love you."

"I love you too." He grabbed his buckets. "Now, stop distracting me. I've got important rancher things to do."

Still, he took the time to watch as she walked away. There was a skip in her step, the sun reflecting off her blonde hair as she left the yard and headed toward their home.

This being in love thing—it was pretty damn good.

CASSIDY WAITED for the entire situation to unfurl like one of the crocuses poking their heads up everywhere in the fields.

He'd never dreamed his life could be like this. A real family surrounded him with laughter and love, getting in his face whenever he made the unwise decision to go it on his own. He was now a part of the Coleman clan—there were no lone wolves allowed amongst them.

Ever since the weekend, Ashley had been damn near buzzing with excitement, and he was pretty sure it had something to do with whatever evil plot she had started a couple weeks earlier.

Travis seemed unaware of the impending doom as he reclined on the couch, a book held in one hand, playing with Ashley's hair with his other hand as she lay with her head in his lap. Her lips twisted into a smile as she stared across the room into Cassidy's eyes.

It was a moment of calm in the middle of the work, a deep breath in the middle of everyday activities that seemed so much richer because he got to share them with two people who he loved.

Finally, he couldn't wait any longer. "Are you planning on sharing secrets anytime tonight?" he asked.

Her smile grew even wider. "Eventually."

Travis put his book aside, his dark grey eyes questioning as he met Cassidy's gaze. "What are you two up to?"

Cassidy raised his hands in protest. "Not me. This is all her doing."

The woman in question twisted until she was kneeling on the couch, her bright blue eyes focused intently on Travis. "You promised if Blake and Jaxi went along with what I had planned, then you would be on board as well."

"Ahhh, you're finally going to tell me your big surprise. Go ahead—I'm all yours."

She leaned up higher and kissed him briefly, unfurling from the couch and heading toward the front hall. "I already knew you are mine, but now I have something that really *shows* you belong to me." She glanced towards Cassidy, crooking a finger at him as well. "You too, sugar."

"I have no objection to being claimed by you." Cassidy rose to his feet and followed after her, smiling as Travis deliberately moved in close enough that they were torso to torso when they paused in the front hall to watch her pull a shipping box from the closet.

Cassidy leaned against Travis, welcoming the warmth of his body and the sure touch of his hand as its weight settled on his hip. Travis spoke quietly, his lips brushing Cassidy's ear. "You have any idea what she's up to?"

Cassidy shook his head. Maybe he could have talked her into sharing details, but it was a whole lot more fun letting her spring surprises on them.

That was part of being a family as well.

Ashley got the top of the box open, dragging out a pair of rubber boots. She beamed up at them as she held them up in triumph. "See?"

They were rubber boots, but the farthest thing from typical Cassidy had ever seen. Instead of black rubber, the boots were bright yellow, and if that weren't enough, brilliant pink flowers were scattered over the surface.

Travis raised a hand to cover his eyes. "Good grief, I've been blinded."

Ashley stood, settling her fists on her hips with the boots still held in her hands, wild colours radiating out like errant sunbeams. "I told you I wanted to brighten up the place."

Because he was leaning against Travis's body, Cassidy felt his partner tense, and heard him mutter a curse.

That was the moment Cassidy realized Ashley really was a genius. "I take it there are two more sets of boots in that box?"

Ashley's nod made him laugh as he faced Travis. "You did promise," he reminded him.

"If Blake and Jaxi—"

"Went along with what I proposed, you said you would as well. And they did. Jaxi told me she had no objections to," Ashley lifted a hand and counted off points on her fingers, "ordering three pairs of awesome rubber boots, and two, seeing that they were worn on a regular basis around the ranch."

Travis narrowed his eyes. "But Jaxi would have ordered rubber boots for their girls, who are all under the age of three."

Ashley shrugged. "I don't see *that* detail makes any difference."

She brought out two more pairs of boots, one neon-blue, the other purple, both dotted with yellow stars. She passed them over, and Cassidy accepted his set with a grin.

Travis hesitated.

Cassidy bumped him in the chest with his elbow. "You promised."

"She cheated," Travis complained, but he grabbed the purple pair.

"Come on," Ashley slipped her feet into her boots and had the door open before either of them could move. "If you find me in the barn, I might have a reward for you" she offered, her tone sheer dirty invitation before she took off like a shot.

There was no way to stop his laughter from bubbling up and

pouring out. *This* was why Cassidy found himself getting up every morning with a heart that was ready to explode with joy. Beside him Travis was shoving his feet into the boots, shaking his head and chuckling at Ashley's evil plot.

Cassidy put a hand on Travis's chest, holding him back so he could let his admiration show. "You look good in purple," he teased.

Between one moment and the next Cassidy found himself being kissed fiercely, the best kind of tension rising between them along with a whole lot of anticipation.

Travis pushed Cassidy toward the door. "I'll give you a five minute head start. And when I find you two, you'd better be ready for me."

Coloured boots on his feet and joy in his heart, Cassidy raced across the yard to where he could see Ashley waiting, her hand held out to welcome him. Playing games in the hayloft might be childish, but there was nothing immature about the feeling inside. They raced up the ladder, and then Cassidy pulled her into his arms to wait for Travis to catch up.

He lifted her chin so he could look straight into the sky-blue depths. "You really do brighten up our lives."

"Always," Ashley agreed. "Just wait until you see the awesome coats I ordered for next winter."

5

LIGHTS AND SECRETS

The original two Six Pack homes lie across a coulee from each other. Blake, Jaxi and their four little ones occupy the homestead ranch, while Travis and his two partners are happily settled on the other side of the creek. Close family who are close friends.

But this holiday season, there's a brotherly rivalry brewing..

Timeline: This vignette takes place after Rocky Mountain Shelter, just before Christmas and a short while before Rocky Mountain Devil begins.

~

*T*ravis Coleman opened the curtain barely an inch, and pure white light rushed past him. A whimper of complaint rose from the bed as Ashley rolled away from the bright streak to bury her face against Cassidy's chest. Cassidy didn't wake, but he curled an arm around her instinctively, one hand landing on her ass.

Sleep-warmed and relaxed, the two people who made Travis's

heart beat lay together with room left for him to join them. Cassidy stretched his other hand to the side as if searching for him.

Travis turned back to the curtain, distracted again by what was *way* too much light for three a.m. in the morning.

Between the Peters house, where the three of them lived, and the main Six Pack homestead, a long narrow coulee divided the land. In the bottom of the dip, a creek ran slow in the winter, edges freezing over as the water faded to a mere trickle.

They'd built a bridge years ago, the shortcut between the two houses well used and familiar—and now wrapped in tiny white lights. It was pretty, and festive.

And a pain in the ass, because while the house Blake and Jaxi occupied was barely visible from Travis's master bedroom, the bridge lay in plain view, a beacon now shining across their bed, brighter than Rudolph's nose.

"What the heck are you doing?" Cassidy complained, his deep grumble dragging Travis's attention away from the wintry scene outside the window.

"Go back to sleep," Travis ordered. "The decorating fairies found the coulee, that's all."

Green eyes blinked lazily, then Cassidy patted the mattress beside him. "Come back to bed while you still have time. "

Ashley was now half draped over him, their legs tangled together, her hand partially covering the tattoo on his chest. The one with three initials tangled into a brand.

Travis was all too willing to resume his place, falling asleep to thoughts of mischief.

~

"Do we have any Christmas lights?" he asked casually at breakfast the next morning. "I thought I put some up."

Ashley whirled on him, wide grin in place. "*Yes!*"

He snorted in amusement. "Well, that's an enthusiastic response, even for you."

Cassidy pressed a coffee cup into his hands. "Probably because a year ago when she asked that same question, you insisted the last thing you wanted to do after a day's work was fiddle with hooks and lights."

"Which is why I only got to put up a tiny tree out front with Cassidy's help." She sniffed. "Grinch."

A squeal escaped her as she clapped her hands to her butt, rubbing the spot where he'd pinched her.

"Your 'Grinch-B-Gone' worked. I'm going to put up a whole *mess* of lights." Travis figured Blake didn't do it on purpose, but one good deed deserved another.

Cassidy brushed past, pausing to plant a kiss on Ashley's cheek before facing Travis. "Joel texted me. We're taking the quads to the back pasture to clear deadfall and set up the cattle. We'll be out of range all day, but if you need a hand, I'll help you tonight."

"I have time this morning. I might start on my own." Travis caught Cassidy by the hips, holding him in place. "No stupid shit like racing my brother. I don't need you breaking yourself before Christmas."

"Why? Did you get me a gift you can't return?" Cassidy smirked, remaining still as Travis caught hold of his neck and locked them in position. "*You* be careful today. Climbing on tall ladders can be dangerous when you're clearly still feeling delicate after last night."

"God, you two." Ashley dropped Cassidy's lunchbox on the island. "Whose dick is bigger today?"

"*Mine*," Travis and Cassidy announced at the same time.

She snickered. "I'll break out the ruler later. Now get out of the kitchen so I can get to work. Vicki and Marion are coming over to put together Christmas hampers, and there's no way I'm letting your mom in the house without double-checking all the toys are put away first."

Cassidy leaned in and kissed Travis, quick but deep. "*Mine*," he muttered under his breath before escaping to the mudroom for his coat and boots.

"Brat," Travis called after him, laughing as he turned back to Ashley. "And that wasn't my fault, you know. Besides, my mom has seen crops before. She probably figured it was from the barn."

"With a heart-shaped cutout in the leather?" Ashley demanded. "What *are* you doing to those poor animals—? Oh my God!! Travis, put me down this instant!"

She continued to laugh as he lowered her to her feet, wondering at the joy he got to experience every damn day.

"Lights?" he asked again.

"Art studio, ground level. All the holiday stuff is in boxes labeled 'humbug'."

Life was never boring with Ashley around. "You were pretty pissed last year, I take it."

She smiled sweetly. "Go. Play. I hit the most awesome sale, so there's a bunch of stuff for you to pick from. I'll come supervise later."

He kissed her. Sweet and passionate—the icing on his morning.

There were at least a dozen boxes labeled *humbug*, and his plan expanded. Ashley had enough lights stockpiled to decorate every outbuilding on the ranch.

Travis had no intention of that. Just *one* spot. Somewhere with a clear view of his big brother's home...

~~** BLAKE **~~

IT WAS bedlam time at Blake and Jaxi's.

Rachel and Rebecca had finally settled down after their bath, curling up beside him as he held Lana in his lap and read about a certain teddy bear for the umpteenth time.

He didn't need to look at the page anymore, just recited the words—with voices—from memory until Rebecca interrupted in an attempt to take charge of the book *and* her sisters.

"No, Lana," Rebecca scolded. "I'm the oldest, so I get to turn the pages. You don't always treat books nice. You need to be older, like me."

Rebecca continued to lecture, waving a reproaching finger in front of Lana's face. Lana watched for a moment before her chubby little fingers darted out. She caught hold of the tempting item, pulling her sister's hand to her mouth as Rebecca squealed and complained.

Meanwhile, Rachel silently turned the page before looking up at Blake, her bright blue eyes blinking innocently.

How had he survived before they'd come into his life?

Across the room in the rocking chair sat the very heart of his body. Jaxi's eyes were closed but a smile twisted her lips as she listened to them. Eighteen-month-old Peter lay on her chest, lingering colds making both of them less energetic than normal.

His wife opened her eyes and their gazes met. She must've liked what she saw, because she lit up, her smile like a star shining over her family.

Over him—as if he was all she'd ever need.

Book reading completed, three tiny princesses rushed her for good night kisses before vanishing down the hall to their rooms.

"You need anything?" he asked Jaxi when he returned after tucking the girls into bed. He reached for his son who had started fussing and was wheezing lightly as he offered up sleepy cries.

"A bucket of Tylenol and three weeks uninterrupted sleep," Jaxi requested.

Even with shadows under her eyes, she was still the most beautiful woman he'd ever seen.

"Grab a shower then crawl into bed," he ordered. "I'll take care of everything here."

She stretched as she rose, curling against him briefly to plant a kiss on Peter's forehead. "I'm too tired to argue with you."

Blake waited until she'd left the room, then lifted his son until he could look him in the eye. "Seems as if the men of this family need to do some work to take care of our ladies. You ready to pull your weight?"

Peter blinked, staring seriously. His fussing forgotten under Blake's focused attention.

"That's what I thought. Dishes first, and we'll get you all bundled up and you can help your papa check the new lambs."

He'd barely walked out the back door, Peter in his arms and clinging tightly to his neck, when an out-of-place glow caught his attention.

Travis had strung lights over the barn that had been converted to an art studio for Ashley. Only, he hadn't just placed lights along the edge of the rafters. He must have hammered up two by fours to attach additional strands where there was no building. Now the structure was shaped like a castle instead of a barn, twinkling lights flashing in pretend windows as if people, or elves, were hard at work.

"Son of a gun."

It was more Christmas spirit than he expected from his brother. Then again, *he'd* put up the lights on the bridge after Jaxi had suggested it, so maybe this was Ashley's idea.

Back at the house, Blake changed Peter and tried to put him down. The little boy clung like a limpet until Blake gave up.

"Bring him to bed with us." Jaxi's soft voice. "Then we can all get some sleep."

Peter burrowed into her warmth like a puppy, cuddling in. Blake sat on the mattress edge and stared as that ache rolled in again. The one in his heart that never seemed to go away, but that he never truly wanted to escape.

Still, there were times when they seemed to have far more chores and urgent things to accomplish than they had hours for in a day, that he wondered.

"You ever regret not doing things differently?" he asked quietly, the words escaping before he'd thought them through.

Jaxi's lashes fluttered open. "Never."

Her instant response and firm tone said it all.

"I love you," he whispered.

"Of course you do." Her lips cracked into a smile even as her eyes remained closed. "And I love you too. Totally, and completely, but you forgot to turn off the yard lights," she muttered sleepily.

He kissed both Jaxi and his son before heading back downstairs, where he was surprised to find that flicking the switch at the backdoor didn't change the light pouring in the windows.

He leaned against the glass, scratching the frost away.

Damn, he'd forgotten. The castle was glowing like a landing beacon. Travis had aimed the main lights directly at Blake and Jaxi's house. At their bedroom window.

Blake plotted as he headed to bed. Drawing the curtains tight, he crawled in and pulled his already sleeping wife and son into his arms where they belonged.

And dreamt of thirty-foot-tall snowmen with waving arms, and spinning spotlights that would follow Travis no matter where he hid.

~~** CASSIDY **~~

CASSIDY TWISTED ON the seat of his skidoo, waiting for Travis to catch up with them.

"He's slow," Ashley teased. "What'd you guys do last night?"

"The Coleman boys Christmas party? I'll never tell." He pretended to zip his lips shut.

Ashley popped off her sled and crawled over him, legs hanging over his thighs as she faced him. "They won't kick you out, you know." She pulled off her mitts so she could press her hot palms to his cheeks. "You are one hundred percent Coleman boy *forever*."

He resisted the urge for all of two seconds, then dragged her over his body to rest fully in his lap where she belonged. "One hundred percent Coleman *man*, you mean."

She rolled her eyes. "Is it something in the winter air? You two are hyper-testosterone-y lately."

"It's the animal instinct," he quipped. "Fighting to be top dog."

"*Woof*," she teased.

Yeah, she was just as likely to come out on top in any battle, except both of them tended to defer to Travis. Usually.

Except when the turkey got up in the middle of the night to go and put up extra Christmas lights. As far as Cassidy was concerned, Travis's current tired ass was his own damn fault.

He pulled Ashley close and nuzzled her neck. "When's the girls' party again?"

"Why? You planning on crashing it?"

"Hardly. Jaxi would rip my ears off. Or those little girls of hers would bat their lashes at me, and I'd end up babysitting and playing Barbies all night."

"Softie." She kissed him then, giving over one hundred percent of her attention, distracting him from the lightly falling snow, and the cold temperatures, and the—

Whack.

Something icy and wet smacked into the side of his toque, snow crystals sliding down his collar as Travis whooped in the distance.

"*Score.*"

Laughter rippled from Ashley's lips. "That's not going to put you in either of our good books," she called in warning, twisting toward where Travis's dark green toque stuck up over the ridge behind them.

His head vanished, the sound of a revving snowmobile engine growing louder as he rounded the corner and pulled up beside them, grinning in spite of the tiredness in his eyes. "You'll both forgive me. You *lurve* me."

Ashley got back on her own sled, and the three of them played in the snow for the next hour, traveling all over the Coleman land before returning home.

Home. It was such an amazing word, and Cassidy wondered if he'd ever walk through that door without feeling complete and utter soul-satisfaction inside.

"You guys grab a shower. I'll get supper tonight," Ashley offered, already digging in the fridge.

Neither of them complained. They weren't stupid, and it meant that five minutes later Cassidy was standing under the full force of the showerhead, hot water streaming over naked skin while Travis's strong hands soaped him up in a way that made Cassidy hope whatever Ashley was making would take a long time to cook.

Lips pressed to the side of his neck, and Cassidy chuckled. "I'm surprised you have the energy for this."

He got a sharp nip as a reward for his teasing.

"I always have energy," Travis murmured, digging his fingers into Cassidy's biceps.

"Except when you're out of bed at strange hours." Cassidy rotated rapidly, grabbing Travis's hands and surprising him enough he managed to pin Travis's wrists to the tile over his head. "What's going on with the Christmas lights?"

Travis's grin grew wider. "They look pretty awesome, don't they?"

He tried rocking against Cassidy, but Cassidy held his ground, leaning in with his heavier weight and trapping him in place.

"Last year, no lights. This year, you've decorated the shop, all the fence lines to the south, and I spotted a dozen new boxes of decorations in the back of the truck." Cassidy leaned closer, stopping only inches away from Travis's lips. "What. Gives?"

"Just feeling the holiday spirit," Travis murmured a second before angling his head and taking control with a devastating kiss.

And suddenly, as curious as Cassidy was about Travis's strange obsession with holiday lights, other things rated higher on his agenda.

Travis's decorating game was forgotten in a hurry.

~~** JAXI **~~

IT HAD BEEN dark for an hour already, which meant every time Jaxi walked past the living room window she was reminded all over again how good her life was.

It wasn't often that she needed reminders—she had them all around her, every moment of every day. In the little boy tugging at her fingers. In his older sisters: Lana who didn't say much, but seemed to shadow him at all times, and his big sisters who would be five years old this spring, and knew *everything* about *everything,* and were intent that Peter should miss none of the significance of their family Christmas traditions.

There were shreds of wrapping paper all over the house, Christmas trees drawn in crayon stuck on the fridge. Letters to Santa waited by the door, ready to be delivered through some secret method Blake had promised.

They had cleared out one corner of the living room, and a growing collection of things to give to others was stockpiled there. Christmas Eve day they would pack it all up and drive around town, delivering baskets, and boxes, and all kinds of presents from their family to their friends and relatives.

And sometime that night, after the kids were in bed, magic would happen. The tree would appear, tall and perfectly suited for their growing collection of decorations.

She knew the girls would be up even earlier than her and Blake. They'd head downstairs to discover tiny princesses staring in amazement at the sparkling lights and brightly colored packages.

It was Christmas, and it was love.

They had each other every day of the year, and their house exploded with joyful noise most of the time, but the holiday season seemed that much richer. That much more meaningful.

That much—*brighter*.

She looked out the window again at all the festive lights she could see. The ones Blake had put up, plus the ones that had magically appeared across the coulee, and she grinned.

For the past week Blake and Travis had taken turns lighting up the countryside. Their un-discussed combat had accelerated to the point they were running out of room for new projects.

There was another new one tonight over on Travis's side. Racing lights twinkled in sequence like a moving train, or the edges of a landing strip. Which made sense when she followed the flickering colours to their final destination to where Travis had a spotlight aimed at an enormous billboard announcing "Private airstrip, reindeer only".

It went well with the enormous Santa sleigh Blake was just putting the finishing touches on. She leaned against the window as she watched them—her three little girls dancing around their daddy, their toddling son picked up out of the snow by his grandpa. The whole lot of them surrounded by glowing red and green and golden lights.

It was as bright as midday outside, and she found a bubble of amusement escaping her. Small giggles gave way to full out laughter as she looked at the dozens of displays covering the Six Pack land.

She had to give it to the boys—whatever they did, they put their heart and soul into it, even if it was decorating for the holidays.

Making spirits bright, indeed.

~~** ASHLEY **~~

HER SISTER-IN-LAW-ISH WAS LAUGHING out loud in the empty house as Ashley snuck into the front foyer.

"Hey, no having fun without me," she called as she stepped out of her boots and hurried down the hallway, nearly bumping into Jaxi as she rounded the corner.

"Have you seen what they've been doing out there?" Jaxi asked with a snicker. "We've got our own Candy Cane lane happening, and we have only two driveways."

"They have been enthusiastic," Ashley agreed, tilting her head toward the door. "You feel up to pulling on your coat? You've *got* to see what it looks like from the road."

Jaxi bundled up, and they stepped out, linking arms as Ashley led her to the best vantage point.

It was nice to have someone like Jaxi living close by. They'd become good friends, although maybe it shouldn't have been so surprising. Jaxi was all about family, and Ashley and Cassidy both loved Travis to distraction, which made *everyone* in the Coleman family happy.

Plus, she and Jaxi had a few things in common, more so now than ever before.

"I convinced Cassidy to move a couple benches to a strategic spot. I think you'll like it," Ashley said cheerfully, the cold night air sharp as she breathed it in.

They walked together, arm in arm, supporting each other over the slippery snow-stomped path. Ahead of them, more laughter rang from where Jaxi's children were chattering and playing with their daddy and grandpa Mike.

Jaxi jerked to a stop. "Is that a...*menorah*?" she asked in amazement.

"Uh-huh. And there's a Yule Log over there." Ashley waved a hand toward the front driveway. "And about twenty giant-sized candles all over the front lawn and fence line."

Jaxi settled on the bench, looking around with satisfaction in her eyes. "Candles. Like the type you would put on an old-fashioned Christmas tree?"

Ashley felt guilty for just a moment before admitting, "I was thinking more of the feast of Saturnalia, but your idea works, too. Let's go with that if Marion asks."

Jaxi covered her grin with a hand. "You are so bad."

"Hey, it's the holidays. I figure everybody who's celebrating this time of year should get a shout-out in the light displays."

"And all it took was you mentioning some candles would look good, and Travis put them up?"

"Of course not. I might have *casually* left a few drawings on the dining room table, though." Ashley squeezed her arm then turned slowly in a circle as she admired the happy beauty all around them. "You were right. Last year I had zero success getting Travis to budge on the light thing. This year?" She leaned forward and offered Jaxi a big smile. "You made one little suggestion to Blake, and *poof*, we're walking in a winter wonderland."

Her sister-in-law-ish shrugged. "The bridge needed lights," she insisted. "It's far safer this way."

"And it's been a good distraction," Ashley said innocently. "Between putting up all those lights, and his regular chores, and the rest of the holiday preparations, I bet Blake hasn't even noticed..."

Jaxi's cheeks flushed red, but it could've been from the reflected Christmas lights, or the cold.

But Ashley bet it wasn't. She just stared at the other woman, daring her to admit the secret she'd been keeping.

Jaxi finally caved. "How did you know?"

"That you're pregnant?" Ashley shrugged. "Peter's nearly two. I figured if you were going to have another, it would be soon. Plus, there were few other signs."

"This is the last time," Jaxi said firmly. "Now, no spilling the beans to anyone before I get a chance to let Blake know. I was going to tell him on Christmas Eve."

That sounded like a wonderful idea...

"Your secret is safe with me." Curiosity demanded she ask, though. "That leaves you with five kids. I thought the family joke is Blake insisted you guys would stop at six."

Jaxi made a face. "If he wants to conceive, carry and birth that last one, I'm good with it. Otherwise, I'm done with five."

Vehicle lights on the gravel road leading to the houses made them turn. More family pulled into the yard—Daniel and Beth and their boys, who raced off to examine the lights up close.

Cassidy brought out a couple more chairs, then tugged Ashley into his arms and kissed her hard enough her toes curled as Jaxi whistled in admiration.

His grin was wide and contented as he proceeded to get a small bonfire going.

"Not that we need it for the light," he teased as Travis, Blake and the kids wandered over, drawn by the fire. "Think you got enough decorations up yet, T?"

"It's so Santa can find the house better," Rebecca offered in his defense. "Uncle Travis said so."

Ashley looked up into Travis's laughing grey eyes, felt Cassidy's arm around her shoulder, and knew she'd landed in the most perfect place of all.

With family.

With people who loved her—completely and forever.

"Christmas Day at our place this year," Mike reminded them

before the group broke up to head home. "And Boxing Day at Whiskey Creek."

Which left Christmas Eve for the individual families, and a growing warmth inside threatened to burst out and make Ashley shout her secret too early.

I'm going to tell him on Christmas Eve, Jaxi had said.

Yes, that sounded like a *wonderful* time to share a secret with her two loves…

"Anything special you want to do on Christmas Eve?" Cassidy asked as they found themselves curled up, all three on the couch in front of their fireplace.

"Dick wars," Ashley deadpanned.

Travis snorted. "Could be fun."

"What are the rules?" Cassidy asked as he leaned on Travis's chest, pulling her feet into his lap so he could dig his fingers into her soles.

Her gaze met Travis's over Cassidy's shoulder. "He wants to know the rules. What have you done with him?"

"Not my fault," Travis insisted. "His straight-and-narrow side rears its head every now and then."

"We should really do something about it," she teased softly, trailing her fingers up Cassidy's leg.

"I'm not moving," Cassidy warned. "You want to do dirty things to me, you do them here."

"Lazy ass," Travis poked.

"Smartest ass in the room," Cassidy countered.

"Biggest ass in the room."

"Biggest cock, you mean."

A short *ha!* exploded from Travis.

"Boys…" Two faces turned toward her, and she shook her head, happiness pouring through her. "Dick wars—they never do end."

So softly she might have imagined it, both of them whispered *mine*, and she couldn't stop herself. Laughter floated up like teeny bubbles, spilling over them all.

It was tempting to spill the beans now, but she resisted. Christmas Eve was the perfect time to tell them her secret.

Then they'd have to wait another seven months to discover who'd won *that* particular round of the *dick war*.

Although, they'd all won, really.

Ashley leaned back, the twinkling lights shining in the darkness outside the window paling to shadows compared to the bright lights shining in her lovers' eyes.

6

A DADDY'S LOVE

Preparing for Valentines Day as a father means vastly different things depending on how old your children are, as Blake and Daniel from the Six Pack Colemans discover.

Timeline: This vignette takes place during the last half of ROCKY MOUNTAIN DEVIL. February 13 to be specific, only a few days after a certain someone left Rocky Mountain House.

~

Blake stepped across the kitchen and slipped his arms around Jaxi, pulling her body to his. "Smells great," he murmured against her neck before kissing the soft spot under her ear.

"Roast chicken and veggies," Jaxi offered.

He hummed, hands moving around her more firmly as he took a deep breath. "Not talking 'bout the food."

She laughed softly before twisting in his arms. Her lips met his full on while she was still smiling, and he swore he could taste her happiness.

Something jerked at his belt loop. Some*one*.

"Daddy, we need you." Two voices in unison made the demand, followed by a softer, more babyish echo, "Daddy, need you."

Blake glanced down to discover he and Jaxi were surrounded by their blonde-haired little girls, all three of them dancing on the spot with excitement.

"We'll pick this up later," Blake promised his wife.

"I'll hold you to that," Jaxi said. "Go. Looks like you have important things to do. Supper's ready in about half an hour." She glanced at her watch. "Oops. Keep an eye on Peter, too? I have to run outside for a couple minutes."

"No problem."

His daughters guided him to the living room where they tugged him to the floor and shoved red construction paper at him.

"Can you make hearts, Daddy—?" Rachel began.

"—because Mama says you can," Rebecca finished

"If Mama says I can, then it must be true. What're we making hearts for?" Blake picked up the scissors, holding back a grunt of pain as his youngest daughter crawled into his lap, stepping on spots he'd rather not have stepped on.

Lana cupped his cheeks in her little hands, her big blue eyes wide as she explained in a serious tone that was all business, "It valenday, Daddy."

"Val-len-*tine*," Rebecca corrected.

"Val-man-*time*," Lana echoed.

"Right." Rachel nodded before her lower lip stuck out briefly in what Blake thought was a fairly adorable pout. "Mama said we can make better cards, but I liked the one at the store with—"

"—Elsa was pretty," Rebecca agreed, "but we can't—"

"—I know. But then we can—"

"—oh, can we?"

"*Yes*."

Rachel grinned at her twin, then they both faced Blake with identical smiles, the shared conversation obviously complete and clear as day. To them.

His heart ached fiercely, and he wondered what he'd ever done to deserve this kind of paradise. "You two should try to finish a sentence on your own once in a while. Just for variety."

"Did you cut out any—"

"—hearts yet?"

Blake attacked the construction paper, dipping his chin and hiding his grin. "I forgot it was Valentine's Day. Who you gonna make cards for?" He lowered his voice. "You makin' one for me?"

Lana was rubbing the glue stick over her heart, getting more on the table under the red cut-out than on the paper. Blake adjusted her grip so he could guide her fingers.

"I'm making one for Mama and—"

"—one for Grampa, and one for Gramma, and one for—"

"—PJ, and—"

Blake held up a hand, glancing around the room. "Hold that list, babies. Where's your brother?"

"PJ in jail." Lana jabbed a stubby finger at the wooden bars between the living room and the kitchen. Jaxi had jammed an old playpen into the gap where she said she could keep an eye on it from anywhere on the main floor.

Blake kissed the top of Lana's head and lowered her to the floor carefully. "The way you keep telling people we put your brother in prison, I'm surprised we haven't had social services drop by yet."

"We need—"

"—more hearts," the twins warned.

"Be right back," he promised, starting toward the playpen. The absolute silence from the "jail" left him expecting to see Peter passed out enjoying the sleep of the innocent.

Instead he found his son lying on his back, staring at the

ceiling with a huge grin on his face. Every stitch of his clothing had been removed...

Including his diaper.

The aroma that rose into the air was damn near lethal, and Blake swore softly. His son's ability to strip like a little Houdini was entertaining at times, but this? Not so much. The diaper had been full. And while Blake spent his days shoveling shit, this was different. Peter poop was a special brand of hell all of its own.

With a sigh, he tossed all the contaminated clothes and blankets on top of his son's naked belly, stripping the playpen of all toxic waste. He wrapped the little man up and hoisted the entire mess into the air. "Just a minute, girls. Your brother needs hosing off."

Fortunately, the new laundry room was right there off the kitchen, the washtub big enough to use as a bathtub. The instant Blake set him down, Peter grabbed the scrub brush off the counter and began driving it like a car over the edges of the basin. Blake hauled open the washing machine with the intent of getting rid of his filthy armload.

But the washer was full. So was the dryer. By the time he'd manhandled the dry clothes into a laundry basket, transferred the wet washing to the dryer and finally shoved the dirty blankets into the washer, Peter had stopped playing and started crying, and there were noises of discontentment rising from the living room.

Blake gave up all hope of keeping his clothes clean. He snatched Peter up against his chest so he could stick his head around the corner and shout a warning at his daughters. "Play nice. I'll be right back."

"Goo stick *mine*," Lana complained loudly.

"Give her back the glue stick," Blake ordered as he stepped back into the laundry room and turned on the water. He got it nice and warm before dipping his son under the stream.

Going by the sounds escaping PJ's lips, anyone within a

quarter mile would have sworn there was a pig being butchered in the room. He ignored his son's complaining as he rapidly wiped him clean. Blake took a moment to shed his now shit-decorated shirt before wrapping Peter in a dry towel and hauling him in close.

"That wasn't so bad, was it?" he offered gently, but Peter was inconsolable, his volume peaking at maximum. As an added bonus, the screams from the living room had also grown louder. Blake resisted the urge to cover his ears. "Jeez, I'm going to be deaf before I'm an old man."

Two-year-old tucked close, Blake hurried back to the living room and found three little girls with tears streaming down their faces all tugging at the pile of construction paper. Blake watched helplessly as the paper ripped, and three miniature blondes fell in different directions, tattered shreds of red falling like bloodstained rain. It looked as if the apocalypse had taken place in what had only moments before been a well-organized and pristine room.

Blake took a deep breath and then let out the laugh that had been building ever since he'd spotted the open diaper. He laughed hard and loud, and the echoing cries of the four children in the room slowly decreased in volume as they looked at him in confusion.

Peter tilted his head to one side, his mouth hanging open as he stopped crying, sucking in little gasps of air that shook his body. He reached up and touched Blake's cheek, as if wondering when his father had lost his mind.

Fortunately, Jaxi stayed out of the house long enough that Blake had time to clean the mess in the living room. He sent Rebecca off to fetch a wet face cloth so he could wipe all four faces clear of tears, and by the time Mama was back in the house, the girls were once again gluing hearts on card stock, and Peter was sitting on the blanket in front of the fireplace, happily playing with a couple stuffed horses.

Jaxi paused in the doorway of the living room, the basket of eggs dangling from her hand as she eyed the room suspiciously. Blake smiled up at her, knowing she was probably reading the clues like a detective, but she didn't say anything other than to admire the cards their daughters jumped up to show off. The ones with orange and yellow hearts on them since there was no red paper to be salvaged.

Then she examined Blake closer, a trickle of amusement in her eyes as she made her way to his side. She knelt behind him, the soft swell of the baby in her belly pressing against his back as she whispered in his ear. "You seem to have lost your shirt."

He twisted his head toward her so he could answer softly, "Just getting ready for later."

She hummed lustily, kissing his cheek before rising and making her way to scoop PJ off the floor. "I'll get him dressed, then it's time to go to the table."

"I'll get the girls there," he promised.

Jaxi smiled. "You're a great daddy."

"He's the *bestest*—"

"—daddy."

"Bestest daddy," Lana agreed.

Their reassuring chorus warmed something deep inside him. Damn if being a daddy wasn't the hardest job he'd ever had.

Although, he figured he had another job that was just as demanding, and considering it was Valentine's Day tomorrow, he needed to make sure he was working just as hard to be the bestest *husband* as well...

Time to make some plans.

~

DANIEL WONDERED how on earth he was going to survive the next five plus years of raising teenage boys.

In front of him, Lance shifted uncomfortably from side to

side, partially blocking the computer screen he'd unsuccessfully attempted to close when Daniel had entered the room. Daniel was pretty sure *he* was fidgeting as well, but it had to be done.

"That's not what sex is really like," Daniel informed his son bluntly as he reached around Lance and stabbed the power button off. "I mean, some of the mechanics are right, but you ever try something like that with a woman who's not one hundred percent on board, she'll chop off your balls with a pair of rusty scissors."

Lance's face flushed beet red. "It's just...acting."

Daniel pinched the bridge of his nose. Not that he wished Beth'd been the one to catch their fourteen-year-old checking out porn, but...

Yeah, actually he kinda did wish she'd been the one who'd caught Lance, because then *she'd* be having this conversation instead. Admittedly, though, he was glad she hadn't witnessed their son ogling a site that could only be considered sleazy by any stretch of the imagination.

He was a guy. He understood the draw of porn, but that still didn't make it right to toss this off as a guy thing. Particularly not at Lance's age. It didn't seem a time for a lecture on the differences between willing and unwilling participants of the sex trade, but—

Damn if this wasn't one of the most awkward moments of Daniel's entire life. And probably Lance's, for that matter.

He took a deep breath. "I'm not trying to make this worse than it is. We've talked about sex, and movies and TV make it pretty clear it's something people do for fun as well as to have kids."

"*Daaaaaaad*," Lance complained, dragging the word out long enough it had multiple syllables. "Just tell me. Am I in deep shit?"

Daniel raised a brow. "Are you in *what*?"

Lance swallowed hard. "Am I in trouble, sir?"

There were so many things that Daniel would rather be doing

and so many places he'd rather be, but this was part of the job description. He thought back to the discussions his father had with him and his brothers, but *jeez*, Mike hadn't had to deal with the insanity of the Internet, just Playboy magazines tucked under the mattress.

Daniel tried his best to channel his dad's wisdom and patience. "Do I understand why you're interested in checking out porn? Yep. Do I want you watching what I just saw and thinking that's hot? Hell, no. And do I want you showing your younger brothers anything—?"

"I'd never show anything like that to Nathan and Robbie," Lance insisted, honest shock in his voice.

"And they never go on your computer, and they would never even think to check your history." Daniel folded his arms over his chest. "Oh, wait. Maybe Robbie knows how to take apart a computer and rebuild it in his sleep. And he's already broken into your system once when you forgot your passwords."

Lance had the grace to look sheepish. "I'd delete my history."

"Scrub it clean. And the laptop stays in the family room from now on," Daniel declared.

"But that means I have to do my homework—"

"*Lance.*"

His son sighed mightily then began to gather up the cords. "Yes, sir."

Unfortunately, the awkwardness was destined to continue. The real reason Daniel had made his way to Lance's room in the first place still had to be dealt with. "You taking Kim to the Valentine's Day dance tomorrow night?"

His son hesitated. He and Kim had been going together since before Christmas. "I'm not grounded, am I?"

Daniel shook his head. "Not unless you think you should be."

"I don't want to be grounded," Lance said quickly. He looked up at Daniel, concern on his face. "I get what you mean. That stuff made me feel funny inside. *Wrong* funny."

"Because it was wrong sex," Daniel said plainly. "To be honest, at your age pretty much all sex is going to be wrong. Our bodies are built to think it would be fun, but sex is about a lot more than bodies."

Lance was now staring firmly at the floor. Thank God, because it made it easier for Daniel to continue.

"Let's see if you're old enough to understand what I'm about to do." Daniel handed over the box of condoms, still not positive he was making the right decision.

Lance had instinctively reached out to take what his dad offered before jerking his hands back as if Daniel had offered a live snake. "I don't need— I mean, Kim and I aren't—"

He stumbled to silence and if possible turned an even brighter red.

"Good to know that you're not having sex, because you're not ready for it. That whole *'your body is interested but your brain's not quite there'* is still happening. You'll understand it all a lot better in a couple years." Daniel shut his mouth to stop from rambling, even though rambling felt natural at the moment. He took a deep breath and forced himself to continue. "And me giving you this box is not in any way telling you that *I* approve of you having sex, but *if* you make the decision to go ahead at some point down the road, you now have no excuse for not wearing a condom. Just in case I haven't made it clear, if you don't use a condom, even your first time having sex, she could get pregnant, or you could get an STD. I hope to hell you're smarter than that. No condom, no sex. *Ever*. No matter what anyone says. Got it?"

He held the box closer to Lance, who finally took it, holding the small package gingerly as if it might snap his fingers like a triggered mousetrap at any moment.

"Also," Daniel pushed himself to finish. "When they're older, I'll have this same awkward conversation with your brothers. But, if by some chance you hear that they're going to do something stupid before I get around to the talk, I expect you to step in and lay down the law. And make sure they're prepared."

"Yes, sir."

Daniel held out his hand, grateful as hell they were one step closer to this whole experience being over.

Lance ignored his fingers completely, rushing forward to bury his face against Daniel's chest. He snuck his arms around Daniel and squeezed tightly, all gangly arms, like a colt that had just been turned out of the barn and wasn't quite sure what to do with its freedom.

"*Iloveyoudad.*"

The words came out in a rush. An instant later, Lance was out of Daniel's arms and back at his desk, sitting down to delete his browser history.

"I love you, too," Daniel spoke the words clearly and without hesitation. "I'll be working in the shop tonight if you need anything."

He paused in the hallway and leaned his head back against the wall as he took a deep breath to clear the tension out of his body. Beth was out with Nathan and Robbie at the swimming pool for another half hour, so Daniel turned on the dishwasher and headed out back to the woodworking shop.

The entire place was lit up. Daniel moved forward quickly, wondering if he had left the lights on when he stopped for dinner.

Blake stood at the jigsaw, protective goggles in place as he twisted a thin piece of dark wood under the rapidly moving blade. Daniel paced slowly around the perimeter of the shop until he was in sight, and his brother turned off the machine then stepped forward to offer him a slap on the shoulder.

"I rang the bell but nobody answered. Hope you don't mind me making myself at home."

Daniel shook his head. "You know it's never a problem. What're you up to?"

"Valentine's gift for Jaxi. You got something done for Beth, yet?"

Dammit. He'd been so busy trying to figure out the best time and way to get the condoms to Lance that Valentine's Day had completely slipped his mind. "Tell me your idea will duplicate easily."

Blake grinned. "I thought I'd make a picture frame with a cut out of a tree. Kind of a twist on the family tree thing."

"That's brilliant," Daniel offered. "Want to go into production and make one for everybody in the family?"

"With a really huge one for Ma and Dad?"

"One tree trunk, six branches," Daniel countered.

Blake nodded, and they both moved around the shop to gather the supplies they needed. While it had been years since Blake and Daniel had worked together in the woodshop, there were some things that even time didn't change. Daniel sketched designs on the wood that Blake ran through the planer, and by the time they ended up with the stack of pieces, they were both ready for a chance to shoot the breeze while they glued the frames together.

Blake adjusted his chair and took a deep, appreciative breath. "I can't tell you how lucky you are to have the scent of cedar around all the time instead of the smell of shit."

"You don't have to use tweezers to pull shit slivers from under your skin."

Blake chuckled then shared his pre-dinner fun involving screaming kids and nuclear waste-loaded diapers.

Poopie diapers and toddler tantrums—two things Daniel had never had to deal with, and he was glad. But then again—

"I missed that stage with the boys, but don't go thinking what's coming down the road gets any easier." Blake's expression grew tighter as Daniel shared his evening's adventure in teenager-wrangling.

Blake shook his head in amazement when Daniel was done.

"You gave Lance condoms? Holy shit, he's only what—fourteen? Even Jesse and Joel waited until they were sixteen."

God, Daniel knew. "I went looking at the statistics. Average age kids try sex these days is fifteen. And it's not just the guys—the girls are pushing for it earlier as well."

Blake's face went white. "That's *not* what I needed to hear. I was feeling thankful I've got girls to deal with first, but it sounds like I should be even more frightened."

"Definitely frightened," Daniel deadpanned.

His brother snorted. "Jerk."

Daniel leaned back on his stool as he considered. Maybe the emotion was wrong, but it was somehow reassuring to know neither of them were completely sure what they were doing. "I don't know that I ever thought about this part. I mean, I knew I wanted kids, and Ma and Dad are awesome parents, but I never really thought about the challenges. The ordinary, everyday decisions we have to keep making. Most of the time I wonder if I'm totally screwing up," he admitted reluctantly.

His brother frowned before making a rude noise. "For what it's worth, I think you're doing a great job."

Daniel took the compliment gladly. "Thanks. You too."

They returned to work, chatting about upcoming plans as they finished their task.

They were stacking the frames to one side for Blake to drop off with their brothers on his way home when Daniel held up the seventh one. The hollow sensation in the pit of his stomach was unfamiliar and uncomfortable.

One brother wasn't around. There'd be no simple way to drop off his gift.

Jesse's leaving was still so brand new, neither of them had remembered not to include him until this moment. "Think Jesse will be back for this soon?" Daniel asked quietly as he traced the tree's outline.

Blake went quiet. "Still don't understand why the jerk took off like that." He paused. "I can keep it at my place until he comes to his senses and comes home."

Daniel wasn't sure why Jesse had up and vanished only days earlier, although he had his suspicions. Between Jesse's leaving and a family funeral, there'd been a lot of tension and sadness in the Coleman clan that week.

Suddenly, it was important to have a way to turn that sadness around. He picked up the larger frame that was intended for their parents. "What about we save this for the next time we have a family meal? I'll get everybody to give me a family picture, and I'll grab a recent one of Jesse, and we can give the frame to Ma and Dad all done up nice."

"Good idea." Blake glanced at his watch. "Shit, I need to run if I'm going to make it home in time to tuck the kids in."

There were headlights in the driveway. "Beth's home with the boys, so I have to go, too."

Yet they stood motionless together for another minute, staring down at the frames they'd made. Daniel's mind was whirling with thoughts about family and growing pains and difficult moments. And love, if Daniel was honest, because it was love that made it all happen and made it worthwhile.

Blake spoke, and pretty much verbalized what Daniel was feeling inside. "We got a whole ton of blessings in our lives, don't we?"

Daniel laid a hand on his brother's shoulder. For all the awkwardness and frustrations that went with their lives, neither of them would give up a single minute. "We've got families. That's the biggest blessing of all."

The evening rushed to completion like most other nights, with post swim-practice snacks and late night homework complaints, and by the time the boys were in bed for the night, Daniel and Beth settled in the living room for a moment's quiet before ending their day as well.

Only his thoughts kept returning to that evening's discussion with Blake. Daniel was so focused on his mental ponderings he was surprised to glance over and discover Beth standing beside his chair, a faint smile on her lips as she gazed down at him lovingly.

"You're not reading. You haven't turned a page in fifteen minutes," she teased gently.

He put the book aside and caught her by the wrist, tumbling her into his lap. He took a moment to appreciate the feel of her soft curves as he cuddled her close. "Just thinking."

"Good thoughts?"

He nodded, stroking a finger down her cheek and under the chin so he could tilt her head back and steal a long, slow kiss.

Beth was breathless when he lifted his mouth from hers. "Ahhh. *Those* kind of thoughts…"

He chuckled. "Some. But also about how much you brought into my life. I don't think I've thanked you for it near enough."

Beth looked bemused. "You took on me and three boys, making us part of your world. You've been raising them with me and loving all of us. You've shared your family and you work long hours to support us. If anyone needs to be appreciated more for all they do, it's you."

"I never would have been a dad without you," he said softly.

She rubbed her nose against his. "Well, you never know what *might* have happened, but I'm very pleased with what *did* happen. You're a great dad, and you're a fine husband, as well."

"Fine?" he demanded, rising to his feet with her in his arms as he mock glared at her.

Beth winked. "Pretty fine? Perfectly fine?"

He carried her down the hallway, speaking softer as they passed the boys' rooms. "And what kind of lover am I? Adequate?"

A giggle escaped her, and his amusement rose again. This was another part of love.

"Definitely," Beth whispered. "Pretty adequate. *Perfectly* adequate."

She was full out laughing as he tossed her onto their bed from a few feet away then turned to lock the door.

By the time he faced her, she'd stripped off her top and wiggled out of her pants. She knelt on the bed, scooting forward so she met him at the edge of the mattress. He closed the distance between them, and she curled her fingers into the front of his shirt as she stared up at him with desire and happiness in her eyes. "You really want to know what kind of lover you are? *Perfect.*"

Daniel moved over her and did his best to make it perfectly true.

~

New York Times Bestselling Author Vivian Arend
invites you to meet the Colemans. These contemporary cowboys
ranch the foothills of the Alberta Rockies. Enjoy the ride as they
each find their happily-ever-afters.

~

Six Pack Ranch
Rocky Mountain Heat
Rocky Mountain Haven
Rocky Mountain Desire
Rocky Mountain Angel
Rocky Mountain Rebel
Rocky Mountain Freedom
Rocky Mountain Romance
Rocky Mountain Retreat
Rocky Mountain Shelter
Rocky Mountain Devil
Rocky Mountain Home
Rocky Mountain Forever

~

ABOUT THE AUTHOR

New York Times and *USA Today* bestselling author Vivian Arend loves to share the products of her over-active imagination with her readers. She writes contemporary, western, and light-hearted paranormal romances. The stories are humorous yet emotional, usually with a large cast of family or friends, and a guaranteed happily-ever-after. Vivian lives in British Columbia, Canada, with her husband of many years—her inspiration for every hero and a willing companion for all sorts of adventures.

www.vivianarend.com